GIVE *a novel* ME
LOVE

GIVE ME SERIES, #1

KATE MCCARTHY

Give Me Love

Copyright © Kate McCarthy 2013

ISBN-13: 978-0-9875261-1-3
ISBN-10: 0-9875261-1-1

Please note that Kate McCarthy is an Australian author and Australian English spelling and slang have been used in this book.

Cover Art courtesy of Okay Creations
http://www.okaycreations.net/

Interior Design by Angela McLaurin, Fictional Formats

Table of Contents

This book is dedicated to Carl Wallis and Marjorie Edith

Chapter One

Performing the transformation into Rockstar Goddess was quite a feat. I'd be up for Heavyweight Champion in the Makeup Application Olympics if I managed to open my eyes under the weight of all the layers. The only other alternative was to look washed out under the bright lights of the stage, so I persisted with my efforts. Many nights performing on stage should have meant I'd perfected the process, but being a natural girl at heart, I still struggled to get it right.

The granite of the bathroom vanity was cool on my near naked form as I finished lining glue on the furry black eyelash, leaning close to the mirror to tack it on as quickly as possible. Time was escaping me, and Mac, my fierce and predictable best friend and roommate, would be busting down the door with impatience soon. I didn't mind too much because I needed her to kick my ass into gear on a regular basis.

"Hurry up, asshead!" I heard her shout from outside the closed bathroom door. It was accompanied by a few loud thumps for emphasis causing me to jump in fright and attach the lash to my eyebrow by mistake. It wasn't exactly the look I was aiming for.

"Macklewaine," I complained loudly.

Mac took it as an invitation to enter because the door burst open hard enough for the knob to whack the back wall with a loud thud, making a dent in the perfectly painted plaster.

"Oh shit!" Apparently, Mac wasn't anticipating an unlocked door.

I folded my arms and flared my nostrils but she just let out a snort of laughter at my expense.

At twenty-four, Mackenzie Valentine was the same age as me but far more beautiful than any one person needed to be. She was tough and direct, leaving me to believe that when God was handing out the looks, she not only jumped the queue, she muscled her way to the front in order to take more than her fair share. She was golden all over, from the shimmery blonde strands of hair to her luminous skin, down to the golden sparkle of polish on her toes. Her eyes were like green emeralds, and not a single blemish marred her perfect complexion. Love her or hate her, there was no in between for a person like Mac. In her defence, she had three older brothers, hence fierce determination wasn't just a way of life, it was a matter of survival learned from the tender years of childhood.

When it came to appearances, the only thing Mac and I shared was height and shoe size, but considering the footwear collection she housed in her wardrobe, this made me a very lucky girl indeed. My hair was dark brown to her blonde, with highlights of caramel littering the strands from the sun. It hung down my back, almost to my waist, in waves of imperfect wildness. My skin was not golden but olive with a hint of rose, and my eyes were a dark chocolate brown. I wouldn't ever call myself beautiful, constantly lamenting my nose was a little too wide and my lips not full enough, however, Mac always told me I had an inner radiance that drew people in, and with such a look of "smouldering sex appeal," she felt prim and proper in comparison. I guess I could deal with that.

"What the hell happened to your face?" Mac said after she finished laughing at me.

I put my hands on my hips and glowered at her but the whole furry eyebrow look was ruining my attempts to look fierce. "You. You happened to my face. Everything was going fine until you busted in here like a fucking SWAT team."

It wasn't really going fine, but she didn't need to know I was struggling or her impatience would reach even greater heights.

I turned back to the mirror and peeled the furry caterpillar off the neatly pencilled arch of my eyebrow. The eyelash was ruined now. Gluey dried clumps coated the surface. I leaned forward and began picking the glue remnants out of my brow. Dastardly stuff.

"You're bathroom hogging again," she complained, and I didn't deny the obvious. It was taking me at least a year to achieve Rockstar Goddess status, but defeat and I were not friends.

Mac put the toilet seat down, sat on the lid, and began buffing the already perfect nails on her left hand while I picked at the glue. I watched her warily through the mirror as I began to re-apply a new set of eyelashes. Something was churning through her brain. I could feel the waves of it powering towards me like a tsunami. I waited for her to get to the point since she wasn't known for taking winding side trips through the willows.

I raised a brow as I turned to look at her properly. "Can I help you?" I prodded, just wanting to get whatever it was over with already.

At my question, she tried to feign nonchalance, but she could never manage to get the expression right. Her eyes went a little too wide, and her shrug a little too exaggerated.

"I just got off the phone with Jared."

Hearing his name made my heart pitter patter, and then plonk somewhere down in the vicinity of my toes. That explained Mac's willow trip. Being direct on the subject of Jared hadn't gotten Mac anywhere in the past. In fact, coming at me sideways on the subject of Jared hadn't gotten her anywhere either. It was a no-win conversation as far as I was concerned.

I turned back to the mirror, finished tacking on the eyelash with smug triumph, and stepped back, doing some rapid blinks to make sure I hadn't glued my eyes together.

Don't laugh. I'd done it before. Granted, the emergency glue I pilfered from the shit draw in the kitchen probably wasn't a good idea.

"Oh?" I replied back with an offhanded casualness that belied the churning of my insides.

Jared is Mac's older brother by three years. Out of her three brothers, Jared is the one she is closest to, and of the three, he is the only one I look at and feel like time has stopped.

"He said he's coming tonight to watch the band."

I was about to burst out with "That's not fair!" but wisely held my tongue. Tonight was an important night for us and required focus, not distraction, and Jared would be a distraction. Of that I was sure.

It was my band's debut in Sydney tonight at the White Demon Warehouse, an uber cool venue to hear up and coming indie rock bands. This meant my stomach was already on the verge of dancing the twist and the slight tremor in my hands was making this eyelash attachment a nightmare.

I sucked in a few deep breaths. I could do this. I could.

I am a cool cucumber.

No, fuck that. I am Snoop Dogg. You can get no cooler than that.

Satisfied that one eye had achieved full Rockstar Goddess status, I leant forward to begin layering liner on the second eye. All the while, I could feel Mac's eyeballs burning into my back, assessing my reaction to her words.

"Is that so?" I murmured, doing my best not to react.

She stopped filing her nails to gift me with a smirk, making it apparent that my lack of reaction was answer enough. Damn! I wasn't good at game playing, and she knew me too well.

"Yes that's so," she replied.

I didn't have the time or the inclination for a man in my life for important reasons. The first of which was that I had a career in the music industry as a lead singer in a band that was going places. Music wasn't just my therapy, it was my life, and as long as I had that, I had everything I needed.

My band had been a family for six years; the four boys were like my brothers. We took it seriously, working long days—and even harder nights—and weekends, playing, creating, and evolving into what I chose to believe was a musical fucking force of nature that would eventually take over, if not the world, at least Australia to start. If we worked hard enough, it would mean months of travel—nationally and internationally—hours, days, and months of recording time, and if successful enough, we'd generate acres of fans and album sales. All of that so we could keep feeding our souls by doing what we loved most in the world.

"That's nice," I offered.

Besides music being my world, my heart had already been broken twice in the past, and I had no intention of revisiting that pain. Once by my ex Wild Renny and subsequently by my ex Asshole Kellar. Deciding that the third time was apparently the charm, I changed mid-stride and began dating dorks like they were my new religion. As long as they didn't fit what seemed to be my type—tall, hot bad boy with the consistent ability to put my life in danger—I was safe. No broken heart there. I had needed to change my ways before I started university because my life was spiralling out of control based on my lack of ability to make good decisions.

I met Jared for the first time during my first year at university when he came to check on his little sister, my very new roommate and soon to be bff. After that, avoiding him became my new mission in life because by appearance alone, he seemed to fit my type. All I had to do was ensure that wherever Jared was, I wasn't. Not an easy feat considering he was Mac's brother and co-owned a business with my older brother Coby, but the fact that he lived in Sydney while I lived in Melbourne kept him at arm's length.

The trouble *now* was the whole distance thing no longer existed since we moved to Sydney a week ago which placed me directly in Jared's determined path.

I risked another glance at Mac through the mirror. She appeared distracted from her current topic choice and was now eyeballing my underwear with a narrowed gaze. It was a vintage blue and black lacy affair with a demi cup bra and little black bows and satin gathering that was both pretty and sexy and so expensive my purse gave out a feeble

5

bleat of protest when exposed to the price tag. I'd only ventured to the shops to pick up milk and bread, but unfortunately that was when all sense went out the window.

"New underwear?"

I nodded because "This old thing?" never worked. She knew more about the contents of my wardrobe then I did. "I bought it yesterday."

"Um, sorry? I thought I just heard you say you bought it yesterday."

I cringed at the unhappy tone of her voice. What meditation was for some, shopping was for Mac. She didn't mind doing it alone, but for some reason, if I shopped without her, I might as well just take myself directly to hell and save the time of waiting around for her to do it.

"We only moved to Sydney a week ago and you've gone shopping without me," she hissed.

When I started putting the eyeliner on in a panic so I could make a quick escape, Henry, my other best friend and roommate, banged hard on the bathroom door to hurry me along.

I jumped again at the noise, eyeliner running wildly up my eyelid, and I wanted to scream in frustration. I'd never achieve Rockstar Goddess at this rate.

"Effing hell, Henrietta," I screeched and tore open the door. "Can a girl not work her freaking Rockstar Goddess magic in peace?"

"Holy shit, Sandwich," he muttered.

Sandwich was their nickname for me because of my surname Jamieson. Jam. Jam Sandwich. Now it was just Sandwich. It wasn't really the best nickname, but you just had to roll with what you got because if you kicked up a fuss, you'd likely end up with something worse.

I pursed my lips as his eyes did a full body scan before finally resting on the eyeballs that were glaring back at him.

"Finished?" I asked tersely.

Henry had long since declared Mac and I as asexual beings, so I took his body scan as the insult it intended to be.

"Tonight's theme is Tartmonkey?" he asked.

Did he think I was planning to hit the stage in underwear alone? Before I could open my mouth, Mac beat me to it, snorting from her seated position on the toilet.

"That's rich coming from your manwhore status, isn't it, Hussy?"

He burst out laughing. "What the hell happened to your face, Evie?"

I raced back to the mirror to see a mad streak of liner, not unlike another furry black caterpillar, trailing up my eyelid and over my brow.

Was the universe trying to tell me something about my eyebrows? I raised them experimentally and turned my head left to right.

"Fucksicles, the pair of you. I have to start over now." I grabbed for a makeup wipe.

"What's with you, Mactard?" Henry asked.

I gave Henry a warning look as I threw the wipe in the bin. It conveyed the message that Mac was on the warpath, and that it was too late for me, but save yourself.

Mac stood up to inspect her perfect make-up job for any flaws as she replied, "I'm stressed and need an outlet. I need shopping, I need chocolate, and I need alcohol. Any order will do."

Mac is like Ellen Ripley of Alien, capable, fierce, and downright scary, but being our band manager, not even those attributes could shield her from the stress levels the job entailed. She had me to deal with, didn't she? And if I wasn't bad enough, there was Henry and Snap, Crackle, and Pop, our other band members, otherwise known as Frog, Cooper, and Jake: the Rice Bubble trio.

Mac became our band manager when we finished uni, having long since given up her lifelong dream to kick ass on the police force like her dad, Steve, and eldest brother Mitch. I think it was all fun in theory—hot bad guys, guns, shoot outs, hot bad guys—but she eventually realised that the whole premise of having to be an upstanding citizen put a crapshoot on that idea.

"Start with alcohol," Henry ordered.

"There's bubbles in the fridge. Get me some too, please," I added.

"Me, too," said Henry.

Mac smoothed her already perfectly smooth golden blonde waves and vacated the bathroom, making sure to inform Henry that Jared was coming tonight before she left because Henry and Mac rode the same wavelength on that particular topic.

Who did the two think they were? The love fairies? I gave a snort as I re-pencilled my brow. The Laurel and Hardy duo was more their speed.

Henry smirked and got out his phone to start texting whoever. "Looks like your avoidance plan hit a snafu."

"Snafu?" I snorted. "That's something my Great Aunt Dottie would say."

"You don't have a Great Aunt Dottie."

"If I did, she would say that."

I finished adding the second set of eyelashes to my eye and blinked rapidly as Henry read a reply to his text with a faint smile.

Henry was the lead guitarist in our band and the ultimate pretty boy. A real live Paul Walker with his white blond hair and blue eyes, and left girls a bit tongue tied. Not me though. I'd known him since the age of five when he was a dirty little snot nosed grub. I got into a fight with Johnny in the schoolyard. I called Johnny a bumface (he'd looked up my skirt), and a shouting (him), name calling (me), hair pulling (him and me) match began. Our interaction had drawn quite the crowd by the time I got in his face and smashed my knee into his boy bits. Everyone laughed, as little kids do, in the face of seeing a bully go down, especially at the hands of a girl.

More yelling (me again) ensued and at that, Johnny's friend came over and pushed me into the dirt. I heard a boy yell out and looked up from the pile of rubble to see a little blond boy leap onto the back of Johnny's friend and pull him into a headlock. I got up and dusted off my hands, ready to jump into the fray, when our teacher Mr. Paul came racing over to pull everyone apart.

We bonded after the mayhem, and afternoons found us trading the guitar we'd bought together with saved pocket money back and forth, or driving our matchbox cars through little dirt tracks we had painstakingly dug out in the backyard. Mum hadn't been impressed about that because we'd turfed up a fair whack of lawn, and after the Big Wet (it had bucketed down rain for two weeks straight) it left quite the mud pit in the backyard. A few of our precious little cars, including my prized black Trans Am, got buried.

"Earth to JimmyJam," Mac sing-songed, waving a glass of bubbles under my nose.

I snatched the glass out of her hand with a thanks and took a sip, followed it with a loud delighted sigh, and finished with a lip smack.

"Big crowd expected tonight, Macface?" I asked.

Henry looked up expectantly from his text fest.

We'd played quite a few large crowds at venues and festivals throughout Melbourne, but The White Demon Warehouse was our biggest break yet and was well known as the launchpad for two bands now headed into the stratosphere of Planet Success. We had high hopes.

"Packed house, bitches."

I grinned at Henry. Henry grinned at me. Mac grinned at both of us.

"Just add a scout to that mix and I'll give you a big pash," I said to Mac, pouting my lips in a come hither if you dare expression.

"Christ, don't say that. You'll ruin my lippie. I spent like ten minutes on it."

I looked at Mac's lips. They looked like she'd spent ten minutes on them.

"Do mine," I ordered.

I guzzled the rest of my bubbles while she scrabbled around in the vanity drawer, producing a lip liner, a tube of lip plumper, base lipstick, top lipstick, and a sparkly pink gloss.

Henry, absorbing the seriousness of what we were about to embark on, rolled his eyes. "Aren't we like in a hurry?"

The front door slammed and the Rice Bubbles could be heard banging around in the kitchen, pillaging our fridge and pantry.

"Christ, Henry!" Mac waved the lip liner around in a panic. I moved my head back, fearing another furry eyebrow fiasco, this time in

Perverted Pink. "Go hide my chocolate stash will you? If those troublemakers so much as breath on it, I'll have them eating through straws."

Henry left with an eye roll, drinking his bubbles and texting madly as he went.

Mac turned to me with an evil grin that evoked feelings of great fear.

"Now, back to Jared," she began.

"Mac," I warned sternly with a finger point. "Don't even go there."

Mac, having heard my warnings before, rolled her eyes.

What was this? The Eye Rolling Convention?

She grabbed my finger and shoved it away. "Bet your sweet ass I am going there. I'm tired of your silly geek parade, Sandwich. You might have no trouble lying to yourself, but I'm not lying to you when I tell you that you're being a giant, fat, retarded idiot."

Mac had obviously decided the indirect route was for the weak.

"Just give it to me straight, Mac, okay? Because I'd hate for you to waste time taking tact pills in the morning."

"Better than the stupid pills you seem to have been overdosing on the last God knows how many years. Come on, Evie, I know you think the dorks you've been dating are safe, and I won't deny that they are because I've seen you more involved in watching paint peel from the walls, but it's no way to live. I don't care about Hairy Parry's time space continuum theory or Beetle Bob's thesis on the evolution of insects and its problems for Darwinism."

Frankly, I didn't care either, but it was hardly the heady stuff that would lead your heart down the garden path either, was it?

"Hairy Parry was cute."

"Was he? How were you able to tell under all that hair?"

I chuckled, disrupting Mac's efforts at layering liner along the edges of my lips.

Hairy Parry had a calm, quiet demeanour and also a beard and a long wavy mane that rivalled my own. I think dating a man with so much hair was more a novelty than anything else, but we did enjoy each other's company. I was loud and he was quiet, and we somehow managed to find a middle ground that worked for the both of us.

Mac smoothed on the base lipstick.

"Rub your lips together, Sandwich," she ordered.

I rubbed my lips and offered a pout as she inspected and then continued with the top coat.

"Beetle Bob was really sweet."

"Beetle Bob lavished more attention on Draco than on you!"

This was true. Draco was one of Beetle Bob's pet bearded dragons, a very social little Australian lizard that would bob his head and swish his tail whenever I visited. Surprisingly, Beetle Bob's little creatures were entertaining and somehow soothing, but they did require constant care, so many nights would find us cozied up on the couch watching television while they overran the house.

"I miss Draco," I muttered. "Maybe I should get my own little lizard friend."

Mac snorted. "You don't have the time involved in caring for one of those freaky little critters and don't change the subject."

With a "Voila," Mac finished slicking gloss on my lips and shoved me out the door and towards my walk-in wardrobe before I could even pout in the mirror to inspect the results.

Hands on her hips, she stared at the contents. "What are you wearing?"

"Well I thought I would—"

"No, you thought wrong."

Of course I did, considering her control issues filtered down into telling me what I should and shouldn't wear.

I pursed my glossy Perverted Pink lips, and let her have her way, flopping down on the bed as she made her way into the wardrobe.

Henry wandered in, phone at the ready. "Top up?" he asked, indicating towards the empty champagne glass I still clutched in my hands.

"No," Mac shouted from somewhere within the dark confines. "She'll ruin her lips."

True. Perverted Pink Perfection was not created in mere moments.

Henry shrugged and walked back out.

"I think that you should ask Jared out," Mac shouted.

"Are you high? Because I'm pretty sure I heard you telling me I should ask Jared out."

"Here!" A pair of Sass and Bide croc-print skinny jeans slapped me in the face.

I winced. Those were going to be hot, as in sweaty. I stood up and began the struggle of wedging my legs into the tight material.

"No, I am not *high*. Okay, don't. He'll ask you. I'm sure of it. Now that we're living in Sydney, there'll be no more avoiding him."

That was what I was worried about, especially after the incident at the Zen bar two weeks ago in Melbourne that simply confirmed my lack of control around the man.

I lay on the bed, sucked in my stomach with everything I had, and zipped up the jeans. As I rolled off the bed and onto my knees, a manoeuvre performed because simply sitting up in said jeans was unachievable, a silver and Lucite studded baby doll top slapped me up the side of my head.

Mac emerged from the wardrobe as I struggled to my feet.

"What are you doing?" she asked in disbelief, as though flopping around on the floor like a trout was something I was doing for fun. "We need to get going."

I glared. "I'm trying to get dressed, asshead."

I smoothed the long curls of hair that ran down my back, an attempt at fixing the mess created from clothing whiplash, and flung the babydoll top over my new lacy creation. As I moved to examine my appearance in the full length mirror behind the wardrobe door, Mac came to stand behind me.

"Just say yes."

I heard a quaver in her voice and had no doubt she believed with all her heart that Jared and I were meant to be. I couldn't help but feel partial responsibility for that particular belief.

I met her eyes. "No."

"Sandwich," she growled. "I want you happy. I want Jared happy. The two of you together would equal giant rainbows of happiness."

I couldn't help but laugh at her earnest, yet idiotic expression which changed to hopeful when I didn't reply.

Mac nodded her head approvingly and pointed at me. "Shoes."

At that, she spun on her heel and vacated the room.

I clambered for a pair of black stilettos from the chaos that was now my wardrobe and gave up breathing as I bent over to slip them on. These shoes were the David Copperfield of the stiletto world. They might have looked like skyscraping gems of leather strappage, but in reality it would likely take threats of scissors and at least half an hour to get them off later tonight.

I stood up with a gasp, my face red from the exertion of performing magical deeds.

"Hurry up, asshead!" Mac shouted up the stairs.

I rolled my eyes, because this was the Eyerolling Convention after all, grabbed my bag, and headed down the stairs to the car where everyone was waiting.

Chapter Two

"Up and in the shower, Sandwich!"

Mac's voice sounded far away because I was happily burrowed deep beneath the fluffy white mounds of my bed, busy reflecting on last night's success.

The White Demon Warehouse had been filled to capacity just like Mac assured us it would be. The venue was more than worthy of launching our band, Jamieson, into success. Only a repeat booking would provide the concrete evidence, so we'd remain on tenterhooks until Mac had spoken to their manager Marcus and received some feedback.

The White Demon was located in the heart of the city, just a drunken stumble to Central Station, and displayed a retro red brick façade, white panelled windows, and high lofty ceilings for acoustical brilliance. Several bars dotted the interior, allowing enough alcoholic lubrication to launch a rocket, and burly bouncers swarmed the four entry points, ensuring drunken degenerates were given the boot.

I felt hands make contact and give a tickle to the body protected by the thick white covers. I chuckled and burrowed in further.

"She's awake." I heard Henry's muffled voice.

The covers were whipped off, and I shrieked at the sudden bright rays of light, squinting at Mac and Henry as they piled on my bed.

I squeezed out a squeal as I yawned and stretched aching muscles, exhausted after last night's efforts. It felt far too early to be doing something as energetic as getting in the shower like Mac suggested.

"What's going on?" I muttered tiredly.

"Mum and Dad are having a barbecue lunch today. Spur of the moment. They were disappointed they missed seeing you last night, so they want us there."

I was disappointed I'd missed seeing Steve and Jenna too. Mac's parents were like my surrogate mum and dad since my own were no longer around. My dad—a very loose term—Ray, was big on sailing, and when I was five, he'd gotten on his boat one day and never returned. It would be nice to believe that the choice of leaving us was out of his hands, even if that meant he'd died, but there'd been a couple of random sightings of him by family friends, so the truth was that he just didn't want us anymore. Sometimes, I think it must have broken my mum's heart more knowing that rather than if he'd died. For me it doesn't hurt, not in a devastating break your heart kind of way, because I didn't know him. There was just an empty space where a dad was supposed to be. Random snippets sometimes flitted through my mind of him on the boat as the harsh sun beat down, laughing, directing my older brother Coby on hoisting sails, urging me out of the way, but they were blurry, and sometimes I wondered if they really happened.

My mum, Nance, wasn't around much. She worked long hours in an investment banking firm. That had never been an issue for me because when she was home and with you, she was *with* you. Her focus didn't waver, and Coby and I knew, without her needing to say, that we were the most important part of her life. The hard work was done for us, a single mother trying to do it all for her kids.

She died the day of my sixteenth birthday. She'd left at four in the morning just so she could get through her work to leave early and help set up for my party. I was bitterly disappointed when she hadn't arrived and set about doing it all myself. I left school early that Friday to be there and angrily strung up balloons, thinking that I'd never asked for much, just Mum's time, and on the day of my sixteenth birthday party of all days, work had come first. Only an hour after the party was under way, Coby found me in the kitchen chatting to my friend Cam. His pale, anxious face and the fact that he'd snatched my wrist, dragging me upstairs to my room without a word, was cause for alarm. When he delivered the news that Mum had died in a car accident, I didn't cry or turn hysterical. Adrenaline kicked in and I nodded quietly and returned to the party, realising Coby had told Henry first because guests were already disappearing en masse towards the door. I calmly accepted hugs and tears from closer friends, and when the door closed behind the last guest, Coby and Henry looked on, their eyebrows drawn together in similar expressions of worry as I set about pulling down balloons, binning rubbish that littered the house, and packing food away in the fridge. I still looked back on my response that day and marvelled at how I managed to just pack it away and pull myself together. Apparently, I was good in a crisis.

Later that night, Coby and Henry urged me into the shower, thinking that maybe the shock of the water might alleviate some of the adrenaline and let the emotion through. The fact that I sat on the floor of the shower for over an hour as the water beat down on my curled sobbing form told me their idea had been a good one. Unfortunately, I'd packed it away again the next day, and that was when my life had started to spiral out of control. Turning to both men and alcohol wasn't the ideal way to heal the horrible sensation of abandonment, but it certainly helped me forget, and for brief moments I felt wanted. Thankfully, Coby forgave me for those years even though I'd put him through hell. At seven years my senior, and in the middle of finals, I figured being saddled with a sixteen year old female was probably already hell in itself.

"Earth to space cadet," Mac sing-songed, snapping her fingers in my face and I blinked away the memories.

"They're putting on a barbecue just for us?"

Mac's parents lived in the Sydney suburb of Balmain, still in the same house Mac grew up in until she moved to Melbourne on scholarship and found us. They'd been excited about coming to our first Sydney show last night, but we hadn't finished playing until well after midnight. Being in their early fifties, they weren't the die-hard mosh pit types, well not anymore, and they left at a sensible hour.

"Yep," she replied.

"That's really nice, but um, why does that mean we need to be up at the hour of...whatever hour it is?"

Henry and Mac shared a meaningful smirk.

"Because Mac wants to head over there early to help Jenna set up," Henry offered as he stole the pillow out from under my head and propped it behind his back.

"Hey!" I made a grab for the pillow. "Does she want me there to help too or do you need a lift?"

Mac didn't own a car and neither did Henry. They hadn't needed one in Melbourne. Most places had been within walking distance, and I had my Toyota Hilux and the Rice Bubbles had their van, so they borrowed either when needed.

"No...no, but maybe you can make your slice?" Henry suggested, pressing his back hard into the pillow as I tried to pry it away from him.

My lemon coconut slice was popular on the Melbourne uni circuit because it had the perfect ratio of biscuit base to lemon icing and had a tart chewy crunch that almost made your toes curl.

"Sure," I said on a yawn, stretching again, and when Henry shifted, I snatched my pillow back in triumph. Fluffing it and then tucking it back under my head I asked Mac, "But how are you getting there then?"

Henry and Mac once again looked at each other with raised eyebrows, and before I could make threats of violence to find out what they were up to, a voice called out from the stairway and my question was answered.

I jabbed an angry finger at both Mac and Henry as they crowded my bed. "You sneaky interfering fuckers," I hissed. "You both need to worry about your own damn love lives and stop interfering in my own."

Shit.

"In here, Jared," Mac shouted.

Double shit.

17

I'd successfully managed to evade Jared last night, but it wasn't through any magical tricks from my bag of, well, magical tricks. After the show, my band mates had left the dressing room for the bar, the roar of the DJ thumping through the air as they'd made their exit. I'd stayed behind, mostly because I was still in the throes of avoiding Jared and somewhat because my makeup had sweated off under the blinding bright lights of the stage and needed a serious overhaul. Then Mac had busted through the door, in the way only Mac could, and delivered the news that Jared and Coby had been called out for work and exited the warehouse half an hour ago. I squashed the feelings of disappointment like a pesky bug and summoned up a smile of delight to put Mac off the scent. Jared was likely off to shoot at a few criminals before blowing up a small building or two.

Jared earned his living dealing in mayhem and chaotic violence, just like my brother Coby. They both co-owned *Jamieson and Valentine Consulting* here in Sydney, along with Mac's other brother Travis. Coby fitted in well with the Valentine brothers, having met Jared when he'd visited Mac in Melbourne one weekend a few months after she'd moved. Happy I was settled and doing well at uni, and seemingly done with my years of spiralling out of control, Coby moved to Sydney and their consulting business was born. To be honest, none of us were sure what the *consulting* part meant; the term was conveniently vague in my opinion, but I knew they had contracts from various government agencies and mostly dealt in hostage negotiations, kidnapping, and ransom.

After being in business for five years, their operation expanded and they now had a huge team in place as well as gaining another co-owner, Casey. I knew they'd been shot at on more than one occasion. Travis was actually hit once in the shoulder. Jared was knifed two different times, and Casey rolled his car during a full-on, hair raising, police flashing, siren screaming car chase down Motorway 5 in Sydney's south-west. It seemed they had their fingers in every dangerous pie across the city of Sydney and would soon be running out of hands. Once, while I was busy trying to recuperate from a hangover on the couch of my Melbourne apartment, I saw Coby on the news running full pelt down a back alley, shouting and gun in hand, before it cut to the news reporter on the street. My heart almost closed up shop and moved to another city. I told Coby he had to remove *consulting* from their sign and change their name to *Jamieson & Valentine: Badass Brigade.*

Henry laughed and Mac smirked as I tried to smooth the birds nest that was my hair and hurriedly wiped under my eyes to make sure no smudged mascara residue lingered there.

Why hadn't I jumped in the shower like Mac told me to? I was now desperately lamenting my laziness. The first time I'd met Jared I'd fared no better.

It was the first time Jared had visited Melbourne and became friends with my brother. Henry and I hadn't known Mac before uni; she answered our online ad to share a three-bedroomed apartment with the two of us. Jared had stopped in for a weekend visit from Sydney to see with his own eyes that Mac was happily settled and not getting into any trouble. He didn't actually say that last part, but it was definitely implied. The fact that we were uni students in a band meant that troubles did abound on a regular basis, however, we weren't housing any plans on announcing said troubles to an overprotective older brother. We had a party apartment. It was within walking distance to the uni bar and featured lots of timber flooring that forgave rivers of vodka spillage and unfortunate barfing with reckless regularity.

His arrival was unannounced, so when the knock came at the door, I was prone on the couch, Mac was on the floor, and Henry was somewhere in between both. The three of us were hungover, motionless, and watching a music video marathon with all the enthusiasm of a goldfish on Christmas day.

A quick and silent rock, paper, scissors ensued, and the loser, which was always me, staggered off with a numb backside to open the door.

My pickled brain and my unfortunate choice of hangover wear (comfy cotton shorts with a hole in the ass, ratty faded to grey Rolling Stones singlet top, hair half dried and frizzed in a ball on top of my head) left me speechless and feeling the immediate burn of embarrassment when I'd flung the door open.

Jared stood there in all his delicious glory, and that, for me, was when time had stopped. The man was absolutely exceptional and not just because of how he looked because I'd already seen photos, and it was evident he shared the same genes as Mac. His eyes were the same shade of emerald, and his skin just as golden, but where Mac was all blonde, his hair was light brown, the ends only slightly blond from the sun. It was obvious he needed a haircut. Most of the photos I saw featured him with shorter hair. I liked the length, how it hung in his eyes and made me want to brush it across his forehead, my fingers itching to feel the silky strands that caressed the back of his neck.

His clothes were nothing special, an old vintage t-shirt and soft worn jeans, but he wore them well. The shirt stretched across a broad chest and revealed the tanned muscles of his biceps. The jeans rode low upon lean hips, leading down the long length of leg to a pair of motorcycle boots that had seen better days.

He didn't appear heavily tattooed, but when he lifted his right arm to scratch at the back of his neck, the underside of his bicep revealed an inky swirl of words you just knew meant something important. I was dying to know what it said, what it meant to him.

It all made up a tantalising package of man, but it was his eyes and his demeanour that spoke to me of something special. His posture exuded a strong, capable determinedness, serious and unwavering, but his eyes radiated laughter and passion, and when they locked on mine, my mouth went dry and my heart quickened to a beat of epic proportions.

Then those eyes did a full body scan of the wonderment that was me in hangover mode, and I watched the corners of his lips curl up in a lazy grin so hot it was a wonder I wasn't already a pile of ash on the floor.

I sucked in a deep breath, letting it out in a whoosh when he opened his mouth to talk and his deep voice rumbled across my skin like rich honey.

"You must be Evie."

I shivered, nodding mutely because upon hearing that voice, I decided I'd be whoever he wanted me to be as long he kept talking.

"Can I come in?" he asked, green eyes watching me intently.

When his voice set off more shivers, I once again nodded dumbly, deciding he could move in if that was what he wanted.

"I'm Mac's brother Jared," he offered, even though I'd already known, and he moved through the doorway. For the third and final time, I nodded because I decided he could be whoever he wanted to be as long as he was standing in my apartment.

"Jared," Mac squealed and leaped into his arms when I'd guided him into the lounge room like a dumb mute.

Mac's squeal was a like a sucker punch. It pulled me out of a time warp that had me sucked in so hard I'd forgotten who I was, leaving me filled me with horror. No man had ever left me at such a loss the way he had done in just a matter of moments. I promptly vacated the room, got dressed, and did what any self-respecting girl would do when faced with such a predicament.

I went shopping.

One pair of shoes, two sets of silk and lace underwear, a dress, and two new kitchen implements later, I descended on Hairy Parry's apartment for the weekend. A good dose of dork was exactly what I needed to break Jared's spell.

The next morning I'd woken up all tangled in Hairy Parry's hair to a text message from Mac.

M: Did you have to disappear yesterday?

E: Yes. Yes, I did :P

I rolled over to my stomach in the darkened room so I wouldn't disturb Parry with my messaging.

M: Why?

I sighed as I thought about my response and decided to just come out with it. God knew she'd get it out of me eventually anyway.

E: Your brother is hot.

M: Your point is?

E: Hello? Did you not see me yesterday? <-- social retard alert.

M: You like him???!!!

This time my sigh accompanied a cringe of embarrassment.

E: Like is a strong word, Mactard.

M: We're going out for lunch. If you don't come with us, I'll tell Jared you like him and give him your number.

I couldn't help but feel I was somehow revisiting my high school years and resisted the urge to message Mac and tell her to suck it. Instead, I got up, showered, and left Parry a note telling him not to leave town because I had plans that involved him and bed for later that evening. I ignored the loud voice telling me to call Mac's bluff. So what if she gave him my number? Were the tickets on myself that big that I thought he would use it anyway? I saw him for all of ten minutes!

I messaged Coby, inviting him to lunch, too. If Mac was going to have her brother there, then by God, so was I. With Coby there I was sure I'd be less likely to make an idiot of myself around Jared. Besides, it was entirely possible my initial reaction to him was simply my brain cells not firing at full speed due to the hangover I'd been suffering.

The four of us met at a café and sat in the sun at a pretty, outdoor table. After finishing lunch, I realised my mistake in not trusting my initial instincts. Jared hadn't looked any less hot, and I hadn't acted any less stupid. Thankfully, most of the conversation was carried by Jared and Coby, making my lack of speech less noticeable. Whenever I looked anywhere other than my plate, it was in Jared's direction, and every time, his eyes would meet mine with an expression I wasn't able to decipher.

Eventually, I was able to relax a little and join in the conversation. At one point, I even had Jared laughing with a story about Cooper's latest stage diving attempt when we played at a small, local festival three weeks ago. It had left Cooper with a twisted ankle and a bunch of female groupies dragging him to safety as he gave us the thumbs up.

As the afternoon wore on, I let my guard down. I decided I could happily sit there for hours and listen to Jared talk. When I was able to forget myself, I could respond freely or talk and laugh loudly with Mac in our usual banter. Then I would find his eyes on me again and clam up until he directed his focus away, speaking to Coby and laughing.

It got to the point where I was gazing freely at Jared, and he must have felt it because he offered me a wink while he kept talking with Coby. By then I knew it was time to go. I stood on shaky legs and informed the table I was going out and that I'd see them tomorrow.

Out of the corner of my eye I saw Jared frown. Coby shook his head at Mac, mouthing "Hairy Parry?"

Feeling annoyed, which I attributed mostly to the fact that I wanted Jared and wasn't allowing myself the chance, I snapped out, "Yes, Coby. I have a hot date with Hairy Parry."

Mac snorted as though the idea of *hot* and *Hairy Parry* together in one sentence was outrageous.

I glared at Mac, and Coby stood up, kissing me on the cheek and telling me to be safe. I offered a smile and a quick hand wave to Jared, not quite meeting his eyes, and left.

I'd only gotten a few steps when I heard, "Wait up, Evie."

I turned, seeing Jared jogging to catch up to me, and my heart skipped a beat. Okay, it skipped a couple. I raised my eyebrows in question.

"I was wondering if I could get your number?"

My first reaction was that I was going to murder Mac, weigh her body down, and throw her over a bridge. Well maybe that might be a bit much, but at the least there would be pain. Did she put him up to this?

I folded my arms. "Did Mac put you up to this?"

He gave a slight head shake, appearing confused. "Ah, no? Actually, I was going to say I have a friend who lives here in Melbourne. His little sister is getting into singing, and I thought maybe if I passed on your info, you could be like a mentor or something. It's just a thought," he added.

Deflated and embarrassed, I made a show of digging around in my bag for a pen to cover the flush. Of course Mac had been all talk, and of course Jared wasn't interested. I wanted him to want me as much as I wanted him, even if I wasn't willing to act on it. How stupid was that?

"You can just tell me you know. I can type it in," he said.

I peered up from the depths of my bag, flush returning as he stood there holding his phone with amusement crinkling his eyes.

"Right." I wiped my sweaty hands down my shirt in the pretence of smoothing wrinkles as I gave him my number.

He typed it in, then casually tucked his phone into his back pocket. "Thanks. So uh, Hairy Parry, huh? He's your boyfriend?"

I nodded, avoiding his gaze because it was giving me shivers.

He stepped closer, tipping his finger under my chin until I met his eyes. The light touch and the heat from his body left me feeling breathless, but it was nothing compared to the burning heat in his eyes. "Hope he knows he's a lucky guy. Well, enjoy your hot date, Evie."

"Um, thanks," I replied, wondering if he'd now ruined Hairy Parry for me, and quite possibly any other man.

Jared turned and headed back to the table, and unwilling to return my gaze to Mac and Coby for their reaction to that little whatever it was, I left for Hairy Parry's.

That evening found me wearing my slinkiest, shortest black dress and highest heels and dragging Parry out to Verve with some casual friends. The plan was to drink and dance the night away in my best effort to remove Jared's image from my head. The barely there underwear I'd worn worked well in capturing Parry's attention, but later that night, naked in bed after sex, I'd felt like an absolute shit girlfriend for wishing it was Jared's tongue that was tasting my skin and his mouth that was doing wicked things to my body.

I woke again the next day, closer to lunch time than morning, to another message as Parry lay snoring at my side. This time though, it wasn't from Mac.

Leaving for Sydney this morning, Evie. Just wanted to say bye and thanks for letting me stay at your apartment. Jared.

I swallowed the lump in my throat at the thought of Jared leaving and typed a casual response.

E: Have a safe flight home!

A safe flight home? Like he had any control over the aircraft? What an idiot.

J: Thanks. How did your hot date go?

What was I supposed to say to that? Shitty, because I wished it was you I was on the hot date with?

E: Great! We went drinking and dancing at Verve with some friends.

J: So can I assume that Hairy Parry's name is because he's hairy?

E: You can. Hair almost as long as mine.

J: So you like guys with long hair? Should I grow mine?

What did that mean? He wants me to like him? He likes me? My pulse raced, making me feel worse because I was lying in bed naked with one man while I was burning up inside for another.

I ignored the question, not sure how to respond, and instead changed the subject.

E: Hey, I didn't ask you what your friend's sister's name was?

Jared replied to my question, and we messaged each other on and off for the rest of the day. I enjoyed the banter. He was witty and smart, and considering he lived such a long distance away, surely chatting to him this way was safe enough.

Then the next day he asked me about a band he was seeing that afternoon with friends and if I'd heard of them. I hadn't but I looked them up, and their songs were fantastic. I commended him on his taste in music, and the rest of that day found us messaging each other on and off, and then the next day, and the next, until it seemed we struck up some kind of texting friendship where the two of us couldn't seem to go a day without texting the other.

Like when I found a particularly expensive, but necessary pair of shoes. I'd snap a photo and message it.

E: Should I buy these?

J: Only if you promise to send a pic of you wearing them.

I would get a message late at night.

J: Drowning in paperwork. Do you know first aid?

E: Mouth to mouth is my speciality, but alas, you will be blue by the time I arrive. Call the medics.

When I'd broken up with Hairy Parry six months later, I found myself forlorn but naturally not heartbroken.

J: Do you need me to break his face?

E: I would, but you would be hard pressed to find it under all that hair.

J: lol

E: Don't you have any girls I can break a face for?

If that wasn't fishing then I wasn't Rex Hunt.

J: I don't do relationships.

E: Why not?

J: That is a story for another day.

Six months later, I met Robert the insect fiend who we'd promptly nicknamed Beetle Bob. Mac and Henry had chortled with glee when they found out our first date was to the Melbourne Museum to view the *Bugs Alive!* exhibition.

Later that night, Jared's message arrived.

J: How was your first date at the museum?

E: Beetle Bob was very attentive & I got to see a feeding demonstration. Very cool.

J: Cool, huh? What was your favourite bug?

E: Praying mantis, I think. Those things were pretty cute.

J: Don't they bite the head off the male after sex?

E: Oh gross. They do?

J: lol. Didn't you learn anything at the exhibition?

E: I guess not!

Four weeks later, I actually received an invitation inside the inner sanctum that was Beetle Bob's house and promptly met Draco. Draco liked a good piece of mango and hung out on my arm while I made him watch *So You Think You Can Dance*. He really seemed to like it. I snapped a photo of Draco head-bobbing and texted it to Jared.

E: Isn't he cute?

J: Is that Beetle Bob? If so, he's much better looking than Hairy Parry.

I laughed like a loon while Beetle Bob gave me the freaky eye, and Draco just kept on head-bobbing on my arm.

Then six months later, Jared got knifed in the side by a drugged up lunatic who thought waving it about inside a store and locking up customers seemed like a good way to earn money.

Panicked and scared, it almost got me on a plane to Sydney.

E: Are you okay?

J: Just a scratch. I had worse at ten years old when I jumped off the roof of our house.

E: What trying to be Superman?

J: Wolverine. His thing is an accelerated healing process. Sadly mine took a metal pin and eight weeks in plaster.

Four months later, our Melbourne festival appearance hit YouTube and received a really decent viewing. That night found us at the local university watering hole dancing and singing and liberating the bar of all alcohol. Unfortunately, Beetle Bob, as usual, decided to leave early to tend the insects in his care, and while the thought was admirable, for a brief moment, I was tired of coming second best to a bunch of creepy-crawlies. Thus began a knock down drag out shouting match that levelled the entire building to silence.

I left in a drunken snit and promptly messaged Jared when I got home.

E: Beetle Bob has been effectively crushed. I will miss Draco.

J: Plenty more dorks in the sea.

Two weeks later, Beetle Bob came by, Draco in tow because he knew I'd do anything for the little lizard dude, apologised, and told me he would be a better boyfriend.

I immediately felt bad because it wasn't like we were in love, and I *was* being a bit of a selfish mole, but Beetle Bob was otherwise a good person, so I took him back. I snapped a photo of me holding Draco and messaged it to Jared.

E: Beetle Bob is back on.

J: You just want him for his big lizard.

E: Guilty :-D

It was six weeks later when I saw Coby on the news as he rushed some random dilapidated brown weatherboard house.

E: What the hell are you up to?

J: You know I can't discuss details. We are all good.

Two weeks later he messaged a photo of what was left of Casey's car after his high speed chase.

J: Walked away, the lucky bastard.

E: He must be the real Wolverine. Lucky you weren't in the car. You would have been in traction for months.

J: Har har.

A few inane messages.

J: What are you doing?

E: Face mask. Can't talk.

J: In that case, a string walks into a bar several times and asks for a drink. Each time, he is turned down by the bartender. Finally, the string asks a stranger to tie him in a knot and frazzle the ends a little. The string walks back into the bar and the bartender asks him, "Hey aren't you the same string I just turned down?" The string replies, "I'm a frayed knot."

I snorted water out my nose, and my mask promptly cracked into a thousand pieces at his lame, dorky joke.

Six weeks later, I met Herringbone, Beetle Bob's new baby python. His greeting was simply a pair of beady black eyeballs peeking out from the inside of my running shoe. I snapped a photo and messaged Jared.

E: So I thought I'd go for a light jog this morning.

J: Nice snake shoes. Bet that made you run fast.

E: Like you wouldn't believe.

Two months later.

J: Finally, a weekend off. Thought I'd come visit.

I panicked.

A long distance friendship was all good and well from the safety of another state, but we all knew how well I managed in Jared's real life presence.

E: This weekend? What a shame. Beetle Bob and I will be away visiting his sister and brother-in-law in Canberra.

We weren't, but Beetle Bob had been making noises about it, so no time like the present. I messaged Beetle Bob, and in a matter of moments, our weekend was arranged.

Two months later, we arrived at the conclusion our musical career would take off better in Sydney and made the decision to move.

J: Mac tells me you're moving to Sydney.

E: Yes, our band is going to be the next big thing.

J: Does this mean we get to hang out?

E: You should be so lucky.

Three months later found us all set to move. Over the internet, we picked out a newly renovated duplex based in Coogee, a pretty beachside suburb just out of the city and a short walk to the beach. It had three bedrooms on one side and three on the other with a joint basement that housed a shared laundry and tons of space for musical equipment. It was perfect for the six of us. Coby did the inspection and when he gave us the nod telling us it wasn't really a fallen down ramshackle in a desperate state of disrepair, he arranged the rental for us. That simply left us with four weeks to pack up our lives in Melbourne and make the move.

Two weeks later, Beetle Bob and I decided to part ways. Long distance visiting was simply not feasible when it came to the care of his creatures.

J: So you and Beetle Bob, huh?

E: Draco and Herringbone will fill the empty void that I leave behind.

One week later, Jared and Travis arrived for an overnight stay to help move some of the heavier furniture. The plan was for us to follow in a few days with the rest of our possessions and the band equipment.

Unfortunately, on the afternoon of Jared's arrival, I'd received some snide comments from Beetle Bob's friends at the local store, and feeling angry and a little let down, I met up with Henry at the Zen bar, our new local watering hole since graduating uni.

It was later that night, after five Metropolitans, that Mac arrived at the bar, Jared and Travis in tow. Metros were like Cosmos but better because they were made with black-currant vodka. I had been busy happily bashing Beetle Bob's friends to Henry to make myself feel better. Henry, who was trying his best to offer support but not used to Metros, was having trouble keeping his seat.

My first thought when I saw Jared venture into the bar alongside Mac and Travis, was thank God I finally looked decent. My long waves of hair were curled into lush waves that very morning. My skin was tinted rose from the summer sunshine. No longer donning ratty pyjamas or the last minute wrinkled outfit worn to lunch, I was dressed in tailored grey shorts with pink pinstripes, a loosely fitted cream blouse, and strappy lemon coloured wedges. It was the perfect ensemble: casual, chic, and pretty.

My second thought was that he hadn't changed one bit since I saw him last. His effect on me was as strong as it had ever been. My breath still lodged in my throat, and my palms sweated so much I had to wipe them discreetly on my shorts. Communicating via messages from another state was so much easier and safer.

I overheard Henry informing Jared of the spiteful comments by Beetle Bob's friends. Soon after, I felt Jared's hand grasp mine as he hustled me into a quiet dark corner of the bar.

"You okay, baby?" he asked, his brow furrowed with concern.

The endearment sent my pulse racing, and up close, those fierce green eyes of his were amazing, the golden flecks highlighting the vivid shade of emerald.

I ducked my head from the intensity and picked at a loose thread on the hem of my blouse. "I'm okay Jared, thanks. I just… We parted on good terms so it wasn't expected."

"Don't let them get to you. They're just jealous."

I huffed out a little laugh at his words. "What? Jealous of me?"

"Jealous that your Beetle Bob managed a catch like you."

"He's not *my* Beetle Bob anymore."

I felt the light brush of Jared's fingers as he gently swept a rogue curl of hair off my shoulder and tucked it behind my ear.

I met his eyes at the touch, unable to look away and not wanting to.

"Good," he muttered.

Slowly, he bent his head, and I felt the whisper light touch of his mouth on my collarbone as though he'd needed the very taste of my skin on his lips.

My heart thumped painfully in my chest, and without thinking, I tilted my neck. At the silent invitation, his tongue came out to trace hot, lazy circles on my skin, slowly and maddeningly making his way up to my ear. I felt my knees buckle, and he shifted towards me until his body pressed me into the wall.

"Fuck," I heard him mutter before his lips came down on mine.

He swallowed the moan climbing up my throat, his tongue flooding my mouth. One hand grasped the back of my neck, reaching up to thread his fingers through my hair. The other hand tugged at my leg until he had it wrapped around him, ensuring I was pressed against him hard. A warm, possessive groan rumbled from his chest and set a slow burn through my body.

Somewhere, somehow, my mind let out a feeble whimper of protest. Panting, I yanked my head back faster than you could say "break your silly idiot heart."

Not realising we had gained such an enthusiastic audience, I faltered when my eyes hit the little group that was comprised of Mac, Henry, and Travis. Mac was watching with unconcealed delight. Henry, squinting in his blurry drunken state, appeared no less delighted, and Travis simply looked on with amusement.

Jared groaned. "Sorry. I shouldn't have done that."

"You shouldn't have?"

He tugged gently on the rogue strand of hair that broke loose and was currently hiding the disappointment on my face.

"We need to talk, Evie."

We did?

"We do?"

"You're moving to Sydney in a week, and I think it's time that—"

I cut him off quickly, worried about the direction the conversation seemed to be taking. "Actually, it's time for me to get going."

His eyebrows lifted in surprise, and shifting around him in a manoeuvre that would impress James Bond, I raced back to the table and picked up my bag.

"I'm sorry," I said to the table, "but I have to go."

Panicking because I could feel Jared coming up behind me, I avoided the questioning gaze directed at me by both of my best friends and escaped the building with all the grace of an elephant charging through the scrub, no doubt making a spectacle of myself that had me burning with embarrassment.

Not quite ready to face Jared, or the cavalry, or *that* kiss, I stayed the night at Cam's apartment, snapping off a message to Henry to let him know where I was. Not long after, messages came through from both Mac and Jared while I struggled to find sleep.

M: It's come to my attention after tonight's events that nothing is more perfect than you and my brother together. I know you, Sandwich. Give it a chance.

When I didn't reply, because I planned on fighting it with all the arsenal I had at my disposal, her messages became, unsurprisingly, more direct.

M: Sandwich, stop being so retarded and come home.

Then there was Jared.

J: I'm sorry, Evie. I didn't intend to upset you. Please talk to me?

I wasn't sure what I was supposed to say, so I didn't reply to that either.

A week later, I hadn't heard from him at all, apart from that one text. I could only conclude that he either thought I was an idiot and decided I wasn't worth the effort, which I tried to tell myself was a really good thing, or he was waiting for our move to Sydney so he could talk to me face to face.

Now, I found myself surrounded by traitorous bastards formerly known as my friends, wondering if it was going to be the former or the latter and knowing that I would soon find out.

Chapter Three

"Sandwich, the two of you need to talk," Mac insisted.

Maybe we did but that didn't mean it was going to happen. Regardless, I tried to curb my irritation with my friends. They meant well and I did appreciate that they wanted to see me happy, but the sooner they realised a relationship with Jared was not in the cards the better.

I heard heavy footfalls on the stairs, followed by Jared appearing in my bedroom doorway. I watched his eyes find Mac first as she bounded off the bed to wrap him in hug and start a rapid fire of questions about what had called him away last night. Henry scooted to the edge of the bed to join the conversation, but my mind tuned out, unable to listen to his answers as my eyes drank him in. His silky hair was damp as though he'd just showered, and he was wearing his usual vintage t-shirt teamed with a pair of low slung cargo shorts.

Jared's gaze cut to mine as he spoke, his eyes lowering lazily in a full body scan. Glancing down at my scantily clad form, I remembered I was still only wearing my usual night time attire of a thin silk camisole and tiny matching shorts. I owned numerous sets in various colours and patterns, and this one, a deep rose with ivory lace trim, was my favourite. I quickly shifted my bare legs, scooting them back under the heavy white covers and out of sight, before turning a scorching glare his way.

His eyes flickered in amusement, and he grinned at me, revealing a dimple as Henry spoke to him. A dimple! How was I supposed to fight that? I could feel battle lines being drawn.

My mind tuned back in after I'd finished pulling the covers to my chin.

"How did you get in anyway?" Mac asked.

Jared's frown included all of us. "No one answered the door, and it wasn't locked. Why the fuck wasn't the door locked?"

The three of us shared a guilty expression because the cab ride home was a little vague. Frankly, we were lucky the front door was even closed after our hard-earned night of celebration.

I winced when both Mac and Henry mumbled awkwardly obvious excuses and vacated the room. I heard a loud thump that sounded like someone banging into the wall and then the bathroom door slammed shut. It was, no doubt, a skirmish for dibs on the shower which was a regular occurrence in our household, and Henry, the bigger of the three of us, was no gentlemen and usually came out trumps.

My eyes warned Jared that he too should also vacate the room, but he ignored it. Instead, he chose to gift me with another grin and shifted to the end of the bed where he proceeded to slip off his shoes and stretch his long, sexy length out next to me. He turned on his back and tucked his arms under his head to contemplate the ceiling.

"I thought they'd never leave."

He smelled nice. I pulled the sheet up higher.

"Maybe you should wait for Mac downstairs," I suggested.

He didn't respond to my words. He lost his smile and small lines furrowed the middle of his brow.

"You didn't return my message, Evie."

He was, of course, referring to the message he'd sent post kiss that I had no idea how to respond to. I itched to pull the sheets up and over my head, but instead, I tried to form a response that came out badly worded.

"That's because your lips on mine was a colossal mistake, and I wasn't sure where we should go from that."

38

My eyes flickered to his lips, and I tried to shake the feeling that it wasn't a mistake at all. When I shifted my gaze to meet his, I almost missed the brief flash of hurt he carefully tucked away.

"Well, I can't say being called a colossal mistake is a nice feeling."

It wasn't how I'd meant it to sound, so I tried to explain without giving away too much. "Not you, just you and I together. It was a nice kiss. I just think we work much better as friends."

Jared's eyebrows raised as he turned on his side to face me, propping his head on his hand. "Just nice?"

I flushed and the urge to burrow reached critical levels. "Um…" I offered in response. Really, what was I supposed to say? *"It was a lip-locking, body-burning, mind-vacating experience like I'd never had in my entire life and please could you just keep kissing me until the end of time?"*

"Was this what you wanted to talk about?" I blurted out.

Then I cringed internally for throwing myself into the fire.

Amusement returned and flickered in his eyes as he noted my flushed skin and seemed to like the reaction. "No, but it's a good start."

It was?

"It is?"

I shifted the covers down a little so my arms could escape the confines. It was getting hot. Jared took the opportunity to reach out and tuck my hand in his, threading our fingers together. He expanded no further at my question, but his gaze on our linked hands was contemplative.

"Jared?"

He took his time answering, now watching me intently with an expression I wasn't able to read. "I'm not really sure you're ready to hear what I have to say."

I frowned. "Isn't that for me to decide?"

Irritated, I tugged my hand out of his and scooted out of bed, hurrying to my wardrobe to shrug on my silk robe, tying it in knots so tight I thought I might have to get the scissors out later just to get out of it.

When I emerged from the wardrobe, Jared hadn't moved.

"I need to have a shower, so you know, maybe you should wait downstairs."

He merely looked at me and pulled the covers up and over his chest, his actions telling me he wasn't planning on moving anywhere any time soon.

"Evie?" he called out when I turned to leave the room.

I rested my hand against the doorframe and half turned. "Yeah?"

"I've missed you. You've always been a good friend, even living in another city, it was nice knowing I had you to talk to. Just a random simple message in the middle of the day meant more to me than... Well, anyway, I've missed hearing from you, so let's get back to that okay?"

Because I'd missed it too, I nodded with smile. "Okay," I agreed.

"Good," was his response. "Wake me when Mac is ready to leave."

He closed tired eyes and before I left the room, I tried not to notice how hot he looked all wrapped up in the frilly white confection of my bed, but really, it was a wonder the sheets didn't catch fire.

After my shower, during which Mac and Jared left, I hit the kitchen of our duplex to start making the slice. As it was newly renovated, the walls were painted in a stone colour, the cupboards were glossy white and housed big stainless steel appliances. Thick, pale caesarstone benchtops ran the length of the room. It suited my kitchen implements fetish seamlessly. A Breville juicer sat on the counter for when I decided to shock my insides with something healthy. It sat next to my kettle, toaster, and KitchenAid mixer, all in cherry red because everyone knew red was faster.

I came out of the walk-in pantry with an armload of ingredients as Henry stumbled in. I shoved some Panadol at him and took some for myself while I was at it.

He swallowed them gratefully. "Thanks, Evie."

"Want some breakie? I could annihilate a bacon and egg burger right now."

Watching Henry flinch and turn green, I realised that he was suffering the effects of the Hangover Stalker. It was when you woke surprised at how great you felt, only to have a shower and start moving around, and then realised you were slowly losing the will to live.

I patted his arm in sympathy, but really, this was karma for the stunt he and Mac had pulled on me this morning.

"Maybe later," he said.

I pulled my cherry red food processor out of the bottom cupboard and sat it on the bench, emptying out the packet of biscuits I'd ripped open.

"Well maybe just a biscuit," he said, rescuing one from imminent massacre and shovelling it in his face.

I smacked at his hand before proceeding to switch the processor on and watch the biscuits rapidly become a pile of rubble before my eyes.

"You making your slice?" he asked around a mouthful of biscuit.

"Yes I am, Detective Hussy. You coming to the barbecue?"

"Fuck yeah."

This was not a surprise. Barbecued food was hot on our list of must eat items. I emptied the rubble of biscuits into a bowl and opened a tin of condensed milk.

"Mac said her mum invited half of Sydney last night," he leaned over to flip on the kettle. "So did you and Jared have the *talk*?" he asked, obviously wanting the low down on what happened after he and Mac vacated the bedroom.

"There was nothing to talk about." Well nothing Jared was prepared to talk about until I was ready, but I wasn't willing to share that little gem with Henry. It would only encourage him.

He rolled his eyes in obvious frustration. "Chook, I may not be Dr. Love, but it's obvious to even me, the retarded relationship bastard, that you and Jared have a thing."

This was true, the part about Henry being a retarded relationship bastard. Henry had broken a heart or a million in his time (pick a number somewhere in between) because his struggle with the concept of commitment was an ongoing one. In his defence, he was always upfront about his unwillingness to commit.

He spooned sugar into two mugs as I began to press the biscuit base into the slice pan.

"Henry, does either Wild Renny or Asshole Kellar ring a bell? I'm not going there again."

"Jared is hardly in the same league as those two losers."

"They weren't complete losers, Henry."

Henry raised one eyebrow at me as I moved to the fridge.

"Okay, well maybe Asshole Kellar was, but his car wasn't. Wild Renny was just misunderstood, you know. I wonder what he's doing now?"

Henry handed me a mug of tea along with a warning. "Wild Renny is out of your life, Evie. I don't want you thinking about him or wondering anything about him. Clear?"

Henry liked to act like the big bossy brother sometimes, and on this particular subject, I usually allowed it because alongside Coby, he was the one who helped pick up the pieces when my life had spiralled out of control.

I pulled him in for a soothing hug, knowing the memories made him tense and angry.

"I'm clear, Henry."

He squeezed me tight before pulling away, nodding and moving to the couch indicating he wanted to watch music videos.

I finished making my slice, popped it in the fridge to set, made a pile of vegemite toast, and joined Henry. I promptly ate the pile of toast and passed out.

A message from Mac woke me up as I lay drooling all over Henry's chest with a piece of vegemite toast mashed into my face.

M: Have you left yet? If you don't leave now, you're gonna be late, asshead!

"Shit, Henry, wake up!"

Henry was lying on his back, lightly snoring into a cushion. I shoved his shoulder. When he didn't move, I shoved harder and he accidentally went off the edge of the couch. I winced when his head bounced off the floor with a crack.

"Evie. *What the fuck?*"

I lifted my chin up in challenge. I didn't mean to crack his head, but I had to roll with it now. "I tried for ages to wake you," I lied.

Henry pounced and we wrestled on the floor like ten year olds. Henry knew all my best moves, and because of my aversion to defeat, I retreated, leaping off him and racing for the stairs instead. I needed to wash my face now that I had vegemite smeared up the side of my cheek.

Henry, realising my intentions, raced passed me on the stairs and shoved into my shoulder so that I stumbled. I should have remembered that move because he surged ahead, flew into the bathroom, and slammed the door.

"Damn you, Henry," I shouted.

I changed into a pair of hot pink capris and a black singlet top, and because it was hot, pulled my hair into a knot of curls at the nape of my neck. Sliding my feet into black flip flops, I was ready to go, and we were only ten minutes late by the time I parked my Hilux in front of Steve and Jenna's house. Coby had bought me the car for my birthday two years ago. It was a double-cab with turbo diesel in tidal blue and kicked car ass. In addition to kicking car ass, it also helped cart around musical equipment when needed while still making me feel like I owned the road just a little, which was extremely satisfying.

Steve and Jenna's house in Balmain was a renovated two storey rendered brick affair with bright green, well-tended shrubbery and a giant wall of jasmine vine currently in bloom along either side of the house. Apparently, the barbecue had just hit full swing if the amount of cars parked in the driveway and street were anything to go by.

I tilted my head to glare at Frog and Cooper through the rear view mirror.

"Cooper," I growled.

"Sandwich," he drawled with a grin.

"Do I look like I need a seeing eye dog?"

I threw up my hands in defeat when no one was willing to meet my eyes, but half the missing slice and coconut crumbed lips told the story that no one needed to verbalise. The boys were like hoovers when it came to food; nothing was safe.

I opened the car door, jumped out, and slammed it shut. As the four of us congregated on the lawn, I snatched the plate of slice out of Frog's pilfering hands and shoved it at Henry.

"You all better be on your best behaviour," I hissed and pointed my finger for extra emphasis. "This is Mac's *mum's* place."

Frog offered a wink. "You can trust us."

"Said the spider to the fly," I muttered under my breath as we made our way to the front door.

Cooper and Frog, named simply because his full name was Jason Froggatt, presented a united front behind me. They were close. I liked to joke that if they had a song, Queen's *You're my Best Friend* would be it, and if they didn't love women so much, they'd try their best to turn gay for each other. They even looked alike: Frog barely an inch taller than Cooper's five foot eleven, silky black hair that fell into their eyes, and golden tanned skin. Though Cooper's eyes were so dark they appeared black, and Frog's were a light hazel. They even dressed alike in their skinny jeans and tight faded Silverchair or Wolfmother t-shirts.

Cooper grew up in Melbourne and transferred to our uni, joining our band when our previous keyboardist of six months quit due to creative differences. Cooper spoke fluent keyboard like we'd never seen and had moved into Frog and Jake's apartment across the hall from ours two weeks later.

Fast friends, they saw each other through a bad break up or two, which included an epic public showdown between Frog and his then girlfriend Rachel. That relationship lasted a whole year before they had a split so publicly volatile it was the talk of uni campus for two weeks, not including the week the breakup dragged on for. Frog remained tight-lipped, but it became public knowledge that she cheated on him. Frog, being wild and crazy and a rule bender, was popular at uni. This made Rachel very unpopular, and three months later, she packed her bags and transferred back home.

One month after that, Coopers girlfriend Natalie copped a mugging and a black eye, blamed Cooper for it in the twisted way that Natalie managed to blame everyone for everything bad that happened in her life, and dumped him on his ass.

No one had ever liked Natalie and the feeling was mutual, so seeing the back of her earned Cooper a one week supply of free alcohol at the uni bar. We would have made it longer, but if you knew how much he could put away you would understand.

At our knock, we heard a voice yell that the door was open. Jenna came out of the kitchen at our arrival, rushing over to envelop me in a sweet smelling hug. I hugged back—hard because I'd missed her. Both she and Steve had visited us in Melbourne every chance they got, and Mac and I would take her shopping on Chapel Street, my favourite place to spend money.

"Genevieve, honey..." she palmed both of my cheeks in her hands "...how are you?"

She looked into my eyes, concern filling her gaze because Jenna was always a mother first. She was sharp and capable, kept herself toned with regular yoga, and wore her blonde hair in a neat bob. She was also pushing for grandkids harder than a drill sergeant on a recruitment drive. With all the Valentine offspring currently unattached, it wasn't looking good for her. Without waiting for my reply, her green eyes gleamed as she leaned in. "Jared is out back, honey. You should go say hello."

She winked at me meaningfully, and I knew she'd been apprised of recent events between Jared and me. It appeared Mac had been busily recruiting while I had my eye off the ball. This did not bode well.

She reached around me to pull Henry into a hug.

"Hey, honey, how are you?"

"Uh, good thanks, Mrs Valentine," Henry managed.

"Jenna, please, honey." She took the proffered plate out of Henry's hands. "Oh, are these for us? You know how much everyone loves this slice, Evie." She smiled at me kindly, obviously remembering I made it for them in honour of their first visit to our Melbourne apartment.

"Well, half of its gone now, thanks to banana one and two there." I rolled my eyes towards Frog and Cooper.

She raised one eyebrow in a mock glare. "Well. None for them later then," she said, putting the slice down on the kitchen counter to grab them both in a hug.

"Hi, Mrs Valentine," they both mumbled.

"Jenna, please," she addressed them. "Go get your butts outside. Steve is manning the barbecue, and the esky is by the big table," she called out as we headed outside.

The yard was half tiled with thick sandstone, and the other half had a lush green lawn with Jenna's prized vegie patch running along the side of the fence. A rectangle pool sat to the left, surrounded by a clear perspex fence, and was half covered under a big cream coloured shade sail. The water rippled invitingly in the early afternoon sun, and a heated game of water volleyball was going on. A bikini clad Mac was smack bang in the middle of a Hot Guy Volleyball Sandwich and looked as though she was in no hurry to rectify the situation.

"Genevieve!" Steve called out and made his way over, waving his tongs about through the throng of people as Henry, Frog, and Cooper made for the esky. He grabbed me in a big hug, lifting me off my feet, and I shivered with delight because Steve was the big gruff dad I never had. Once again, I squeezed back hard.

"You look beautiful, my girl," he said, indicating my outfit.

"Thanks, Steve. How's it going?"

"Good, good, apart from the fact that Jenna invited half of Sydney," he muttered covertly, though I could see the twinkle in his eye. He loved entertaining since his retirement from the force, living for the weekends when he could crank up the barbecue. We chatted for a moment on recent current events; Steve liked to follow the World News religiously and felt it was his duty to then inform everyone else.

"Why don't you have a drink yet?" he demanded, looking about. "Where's Jenna?"

"She's busy in the kitchen I think. It's okay, I can get my own."

"Rubbish. Ah, here's Jared to the rescue."

Jared was strolling my way, juice in one hand, glass of wine in the other, eyes glittering hotly as he took me in.

Henry trailed along behind carrying two beers. No doubt his purpose was to eavesdrop on all verbal (and non-verbal for that matter) exchanges and report back to Mac at the next available opportunity.

"I better get back before those steaks catch fire. Leave you kids to it," Steve muttered distractedly as he made his way back from where he came, slapping Jared and Henry heartily on the back along the way and stopping every so often to chatter with the people milling about.

"Hey, baby," Jared leaned over and planted a kiss on my cheek.

The gesture had my skin tingling where his lips touched me, and despite the insistent voice telling me to move away, my legs appeared unwilling to listen.

"Jared," I replied.

He grinned, displaying his dimple. "Wine or juice?"

"Juice, please."

I took it with a grateful sigh as I watched Steve's retreating back. Jared sat the wine down, and Henry handed him the second beer.

"Thanks. I love your dad."

I took a massive gulp of the nice icy cold drink, and my eyes found Jenna who now stood next to Steve at the barbecue, watching us with delight as she tittered something in Steve's ear.

"I love your mum too."

Jared put an arm around my shoulders comfortably and tucked me into his side. "You know they love you like a daughter."

I did know this. Jenna made sure to inform me on a regular basis, but I appreciated the reassurance of his words.

I listened quietly as Jared and Henry chatted about his work and how busy they were lately when I heard a voice in my ear and felt a wall at my back.

"Hey, there's my dancing partner." Two well-muscled arms encircled my waist to give a quick squeeze.

"Travis!" I grinned delightedly as Jared frowned at the both of us.

Travis was almost a carbon copy of Jared only his green eyes were a little lighter, his hair a little shorter and more blond, and he was maybe an inch taller. Travis was at the White Demon last night for our show and after party. I loved to dance and the fact that Travis wasn't bad at it, and rarely left the dance floor, meant we'd stuck close to each other for most of the party.

He came around to stand in our huddle.

"Jared was just telling us how well the business was going because you all seem so busy."

"It is going well," he said. "Jared and I are lucky enough to have a rare day off while Casey and Coby are stuck working, so let's not talk shop."

"Agreed," said Jared. "In fact..." he grabbed my hand and yanked me away "...we're going for a swim."

"We are? But I didn't bring swimmers."

He changed direction. "This way then. Mac keeps a heap in her old room."

He led me inside the house and up the stairs to Mac's old room. I started to snoop about with great interest because Jenna had left their rooms intact after they'd all eventually moved out, giving the impression she was keeping them that way for future grandkids. Jared went straight to a drawer, yanked it open, and pulled out a pretty little yellow bikini.

"Here." He walked over, interrupting my perusal of Mac's hoard of historical romance novels. Who knew Mac had such a romantic side?

I took the bikini he held out and went to step away, but he effectively blocked me in.

Dammit. He still smelled really good.

My head tilted back to meet his eyes.

"Why do I get the feeling you're keeping things from me?" he asked, his voice low and gentle. His face came close to mine, and my pulse raced. Once again, my gaze was drawn to his lips, unable to forget their heat.

"I don't really know what you mean," I mumbled.

I put my hands on his chest in a half-hearted shove because he was standing too close and it was making me dizzy.

He didn't budge.

"We're supposed to be friends, but there are pieces of yourself you're keeping locked away. What is it? It's got something to do with this geek parade that Mac keeps yabbering on about doesn't it? What's *that* about?"

"Nothing," I lied. "Smart guys are cool, you know."

"I didn't say they weren't. Is it me? Have I offended you in some way? I might have thought it was because I kissed you, but it's like you've had your guard up since the moment I met you."

His words threw me off balance, and I wasn't sure how to respond.

"I think that—"

"No. Don't think. You've been doing too much of that. Just tell me what's going on."

"It's not any of your business, Jared."

He leaned in close, too close, and I thought he might actually kiss me again.

49

"Evie." He breathed against my mouth, his lips hovering over mine. "That hurts. You're my friend and that makes you my business."

If I was just your friend, why did you kiss me the way you did back at Zen that night, and if that was all I wanted you to be, why did I let you?

Jared's phone saved me from verbalising my inner confusion.

He stepped away, pulling it out of his back pocket, and looked at the screen before answering.

I dragged in a few deep breaths, both grateful for the reprieve and disappointed in a way I wasn't prepared to acknowledge.

"Coby." Pause. "Where?" Longer pause. "Fifteen minutes."

He ended the call, tucking the phone away, and locked his eyes on mine. "I have to go."

The best I could manage was a mute nod because he was leaving, and even before he was gone, I felt bereft.

"I have to go away for a couple of weeks for work tomorrow. I wanna hear from you."

I nodded again and his eyes went warm as he tapped his finger gently on my nose.

"See you, Evie."

"Bye, Jared," I whispered.

He turned and left so I changed into the yellow bikini and sat quietly on the bed for moment, wondering how on earth I was going to manage denying myself what I wanted. Seriously. It was like waving a bag of lollies in front of a starving child.

"There you are!"

Mac rounded the doorway and her gaze swept the room for Jared. Remembering Mac's recruitment drive, I thought I'd try catching her off guard. "I saw your books, Mac."

It worked when she paused in confusion. "My books?"

"Do you think Jared is going to come in, rescue me, sweep me over his shoulder, carry me to his giant steed, and we'll ride to his moat-surrounded castle and live happily ever after?"

With guilt filling her eyes, her gaze slid to the books on her shelves.
"No," she lied.

"Mactard," I said in warning.

She sighed dramatically and flopped down on the bed. "Jared is a good guy, Evie."

"Good guys still break hearts," I snapped.

"Where is he anyway?"

"He had to leave."

"Pity."

"Oh yeah? Why's that?"

She gave my boobs, currently busting out of her yellow bikini because I had a way bigger handful than she did, a pointed glance.

"Jared is a boob man," she said knowingly.

I smacked her in the head with the pillow that was on the bed and flounced out of the room and down to the pool, proceeding to cannonball the five current occupants, dunk Henry three times, and eat a late lunch before we said our goodbyes.

Chapter Four

The next two weeks flew by like a supersonic jet, hurtling me towards certain doom because Jared would be home any day now, and I still had no idea what to do about him.

Mac, bless her managerial bossy soul, had gotten us another booking at the White Demon in a week, assuring us the feedback was high enough to go through the ceiling. If that didn't say potential scout, then I really did have a Great Aunt Dottie.

Jared and I seemed to have moved passed the kissing incident and were back to our daily texting as friends.

E: What are you doing?

He messaged a photo of a huge dull conference room full of people.

J: Stuck inside a conference room in Brisbane.

I snapped a photo of the brilliant sunshine and blue surf.

E: I am at the beach :-P

Later that night, I snapped a photo of my sunburnt face. Even my olive skin wasn't used to the harsher sunshine.

E: Thinking of changing my name to Hellgirl: Beast of the Apocalypse.

J: Get some aloe on that beautiful face of yours, Hellgirl.

I refused to admit the burst of warmth flooding my body was complete and utter pleasure at being called beautiful by Jared.

Two days later while I was out jogging I received a disturbing text.

J: Who is Asshole Kellar?

I stumbled mid-jog and stopped to ping off a message to Mac, suddenly fuming that Mac had told him. I was not proud of my spiralling years and didn't want them advertised. To anyone.

E: What the hell did you say to Jared about Asshole Kellar?

M: Chill, tomato face. His name slipped out. I didn't say anything.

I messaged Jared.

E: No one. Just an ex.

J: I've heard about Hairy Parry and Beetle Bob, but no one has mentioned Asshole Kellar before. Who else don't I know about?

Wild Renny.

E: No one. It's nothing.

Six days later, I received a photo taken from the top of the Giant Drop at the Dreamworld theme park located about an hour's drive south of Brisbane.

E: Working hard I see.

J: Have friends up here with two teenage boys. Feel like a kid again.

Jared was only twenty-seven, hardly in his twilight years.

E: Yes, oh aged and wizened crone. I want a photo of you in the diary chair at the Big Brother house.

The house for the Australian version of the Big Brother reality show was located at the Dreamworld compound. I had a friend almost make the final cut on the show, but I couldn't imagine being shut away from the world for so long. Mac had laughed when I told her this, assuring me I would have only lasted a week before getting voted off. I chuckled when later that afternoon a photo arrived of one of the teenage boys *planking* on the diary chair while Jared stood behind with an obvious look of exasperation.

J: I don't get the whole planking thing, but they seem to find it amusing.

Three days later.

E: Mac has us booked at a place called the Florence Bar tonight.

Supposedly, It was an intimate bar somewhere along Darling Harbour. According to Mac, the place was a bit tamer than our usual wild atmosphere, so we worked at putting a set list together that Mac thought would fit in with the classy vibe.

J: Nice place. Am about to board flight home so save me a ticket, okay?

My heart fluttered at his words.

"It's all useless crap," Mac shouted from the bowels of my wardrobe while I sat on the bed busily messaging all and sundry. "You have nothing sexy and glamorous."

"Jared is coming tonight," I announced the words that a few weeks ago had me spiralling into a panicked frenzy.

"I know. I've already put a ticket aside for him. Right," she muttered as she came out, dusting off her hands as though she was emerging from the murky depths of the great Australian Jenolan caves. "I need to go shopping, like right now."

"Macface, I have plenty of sex and glamour in there. You're up to something."

"Don't be silly," she muttered, not meeting my eyes. "Right, I best get a move on. Won't be long."

Deciding not to make an issue of her subterfuge, I waved her off warily and went to have a shower. When I was done and my hair dry, I pulled on my favourite silky robe from Pretty Plum Sugar and popped a set of heated rollers in my hair. Then I descended the stairs, grabbed a bottle of water from the fridge, and sat on the couch with Henry to watch the Saturday afternoon footy.

Henry watched it for the game. Me, I had no clue what they were doing running around tackling each other for a ball. As much as I could commend them for their athleticism and fiery determination to pound each other to the ground, I just watched it for the little shorts.

E: Go Melbourne Storm.

J: Are you serious? They have three injured star players. Manly Sea Eagles will kick their ass.

I didn't reply because that was about as technical as I got when it came to football.

Half an hour later, a knock came at the door.

"Are you expecting anyone?" I asked Henry.

Henry took a break from shouting at the referee on the television to shake his head. "Nope."

"I'm not answering it with freaking rollers in my hair."

Henry gave my rollered hair a speculative look.

"You should. Then maybe whoever is at the door will see your freaky assed hair-do and think twice before knocking on the door again in the middle of a footy game."

He didn't budge and I sighed as we did a silent rock, paper, scissors, and I squealed in unconcealed delight when I pulled out the scissors to Henry's paper. That was unheard of.

E: I just won my first RPS in like two years.

J: Woohoo. What do you win for that?

E: Not having to answer the door to whoever is knocking of course.

I snatched the packet of chips out of Henry's hand and made for the stairway.

"Hey," he grumbled, getting up to answer the door when the knock came for the second time.

I slammed the bathroom door behind me and began makeup preparations for Glamour Goddess. Glamour, as every woman knew, involved understated eyes with thick black lash extensions and full red lips. When I stepped back to view the results, I knew Mac would approve. I finished pulling the rollers out of my hair and pinned the long thick curls across to the side so they fell in a waterfall over my shoulder.

Hearing voices, I wandered back downstairs in search of Mac and my new and supposed sexy and glamorous outfit. Instead, I found Henry, Mitch, and Tate standing around the kitchen chatting and drinking beer.

Mitch was Mac's other older brother and a detective with the Sydney City police. Tate was his partner. Twenty-five to Mitch's thirty-one, Tate had a short black buzz cut, pale blue eyes, and a penchant for playing online Halo, which was some kind of science fiction slash war type computer game. Apparently, it was serious business in his books and involved an online international team of like-minded individuals and a headset. I wondered if that meant he fit my geek requirements.

"Hey, beautiful," Mitch exclaimed when I rounded the kitchen.

"Hey, Mitch." I smiled and leaned in to kiss his cheek.

"You remember my partner, Tate?" He motioned to Tate standing next to him.

"Of course," I murmured and gave Tate my best smile when I leaned forward to take his hand. I'd met Tate at Steve and Jenna's house once when we visited one weekend.

Tate looked a bit dazed, so I was pleased to know I didn't look like complete ass.

He smiled back. "Nice to see you again."

"Are you both right for a drink?" I asked, and they both nodded as I opened the fridge to grab another bottle of water.

"Hussy?"

"Nah, I'm good, Sandwich."

"To what do we owe the honour of your presence?" I asked, unscrewing the lid and throwing it in the bin.

Mitch raised his eyebrows. "Mac didn't tell you?"

I looked to him in confusion. "Uh, no?"

"I told her we'd come to your show tonight at the Florence Bar and thought we'd stop by for a drink first."

"Oh, that's so nice!" I said, my eyes sparkling excitedly.

"It's purely selfish. Having all of you here is awesome, Evie. It gives us an excuse to go out and listen to music and pick up hot chicks."

All three chuckled in a male bonding moment, and I rolled my eyes.

"Have either of you been to the Florence Bar before?" Henry asked Mitch and Tate.

Mitch nodded in reply as he took a sip of his beer.

"I have too," Tate said and paused. "To arrest someone."

I looked at him in horror. "Oh my God, seriously? What kind of dive is Mac sending us to?"

Tate laughed. "I'm just kidding. I have been to that bar before, though, and it's really nice, classy."

"Yeah, Mac did say that."

Speak of the devil.

Mac came rushing through the front door, kicking off her shoes and throwing all her shopping bags in the direction of the couch.

"Lordie, give me that drink," she ordered, snatching the bottle out of my hand before I'd even managed a sip.

"Hey!" I went to grab it back but she danced out of reach, and I was not prepared to wrestle her for it wearing nothing but a robe over my silky underwear.

I grumbled and went to the fridge to get another one.

"Hey, Mitch, Tate," she said, giving them both a kiss on the cheek before guzzling down the water. "Christ, the shops were bloody awful. You owe me big, Evie."

I whirled around with the new bottle in my hand. "Excuse me? This is all on you. You're the one that bitched about my clothes and insisted on the shopping expedition."

"God, you're a bloody whinger. Wait till you see what I got you!" She smiled wickedly and I felt my hands grow clammy with fear.

Three sets of male eyes glazed over at the talk of shopping, and they rapidly evacuated the kitchen for the greater comfort of the couch and the last quarter of football.

"Where is it?" I asked.

She picked up all the bags off the floor, where Henry had flung them to make couch space, and came back over just as the Rice Bubble trio put in an appearance from next door.

I scanned the pile of bags on the kitchen bench, eyes wide with disbelief. "All *that* is my outfit?"

"As if!" She snorted.

She picked up a tiny little bag out of the massive pile and thrust it at me. "This one's yours."

"You two been shopping again?" Jake asked as he entered the kitchen to inspect the contents of the fridge. This went on for several moments as Jake appeared to be willing something magical to appear from the barren shelves. When nothing did, he grabbed a beer.

"Mac's been shopping. Has she ordered all of you about what you have to wear too?"

He rolled his eyes as he twisted the top off the beer and threw it in the bin. "Yep. Honestly, I have to wear a shirt." He shook his head in disgust.

"A shirt?" I squealed in mock horror. "No!"

He flipped me the finger as he escaped to the lounge room.

I put down my drink and had a peek in the bag. It didn't look like much, just a couple of black scraps. I sighed.

"What time do we have to leave?"

She glanced at her watch. "Shit. Half an hour!"

Mac grabbed an armload of the bags and raced up the stairs.

I chatted with the guys for a few minutes before Jake, Frog, and Cooper headed off to the bar early to help with the setup. Just before we had to leave, I hit my room with my little bag of scraps to get dressed. Mac was ready in record time because she was just leaving her room when I got to the top of the stairs.

I stopped to admire her form. "Wow, Macklewaine!"

She winked and did a posh twirl to show off her gorgeous red dress. It was short, showing off her long golden legs, with a high neck and long sleeves, but the back dipped dangerously low, like to the top of her ass crack low. Mac was the master of deceptively modest clothing.

"Don't be long," she called over her shoulder as she headed down the stairs. "We need to get going soon."

I went to my room and threw the two black scraps on. The top turned out to be a little bustier, nude underneath with black lace over the top. It was strapless with a sweetheart neckline and built in underwire so I didn't need a bra. The skirt was a black leather mini and not fully fitted. It had a band around the top, little pleats that helped it flare out at the hips, and lovely pockets, but it was short. It probably wasn't meant to be that short, but I had long legs, and they were definitely on display.

I wondered what the hell Mac was thinking.

Opening the bedroom door, I shouted down the stairs.

"Macface!"

"Yeah?" she shouted back up.

"Can you come here a sec?"

"No. Just hurry up and get dressed. We need to get going!"

"Mac! I can't wear this. There's too little of it!"

"Christ, Sandwich, stop shouting nonsense and hurry up downstairs. There's no time to bugger about trying to find something else to wear. It's too late."

I could hear the smugness in her voice. I wanted to stomp all over that smugness. Instead, I went to my wardrobe, grabbed my bag and my big black trench coat so I could cover my almost naked chest, and stomped angrily down the stairs to the lounge room.

"Jesus," Henry muttered as everyone looked my way.

"Evie," Mac exclaimed innocently. "I don't know what you're talking about. You look fine. Right, guys?"

Mitch and Tate were eyeballing my cleavage with equally glazed expressions.

"Christ," Mitch muttered.

"It certainly does show off your chest to advantage, doesn't it?" She smirked with satisfaction.

My glare at Mac was a frosty promise of retribution. She raised one eyebrow to tell me that she didn't really give a shit.

I started to shrug on my coat before she ripped it out of my arms and tossed it away. "You're not wearing that thing. It's too bloody hot."

"Mac," I wailed in exasperation.

"Nope. Come on," she bossed. "Mitch has ordered us a cab, and I just heard it tooting out the front."

Mac wrestled me out the door and into the warm night air, piling me into the cab that would take us to the Florence Bar.

"I know you're up to something, Mac, and I don't like it."

"Rubbish." She snorted. "I'm not up to anything. There's nothing wrong with one friend wanting another to look her best."

"I don't think almost naked is the way to do that, Mac."

Mac ignored me and started up a conversation with Tate the whole way into the city.

The bar turned out to be gorgeous, really dark and intimate with an old Hollywood style feel. There were old fashioned button leather booths that surrounded the walls, and the bar was a black painted timber affair which currently boasted a crush of people all trying to order a drink while our band took a break mid-set.

I was standing at the bar with Tate, and we chatted while waiting for the attention of one of the bartenders. I found out that Tate's brother was a drummer in a Melbourne band that I'd seen a few times, so we talked about their music, and I made him promise to let me know next time they made their way to Sydney for a gig.

"Yo, Evie," the bartender shouted.

I smiled. "Hey, um…"

"Vince."

Vince was cute with his tight black shirt and skinny black jeans and gay when I saw him give Tate a sexy wink.

I ordered a round of beers for the table and a bottle of water for myself. The boys usually had a beer or two before or during a show, but I preferred to keep a level head when it came to the serious business of singing.

"Liking Sydney so far?" Tate asked.

"Are you kidding? The beaches are amazing. I've already been burnt to a crisp."

"Soft Melbourne skin." He grinned. "Have you seen all the sights yet?"

"Sorry?" I shouted over the noise of the bar.

"I said have you seen all the sights yet?"

I shook my head. "Not really. We moved up here and got sucked straight into work, so there hasn't really been a chance yet."

He leaned down to my ear so I could hear him better.

"Maybe I could take you out some time?"

I cautiously agreed. I didn't know him all that well, but he certainly didn't seem to fit the type that would cause me any heartbreak. A few casual dates might be nice. I would just be sure to tell him I wasn't looking for more than that.

Tate grinned. "Can I have your number? I'll ring you and we can set something up."

I held out my hand. "Sure. Give me your phone."

He handed it over and I punched my number in before giving it back. "There you go," I said with a flirty smile.

He winked. "Thanks."

My eyes flicked to our booth near the front door while we waited for Vince to finish our drinks order, and I saw Jared had arrived. He was wearing a pair of dress pants so black they had a blue tinge and a fitted white and grey pinstripe dress shirt. The sleeves were rolled up, revealing tanned muscular forearms. I also saw that every woman in the room was eyeballing our booth, flicking their hair like the whole bar was participating in a Clairol commercial.

Skanks, I muttered to myself.

I also saw that our table, including Jared, Mac, Mitch, Coby, and Travis, was watching the two of us with avid interest, though Mac's interest was an unhappy one, and Jared appeared troubled.

Our drinks arrived and Tate leaned in. "Do you want to go put these on the table and have a dance?"

"Maybe later? I need to get back to the band in a minute. Our final set is gonna start soon."

"I'll hold you to that," he replied and put a hand on the small of my back as he guided me over to the booth. We put the drinks down, and Jared immediately took my hand and pulled me aside.

He glanced at my chest and then cleared his throat awkwardly. "What is that you're wearing?"

"Hello to you too, Jared."

He folded his arms. "Well?"

"Blame Mac. She made me wear it." I bit my lip. "Does it really look that bad?"

Jared swallowed visibly. "No, you look sexy as hell, Evie, but every guy in this whole bar is eye fucking you. I can't say I like it."

"I don't really care if you don't like it." I saw his eyes flare unhappily and attempted to soften the blow. "Besides, I haven't been approached by anyone."

"That's because you're a hot singer with a sexy voice in a shit hot band. You're too good for any of them."

Jared glared at a couple of guys who were heading our way, and they quickly changed direction.

"Not to mention Tate has been hanging off you since you got to the bar," he muttered.

"Tate is a nice guy," I offered. "He's going to teach me how to play Halo."

Jared's look turned to one of amusement which confused me because I didn't recall saying anything funny. "What?"

"Saying a guy is *nice* is the kiss of death from you, Evie."

"What?" I sputtered. "I don't know what you're talking about, Jared."

"Is he another one of your *geeks*? Does he get a name too? How about Tetris Tate?"

Tate chose that inopportune moment to come over as I finished the last of my drink. "Walk you back to your dressing room?" he asked me, looking around at the crowd. "It's a crush in here."

Jared glared at Tate. Tate ignored Jared. I was just relieved to be making my getaway.

"Thanks, Tate."

I placed my empty bottle on the table, and he took my hand and guided me through the throng of people to the side of the stage. "I'll see you after?" he asked.

I could see him struggling to be polite and not stare at my chest.

"Sure," I replied.

As he walked away, I saw we were still being watched avidly by all. I laughed at Mac when it was her turn to give me a frosty glare. Jared simply raised his eyebrows, so I childishly poked out my tongue before I headed through the back door.

The band was already backstage and waiting for me.

"What's going on out there, Evie?" Cooper asked as I came through the door. We saw you in a Tough Guy Sandwich."

"It's her top," Henry muttered. "It's causing riots."

I powdered the shine off my face and re-did my lipstick before pulling at my top, trying to lift it up to cover my boobs a bit more without success.

"I keep worrying that they're going to just pop out in the middle of a song."

"Awesome," said Frog with a laugh. "It's no wonder every male in the room seems so focused tonight. Maybe if one did pop out it might get us a good write up in the paper."

Henry whacked him up the head. "It's not a live sex show, Frog."

Frog looked suitably chastened. "Jesus. I was only teasing. Sorry, Evie." He frowned at Henry.

"Hey, guys." Jack, the entertainment manager, poked his head around the door. "How are you all going?"

"Great!" I answered with a smile. "I've never been to this bar before. It's really beautiful. Thanks so much for having us play here, Jack."

"My pleasure, Evie." He gave me a winning smile, his eyes shining brilliantly. "Can I get you anything? I've left you some fresh bottles of water by the side of the stage. You just let me know."

"We're all good. Thanks, Jack."

"Okay, well you're on five."

I gave him the thumbs up, and he shut the door.

"Can I get you anything, Evie?" Cooper mimicked in a high pitched voice. "What are we, invisible?"

The guys all laughed.

"We may as well be while Evie's wearing that." Jake snorted.

"Shut up, assheads, and stop picking on me because I have boobs. You're all just jealous."

"Yeah," Cooper muttered. "We all wish we had boobs right now."

Jake laughed.

"That is not what I meant." I gave them all a glare as I tried not to laugh. "Let's go and if you don't let up about the boobs, then when I get on that stage, I'm going to announce that you're all gayer than an Easter Parade. Then you'll be wrestling with male groupies rather than female ones."

That seemed to shut them up, and we hit the stage to the cheer of the crowd, playing the final forty minutes of our last set. The last song was a slow acoustic song I wrote after my break up with Wild Renny. It was one of our most moving songs, and the crowd didn't disappoint by going silent and listening intently.

Standing at the microphone, I let my voice hang on the notes as Henry hunched over, plucking at his guitar, the corners of his lips turned up. I loved seeing the look on his face, his eyes downcast and completely absorbed as he floated somewhere along cloud nine, immersed in the bliss of doing something he loved more than anything.

My eyes picked out Mac in the crowd. Mac was a sucker for this song. I hid a grin, knowing she would be teary and that would piss her off.

My voice rang out huskily on the final note, and Henry stood up from his stool and gave me a hug as the crowd went crazy and roared around us.

The spotlights went off and the stage went black.

"Okay?" Henry asked.

He always asked me that after that song.

I was more than okay. We might not have been on fire like we were for a bigger crowd, but the intimate setting felt more personal, and that was a rush as much as a massive wild crowd was.

"Are you kidding?" I waved my hand towards the crowd surrounding us. "Look at this shit, Henry. We are so hot right now." I grinned.

The crowd continued their whoops of delight, and Henry chuckled as he picked me up in a big hug and carried me off the stage.

"You know I love you, Evie."

"Don't turn into a sappy bastard." I mock groaned as he set me down on my feet backstage. "I love you too."

"Damn straight you do. Now go get us all a drink while we sort out our equipment," he ordered with a slap on my bum.

"Bossy bastard." I saluted him.

I smiled happily because I didn't mind being the drinks lady, better being at the bar than stuck sorting out cables and amplifiers.

Mac enveloped me in a hug when I arrived at the bar, which was high praise for our performance, before standing back to wipe a little tear from her eye.

"Damn you, Evie. Playing that stupid song. I didn't put it in the set list because you know I freaking hate it."

Mac, of course, loved the song. She just hated being teary.

I patted her shoulder in sympathy and placed a drink order with Vince while Mac pestered me for details about what was going on with Tate.

I looked at my shoes. "Tate's nice. He's going to teach me how to play online Halo." He hadn't said this, like I'd told Jared earlier, but I assumed it would be a given.

A smug smile danced across Mac's lips. "Well, that settles that then."

"Settles what?"

"Tate doesn't do it for you. Nothing to worry about there."

Mac opened her mouth to speak, but Travis interrupted our verbal tussle.

"Great show, Evie," he said, stifling a yawn.

Coby nodded in agreement as he tucked me into his side. Coby might have been seven years older than me, but apart from being almost a foot taller, we could be mistaken for identical twins.

Coby had the same dark chocolate eyes, dark brown hair tinted caramel from the sun, and the same rosy olive skin. Unfortunately, he was the one that ended up with the long black eyelashes which he selfishly complained made him look too girly.

"Thanks, Travis. You two look wrecked. Going home?" I asked.

"Yeah." Coby looked disappointed. "Sorry to bail."

"That's okay." I patted his back. "Dodging bullets and bombs exploding into towering inferno's of hell must really take it out of a guy."

"Are you kidding?" Travis muttered. "That's the best part. It's the paper work that is slowly killing us."

I nodded. "So I've heard."

I waved them off, had Vince put the drinks on our tab, and Mac and I hit what was left of our table, which was Henry, Mitch, and Tate. I wasn't sure where Jared had gone to.

"You have an amazing voice, Evie," Tate murmured close in my ear.

"Thanks, Tate."

My eyes flicked to Mac who watched our exchange unhappily. The DJ cranked her next song, loud and eager to escape the tense vibes, I took Tate's hand. "Ready for that dance?"

"Sure, lead the way."

I turned a smug gaze to Mac before I headed towards the dance floor, and I felt her death ray eyes burning into my back. It was a wonder they didn't laser a giant hole through my middle.

I found Jared on the dance floor wrapped around a blonde who looked like she'd been busy that day maxing out her credit card at Skanks 'R Us. I stumbled in my haste to look away because what he did and who he did it with was of no consequence to me.

"Are you okay?" Tate asked.

"Sorry," I murmured. "These heels are a death trap."

I leaned in and put my hands around his neck. Tate felt warm and comforting.

"They look sexy on those beautiful legs of yours, Evie," he whispered in my ear.

The compliment had me flushing with pleasure, making Tate seem a bit smoother than Hairy Parry or Beetle Bob.

I murmured a thank you while I avoided all the eyes I could feel watching us.

"What are your plans tomorrow?"

"No plans except to maybe hit the beach," I replied.

"I'm on call with Mitch tomorrow, so we really should get going. I told him we had to stay so I could have a dance with you first."

My eyes flicked to Mitch as we turned around. He looked a little bit impatient as he glanced at his watch.

"Okay. You two better get going then so poor Mitch can get his beauty sleep."

"Walk us out?"

He didn't wait for a reply, simply took my hand and led me over to Mitch.

"Ready to go?" Mitch asked.

"Yeah. Evie's gonna walk us out."

Mitch nodded and downed the last of his beer.

"Be right back," I said to Mac and Henry.

I felt the cool fresh air wash over me as we approached the loud chatter of the cab line, and I pulled Mitch in for a quick hug. "Thanks for coming, Mitch."

He hugged me back. "Great show. Killer voice. Sexy outfit. The pleasure's all mine, beautiful."

"Sweet talker," I muttered and he chuckled. I turned to Tate. "Call me?"

"Sure," he replied and placed a kiss on my cheek.

I winked at them both and headed back inside.

Chapter Five

When I returned to the bar after being waylaid for several conversations along the way, Jared, Mac, and Henry were well on their way to complete inebriation.

Mac was trying to sing (she can't), Henry was laughing at her singing (when he usually cringed), and Jared looked a little unsteady. Mostly though, the empty shot glasses on the table were a dead giveaway.

"Without me? You started shots without me?" I whimpered in mock sadness when I reached the table.

"Evie's back!" Jared shouted. "Another round of shots, Vince!"

Vince didn't seem to mind the shouting. He looked at Jared like he was God and rushed to do his bidding. He placed our drinks on the bar, and I told him to put it on our tab as I reached for them.

Jared appeared beside me and handed over money. "I'll pay."

"Thanks, Jared, but it's okay. We have a tab. Put it on the tab please, Vince," I said.

Vince waited, undecided about picking up the money.

There was a tense pause that appeared to indicate Jared wasn't backing down, his determined stance speaking for him.

Vince took the money.

"So you and Tetris Tate, huh?"

I grabbed the shot and downed it fast.

"Yep." The words burst from my mouth when the alcohol's vertical burn travelled to my toes.

"We need to talk," Jared muttered.

I felt a sense of déjà vu, and I looked at him with surprise as we walked back to the table. "We do? I thought you said I wasn't ready to hear what you had to say."

"Yeah, but that's about something else. Later, okay?"

In the early, messy hours of the morning, I decided that Drunk Jared was fun. In fact, everyone was fun. Even Mac managed to lose her Tate snit, and I laughed uncontrollably as she tried to do an exaggerated imitation of how I sang on stage, but only managed a pathetic drunken warble before stumbling in an embarrassed heap on the floor. She tried to make a recovery, pretending she was just showing us the worm dance, but the bar's owners were likely not fooled, and I imagined that an eviction was imminent.

Jared and Henry managed to pick her up off the floor before she made too much of a spectacle of herself, and on that high note, the bar closed, and we found ourselves stumbling out onto the dark streets to find a cab and head home. The cab driver politely chatted to Jared the entire way, and Henry drunkenly threw some money his way when we reach our duplex, insisting on paying because Jared kept buying all our drinks.

After staggering inside, Mac and Henry made a beeline for the fridge, and I hit the stairs, Jared following behind. He flopped down on my bed with a sigh, and I had to physically restrain my body from flinging itself on top of him by grasping hold of the dresser. I then decided that Drunk Evie around Drunk Jared wasn't a terribly smart idea.

I poked his shoulder because that was as close to Jared I was willing to allow myself. "You're not sleeping in my bed."

He rolled over and blinked at me sleepily. "I'm not sleeping with Henry, and I'm definitely not sleeping in a bed with my sister." He winked. "That leaves you."

I blinked at him drunkenly as I tried, unsuccessfully, to focus. "We have a couch."

"It's too late to walk down the stairs now, Evie. What if I fall?"

71

This was true. Drunken stumbles down stairs never ended well.

"You have an answer for everything. Fine." I wondered how Drunk Jared managed such feats of logic while I'd lost all mental faculties. "No wandering hands," I added.

I grabbed my usual sleeping attire from my drawer, lemon striped silk with ivory lace trim set, and went to the bathroom to change and perform my nightly skin routine. When I came back, Jared was under the covers and sleeping peacefully.

Not really sure what the hell I was doing, I sighed and slipped under the cool sheets, blissfully closing my tired eyes and trying to pretend that Jared wasn't there. It wasn't working. I could feel the heat emanating from his body, and I wanted to roll over and wrap myself in it.

When I felt him shift and whisper my name, I considered playing possum, but I didn't know what the outcome would be, and I wasn't willing to risk it.

Mac and Henry stomped loudly up the stairs after their fridge binge, and I heard a bang as something hit the wall, then a muffled "ouch" before the bathroom door slammed.

"Yeah?" I whispered quietly to Jared. If Mac opened the door and saw the two of us here together, I would be screwed.

I opened my eyes and found Jared on his side, watching me in the dark. "It was Asshole Kellar that broke your heart, wasn't it?"

The man was far too smart, but even as drunk as I was, I was still not prepared to share. "I don't know what you're talking about."

"The geek parade that Mac talks about, Evie. It's because they're safe, isn't it? It's obvious. You can talk to me."

I huffed, annoyed at Mac for her loose lips, and rolled over so I was facing the wall. Jared reached over and put a hand on my hip. The heat from it burned so hot I was sure I would wake up in the morning with an imprint on my skin.

"Do I need to go break his face? Will I find it? He's not another hairy one is he?"

My breath hitched and I let out a giggle as he chuckled.

"Jared," I whispered. "I'm not talking about this, okay?"

"Okay. Not now, but you'll tell me eventually."

His fingers gripped my hip tightly before pulling away, and when I woke the next morning feeling completely exhausted, the bed was empty.

Jared was gone.

The disappointment in my belly was too great to ignore. My heart wasn't just heading south, it was also heading north, east, and west too, scattered to all four corners. Maybe going out with Tate would be the best thing to do to help slow down its direction.

Snoop Dogg, I reminded myself.

I let out the breath I'd held in with a loud whoosh and rolled over to stare blindly at the litter of framed photos on my wall. Most were black and white prints in thin black frames of varying sizes. My favourite was a huge photo of Henry and I on stage, a birthday gift from Mac. A giant fan was whipping my wild hair across my face, and I was laughing into the microphone and pointing at someone in the crowd. Henry, guitar slung over his shoulders, was plucking a string and grinning at my antics. There was something about that photo that made me feel full whenever I looked at it.

"Morning, baby."

My eyes whipped to the door, and I watched a shirtless Jared walk in and place a mug on my white vintage bedside table.

I hadn't seen a shirtless Jared before. My breath packed its bags and headed for higher ground. His shoulders were wide, abs hard and tanned. A treasure trail of golden hair led from his navel down to where I could see the top button of his pants still left undone.

"I made you some tea because I know you don't drink coffee."

"Thanks," I croaked out and cleared my throat. "I thought you must have gone." It would have been the best idea, but being deprived of a vision like him in the morning was surely some sort of crime.

"No, I slept in." He looked surprised. "I never usually do that."

He stretched and yawned noisily, and I caught another peek of the tattoo on the underside of his right arm.

"What does it say?" I asked, pointing to it.

His bicep muscle flexed as he lifted his arm for me to see. "To thine own self be true."

"Hamlet? To be reminded not to lie to yourself?"

It sounded like something I needed inked on my skin.

"No, not lie," he said patiently. "Be true. There's a difference."

"So explain it to me."

The intensity of his gaze lessened until it almost felt like he'd left the room, but he was still there with me because he finally spoke. "It means not giving myself to someone else at the cost of who I am. Not allowing someone else to define me. It means letting go of personal misconceptions so I can be a better person...not just for me, but for others."

His words set in and my gaze softened on his face because I knew he was someone who would only mark their skin for something that held deep personal meaning. I could sense there was more to it, but before I could ask the question he continued, his eyes regaining their passion.

"It's too easy to suffer under mistaken beliefs, Evie. There's already far too much suffering in the world."

Not being able to stop myself if I tried, I reached out a hand and brushed it down the side of his face. The corners of his lips turned up slightly at my gesture.

"It's a good way to be, Jared."

His mouth opened to speak but my phone buzzed from the bedside table, and he turned and snatched it up. He looked at the screen and a frown furrowed his brow. He tossed it at me irritably.

"It's from Tate."

"Hey!" I responded when it hit me in the shoulder. "What was that for?"

"I don't like Tate. He's shifty."

I snorted with laughter at how ridiculous that sounded. "Tate shifty?"

Jared crawled back into my bed with his own coffee while I opened the message.

T: Morning, Evie. How did you pull up last night?

E: Didn't get home till early hours. Just woke up. How about you?

"What'd he say?" Jared asked.

I yawned and stretched. "Just asking how the night went."

T: That's a nice visual, you waking up in bed. Can I take you out tonight?

I flushed and Jared leaned over my shoulder. "What is it?"

"He just asked me out."

"Show me?"

I handed over the phone and watched Jared read the message, lips pressed together firmly as he handed it back.

I took the phone in my hand unsure of what to say in the unnatural quiet. I typed out a response as Jared fluffed the pillow to sit back more comfortably and took a sip of his coffee.

E: Ok. What time?

T: Pick you up at 5?

E: See you then.

T: Will look forward to it. Dress casual. Wear non slip shoes.

"Well?" Jared asked impatiently as he watched me messaging.

"He's picking me up at five. It sounds a bit exciting. I have to wear non slip shoes."

"I don't like this, Evie."

"Who I date is my business. If you don't like it, then you should just leave."

"So you just do whatever you want without a thought or care to anyone else, huh?"

"Am I supposed to check in with all and sundry for approval before I date someone?" I folded my arms and narrowed my gaze. "Or just check in with you?"

Jared tipped his head to the ceiling with a deep breath as though frustrated, and I waved my hand at the door.

"Don't you have some criminals to round up and shoot at today?"

"Shit. Look, Evie, I'm sorry. We're friends, okay?" His eyes returned to me and softened. "I care about you. A lot."

My eyes searched his face and seeing only sincerity, I nodded. "I care about you too, Jared."

His lips curved in response, and he stood up quickly as I placed the phone on the bedside table and picked up my tea. When he flipped open the blinds, I squealed in agony, sure my retinas turned to ash from the blinding glare flooding the room.

I put my tea back down and burrowed deep down beneath the covers.

"Come on, friend. Let's go to the beach instead of wasting the day away." He came and ripped the covers off, grabbing my hand and yanking me out of bed.

"Jared!" I squealed again. "I'm not dressed."

He stopped to rake a roasting gaze over my silk and lace clad form.

"Rubbish." He pushed me towards the wardrobe. "I saw you wear less last night. Get dressed," he ordered and sailed happily out the door.

Happy at the idea of a trip to the beach, I resigned myself to the fact that avoiding Jared was going to be an impossibility. Frankly, when I got past the part of the breath-losing, heart-thumping, speech-muting feelings whenever he was close, I really enjoyed having him around. He had a way of making me feel like I could be myself in his company, like he enjoyed me for who I was. There was no criticism or reprove, just a sense of warmth and acceptance that I'd never found with anyone else. This friendship was important to me for those very reasons, and I wasn't willing to lose it.

Sipping at my tea, I perused the chaos that was now my wardrobe after Mac's petty attack from yesterday. I pulled a white and navy string bikini from a drawer, a pair of denim shorts from the floor, and a plain white tank top. Dressed, I passed a prone Mac and Henry lazing motionless on the couch and headed for the kitchen to flick the kettle on.

"Who wants a cuppa?" I yelled out.

"Me," Mac and Henry both shouted back from the couch.

I peered out the kitchen window to see Jared wearing a t-shirt and pair of Henry's boardshorts sitting on the back deck talking seriously on the phone.

"Mac, how does Jared have his coffee?" I called out.

"White, no sugar," she called back feebly.

Frog walked in from next door and gave Henry a slap up the back of the head on his way to the kitchen. Henry, to his credit because no one has reflexes when hungover, managed to stick out a foot and trip him up. Frog stumbled into the kitchen with an "oomph" and opened the fridge door.

"Where's the milk?" he asked after peering in there for about an hour.

"Are you having a man's look?"

I pushed him out of the way with a huff and looked into the fridge to see if we were actually out of milk and found the fridge completely barren.

"No beach today," I told Jared when he walked back inside. "I have to go food shopping." I waved my hand at the empty fridge as evidence before slamming the door shut.

In response, he grabbed my car keys off the bench and flung them at me. "Well, let's go then."

"You're not going to spend your day off at the supermarket with me, are you? What a total drag. Hungover, people ramming their trolleys into your ankles, mile long lines at the checkout, screaming kids. I could go on."

The list really was endless considering food shopping was not high on my list of fun things to do. It was also unfortunate that food shopping brought out the indecision in me. I could spend ten minutes trying to decide whether I wanted to buy barbecue or salt and vinegar flavoured chips. Then it was whether they should be crinkle cut or thin and crispy. Serious decisions like that could not be made lightly.

Mac, her impatience rising to the fore, couldn't handle my indecisive side. She would solve the problem by throwing both packets of chips in the trolley, and then we would end up spending way more than we should.

"Better you than me, dude," Frog said before making a quick escape next door, making sure to slap Henry up the back of the head again on his way out.

"With the two of us, we'll get it done faster, and then we can still go to the beach."

My eyebrows raised to my hairline in disbelief because obviously if he thought food shopping with me would be quick, he had another thing coming. "If you say so."

I picked my handbag up off the counter and slid my feet into my flip flops by the door. Mac and Henry were still motionless on the couch. "You guys wanna come?"

Henry groaned pathetically in response to my question. Mac was obviously asleep. Otherwise, I would be watching her smug grin of delight at the thought of Jared and I doing something as domesticated as food shopping together.

When we arrived at the supermarket, I discovered that Jared was surprisingly health conscious. How this was something that hadn't come to my attention over the years I did not know. This was not good news. In fact, there was only bad and worse news. The bad was I was watching Jared busily fling healthy food in the trolley. The worse was none of us would actually eat any of it. Our systems would declare war. Not only that, there would be riots. Without chips and chocolate, we would all turn on each other. It would be like *Lord of the Flies.*

Panicked at the notion of being flayed alive with a stick, I started flinging chips and chocolate in the trolley with unprecedented reckless abandon. I watched in horror as Jared kept putting it all back on the shelves, and I literally gagged when he replaced it with bags of brown rice and chickpeas. In desperation, I resorted to hiding whole blocks of chocolate underneath the packets of wholemeal wraps I found in there. I would have slid them into my handbag as well, but I didn't want Big Brother to think I was shoplifting and then get arrested.

"Jared," I growled, fed up when he grabbed the garlic bread I threw in and put it back on the shelf. No one messed with my garlic bread. "Put it back." I revved up for a garlic bread face off.

"Evie," he retorted, clearly exasperated. "You can't eat that crap; it's all white bread and butter."

I reached back to the shelves, grabbed the bread, and threw it back in the trolley. "I know. Yummy!"

He took it out again. People gave us odd looks as they darted in between us like birds, trying to grab at the produce we were blocking during our OK Corral showdown.

"Jared, it's not like you'll be eating all this food. You don't live with us."

"No, I don't, but I plan on hanging around a hell of a lot, so I will be eating it."

Clearly fighting a losing battle, I hissed at him. "You suck."

He pushed the trolley along quickly, ignoring my juvenile retort.

"Fine, but you just wait 'til the guys see all this vegetation..." I waved my hand at the trolley "...and then I'll be the one that has to deal when it degenerates into savagery."

"Evie." He stopped the trolley. "I think you're exaggerating. I'm just looking out for you that's all."

"Seeing me pounded by a bunch of savages with sticks is a mad way of showing it," I mumbled under my breath.

The checkout involved another scuffle over who would pay for the food, then we left, Jared smug in his victory. We came home to a deserted lounge room as we chucked shopping bags on the kitchen counter.

"Mac," Jared yelled up the stairway.

"Yeah?" she bleated back feebly.

"Groceries on the counter. We did the shop, you can put them away."

I picked up the beach bag I'd packed and placed by the front door earlier, and we walked down to the beach, stopping to pick up lunch: sushi rolls (Jared) and a hamburger with the works (me).

The beach was busy which was not unusual for a hot summer's day. People were playing beach footy and flinging frisbies and little kids were making sandcastles and giggling as they made grabs for the little crabs that scurried frantically for their lives.

Finding a nice spot, we laid out our towels before hitting the water. I decided I like Beach Jared way better than Supermarket Jared. He was actually fun to hang out with. We spent an hour body surfing and dunking each other, and I was a prune by the time we flung ourselves down on our towels to dry off under the hot sun.

Fearing another Hellgirl episode, I re-slathered on the sunscreen before grabbing my book out of my beach bag to have a read. It was the latest book in a popular vampire series, and I'd been itching to start it for ages.

Jared lay on his stomach, head on his folded arms, facing me with his eyes closed. I ignored how delicious the spots of water that dotted his skin looked and opened my book.

Jared peeked one eye open at my movement and took in the cover. It depicted a huge muscle chested guy with serious tattoos and green eyes that glared at you fiercely.

"Whatcha reading?" he asked.

I rolled my eyes at the question. If there was ever anything more annoying. "A book."

He huffed a little bit at my deliberate ignorance. "What's it about?"

"Vampires," I said as I re-read the same paragraph again.

"Is there lots of sex in it?"

I threw my book down in exasperation and half turned to glare at him. "I hope so but I'll never find out if you keep chatting to me while I'm trying to read it!"

I saw his eyes hit my chest. Remembering that Mac said Jared was a boob man, I quickly rolled on my stomach.

"Will you read the sex parts to me when you get to them?"

Read them to you? I'd rather re-enact them with you.

Oh God, I really would and not even Supermarket Jared could throw me off the path my mind was wandering down.

"Maybe."

That would be hot.

Jared obviously thought so too because the laziness left his eyes and they started to sear my skin.

Stop flirting, you idiot!

I picked up my book again and stuck my head in it so closely I couldn't even read the words. Jared sighed and flopped over to his stomach.

"Ready to talk yet?" he asked.

"No."

"How about if I ask you the questions?"

"No."

Jared looked amused rather than deterred. "I'll find out eventually."

I put my book back down with a huff. "Yeah? How do you suppose you'll do that?"

He rolled onto his side and his eyes did that warm and gentle thing again that made my heart turn to mush. "Because one day you'll belong to me, Evie, and I'll know everything about you."

Jared looked completely serious and left me with absolutely no doubt that he meant what he said.

Chapter Six

J: Ok, so give it up. Where did he take you?

E: You are just dying to know aren't you?

Tate and I were just sitting down on a blanket at Mrs. Macquarie's Chair along the city's harbour for fish and chips when the message arrived.

J: Give it up.

I replied by messaging him an earlier snapped photo of our twilight Sydney Harbour Bridge climb. It was epic and far removed from the Computer Convention I was originally expecting. The views were amazing, and the sunset was a riot of pinks, oranges, and reds. Heady stuff for a first date and Tate seemed a nice enough person, but with the huffing and puffing of climbing the huge Australian icon, there hadn't been much of a chance to talk.

J: I'm impressed. Where do you go from there – base jumping off Centrepoint Tower?

I shuddered at the thought Tate might be a potential adrenaline junky. I wasn't scared of heights. Okay, I was a little. Alright, maybe a lot. It would explain the jelly legs at the top of the bridge as I stood there sucking in deep breaths and gazed at the cars whizzing by beneath us. Jumping out of an aeroplane seemed to me a perfectly reckless pursuit of finding a high and would never make it on my bucket list.

A message arrived soon after from Henry.

H: *Message me if you need rescue.*

I knew I wouldn't hear from Mac. The fiery laser beams she shot my way when Tate picked me up could have been seen from space. I tried to respond with my own laser death rays. Unfortunately, Mac was made of Teflon, so they slid right off.

Tate began unwrapping the paper holding our fish and chips. "So you and Jared seem pretty close. Do I need to be worried?"

I smoothed out the edges of the wrinkled paper, buying some time while I figured out how to respond, and Tate watched me as he munched on a chip.

"Jared and I have been friends for years, and I don't want to compromise that," I explained as I picked up a chip. "Otherwise, you should probably know that I'm not looking for a relationship. They tend to get really complicated, and right now I need to focus on my music career, you know?" I waved my chip about before popping it in my mouth, chewing and swallowing. "I can't really offer any commitment, Tate. I work every weekend, even some week nights, and hopefully there'll be a lot of travel in our immediate future, so it's not really fair to expect someone to deal with me not being around."

It wasn't the full story, but a first date with Tate hardly qualified for soul baring confessions about why I wasn't willing to open up my heart.

My phone buzzed madly again. Not wishing to be rude, I ignored it and tore a piece of battered fish in half and started eating it.

"I'm happy with casual," Tate replied and undid the tops of two bottles of coke, handing the diet one to me. "Hell, do you know how hard it is trying to work a relationship when you're a copper? Late night shifts, call outs, constant danger. Who wants to marry that? I can't do anything else though. It's who I am, same as Mitch. Besides," he said with a wicked grin, "I'm still young and if it means I get to date gorgeous girls like you, then I'm cool with that."

My phone buzzed madly again, and I shrugged my shoulders in apology. "Sorry."

"Popular, huh? Better answer it in case it's important."

I somehow didn't think so, but I checked it anyway.

J: So what's for dinner?

Someone had nothing better to do tonight than harass me on my date.

E: Fish and chips on the harbour.

J: Is he trying to clog your arteries and kill you?

E: Yes, it seems that is his fiendish plan, and after several decades when I suffer a heart attack, it will reach its heinous fruition.

J: Smart ass.

E: Isn't the football on?

I switched off my phone and shoved it back in my bag.

"So..." I took a sip of my drink "...tell me why you decided to be a detective?"

Tate and I chatted for another hour while we finished our dinner before leaving at a respectable hour, Tate citing a dawn start for work tomorrow morning.

He walked me to the door, and before I'd even had time to blink, he leaned in and kissed me, sealing his mouth over mine. His tongue slid over my lips, and I opened my mouth, letting it sweep inside. I kissed him with everything I had, giving him all my best moves, seeing if it was at all possible to replicate the kiss I'd shared with Jared. When Tate's hand shifted lower and gripped my ass, I pulled back. Disappointed that it seemed only Jared it could evoke the feelings I longed for when he kissed me, I was also relieved because they weren't the sort of feelings I wanted to have with Tate if things were supposed to be casual.

"Jesus, Evie," he panted. His eyes were glazed over, and I almost thought he was trembling. "You're really good at that."

I nodded in mock seriousness to lighten the moment. "I get that a lot."

"You do?"

"No." I grinned. "I'm just teasing you."

He chuckled and brushed a finger across my cheek. "I'll call you."

I nodded and ducked inside the front door, latching it behind me. I was greeted by my beautiful band boys with whoops and drunken laughter as they sat around the dining table playing poker, yelling loudly, and getting through what appeared to be every single drop of alcohol we had in the house.

"Evie's home!" Frog bellowed.

"Woooooo, Evie McStevie," Cooper shouted.

They tried to enact a Mexican wave at my arrival, but with only the four of them, and drunk to boot, it came off pretty poorly.

Jake got up, poured a glass of wine, and shoved it in my hand. "Drink up, Tweety Bird. It's a poker party. Join us?"

I raised my brows. "So I see and not on your life."

I hated card games. I hated board games too for that matter. It wasn't because I was a sore loser, though when I did get roped into playing, I did happen to lose a lot. It was mostly because card games and board games were something Mum loved to do with me as a way to laugh and unwind from a long day at work. Maybe it was selfish, but I liked to keep those memories for myself.

"How was your date with Tetris Tate?" Henry asked.

I sighed at the name. It didn't take long to make the rounds. Rather than telling him, I pulled my phone out of my bag and called up the bridge climb photos and handed it over.

"Holy shit, a bridge climb? That's fucking alright. We were expecting a computer convention."

He chortled and passed around my phone to show off the beautiful photos while I sat on the arm of the lounge chair.

I pointed to the giant bowl of chips in the centre of the dining table. "You got chips!"

"Yarh." Cooper for some reason decided to use a Swedish accent.

"Jake ducked to the store earlier," Frog told me.

"Did you—"

"Yes, Chook, Jake bought you some chocolate. It's in the fridge because the heat tonight would've melted it."

I grinned in delight and gave Jake a big smoochy kiss on the cheek. "Love you, Jakie, always looking out for your Evie."

He gave my bum a pat with a silly smile, and I let that one go because he was drunk and he'd bought me chocolate. "Of course we have to look after our favourite girl, don't we?"

Abandoning the glass of wine Jake had thrust in my hand, I skipped to the fridge, grabbed my chocolate, and cozied up on the couch, settling in for a late night movie and a chocolate coma.

The next morning found my feet pounding the pavement in a river of sweat as I paid the price for my fish and chips and half a family block of chocolate. That shit did not come cheap. When I let myself back in the house, I ran into Mac's room with a grin and a loud squeal and jumped on the bed until her face smacked the headboard and she woke up.

"Oh shit," I squealed, bringing my hands to my face. "Mac, sorry, are you okay?"

I pulled back the sheets as she grumbled and rubbed at her head. "What's going on?"

Deciding she would live, I locked her in a big sweaty hug until she started screaming her head off.

Henry came running in, wild-eyed and hair every which way, to see what the noise was. When he saw Mac pinned, he jumped into the fray and began a tickle fest.

"Henry," Mac cried, "get her off me. She stinks! Ew!"

I rubbed my sweaty armpit in her face. "Take that back!"

"No," she spat.

"Jesus, Evie," Henry laughed. "You do stink."

"Hey!" I shouted as he pushed me off the bed and onto the floor. They both leaned over the side to look at me.

"First dibs on the shower!" I yelled, scrambling to get up off the floor and make a run for it. Too late, I realised my mistake was in declaring my intentions because Henry grabbed my arm and shoved me back on the floor. He raced in to the bathroom ahead of me and slammed the door.

I sighed and Mac gave me the evil eye.

"Don't be like that, Macky Wacky," I said and pulled out my bottom lip.

She tried to hold the glare but giggled. "Shut up, Evie McStevie. Now I stink too."

"Har har." I giggled. "At least everyone's awake now," I sing-songed.

She gave me a speculative look. "How was your date last night?"

I gave her the quick lowdown, and she sighed. "Why can't you and Jared just get your shit together already?"

The sound of my phone buzzed from my room, so I politely gave Mac the finger for her interference.

She sneered in return.

Satisfied with the exchange, she got up to bang down the bathroom door and I went to my room to check my phone.

"Mac?" I yelled.

"Yeah?"

"Travis wants to know if we want to go to the shooting range with him and Coby."

"Cool. When?"

"Wednesday. Can we squeeze that?"

"Maybe. Let me check the diary."

Out of the corner of my eye, I saw Henry walk out of the bathroom, a towel wrapped around his slim hips. I threw my phone on the bed and raced for the bathroom. Mac cackled evilly when she beat me to it, slamming the door in my face.

Two days later found us at the shooting range with Coby and Travis. Oddly enough, it was a regular outing for most of us. Guns ran in both families because of our brothers' careers, and heavy betting usually ensued with the loser having to pay for either lunch or dinner. As usual, I busted everyone's targets out of the water because firing a gun seemed to be my second talent, and Mac, the worst shot of the day, was gearing up to buy us all lunch.

Unfortunately, when we were pulling out of the carpark of the shooting range, Coby and Travis got a call from Jared. All Mac and I managed to make out was that some kind of kidnapping slash hostage stand-off was going down in Penrith. It meant we were abandoned at the shooting range and had to call Henry for pick up duty. Apparently, hostage negotiation waited for no man, or in this case, Coby and Travis.

My phone buzzed madly at three the next morning. Panicked, I sprang to a sitting position and snatched it up.

J: Baby, need you to come get me.

E: What? It's 3 am!

Was he high? And enough with the 'baby' business already. I liked it too much. I threw the phone on the bed and huffed my way back under the covers. When it buzzed again, I eyed it evilly and considered turning it off but picked it up instead.

J: At the hospital.

The words had my heart leaping into my throat, and I shifted to the edge of the bed and planted my feet on the floor.

E: Are you okay?

J: Just a couple of scratches.

I knew Jared and his scratches.

E: What hospital? I'll come get you.

J: Prince Alfred. Thanks. Can't sleep here. Horrible asshole next to me is snoring like a freight train.

I padded to my wardrobe and changed into a pair of soft worn jeans and a hooded sweater. Tying my hair into a messy knot at the nape of my neck, I grabbed my car keys, phone, and wallet and quietly let myself out of the house. I set the GPS and drove along the quiet, dark deserted streets to the hospital.

The help desk directed me to level four, and I waited patiently while Fiona, according to her name tag, finished tapping away at whatever it was she was doing at the nurses station. She stopped and her kind, tired eyes gave me a questioning look.

"I'm here for—"

"Jared?" she interrupted.

"I...yes. How did you know?"

"I didn't. Just hopeful I guess after he told me he was 'busting out of the joint'." She air-quoted with an amused roll of the eyes. She stood up, tucked a pen neatly into her breast pocket, and walked around the counter with a capable efficiency all nurses seemed to possess.

"Follow me, love."

I followed her down the corridor. "Is he okay?"

She turned her head to meet my eyes as she moved smartly along the corridor. "Two stab wounds to his back. They're not deep, love, so there's no internal damage." My eyes went wide and my breathing faltered. She attempted to reassure me, but it didn't ease any of my panic. "We were just keeping him overnight for observation and the possibility of infection."

"Stab wounds?"

"He'll be fine, love." She gave a reassuring pat to my hand. "He's all stitched up, but he'll need complete bed rest for at least forty-eight hours to give the wounds time to heal. We've dosed his IV up liberally with morphine, so he'll likely be off his rocker. I'll write you a script for some heavy duty painkillers before you leave, but I'll give you a couple in a little packet to take with you for the morning because he's going wake up in a lot of pain."

We moved into the room where Jared lay awake, half-reclined, and beaming a silly smile at me.

"Evie!" he slurred.

Fiona rolled her eyes. "Morphine," she whispered and giggled.

I moved to the bed and he latched onto my hand. I tried to snatch it back as I looked him over. "Jared, I'm not sure it's a good idea that you leave."

He tugged my hand back, and I stopped struggling when I saw him grimace in pain. "Not you too, Evie," he grumbled. "How will I get any better if I can't sleep?" He rolled his eyes over at the other bed where, true enough, a big man lay snoring like a freight train.

"Okay, okay." I conceded. I wouldn't have been able to sleep with that either, and he did look tired. His lovely golden skin was pale.

Fiona pottered around unhooking his IV and writing in his chart. She handed him a form which he signed before she left and came back with a wheelchair. "If I catch you trying to walk out of this hospital not using that wheelchair, then you won't be going anywhere."

"Tell me what happened, Jared," I ordered.

"Can I tell you later?" he asked as he slowly got out of bed. "I'm a bit knackered right now." He turned his back to me so he faced the bed and ripped off his hospital gown.

"Jared," I squealed. He wasn't wearing anything underneath, and I almost passed out when I got a glimpse of his bare ass. It met the tops of his legs in a tantalising package of firm, smooth skin that had me diverting my eyes before the urge to get grabby overwhelmed me.

He chuckled in the face of my modesty when I turned around to face the wall as though it held all the secrets of the universe.

"Put some clothes on!"

"Like you've never seen a bare ass before."

I muttered under my breath. "Not one as fine as that."

"Right, let's go," he said after a minute.

I turned back around to see him wearing jeans covered in blood spatter. Knowing it was his had me closing my eyes at the swift onset of anger until I felt myself shake with it. "Who did this to you?"

He smiled a silly grin and his dimple deepened with amusement. "Why? Going to give them a knuckle sandwich for me, baby?"

"Damn straight," I muttered valiantly. "I'll kick the fucker's ass."

"Maybe you'll get your chance later today," he chuckled.

"Where's your shirt?"

"It got thrown out. It was all torn and bloody." He gave me a pitiful look. "Can we just go?"

"Come on then." I sighed.

By the time I started the car, I realised I hadn't been to Jared's place before. I only knew it was a loft somewhere in Woolloomooloo that he shared with Travis. Putting the car in gear, I look at him. "Where do you live, Jared? I'll drop you home. Will Travis be there?"

"Travis will still be working. Evie..." He smiled his silly grin again as I drove out of the hospital car park. "Beautiful Evie," he sing-songed, and I wondered how much morphine they pumped into that IV of his. "Have I ever told you how beautiful you are?"

Droopy eyelids and a soft smile, I laughed at the dreamy expression, but I couldn't leave him like that on his own. "Come on, Romeo, I'll take you home with me."

He grinned in smug satisfaction. "I like hearing those words on your lips. I like hearing everything on your lips. You sing like an angel. Sing me a song?"

"Jared, I'm trying to drive."

"How about I sing you a song?" He started to warble a little tune, and it grated painfully on my ears. Bad singing, I realised, ran in the Valentine family.

"Don't. Stop! Please," I pleaded, laughing as I began the return journey home through the still dark streets. "My ears are bleeding."

"Don't stop? Okay," he joked and kept singing. His little song faded out pitifully, and when I took a quick glance at him, I saw he was fast asleep. When I pulled into the driveway, I gave Travis a quick call to let him know I had him at my place. He seemed relieved, asking me if we could keep him for a couple of days to rest up because he'd be working around the clock. I agreed and hung up on his promise to come by in the morning with Jared's laptop and some clothes.

When I shut off the ignition, Jared stirred. "Evie?"

"Yeah?" I replied as I tucked my phone back in my bag.

I looked up and was met with sober and serious eyes.

"I feel like everything is so much brighter when I'm with you. When you're not there it's like someone turned out the lights."

It had to be the morphine talking, but still, I grasped his hand and squeezed tight, feeling the warmth of it wrap around me soothingly.

"I know. I feel the same."

I let go of his hand and fumbled with the door handle.

He reached out and snagged my wrist. "Evie?"

I stopped. "Yeah?"

He looked at me intently, and after a long pause, let go of my arm. "Nothing."

Chapter Seven

I heard an alarm go off at a time that should have been reserved solely for bakers and crazy people. Was it some kind of hideous cosmic joke or simply Henry playing another prank? He'd done it before when I'd eaten the last of the chocolate biscuits. I racked my brain but I couldn't think of what I'd done recently that deserved this kind of retaliation. Maybe it was from lack of real food in the house. Perhaps *Lord of the Flies* was now a reality and Henry was the first of us to fall.

I opened one eye when I heard a male grunt and the alarm stopped.

"Sorry," Jared muttered. "Forgot it was set."

Hair mussed and eyes half open, he turned his head to face me, giving me the urge to snuggle close and feel the heat of his bare skin against mine.

His grimace of pain had me scooting to the edge of the bed and reaching for the pills and water I'd placed nearby last night. "Here." I handed them over.

Jared propped himself up on an elbow and put them in his mouth before reaching for the water I held out.

"Thanks," he offered gratefully after swallowing them down.

I took back the empty glass and sat it back down. "You wanna tell me what happened?"

He sighed and snuggled into the fluffy white covers, wincing a little. "It was the hostage situation from yesterday at Penrith. We've been consulting on this case that started as a kidnapping a couple of weeks ago. Jimmy Farrell took his two young kids in a custody dispute, and believe me, Jimmy is not the kind of father you'd want around your kids."

As he explained some of the things Jimmy had done, I agreed it was better to have no father at all than to have one like that.

"We located him in a house yesterday morning with his brother Joe. They'd barricaded his wife and kids inside, and he was refusing to let them out. It spiralled from there. We had the house surrounded and they started taking shots at us through the front windows."

I grabbed his arm, fingers digging in. "Jesus, you all wear vests, right?"

"Babe, of course we do," he replied, exasperated. "Anyway, Jimmy's wife moved at the same time one of the cops took a really bad shot and it nicked her in the arm. She started screaming and shouting, and Joe turned and shot her dead right in front of the kids."

"What the hell?" I shouted. I shot off the bed and stood up, pacing the length of the room before I planted one hand on my hip. The other I used to jab fiercely towards the window. "I can't believe there are people out there who do that. How could anyone do that? Those poor kids."

He nodded his agreement at my outburst and rolled further on to his stomach with a wince.

I rushed back to the bed, and sitting on the edge next to Jared I peeled back the bandages to check his stitches. I was no nurse but they didn't look red and angry, and I assumed that was a good thing. I put the bandages back in place and asked him if he was okay.

"Yeah." He nodded. "Just sore. I got a clear shot and took Joe out, and then Jimmy started threatening to shoot his own kids. Coby and I and two others stormed the back of the house, but Joe mustn't have been down like we thought and next thing I knew he was behind me with a knife."

"Christ, you're lucky he didn't come up behind you with a gun."

It was like a bad Steven Seagal movie. No particular one, they were all bad.

"So what happened to Jimmy?" I asked. "And Joe?"

"Jimmy disappeared in the scuffle. Fucking Houdini. The cops have likely been out all night looking for him. I know Travis and Coby would still be out there. Don't know about Joe."

Henry chose that moment to walk into the room, busily texting on his phone. "You doing a food shop today, Sandwich?"

"Is Sandwich doing the shop?" I heard Mac call out from behind him.

As I turned around on the bed, Henry looked up from his phone and caught Jared lying there. His eyes went wide as he stopped dead.

"Ouch, fucktard," Mac mumbled as she smacked into his back.

She came out from behind Henry and took in the scene before her. I knew it didn't look good. I was in my silk nightwear, and Jared was shirtless. She rubbed at her eyes as though she'd woken up in an alternate universe.

Henry pointed at me threateningly. "You're not taking him with you."

Mac didn't even respond, clearly having forgotten what food even was. Her eyes had glazed over and she looked almost giddy.

"Yes, I'm doing the food shop, and no, Jared isn't coming with me. You are. Besides, Jared's injured so you can just stop thinking whatever it is you're thinking."

Mac's eyes whipped to Jared. "You are?"

"Just a couple of scratches, Mac," he replied, his voice low and husky.

I folded my arms, hiding a shiver at the sexy sound. "Yeah, with a knife."

While Mac and Henry were effectively distracted, I made a hasty exit for the bathroom and slammed the door with glee. Showered and dressed, I missed Travis by five minutes, so I set Jared up with his laptop, a coffee, and breakfast, and Henry and I hit the shops.

J: Can you get me some Gatorade while you're there?

I handed over the shopping list to Henry as he pulled out a trolley. "Here. You make a start. I have to go to the chemist to get the prescription filled for Jared."

He took the list.

"Wait." I snatched the list back, got out a pen, and scribbled Gatorade on there and handed it back over.

"Make sure you only get the lime flavour," I ordered as Henry looked over the list. "He doesn't like any of the other flavours."

Henry laughed.

"What?"

"You two. Like an old married couple already."

I stopped searching the bottomless pit that was my handbag for the prescription so he could see my look of exasperation. "We are not! We're just friends. I'd be doing the same for you, Henry."

He rolled his eyes as he started moving off. "Whatever helps you sleep at night, Sandwich."

The next three days found me running around between band rehearsals in the basement and looking after the big baby formerly known as Jared. I could only blame myself for telling him to message me if he needed me. I was worried I wouldn't hear him over the noise of our music otherwise.

J: Can you bring me up a juice?

Or

J: I can't find my USB. Have you seen it?

Sure he may have been milking it a little, but I was happy to oblige. Sometimes it was nice to be taken care of, and the man had just saved the lives of two young kids. Someone should have been giving him a medal for God's sake, not just a glass of juice.

When he wasn't in bed and had moved to the couch, he could simply shout down the stairs to the basement rather than message me.

"Evie, what's for lunch?"

Or

"Have you seen my painkillers?"

By the time Saturday rolled around, I was walking on air. Not because I had another date with Tate later that afternoon, but because I was getting to escape the house.

"Babe?"

"Yeah," I shouted back from the confines of my wardrobe.

"Can you get me some pills?"

I tossed another crappy outfit selection on the floor and walked out of the wardrobe. "You okay?"

"Yeah. Just wanna make sure I'm up for seeing you guys play at the White Demon tonight."

I arranged his pills and headed off for a shower, spending so long under the hot water I could have filled an Olympic pool five times over. Mac was obviously thinking the same thing. By the time I was pulling on my underwear, she barged through the bathroom door, her face like the black thunderclouds of a tropical storm. She didn't even bother to check the wall this time when the door bounced off because the dent was already there anyway.

"Would you hurry up, asshead? You spend more time in this bathroom than I do sleeping."

"I do not, Mactard. I have to get ready for my date. Tate is gonna drop me at the White Demon straight after. Is that okay?"

She sat the glass of wine in her hand down on the vanity with an angry clank at my mention of Tate. "Whatever. Out you get. I need a long hot bath."

I adjusted the twisted strap of my bra as she started running the taps using short, angry movements. "Why are you being such a cow this afternoon?"

She finished adjusting the water temperature and turned to face me as she pinned her hair into a giant knot on the top of head. "Because I'm in a shitty mood. I haven't been shopping in days, Travis is being an overbearing asswad brother, and my best friend has turned into the village idiot by dating Tetris Tate rather than my other brother." She finished her rant in a shout and I flinched.

"I am not the freaking village idiot. Stop being an interfering bitch."

She waved her hand. "What the fuck ever, Sandwich."

Huffing, I grabbed my makeup bag, slammed the bathroom door on my way out, and stormed angrily into the bedroom.

I slammed my own bedroom door behind me, moved to the dresser, and yanking open a drawer, tossed clothes about in a mess while muttering angrily to myself.

"Jesus Christ."

"What?" I growled, whirling around from the dresser that now looked like a casualty of war with clothes hanging out the sides.

"Babe, fuck. Is all that for Tate?" He waved his hand at me.

I glanced down realising I was still in my gold satin and ivory lace creation and swore, stomping over to the wardrobe to get a robe.

"You've got to stop calling me babe, Jared. We're friends. You don't call Coby that, do you?"

As I reached for the hanger, I felt Jared's arms slide around my waist and I stopped, the feel of his rough hands on my skin sending shivers down my spine. I closed my eyes as he pressed his warm chest up against my back and leaned down to press a kiss against my neck.

"You don't like it when I call you that?" he asked me softly.

I did. I loved it. I didn't want him to stop, but if we were going to make a go of this friendship, he couldn't keep doing it. Lines needed to be drawn somewhere.

"No, Jared. I don't like it," I muttered weakly.

I turned around in his embrace and pushed against his chest. Ignoring my struggles, he leaned down to kiss me, and I sucked in a breath and turned my head. The effort cost me. My chest felt tight and tears pricked my eyes.

I renewed my efforts and shoved him, hard. "Let me go."

He sighed, letting go and holding his hands up in surrender. "Friends. I know. Sorry." Backing up, he sat on the edge of the bed, watching me as I shrugged quickly into my pretty silk robe.

Recovered, I replied to his question. "No."

"No what?"

"The underwear isn't for him. I always wear stuff like this."

His eyes widened. "You mean all this time I've known you, you've been prancing about with that on underneath your clothes?"

I picked up a random item of clothing off the floor and flung it at his head. "Prancing? I don't prance!"

"Prance, flounce, strut." He shrugged his shoulders, grinning. "You do it all, baby."

Completely amazed at how he managed to evoke such a range of emotions in just a few short moments, I shook my head in laughter and flopped to the floor to sit cross legged in front of the mirror on the back of the wardrobe door.

"What are you doing?"

I rubbed some pore minimiser into my face. "Putting my makeup on. Mac is operating under Diva mode and hogging the bathroom, so I have to do it in here."

I looked at him through the mirror as he sat there watching me go through my makeup routine. It was slightly unnerving to have him study my every moment.

As I pulled the mascara out of my makeup bag, he snatched it out of my hand.

"Let me do that." He grinned cheekily.

I looked at him in disbelief. "You want to put my mascara on?"

He shrugged. "What is it about women and mascara that they always have to put it on with their mouths open?"

I laughed. "It helps us concentrate."

He grinned wickedly and grabbed his crotch. "I could find you something to concentrate on, baby."

"Jared!"

"I'm kidding." He laughed. "Come sit on the bed," he ordered and pulled me over, sitting me down, kneeling between my legs.

"You better not muck this up, Jared," I warned, "because you can't come back from a bad mascara jab. I'll have to wash my whole face and start again." I was not looking forward to another caterpillar eyebrow.

"Relax, Evie. I do a mean panda face," he joked.

I arched a brow.

"I've done this before, granted it was a long time ago when Mac was seventeen, but if she let me at her face, then you know you can trust me."

I found that very hard to believe, and my mouth opened wide in shock. "Mac let you at her face with a mascara wand?"

He nodded, amusement curling his lips, but still his face was sincere. "It was Mitch's fault. We were lifting weights at home, and you know how competitive Mac gets. She sprained both her wrists on a weight she shouldn't have been allowed anywhere near. The next night she had a date with Tom Fraser who was apparently the man of the hour. With Mum and Dad away, Mitch being on her shit list, and Travis conveniently disappearing, who do you think was left with helping her get pretty?"

I laughed wholeheartedly at the image of Mac ordering Jared about with makeup. "How have I never heard this story?"

He grinned at my response. "I've got plenty more where those came from." He held up the mascara. "Now will you let me?"

Thoughtful, I pursed my lips. "On one condition."

He raised an eyebrow. "What?"

"Give me more stories."

"Okay," he agreed.

He leaned forward, gently brushing the wand across my eyelashes, and proceeded to do just that. I stared into his green eyes as he spoke.

They were focused in intense concentration on my eyelashes, and the little flecks of gold had me mesmerised. He pulled back now and then to check on his progress. Then he grinned, flashing his dimple.

"What?"

"You're beautiful, Evie," he whispered quietly.

I flushed. "Thanks."

He leaned in to do the other eye. "You know, we've never sat down and watched a movie together. Tell me what your favourite movie is. We can watch it tomorrow."

"Anchorman," I said without hesitation.

He pulled back, raising his eyebrows in surprise. "Yeah? Will Ferrell, huh?"

"I don't know how to put this, but I'm kind of a big deal," I said with a chuckle.

"Would you like to come to the party in my pants?" he asked, laughing. Putting movie quotes aside, his face turned serious. "I would've thought you'd say something like *The Notebook* or *Sleepless in Seattle* or some other girly crap."

I flushed. "*The Notebook* isn't girly crap. It's a beautiful movie."

"Course it is." He nodded unconvincingly.

"You haven't seen it, have you?"

Worried I'd ask him to watch it, he ignored my question.

"You're all done." He sat back on his heels to inspect his handiwork.

Feeling mild panic at the thought of having black streaks all over my face, I raced to the mirror. "Jared!"

"What?"

He came over to stand behind me as I pursed my lips, examining my eyes closely. "You actually did an excellent job."

He winked. "I excel at anything I do if you'd care to find out."

I laughed at his playful attitude, and forgetting about his stitches, shoved at his shoulder.

"Ouch!" he yelped.

"Sorry, sorry." I patted his arm soothingly as he grumbled. "You should leave so I can get dressed. Tate will be here any minute."

Jared frowned at the mention of Tate's name and stalked over to the dresser where he'd shoved my clothes over to make room for his own.

"Right, Tate. How could I forget?" He grabbed a shirt and shrugged it on before he walked out the door, closing it quietly in his wake.

Surrounded by silence, I sat down on the bed and worried that I was somehow ruining everything with my idiocy, but I wasn't sure how to fix it without risking anyone getting hurt.

Chapter Eight

J: So what was on this afternoon's agenda? A heavy bout of Halo?

E: Do you have to message me during every date I go on?

J: Of course. Where's the fun otherwise?

Tate gave my phone an eye roll. "Does that thing ever stop?"

"Apparently not," I muttered and tucked it carefully back in my purse.

We pulled into the car park at The White Demon Warehouse after a late afternoon trek around Paddington Markets. We were only there a couple of hours, so there wasn't time to see everything, but Tate said the markets were on the *Things You Have to do in Sydney* list. I had to agree if the mountains of bags in the back of the car were anything to go by.

E: Paddington Markets.

J: Seriously. He took you shopping? That guy is good.

E: Yes. You be good or you won't get your present.

Tate switched off the ignition and turned to me. "I think we're a little early. Do you wanna go in and have a quick drink?"

I checked the time and nodded. "Sure, but I need to be back stage in twenty minutes to help set up and start my vocal warm up."

"Yeah? How long does that usually take?"

"I usually just do some scales for about half an hour."

J: You got me a present? What is it?

E: It's a surprise.

"You don't happen to have an older sister you haven't mentioned, do you?"

He pulled the keys out of the ignition and gave me a puzzled glance. "No, why?"

I explained my first date with Beetle Bob. "The bridge climb and the markets were unexpected."

He laughed. "You were expecting a Halo marathon? I can teach you how to play if you really want, but I didn't think it was your kinda speed."

I grinned. "I have several speeds. I don't mind a computer game now and then. I just thought maybe you might have had a little double X chromosome whispering in your ear on the best places to take your date."

He got out of the car and came around to open my door sheepishly. "One of the girls at the station might have done that a couple of times."

J: Mac has a surprise for you too she says.

Mac's message came through a second later.

M: Brace yourself, Sandwich. I have an epic surprise for you.

I got out of the car wondering what the hell was going on but confident her surprise wouldn't outdo the present I got for her. What could possibly beat an acre sized piece of homemade double chocolate fudge and a pair of jade earrings that matched her newest dress purchase from Collette Dinnigan?

Before I could reach into the car for my bag, or even blink, Tate had me pushed up against the car, his legs between mine and his lips on me. Not even a second later, I heard someone shout my name.

Tate rested his forehead against mine. "Christ," he muttered. "Between your friends and your phone, I feel like I can never get you alone for five minutes."

I peeked over Tate's shoulder. Mac, Henry, Travis, and Jared were walking towards the car.

"Evie," Mac shouted again, grinning and waving happily.

This left me feeling confused. Mac was in Diva mode when I'd left earlier, and being caught in a passionate embrace with Tate should've turned her rabid.

"Hey, guys."

I pushed away from Tate, untucking his arms from my waist, but he used the opportunity to hold my hand in his, tugging me close and rubbing his thumb across my palm in lazy circles. Jared's eyes cut to our linked hands and he frowned.

"What's going on?"

Mac dragged me away from Tate and grabbed me in a hug, jumping up and down. "We've got a scout, baby!" she screeched.

I stopped breathing. "Wait, stop."

She stopped.

"What? A scout?"

She grinned, nodding her head like a maniac. "Not just some random scout, Sandwich. One who's come *specifically* to see Jamieson."

"You got us a fucking scout?" I whispered, tears in my eyes.

She started madly jumping up and down again, and I screamed, joining in with her lunatic behaviour.

"We got a fucking scout," I screamed at Jared in excitement, and he laughed at my hysteria. I pulled Henry into a hug and three of us jumped up and down like we were eight year olds on pogo sticks.

I stopped and squeezed Henry hard. "Henry..."

He squeezed back hard. "I know my beautiful girl."

"Tell me," I ordered Mac when I gained control of my mental faculties.

"Okay," she said happily, "let's all go get a quick drink."

"Fuck a quick drink. Let's get a bottle of champagne."

I leaped on to Henry's back in excitement, and he hollered as he piggybacked me towards the entrance of the bar. Laughing, I turned my head to wink at Jared as the group followed behind us.

"Will you still love me when I'm famous, baby?" I joked.

Jared shook his head and I turned back around. Tate hadn't missed the complete and utter look of adoration on Jared's face and eyed the two of us warily as Henry set me down inside the door.

I started to tremble with nerves when Henry, Travis, and Tate hit the bar. Mac took my hand and squeezed it hard when she realised I was losing it.

"Mackerelface, I love you." My voice wobbled as the emotion overwhelmed me.

"Oh shit." She pointed a warning finger at me. "Don't you start the floodgates, Sandwich. You'll ruin my makeup."

Deep breaths helped me pull myself together, and the next half hour was a blur of champagne and chatter.

"Famous rock star now, hey Evie?" Travis winked at me from across the table with the words he said as more of a statement then a question.

"Yep. Too good for any of you plebs." I arched my brow loftily before laughing. "Oh my God, Mac, we have to go backstage and talk to the Rice Bubbles. Do they know?"

She shook her head. "Not yet. I wanted to tell you first."

With Tate saying he'd hang around to watch the show, Mac, Henry, and I left for the dressing room.

Henry busted open the backstage door with force in his excitement. "We're here, motherfuckers!"

Jake, Cooper, and Frog greeted our arrival from their various positions on the floor where it looked like a heated argument was going on. It was fierce and after a moment became apparent they were arguing about whom of the three could "pull the most chicks," a guitarist, keyboardist, or drummer. Bets were being placed. I grabbed my purse and handed over a twenty in favour of Jake.

Cooper protested. "Evie baby, say it ain't so?" he said in mock sadness.

"Shut up, asswad." Jake smirked and flexed his big ass muscles. "We all know who has the bigger dick here."

Everyone looked at me, assuming I was the expert on Jake's size considering I gave him such good odds.

"Hey!" I held my hands up in surrender. "Just because my bet is on him doesn't mean I've seen his package."

"You can't miss it, Evie." Jake winked. "It precedes me in every room I walk in." He grabbed his crotch suggestively.

Loud ribbing came from the boys at his lewd gesture, and Mac threw a cushion at his head. I wanted to say it was unbelievable that he was the second man that day to grab his junk in front of me, but that would be a lie.

"I'm sorry," I shouted over all the noise, "but look at Jakie's arms. You don't get those playing keyboards or guitars."

"Nooooo!" Frog shouted and threw a paper missile in my direction.

"Hey!" I shouted and tossed it back.

"Everyone shut up," Mac ordered.

They all ignored her as they fought to be heard over each other. I placed two fingers in my mouth and let out a piercing whistle. Everyone shut up and looked at me.

"Be quiet, assheads," I ordered. "Mac has important news."

I turned to Mac and rolled my hand down theatrically before moving through the throng and sitting down on the couch. Henry came and threw himself down next to me, placing a hand over my shoulders and hugging me tightly.

Mac brought them up to speed. Our scout wasn't just anyone. It was Gary Gilmore of Jettison Records, one of the top labels in the country. He'd told Marcus he was coming in to hear us play because their record label was interested and Marcus had spoken to Mac.

The six of us jumped about excitedly until it somehow evolved into who could do the best flying leap and ended with Cooper crashing into a side table, earning a slight gash to the back of his head. We declared him the Grande Jete winner, and Mac was busy patching his head while I started warming up my voice.

A knock came at the door and Marcus peeked his head in, grinning when he saw our level of excitement. "I take it you got the good news?"

I nodded happily. "Sure did. We're going to kick ass tonight, Marcus, thanks."

"I don't doubt it. I'll leave you to it. Just wanted to let you know that Gary just arrived." He winked at Mac before shutting the door.

All eyes swivelled to Mac and she blushed.

"Marcus, huh?"

"Maybe," she muttered mysteriously.

A little under an hour later Marcus hit the stage to introduce us. As we stood off to the side, Jake ran out first to the cheering crowd and sat down and did a frenzied solo on the drums while they all whooped and hollered. I laughed when I heard a girl in the crowd scream out "Take your shirt off, Jakie!"

I nodded knowingly to Frog. He poked me in the shoulder before heading out next, holding up his hand and bowing as the girls screamed his name. He looked over at me pointedly, pulled on his guitar, and plucked a bass tune along to Jake's drums. Cooper came out next to stand at his keyboard, running his fingers up and down the keys, and

Henry gave my hand a quick squeeze and moved out next, putting on his guitar and taking it all in stride as the girls went wild.

I peeked my head around the corner to peer into the darkness of the crowd. I could see Mac, Jared, and Travis front and centre, whooping and clapping at the guys antics on stage, but no Tate.

Henry gave me the nod, and my heart thundered hard in my chest. My throat went tight and my stomach did a long, lazy roll. I wiped my sweaty hands down my pants, fluffed my hair, and strutted out into the blinding lights.

Fake it till you make it, I muttered to myself in encouragement.

The crowd roared and clapped as I pulled the microphone out of the stand, and Mac gave me two thumbs up.

"Hey, Sydney!" I yelled.

They clapped and hollered back.

"You'll have to forgive me because I'm going to get serious for just a moment before we get started," I said to the crowd conversationally.

They tittered and quieted down, and the band stopped fooling around, waiting to see what I was going to say.

"It seems there's a bit of a problem. My boys here..." I waved an arm out behind me "...all seem to be single."

The girls (and a few guys) began screaming madly, Henry laughed out loud, and Frog moved closer to the edge of the stage to offer a wink and a wave.

I nodded at the crowd in mock seriousness. "That's right, see the dilemma? I just thought I'd put that out there in case we have people in the crowd who can help fix the problem."

I shook my head playfully as a guy screamed out, "Are you single, Evie?" and laughed when another yelled that he'd "fix my problem."

"Two more things quickly. Thanks, Marcus, for having us." Marcus offered a little wave from the side of the stage. "And thanks to you guys for a hot shit welcome on our first night here a few weeks ago. We wouldn't be back here if it wasn't for you." I finished on a shout and the

110

crowd yelled and clapped as Jake hit the drums hard, leading into our first song of the night.

"This is our first song, *Follow Me*," I said.

We worked through all our songs steadily over the night and rather than kicking back for a breather during our break, we worked through a cover song we'd chosen to do at the end of the show.

When it came time to wind things down, I brought the microphone up to my lips. "Last song people," I said quietly and the crowd went silent. "We're going to do a cover song, so I hope you don't mind. We've chosen this song as thank you to our beautiful Macklewaine because it's one of her favourites and we love her guts."

I laughed as I glanced at Mac to see her pointing at me fiercely.

"I love you too, Evie!" I heard a guy scream at the top of his lungs, and I laughed again as the crowd tittered.

Henry was singing this one, so I handed the microphone over to him, picked up my guitar, and adjusted the strap over my shoulder. He was my backup vocalist when needed, but he had a fantastic voice, and I enjoyed watching him take the lead.

I nodded at the boys, then I began playing the brief solo intro to *Drive By* by Train. Glancing up as my fingers flew across the strings, I caught Travis and Jared grinning at me from the front of the stage. Travis put two fingers in his mouth and let out a piercing whistle.

Jake thundered in with the beat before Cooper and Frog joined in. I walked to the edge of stage near the three of them so Mac would catch my wink. She laughed and I shifted back over to Henry, and he sang to me for a moment as I played close. Adrenaline pumped through my veins hard, and I hoped that wherever Gary Gilmore was, he was enjoying the show.

Met with a thunderous applause and foot stomping, I unshouldered the guitar and pointed my finger at Mac with Jared and Travis watching on with identical grins. I waved at the crowd before Henry grabbed my hand, had us take a bow, and we bounded off the stage.

We hit the backstage dressing room, beers were handed out, and I took a huge swig. I was hot, sweaty, and thoroughly high on the whole night.

"Group hug!" I shouted, and we all huddled together. "I only want to say one thing. I love you guys!"

They all groaned theatrically.

"Someone gag her before she drags us all down with her," Cooper moaned.

I slapped him on the back of his head, and he shrieked like a girl when I made contact with the gash I had forgotten was there. Cooper tackled me to the floor, and my drink went flying across the room when the door burst open and Mac, Jared, and Travis came in.

"You guys!" she screeched and then gave Cooper and I a raised eyebrow. "I don't even wanna know."

I dusted myself off and reached for a new beer, popping the lid as Mac snatched it out of my hand and took a huge gulp.

"Hey!" I yelled, trying to grab it back.

She pushed her hand into my chest, holding me back. "I need it more than you right now. Thanks for trying to make me cry, asshead."

I grabbed another three beers, passing one to Travis and Jared and keeping one for myself.

"Where's Tate?" I whispered in Mac's ear.

She shook her head and shrugged her shoulders. "He said to say sorry. He got called away."

"Oh," I muttered. Life of a copper. I was warned but I still felt a small sliver of disappointment. I forced a bright smile at Jared as he took hold of my hand and pulled me close. The feel of his body and the heat in his eyes was enough to smother the disappointment and the smile came more easily.

"Evie. Up there? Wow. I already knew you were the hottest fucking thing I'd ever seen in my life, but that voice of yours..." he leaned in close until the warmth of his breath tickled my ear "...makes me want to fuck you."

The words, spoken in a voice that was both deep and husky, left me scrambling for air.

His face close to mine, I gazed up into the intense, unwavering green eyes, and I was floored. In that one single moment, high on adrenaline and life, I realised Jared's words had led me to a fork in the road. Did I continue the cycle of dating and meaningless sex and the fight against the fear of being hurt? Or should I choose what felt right and for once, trust what my heart was trying to tell me—that this man was the one I wanted more than anything, more than Tate, more than any other man I'd ever known. This one, so smart and capable, strong and determined, relentless and funny, caring and gentle and so. fucking. beautiful. I was tired of fighting it, and the overwhelming relief I felt at finally letting it go threw me off balance.

I put down my drink, palmed both his cheeks in my hands, and set myself loose on his lips. The minute he felt the touch of my tongue, he dropped his beer and lifted my legs up off the ground until I was straddling his body, legs wrapped tightly around his hips. He turned and slammed my back into the wall—hard, and I kissed him with every bit of feeling I'd been bottling up inside for weeks, fuck that, years. He groaned as he ravaged my mouth, and I wound my arms around his neck, trailing my fingers through his silky hair. My body was pinned against him and the wall, and I was throbbing with heat as he sucked on my tongue. His hands, gripping the backs of my thighs as he pushed against me, dug in at my whimper. He tore his lips away, his breathing ragged, and rested his forehead against mine. Loosening his grip on my legs, Jared gently set me back to my feet and pressed his lips to mine for a last, swift kiss. I looked over his shoulder and realised the dressing room was levelled to silence.

"Uh..." Lost for words, I flushed.

Jared grinned and grabbed my hand in his. The warmth of his rough palm against my skin sent shivers down my spine, making me forget my embarrassment.

Mac cheered, looking elated. "Well let's go fucking start this party, bitches."

Everyone had left, but Jared and I chose to ditch the after party and head back to the duplex. He was tired from the painkillers, and I was crashing hard after the high, and honestly, I just needed him to myself.

I washed off the makeup and sweat under the warm spray of a shower and changed into my sleepwear, choosing a deep emerald green camisole and matching shorts with rose lace trim. Quiet music was playing in the background, and Jared was busy texting when I came into the bedroom.

"Drink for you over there." He waved at the bedside table, not looking up as he tapped at his phone.

I picked it up and took a sip of icy cold wine. "Ah, that's good," I muttered and walked over to flip up the blinds and open the window to let the faint warm breeze blow through. I switched on the lamp and turned the top light off, making the room cosy and inviting.

"Did Mac tell you about Tate?" Jared asked as he put his phone down and looked up. He scanned my body, and this time I allowed myself to enjoy the heat in his eyes.

"What about him?"

"Why he left."

I nodded. "Do we need to talk about Tate right now?"

"That depends. Are you still going to keep on seeing him?"

I hesitated. Not because I couldn't answer the question but because I was thinking about what I would say to Tate tomorrow.

As I hesitated, I missed the anger swirling in the depths of Jared's eyes, so when he stood up and threw his drink, I flinched, watching it smash against the wall, glass shattering to the floor.

"What the hell, Jared?" I yelled. I ran my hands through my hair in disbelief, holding it back and then releasing it to fall around my shoulders.

"Do you know how fucking hard it was to stand there and see his hands all over you, his lips on you?" he shouted. "I felt sick. I wanted to break his face."

I sank to the bed. "I didn't know. I thought you and I—"

"Please don't start this just friends bullshit, Evie. Because you know that's not what this is, right? You and I are way more than that. Don't try and tell me you aren't feeling what I am, especially after that kiss in the dressing room." Jared's entire body was tense but then he swallowed hard, the hurt in his eyes a brief flash as he made for the door.

I grabbed his arm in a panic. "Jared, wait. Please." He shrugged me off and kept walking. "Look at me."

Clenching his fists at his side, nostrils flaring, he turned around, and I felt his anger crash over me like a wave. Tears pricked my eyes because I hated being the cause of it.

He looked up at the ceiling in frustration and let out a huff. "Baby, don't cry." He pulled me towards him and into a tight embrace. "You know what you have to do, Evie," he whispered in my ear and I shivered. "Just be with me." His voice, low and husky, shook with need.

The gentle plea almost broke my heart, but the longing made my body throb, giving me the confidence to push him backwards until he was sitting on the bed. Then I walked towards the door.

"Evie, what are doing?"

What I should have done a long time ago, I thought. I closed the door and returned to the bed. Flipping my leg over, I sat down and straddled his lap. "Just be quiet and kiss me."

He slid his arms around my waist, his big, warm hands moving up my back until they threaded into my hair and pulled my head down towards his lips.

"Come here," he said in a lust filled whisper.

His lips crashed hard against mine, and my hands rested on his shoulders, feeling muscles bunch and shift as he moaned and rubbed his hands up and down the small of my back. He sucked hard on my tongue, tugging it into his mouth.

"Jared," I murmured, pulling back so I could breathe for a moment.

His eyes shifted down, following the movement of his hands from my back to the bare skin of my thighs. He traced lazy circles with his thumbs, watching his hands move as they slid their way slowly up along my shorts until they reached under the camisole to rest on my hips. I felt his hard length press against me as he gripped my hips tight.

Letting go for a moment, he impatiently tugged at the hem of my camisole, taking it off in one quick movement.

"Christ, baby, you are so fucking beautiful."

Jared traced his fingertips over my stomach, fluttering them softly up my ribs until his hands rested on the undersides of my breasts. His thumbs rubbed the soft skin there, back and forth, setting my body on a slow burn as he tilted his head for another kiss.

My arms shifted around his neck, tugging playfully at the silky hair like I'd been itching to do since what felt like forever. He chuckled against my lips until I gasped when his hands covered my breasts, rubbing the soft skin, rolling my nipples in his fingers, and setting off tingles all over my skin.

"So fucking beautiful," he murmured as his mouth left mine.

Still straddling his lap, I threaded my fingers into his hair as he kissed his way down my neck, bending his head to take a nipple in his mouth, tracing it with his tongue before taking it deeply into his mouth.

"Jared," I moaned, arching my back. He moved to the other one, swirling his tongue and sucking before leaning back to tug his shirt over his head, mussing his hair and revealing the smooth expanse of golden skin and toned muscles as he reached for me.

That was when things progressed from gentle and soothing to wild, and from wild to uncontrolled. Clothes disappeared quickly and hands and mouths moved frantically until he finally picked me up, flipped me to my back on the bed, and slid inside in one swift movement. I sucked in a sharp breath and he paused, breathing hard while waiting for me to adjust to the hard length of him. I exhaled and finally let go.

After years of wanting, we were impatient, our movements hard and rough. The promise of gentle was for another day. Tonight was for urgency and fierce need.

"Jared!" I cried out, feeling the heat explode inside me, starting from my toes and travelling the length of my body. He groaned loudly as he ground his hips hard against mine, kissing me forcefully as he came apart in my arms.

He collapsed his hot, heavy weight on top of me, breathing into my neck before rolling over and taking me with him. Ducking his head, he kissed and nibbled along my neck, moving his way over to tug on my earlobe with his teeth.

"You okay?" he murmured.

"No," I whispered weakly, still struggling for breath but revelling in the feel of being naked and sweaty and plastered over the length of him, "but I will be if we can do that again."

He grinned up at me. "Whatever you say, baby."

Chapter Nine

I woke to the sounds of voices downstairs. Feeling sore and happy, I yawned and stretched loudly as my stomach growled in anger. I decided I could easily eat a small animal and began doing a mental inventory of the contents of our fridge. I wondered if Jared could cook. Breakfast in bed would be the perfect start to my day right now.

Wait a minute. This was Jared I was talking about. Most likely, he'd bring me fruit salad and a piece of non-buttered toast riddled with birdseed. While the effort would be appreciated, I realised that Jared's eating habits did not bode well for my future. It was quite possible I'd die from the stress involved in absconding with secret food and designating it to *secure* points around the house where I could binge in safety.

Just as I was realising the horrific conclusion that I would forever be a closet eater, the bedroom door opened, startling me out of my trauma.

"What the fuck is going on here?" I heard Tate ask.

Shit. What was he doing in here?

I wondered if playing possum was a viable option in the unlikely event that my bed would swallow me whole and spit me out at a safe location (albeit with clothes, please). Maybe he'd just say, "Oh, Evie's asleep. I'll just leave them to it."

Um, no, I didn't think so either.

I attempted to resolve the situation by sitting up in a panic, but unfortunately that didn't solve anything.

"Shit." Jared sat up next to me, holding up the sheet to cover my chest, and I clutched it in my fist.

Tate looked a bit pissed off, and I imagined that was to be expected.

"Thought I remembered you saying there wasn't anything going on between the two of you."

"Well…," I drawled out slowly, trying to buy more time so I could work out how to be tactful. This was definitely not the way I envisioned telling him that all casual dating was over for me.

Henry interrupted my intelligent offering by entering the room and promptly beginning what looked like a choking fit. All eyes swivelled to Henry as he struggled to control himself.

"Chook," he wheezed after a few awkward moments. "I uh, didn't realise, that uh…hmm," he trailed off weakly and looked at me in apology.

Tate folded his arms just in case I didn't get the point that he was not delighted with recent events.

"Jesus, Evie, I came in here to apologise for skipping out on your big night to find this?" He waved his hand at the two of us.

Jared slid to the side of the bed and slipped on his jeans. He pulled them up quickly as he stood, doing up the zip but still leaving the top button undone, and I was momentarily distracted by the brief glimpse of bare ass.

Henry cleared his throat, and I saw amusement flicker in his eyes.

Jared moved to stand in front of Tate. "You get first shot."

"What?" I whipped out sharply. "What does that mean?"

Henry, despite a slow recovery from his choking experience, still managed to keep his wits about him and stood out of the way. He obviously knew what it meant. I scrambled to rip the sheet out of the bed and wrap it around myself when Tate cocked back a fist and smashed it into Jared's face. Jared's head slammed sideways from the impact, and he rubbed at his jaw.

"What the fuck are you doing?" I screeched at Tate as I writhed about on the bed wrestling with the sheet.

"Stay there, baby," Jared ordered.

I fought the urge to laugh hysterically at the thought that I was about to go anywhere. It always looked so easy in the movies, the beautiful goddess silkily glides out of bed and the sheet practically wraps itself around her like a Grecian robe. Obviously, I was a bit retarded, my struggles heading to what appeared to be major strangulation. My legacy wouldn't be memorable rock songs; it would be Death by Sheet. What an embarrassment.

Henry, anticipating mayhem on my part, made a move to lock me down. He decided I was doing a good enough job of that myself with the sheet, so instead, he chuckled before turning back to watch the scuffle.

"That's one," Jared muttered as he slammed his fist back into Tate's face and blood spurted out his nose.

No way.

Not happening.

"Fuck off, Henry," I muttered as he continued to laugh at my situation.

Finally disentangled (but modestly wrapped), I slid to the edge of the bed and watched in disbelief as Tate tackled Jared, and they crashed to the floor in a flurry of arms and punches. How had two dates with Tate resorted to this?

"Henry, if you don't do something, I will," I hissed, watching Tate land a gut punch.

"Oomph," was Jared's reply.

Appraising me, Henry shrugged, obviously finding my threat lacking any substance.

"Right," I muttered, and fisting the sheet in one hand so it wouldn't unravel, I strode with determination to put a halt to the scuffle.

Henry, realising I was actually able to move, yanked me back with a sigh. "Chook, stay out of it or you'll get hurt."

He shoved me back and I faltered from the unexpected hurling motion. Henry helped pull them apart, and I folded my arms indignantly as the three of them stood panting from the effort.

"What are you both, like ten? I've never seen such juvenile behaviour in all my life." I added a look of disbelief to make my statement more believable because it was only the other morning that I had a floor tussle with Henry.

Henry snorted, clearly remembering said tussle himself.

I shot him a warning look before doing a body scan of Jared to inspect for injuries. He looked no worse for wear, just a reddened jaw and some mussed hair. He was breathing heavy, his muscled torso tense and on display.

I know I shouldn't have thought it because I didn't condone violence, but God he was fucking hot, and I wanted him.

"You should be ashamed of yourselves," I continued. "Tate, Jared is still recovering from knife wounds." Tate managed to look a little guilty at this reminder as he wiped at a trickle of blood from his nose. "Besides, you know you and I were just casual. No promises were made. I thought you understood."

Tate wiped his bloody hand on the back of his jeans. "Jesus, sweetheart, not in any stretch of my imagination did I think you would have thought that entailed sleeping with whoever the fuck you felt like along the way. I didn't realise you were that easy," he said in disappointment.

I sucked in a breath and watched Jared's face turn so furious I thought the windows would blow out.

He fisted his hands and rounded a punch to Tate's jaw with a loud crack. Tate's head snapped back, and he held his hand up to gingerly touch the side of his face.

"Don't you dare say another word about Evie, you motherfucker," Jared growled.

"Okay, that's enough the pair of you. Tate out," I ordered, pointing towards the door as he prodded his injured jaw with his fingers. "Wait for me downstairs. Jared, you…" I paused. He what? "You sit down and I'll check your stitches. Henry…" Henry waited in amusement for my order. "Go make me some bacon and eggs. And pancakes," I added.

Amazingly enough, everyone listened to what I said, except for the part where Henry made me breakfast.

"Christ, Jared, what the fuck was that about?"

I threw my arms up in frustration as I flung the sheet to the floor in a giant fit. I shrugged on my robe and moved to the bed where my hero now sat so I could inspect his stitches.

"Lie down and roll over," I ordered.

Ignoring my order, he yanked me down hard and caught my mouth in a hot and hungry kiss. Forgetting myself for a moment, I returned it with equal enthusiasm.

"Morning, baby," he murmured when he pulled away for a breath.

Me? I didn't need to breathe.

"Morning." I grinned.

He groaned when I moved in for another kiss, and one of his hands slid underneath my robe, moving over to cup my ass while the other started to yank at the knotted belt of my robe.

"Christ," he muttered, breathing heavily as he pulled away. "You're all tied up like Fort Knox."

"I know." I smacked his hand. "Hands off. Tate is waiting downstairs. I need to go clean up your mess."

"My mess?" He laughed. "You're the one that dated him."

This was true but relationship rule number one was to never admit guilt.

"Yes, but you're the one that decked him," I replied logically.

I eventually got him to roll over and checked his stitches, which were okay, amazingly enough.

After getting dressed in a short pair of denim shorts and a fitted neon pink cotton shirt that read in sparkly blue font: With a shirt like this who needs pants? I went downstairs, picking up a wet wash cloth along the way for Tate.

The duplex appeared deserted apart from Tate who was perched on the edge of the couch. Shifting closer, I gently dabbed away the blood on his face while he eyed me carefully. It wasn't too bad, just a small trickle.

"I'm sorry, Tate. That wasn't planned."

He grabbed my wrist so I'd stop my ministrations and look him in the eye. "No, Evie. *I'm* sorry. I didn't mean what I said. Fuck it…I was angry because I really like you."

He let go of my wrist and I folded the cloth awkwardly. "Tate… I—"

"No, you don't need to explain. I know you were upfront about casual and so was I. Hell, we've only been out a couple of times."

I moved backwards as he stood up. "I should get going."

"Okay, um, friends?" I cringed at the cliché, but I'd enjoyed Tate's company, and I wanted him to know he was always welcome to keep in touch.

"Ah, sure, okay."

I saw him to the door before returning upstairs where Jared was pacing the room like a caged lion. He pounced when I came back in and tossed me at the bed like I was a lightweight.

"Wait!" I shouted when he stalked up the bed on his hands and knees. Glaring, I pushed at his chest to stop his advance. "I'm still mad at you."

He paused, frowning. "Mad at me for what? Defending your honour?"

I had to bite my cheeks to stop the laugh. Defending my honour? How sweet was that? My voice softened as I spoke. "Jared, you did it with your fists."

"That's how men work, Evie. We punch it out and move on. You women have your own way, and I'm not interfering in that."

I raised an eyebrow. "Oh yeah? What's our way?"

"Talking it out, baby. Women use words," he replied smoothly and hovering over me, leaned in to plant a kiss on my neck.

I figured that was his polite version of *our way* but with his heavy weight pressed against me and his lips nibbling their way up my neck, I slowly lost the will to be angry. "Wait. I need a shower."

Food too, I thought, but I left that part out at the risk he might offer to make me something.

"Shower it is," he conceded.

Since I was heavy into water conservation, we *had* to shower together. The fact that it involved being able to ogle Jared's naked body had nothing to do with my commendable pursuit of saving the earth one shower at a time.

Wasting no time, Jared, in what I was delightfully beginning to think was his signature move, picked me up and pressed me into the tiled wall, muttering something about not being done with me yet.

I didn't object, the urge and the moment to speak had long since passed. In fact, all I could manage was a moan as he slid his way inside my body, his mouth meeting mine. I held on tight as my tongue twined with his and was eventually rewarded with a trip to the stars, seeing them dance wildly behind closed lids as my head tilted back in utter pleasure. His hands gripped the skin under my thighs forcefully as he moved and shuddered. When he groaned and looked into my eyes after he'd buried his head in my neck, I was rewarded with hooded eyelids and lips curved in a sexy smile when he set me on my feet. It was a look of pure male satisfaction and had me looping my arms around his neck and pulling his head down so my lips could meet his in a long, sweet kiss.

Dried and dressed again, I was now starting to feel faint, but watching Jared, a towel wrapped about his slim hips while he stood in front of the bathroom mirror shaving, was fantastically distracting. His muscles contracting as he swiped and rinsed was making me feel positively sweaty.

"You hungry?" I asked.

"For you, baby." He grinned wickedly as he looked at me in the mirror.

I licked my lips suggestively and squealed when he grabbed my hand, spun me around, and slammed me up against the vanity. He nudged my legs apart with his knee and wedged himself between them.

"Teasing me?" he murmured.

I giggled when he rubbed his face in my neck, tickling me with his teeth, and I gasped and writhed as shaving foam flew everywhere.

"You taste like shaving cream," he muttered, pulling back.

"Really?" My sarcasm came to the fore as I snatched a towel and wiped at the mess on my neck. "Well, I hope that'll hold you till lunch."

He grinned at me as I wiped his face with the towel, revealing a smooth jaw and a dimple. His green eyes were assessing me tenderly and as a sharp twinge pierced my heart, my stomach pitched. I was starting to think that maybe I was going be sick, and it had nothing to do with lack of food.

"Shit."

I looked up from tossing the towel into the sink to see Jared's gentle expression shift to concern, his body tense.

I froze. "What?"

"Baby, I didn't use anything. Shit. Got carried away."

My mouth opened in shock.

Shit was right. Safe sex spokespeople it seemed we were not. I wasn't even on the pill because I had the memory of a goldfish. I was unreliable.

He placed his hands firmly on my shoulders, rubbing them up and down as he looked at me. "I'm clean, baby, you should know that."

"Well goody for the both of us because I've always been safe, but one thing I'm not... is on the pill."

His hands held firm on my hips and I felt his fingertips dig in at my words. "You aren't? Why not?"

"I'm unreliable," I said. "I forget to take it."

Jesus. What if I got pregnant?

I felt his hands relax, sliding up my waist to wrap around and hug me close. "Baby..." his green eyes glanced down at me possessively as he read the panicked expression on my face "...we'll cross that bridge if we come to it. Don't stress, okay?"

Easy enough to say, but somehow this relationship seemed to be moving at the speed of a supersonic jet. We'd been together all of one night, had sex twice, and already there was smashed glassware, mayhem and fisticuffs, and now a potential pregnancy scare. Not to mention he was looking at me softly as though the idea of me carrying around a mini Jared was a freaking marvellous one.

I fought the urge to laugh hysterically and sucked in shallow breaths until hyperventilation seemed imminent.

"Are you okay?" he asked, watching me with concern as I struggled for breath.

"Yep," I squeaked. "Peachy."

Surprisingly, the bathroom door had yet to be bashed down, so I opened it and headed for the bedroom.

He followed behind me, and dropping the towel, started to slide on underwear and a pair of faded, worn in jeans.

"Make a doctor's appointment for this afternoon to go on the pill. I have to get to work soon, so message me the time, and I'll come pick you up and go with you," he ordered. "I'll ring you every day to remind you to take it if that's what we need to do. Babe?"

"What?" I muttered.

"Did you hear me?"

I nodded distractedly as my eyes scanned his shirtless torso. I loved his lack of tattoos. Too much ink was becoming common these days, and I admired just the one on his arm, its complex, heartfelt meaning not detracting from all of his beautiful, golden skin. I still hadn't had my chance to run my tongue along the words and bit my lip at the thought of doing it later.

"Appointment with doctor. Message you," I repeated, pulse racing as I watched him shrug on a shirt. "Will you be okay to work today?" I asked, eyeing his stitches.

He sat down on the edge of the bed and started slipping on his shoes. "Yeah, all good. I've got shit to do. Coby and Travis will be here soon. Got a meeting to deal with."

My stomach growled loudly as I brushed through the waves of my hair.

"Right. I'll make breakfast," I offered and left for the kitchen.

Frog and Cooper wandered in from next door. Cooper headed to the chair at the breakfast bar in the kitchen while Frog took a running leap for the couch, grabbing the remote and flicking fast enough to give me channel whiplash. I looked away as white spots dotted my vision.

"Lunch time, Sandwich," Cooper announced as he watched me peruse the fridge. "Watcha making?"

I turned so he could see my raised brows. "Do I look like Martha freaking Stewart to you?"

I didn't actually mind cooking food for all and sundry, but I didn't want to advertise the fact. Otherwise, I'd be pestered to do it all the time. Besides, it's not like I was doing their laundry or anything. In fact, I'd never seen them do laundry, yet they always had clean clothes. "Who does your laundry?"

He winked. "Do you really want the answer to that question?"

"Uh, no, let's keep the mystery alive."

Realising Cooper was right, and it was actually lunch time, I smirked to myself. Time flies when you were having fun. I pulled the milk from the fridge and flicked on the kettle.

"What are you smirking about?"

I arranged my face in a blank expression and turned around to grab some mugs before moving back to the fridge. "What are you talking about? Where's Jake?" I deflected.

"He's still asleep," Cooper replied.

I peeked furtively from the opened fridge door and saw Jared sitting out on the back deck chair, phone glued to his ear. I knew everyone caught the kiss last night, but as long as everyone remained ignorant, there was no need for them to know how quickly things had progressed. I made a mental note to tell Henry to keep his mouth shut.

Cooper, not buying my blank expression, was watching my actions intently, taking in my flushed expression and shifty behaviour. He followed my line of sight.

I flinched as he leaped off the seat, pointed at me, and squealed like a girl.

"Oh my God, you guys did it!"

"Jesus! Did you put your girl pants on today?" I hissed. "Keep it down."

Frog did a full swivel on the couch so his arms were resting over the back in order to watch our exchange. He wagged his eyebrows at me. "Wow, Evie, finally. Does Macklewaine know?"

I grabbed the bacon and eggs out of the fridge in a panic, slammed them on the bench, and whirled to point my finger warningly at the pair of them. "If you so much as breathe –"

"Does Mac know what?" I heard shouted from the front door, interrupting my important warning.

Mac was home. Impeccable timing as usual.

"Keep your mouths shut," I hissed.

I shifted to the walk-in pantry to get the bread and sauce out when I heard Cooper wasting no time informing Mac of recent events.

"Jared and Evie did it."

Jesus, this was like high school.

I heard a loud squeal, and I felt a shove from behind. I turned around to see Mac crowding me into the pantry as she shut the door behind her.

Everything went dark.

"Mac! What the fuck?"

I scrambled for the light switch, and it stayed on long enough for me to catch the euphoric gleam in her evil eyes before the bulb blew.

"Shit," she muttered. "Why the fuck does the pantry light always blow?"

"Maybe because it knows you're up to evil deeds."

"Evil deeds?" she returned.

"Yes, locking me in the pantry is hardly the stuff of—"

"Whatever. Apparently, shit has gone down while I've been shopping and I want details."

"Shopping?" I squeaked, aiming for deflection. "You went shopping without—"

"Shut. Up."

"Talk, shut up, talk, shut up." My stomach growled painfully. "I don't suppose this can wait until after lunch?" I asked hopefully.

Mac tinkled an evil laugh in answer. I was fading from hunger. I reached for a shelf and hung on tight before I fainted at her feet. In the interest of food, I gave up and laid it out really fast. There wasn't much to say anyway except we did it, and now I was off to the doctors for the pill at some stage this afternoon. I still needed to make that appointment. How long did it take to get pregnant anyway? I didn't mean for the last part to slip out. I could really relate to that Snickers commercial right now: *You're not you when you're hungry.*

"Oh my lord." Mac breathed. "I'm going to be an aunty!" she finished on a yell.

"Jesus, Macface, don't get carried away. We had unprotected sex *once*, okay, twice."

I winced, knowing I had opened up a whole new avenue of shopping heaven. Frilly baby pink dresses with bows and ruffles, pinafores, booties, hanging fairy mobiles. If it wasn't so dark, I'd see all that and more flashing across Mac's face.

"Oh, Sandwich."

Somehow finding me in the darkness, she yanked me towards her and squeezed me in a hug. "I'm so excited and happy for you. It's going to be perfect. Trust yourself just this one time, and I promise you it will all be worth it."

Tears pricked my eyes at her sudden kindness. I wasn't used to it. "We'll see," I muttered. "Now let me out of here so I can eat something."

Mac opened the pantry door and shoved me out, bread and sauce in my arms. Everyone was sitting around in the lounge room talking, and by everyone I meant Henry, Frog, Cooper, and Jake who had conveniently woken up and come over. Travis and Coby were there to collect Jared and go do whatever it was that they did. Dining room chairs had been pulled over to complete the huddle.

I took a moment to hope they were discussing the Jimmy Farrell knife wielding incident rather than updating on the morning's events.

Conversations ceased and all eyes swivelled to me as I burst out of the dark pantry, wincing as the sudden light burned my eyes.

"So," Mac shouted cheerfully from behind me as she boogied over to the kitchen counter and started pulling bacon rashers out of the packet. "Who's up for a bacon and egg sandwich?"

Jared ignored Mac's question, instead asking me if I'd managed to make the doctors appointment yet.

"The doctors?" Coby interjected.

"Not yet. I'll do it in a minute and let you know what time we need to go," I said as I got a pan out of the cupboard.

"What time *we* need to go?" Coby echoed.

"What is going on?" Henry shouted over the top of everyone.

Mac laughed delightedly. "Evie's having a baby!"

Mac, it seemed, had a death wish.

I gave her a look that promised payback was a bitch while everyone in the room froze. Except for Jared, who was looking at me with what appeared to be a tender expression.

"Mac!" I hissed. "What are you doing?"

I started stalking towards her with the pan, intent on carrying out my threat, and she shrieked and ran in to the lounge room to hide behind Frog. I looked to Jared for help, but he just sat there, arms folded, looking amused.

Jake looked doubtfully at my stomach. "You're having a baby? You don't look pregnant."

All eyes then swivelled to stare at my stomach.

"Who's the father?" Henry demanded to know, obviously starting to wonder how long I'd been sleeping with Jared and what had been going on with Tate and I. Really, what sort of skank did everyone think I was?

This was getting out of hand. I shoved the pan back on the bench, lamenting the fact that the end of time would arrive before I got to eat something. God, I'd take a piece of Jared's birdseed bread at this rate.

"No one is the father," I ground out through clenched teeth, hands fisted by my side. "I'm not pregnant. Mac has clearly lost the plot."

"Evie," Coby warned. "Maybe we need to have a chat?"

"It's a bit late for the birds and bees man," Cooper threw in.

Frog and Jake laughed. I started pulling out slices from the bread packet and laying them out in a frenzy. Not waiting any longer, I started shovelling a piece of bread in my mouth.

"If you're not pregnant, then why are you going to the doctors?" Coby asked, sounding doubtful of my pregnancy denial as he watched me shovel bread in my face like the world was ending (which it must have been considering I was actually getting something to eat). "Are you sick?" He gave me the once over, apparently concluding with confusion that I looked healthy as a horse.

"I'll tell you later," I said.

"No," Jake ordered. "If you're not well, I want to know too, so you can just tell all of us."

"Yeah," echoed Henry and Frog.

Jared, obviously having had enough, finally entered the conversation. "She's going on the pill."

"Oh my God!" I wailed around a mouthful of bread. "Did you have to tell everyone that?" I folded my arms and glared at him as I chewed.

So not only does everyone now know we did it; they all knew we planned on doing it *regularly*. Well, Jared was shit out of luck now

131

because I decided my girl parts were going into hibernation. He shrugged at me, not grasping the situation.

"Christ, Jared," Coby interjected. "Maybe it's you and me that should be having that talk." Coby looked pissed off.

Jared looked at Coby and nodded. "Later."

Everyone turned to eyeball my stomach warily as it growled loud enough to be heard in the next state.

Determined to take the focus off me and deflect it elsewhere, I gave Mac a malicious smile.

"So, Mac," I asked. "What's the deal with you and Marcus?"

She glared at me. Everyone turned from staring at my stomach to look at Mac, apparently rather interested to hear what she had to say.

"I don't know. He asked me out," she admitted.

"Seriously?" I squealed. "He's hot, Mac."

Jared glared at me for that comment. Jesus, I wasn't blind.

"Would you sleep with him?"

"I wouldn't kick him out of bed." She grinned.

I laughed as I saw her look of panic when she realised what I'd made her say. My work done, I put the pan on the stove and started heating it for the eggs.

"You're not sleeping with him, Mac, or anyone else," Jared ordered.

"Sleeping with who?" Travis butted in on the conversation as he came back from bathroom.

I turned to face Jared, narrowing my eyes. "So what?" My tone was still a little pissy after Pillgate. "It's okay for me to sleep with you, but Mac can't sleep with anyone?"

Travis' eyes bugged out at this particular comment.

"That's right," Jared nodded.

Coby started going red in the face, and I winced as I imagined the type of *words* he'd be having with Jared later.

"Jesus, I'm not a nun. I have slept with guys before," Mac unwisely added.

I saw Jake shake his head and Travis winced. "Well make like a nun, Mac," Travis demanded. "Don't wanna hear about you fucking anyone."

Mac threw her hands up in the air. "Fine, I'll just be sure not to tell either of you when I do," she barked at the both of them before stalking over to the kitchen to mash the bread around that I'd laid out and buttered.

"Thanks a bunch, asshead," she hissed.

I waved the butter knife in her direction. "At least I stood up for you there. You just threw me to the wolves."

She sounded a little hurt. "I had a reason, Sandwich. You and Jared need to get your shit together. I was just trying to speed up the process."

"Jesus, Mac. It's been like an episode of *Days of Our Lives* here this morning, and now Jared and I seem to be on the fast track to God knows where. I've not only slept with him, but now I'm having a pregnancy scare, and we're off to the doctors for the pill!"

How much faster did she need things to progress?

She smiled and nudged my shoulder. "I'm happy for you, Evie."

I sighed and got back to the more important business of finally getting the bacon and eggs I'd been almost dying for the moment I woke up.

Chapter Ten

Four days post Pillgate, and three days after Jared left for a trip to Adelaide for work, I was pulling into the driveway of Coby's hillside split level home in North Bondi for *the chat*.

I sat in the car, not looking forward to what Coby would have to say. As you can imagine, I had several relationship type chats with Coby over the years. They were never a delightful experience and usually included several stern words on his part and excessive use of internal eye rolling on my part. Obviously, Jared would be the main feature in tonight's topic of conversation.

I grabbed the two bottles of wine that were sitting on the passenger seat of my car (one would simply not do) and using my key, let myself into Coby's house.

"I'm here," I yelled out.

"Kitchen, honey," he shouted back.

I made my way down the stairs through the split level home and looked out to see Coby give me a wave from the kitchen below. I waved back and walked across the balcony and down the stairs towards the open concept kitchen, lounge, and dining area. Bi-fold doors off to one side sectioned off a huge room that housed a bar, pool table, and television the size of a small country.

I reached the kitchen, sat the wine on the bench, and wrapped my arms around Coby for a giant bear hug, pulling back to inspect his face.

"You look like you could drop. You look like shit."

He snorted. "Lucky you don't work in PR, honey. You suck at it. I'm tired, that's all, but I've got a day off tomorrow. I thought we could spend it together. I haven't seen you properly since you moved here. Can you swing it?"

Tomorrow was Thursday. We had rehearsals and were halfway through writing two new songs. Plus, we needed to hit the store to upgrade some of our equipment.

"Of course I can swing it," I said with a confident smile, vowing to text Mac and plead for the day off. The bribe of a shoe purchase would grease the wheels.

"Okay." He gave the bottles of wine a pointed glance. "You driving? You can stay over if you like. Tomorrow we could pack a picnic and spend the day at the beach."

"Sounds great." I nodded happily. "We'd just need to stop at my place on the way in the morning so I can grab my beach things."

He opened up the bag of food on the counter and the scent of Chinese hit my nose, sending me into the giddy heights of takeaway heaven.

"Mr. Chow's?" I asked excitedly as I opened the cupboard for a couple of wine glasses. I'd had Mr. Chow's on a previous visit to Sydney once. Even getting a takeaway booking from that place was the equivalent of winning a ticket for a round trip flight to the moon.

He grinned. "Is there any other kind of Chinese?"

"Um, no! How did you manage that?" I asked as I poured out two glasses of wine, keen to know the secret for future use.

"Forget it, honey, you don't have the right equipment," he said with a laugh and started carrying plates to the dining table.

I scowled as I followed him and carried in the wine.

"We're pretty sure the manager is gay. None of us guys seem to have a problem getting takeaway there," he explained.

Of course they didn't. They were like part of the *Awesome Hot Guy Society*. Instead of *Jamieson and Valentine: Badass Brigade*, maybe it should be *Jamieson and Valentine: Bootylicious Boys*, or *Jamieson and Valentine: Bootylicious Brigade of Badass Boys*.

I sat down at the table and started dishing food out on my plate. "How do you know he's gay? Is there a secret gay handshake that I don't know about? That has to be discrimination against people with girl parts," I complained, unhappy at the thought of having to bribe Coby to get my Mr. Chow fix in the future. "There must be a name for it." I pointed my fork at Coby. "Vaginacrimination. I'll Google it."

Coby snorted and shook his head as he chewed and swallowed. "You know, he's patted Jared on the ass more than once."

I choked on an egg roll. "Seriously?"

Coby nodded with a laugh as I coughed and spluttered. "Yep."

"No, seriously as in Jared bought Chinese takeaway?"

Was there hope for him yet?

"Chinese isn't all egg rolls and honey chicken, Evie. They make steamed vegetables and rice too."

I shook my head sadly at the waste of using a Mr. Chow's order for something that sounded about as yummy as a pile of dirt.

Coby stood up. "Another glass?"

"You plan on getting me shitfaced so I'll spill my secrets?"

"Maybe." He grinned. "Do you have secrets?" he asked as he grabbed the wine bottle out of the fridge and came back over to top off our glasses.

"Of course I don't have secrets," I lied around a mouthful of food. "I tell you everything, Coby."

He sat back down and took a sip of wine. "I know you, Evie, and if you think I believe that, you must think me stupid."

"What you choose to believe or not believe is beyond my control, Coby."

"That's probably the smartest thing I've ever heard you say."

"Why, do you think me ordinarily stupid?" I asked, starting to build up a good snit which had nothing to do with me trying to deflect the conversation bearing down on me like a freight train.

"Of course not. I just simply question your judgement sometimes."

"You think I don't?"

"Speaking of which," he continued without acknowledging my question, "it's time to tell me what's going on with you and Jared."

Obviously my deflection wasn't worth the effort; that was the trouble with having conversations with people who knew you too well.

As I took a gulp of wine my handbag buzzed a message, and thankful for the interruption, I reached in my bag to retrieve my phone.

J: Home from Adelaide, baby. Where are you?

E: Dinner at Coby's for our chat.

He knew it was coming. He and Coby had words the other day. Jared had told me, though he refused to give a blow by blow commentary of what was said, much to my disgust.

I put the phone down and picked up my wine. "What did you say to Jared?"

He pointed his fork at me. "That's between him and me."

I took a sip of my wine to calm myself. It didn't work, so I sat my glass down, picked up my fork, and polished off the last mouthful of food. "If it involves me, which it did, then I have a right to know."

"Ask Jared then."

Argh, bloody men.

It was lucky I was being plied with wine and exceptional Chinese food, otherwise this conversation had the potential to escalate into sibling violence.

J: Do you need me there?

Oh would you look at that? Jared had my back. The mere thought calmed me instantly, and if I'd have realised it did that, it would have thrown me into a complete panic and reversed the whole effect.

Coby put down his fork and gave me a look I couldn't interpret. "Evie, he's not who I would have chosen for you."

I played dumb. "Who's not?" I might've been summoned for *the chat*, but it didn't mean I had to make it easy for him.

He rolled his eyes at me in exasperation.

"Okay," I relented. "Who would you choose for me?"

I sat back in my chair, holding my wine as I waited to hear of the supposed virtues of the chosen one.

He looked thoughtful for a moment. "Honestly? I don't know. I just know I don't want Jared to be the one for you."

"Newsflash, Coby, it's not about what you want."

"Dammit, Evie!" He stood up so hard and fast his chair tipped over. "No, it's not about what I want, but after everything that you've been through, that I've been through watching you, I should get a goddamn say."

J: Baby?

Jared was waiting for a reply, and Coby was standing there waiting for a reply. Angry that choices I'd made left me unable to trust myself, made me a person that Coby couldn't trust, and feeling backed into a corner, I snapped off a reply to Jared.

E: No, dammit. I don't need you.

I put the phone down. "Fine, Coby. You don't trust me. I don't trust me. Where do I go from here? If you want your goddamn say, tell me what the fuck I do now?"

Coby righted his chair and sat back down, seemingly unsure on what to say for once.

"You...he..." He cleared his throat and tried again. "I see you two together. I see you look at him and him look at you, and it's like...that's how it's supposed to be. You both share a joy of simply being in the same room as the other. Two people who can be loved just for being who they are is a special thing, honey, and I see that potential in the two of you."

My mouth opened and closed like a fish as his words sank in, and I frowned in confusion. "You see all that? Why, if you see all that, would you not choose that for me?"

"His job, the work we do, it's not safe. I know he wouldn't ever deliberately hurt you, but if one day he was to never come home..."

My heart pounded at his words. It was not something I hadn't thought of, but pushing it to the back of your mind and hearing it vocalised from someone else were two different things.

"You'll have to trust me to make the decisions that are right for me. I know it's not an easy task, considering my past decisions have been downright woeful," I conceded, thinking of Wild Renny and Asshole Kellar, "but in this...you don't get a say." I held up a hand as he started to interrupt me. "I don't say that to piss you off or shut you out. I believe that no one chooses who they love, so if you don't get a say, I don't get a say. The only thing I can control is what I choose to do with those feelings, and I'm tired of being too afraid to trust them."

I sat back in my chair feeling completely wrung out. I needed chocolate and I needed this chat over with because I didn't deal well with emotion. Lying to myself, pushing things down into the dark recesses where I couldn't think on them, flippant remarks, I wasn't above any of it.

"It's not just you I'm worried about."

He was worried about Jared? Did he think I was going to stomp all over him?

"What does that mean?" I asked.

Coby sighed and waved his hand. "Nothing." He had a look that told me he was keeping something from me.

"You're keeping something from me."

"It's not my place to tell you, Evie."

Coby eyeballed my phone as it buzzed and vibrated across the table.

J: Okay then. Did you take your pill?

Shit.

I wasn't popping it in front of Coby, no way.

"Evie." Coby cleared his throat as though embarrassed. "I know I don't need to discuss the birds and the bees, but promise me you'll be safe."

I gave him a suspicious look. Did he read my message somehow?

"We're not going there," I announced with as much authority as I could muster.

E: No. Remind me later?

J: You can't take it now?

E:Negative.

I stood up and walked into the kitchen to get the second bottle of wine out of the fridge. "Jared and I are just taking things slow anyway."

Carrying it back to the table, Coby gave me a look of disbelief as I added more to his glass. "Right," he stated dryly. "Do you think that Jared is on your page?"

Absolutely not. After what had gone down the past few days, it appeared that Jared was heading towards Relationship Hyperdrive.

"Let's go sit on the couch and watch a movie," I suggested instead of answering the question.

"Okay," he agreed.

This, obviously, signified the end of the chat, and I felt so pathetically grateful I staggered to the couch and collapsed on it like a starfish.

Sound blasted from the surround speakers as Coby shoved me over to make room on the couch, wine in one hand, remote in the other.

"What are we watching?" I asked tiredly as I felt my eyelids droop.

I heard my phone buzz from somewhere but the couch and I had already become one.

"I thought we could watch *The Notebook*."

I sat up excitedly, all tiredness immediately forgotten. "Really?"

He snorted. "No. We're not watching that rubbish."

I relaxed back into the couch, wondering why it appeared all men had it in for that movie. My last thought before my eyes drifted closed was that perhaps it was because Ryan Gosling set the bar too high.

Coby kept frowning into the rear view mirror as he drove.

"What's wrong?" I asked.

My head thumped as I asked the question because I was suffering the Barnacle Hangover. It was like someone bashing my head with a hammer, and no matter how many painkillers I took and no matter how big my sunglasses were—and they almost covered my entire face—the hangover latched on and refused to let go.

We were cruising down Mount Street in my Hilux to the duplex so I could get changed and pack a beach bag, though at the moment crawling under my doona and staying there until the end of time sounded like an excellent idea.

"I'm not sure," he murmured as he continued to frown at the rear view mirror. "I think someone might be following us."

"Pffft." I snorted. "You James Bond types are a suspicious lot. How close is our tail? Can you see if he has a mouthful of metal teeth?"

I laughed at my own joke, and then hissed when my head pounded painfully.

Coby rolled his eyes at my lameness before continuing to eye the rear view mirror. I ignored his daft antics and flipped my seat back so I could recline in all my hungover glory. I felt the car pull to the curb and peeked one eye open.

Coby picked up his phone from the centre console and began dialling. As it rang, he put it on speaker and pulled back out into traffic.

"Coby," I heard someone answer. "Aren't you supposed to be lying on a beach right about now?"

"Frank. We were on our way to Evie's, but I think we might have had a tail."

Who would be tailing us in my car?

"Make, model, rego number?" Frank asked, sounding very capable.

"Toyota Camry, silver," Coby replied before rattling off the registration number. "Can't see it now but I don't want to take any chances driving to Evie's place if we're followed there."

"I'll run it. Call you back." Frank hung up.

Coby drove down to the end of the street, turning left again and heading in the totally opposite direction of both my house and the beach.

I sighed. So much for our day out together, and I owed Mac shoes for this. "Who's Frank?"

"Frank's the operations manager, heads up the office control room," he answered as we sped down Coogee Bay Road.

I raised my eyebrows. "You have a control room? Do you have a watchtower? And a moat?" I snickered.

Coby ignored my inane questions and pressed a button when his phone rang. "Yeah?"

"You know a Sarah Jenkins?" Frank asked.

Coby was silent for a moment. "Nope."

He gave me a quick glance. "Do you?"

I shook my head.

"That's who the car is registered to. I'll keep digging. You coming in?"

"Yep. See you in twenty," Coby replied.

"Righto." Frank hung up.

Wow, did this mean I finally got to visit the Batcave? Not even Mac had visited the Batcave yet. I could dine on this for weeks.

Coby looked at my gleeful expression as we stopped at the lights. "What?"

I shrugged and tried to look blank. "Nothing," I replied and grabbed my phone to message Mac.

E: Guess what, Macface?

M: You're pregnant and eloping with Jared?

Oh shit. I didn't take my pill last night. I *told* Jared I was unreliable. I checked my messages and saw that he both messaged and rang me last night, and I'd missed both. How did that happen?

E: No, I'm on my way to the Batcave!

When we pulled into the underground car park of a two storey nondescript building in Darlinghurst, just outside the city centre near Hyde Park and the Sydney Police Centre, I felt like I literally deflated. I was hardly expecting a real life version of Get Smart's control headquarters, but this was, well, not exciting.

M: Holy shit. How did you manage that?

Coby parked and turned the engine off, starting to get out of the car as I madly messaged Mac back.

E: Gotta go. Can't talk now.

Coby eyeballed me impatiently. "Coming?"

I hit send and winced when I lifted the sunglasses to my head. I promptly lowered them back on my face as I staggered out of the car. Doing a scan of the car park, my heart skipped a beat seeing Jared's black Porsche parked two cars down. I had a thing for hot cars, and this one was definitely a car that suited the man.

I followed Coby up the inside stairs and into a plush carpeted reception area via a side door. A young looking guy that I could only describe as pretty with his short black hair, blue eyes, and long black lashes, was manning the sleek dark desk and looked up as we came through.

"Hey, Coby." He gave a small wave. "Oh, this must be Genevieve," he squealed and came running out from behind the desk to wrap me in hug. "The two of you look so much alike," he gushed.

"Uh," I managed as he hugged me in a vice grip while my arms were trapped at my sides. If he wasn't so little, I would have expected him to actually lift me up and start swinging me from side to side with his enthusiasm.

Coby grinned at me. "This is Tim. Tim, this is my little sister Evie."

Tim pulled back, grabbing both my hands in his. "I can't believe I get to meet the big bad rock star!" he gushed again, pumping my hands about in excitement before letting them go.

I waved my hand about in mock weariness. "No autographs please."

He pouted. "A photo then?"

Coby rolled his eyes at us. "Maybe later. We need to get upstairs."

Tim shooed him away. "Go then. I'll show Evie about and bring her up in a minute."

Coby looked at me and I nodded to say I was fine.

"Okay," he muttered and disappeared through a door behind the reception desk.

"Oh, I like your jeans. Are they *Sass and Bide*?"

I was still wearing last nights outfit of jeans and a loose satin dark blue top with little silver chains that dangled from one side to the other all the way down the front. "Yeah, they're my favourites."

He nodded approvingly at my outfit. "You have good taste. We should go shopping together."

I agreed. The more numbers you had, the more terrain that could be covered. Shopping was like preparing for battle, you needed to strategise, plan targets, assign buddy's, spread out, coordinate food stops, and finish on the high of spending money you hadn't yet earned.

We exchanged phone numbers and Tim took my hand. "Come on, I'll show you around."

The phone rang.

"Blasted phone," he muttered. "Hang on. Jamieson and Valentine Consulting, Tim speaking. One moment please." Pushing a set of buttons he said, "Geoff on line two," then hung up.

He put a little phone headset on, hit a button, and turned to me. "Kitchen, coffee, biscuits. Let's go."

I followed because the pretty boy spoke my language. He led me through the door Coby had disappeared behind and past a row of five large open style offices.

Tim pointed at each as he led me past them. "That's Coby's desk, Travis, Jared, Casey, and Carol."

They were all empty. "Where is everyone? Who's Carol?"

He led me into a large kitchenette out back that housed a couple of lounges, a casual dining table, a fridge, and a kitchen bench that ran along one wall with a coffee machine, microwave, and sink.

"Travis, Coby, and Jared are upstairs. Casey's overseas on assignment. Carol is our office manager. She's out running errands. Coffee?"

"Tea, please," I asked as I took a sticky beak in the fridge to find nothing but milk. I waved my hand at the vast emptiness. "This is woeful. What do you eat?"

Tim rolled his eyes. "We never know who is going to be here at any given time, so we order in lunch each day once we do a head count. We do have fruit." He indicated to a large bowlful with a distinct lack of enthusiasm.

I raised a brow. "Jared's doing?"

I got the milk out and handed it over as Tim gave me a speculative look. "You and Jared are dating, aren't you?"

"Is this a trick question? What if I say yes?"

He finished making the tea and opened a cupboard, giving a furtive look left and right. "Because I have these..." he half pulled out a packet of Tim Tams "...or you can have an apple," he said in disgust, "if that's what you want."

The phone rang and Tim pressed a button on his headset. "Jamieson and Valentine Consulting, Tim speaking." I absconded the packet of Tim Tams from his hands and made a mad dash for the couch. It wasn't really a mad dash, but if I wasn't under the effects of the Barnacle Hangover it would have been.

"Casey is out of the country at the moment. Is the matter urgent or can I take a message?" He moved to a notepad and pen by the fridge. "Of course. I'll be sure to let him know." He hung up, grabbed the tea and coffee, and came to settle on the couch next to me.

I had half a Tim Tam packed away already, and he gave me an approving look. "Well you pass the test, but I don't foresee fun times ahead for you and Jared."

"Tell me about it," I agreed around a mouthful of chocolate biscuit. "The whole idea of it makes me break out in a clammy sweat."

He took in my mournful expression and patted my hand in sympathy, confiding that it was always a good lunch day when Jared wasn't in the office.

"So what's upstairs?" I asked as I took a cautious sip of hot tea.

"The control room, an overnight room, and a gym." He dunked his biscuit in his coffee and took a bite, swallowing before he explained, "The control room is where they plan and run their operations from. Frank works up there along with five others who assist in just about everything. The overnight room has a few bunk beds and a small en suite for when they pull overnighters, and the gym is here because they're always working, so it's convenient."

"Working hard, Tim?" a loud voice came from the doorway.

Tim shrieked from being startled, and the Tim Tam packet went flying up in the air. All eyes swivelled to watch it fall face up on the floor.

"Crap," Tim muttered.

Jared was standing just inside the door with his arms folded, casually leaning up against the doorway, amusement flickering in his eyes. He was wearing a pair of dark denim jeans, a fitted white t-shirt, navy jacket, and brown boots, but he'd trimmed his hair.

My face fell in disappointment.

"Hey, baby." He grinned at me and stalked across the room. "I was waiting for you to come up but..." he gave a pointed glance at the biscuit packet "...I see you had other priorities."

I put my tea down on the side table, and Jared yanked me up off the couch and planted his lips hard on mine. I whimpered and I wasn't sure if it was because my head was going to wobble off or because the feel of Jared pressed up against me was more delicious than my feeble body could stand.

He moaned as I wound my arms around his neck and opened my mouth to let his tongue slip inside.

"I'll...ah...just get back to the front desk," Tim muttered from somewhere far away.

Lips still locked, Jared turned me around and sank down on the couch, pulling me with him. I shifted so I straddled his lap and met his tongue with my own. The kiss swiftly turned from tender to hot, and he broke away and sucked in a breath.

"Christ, you're fucking hot," he muttered as he stared at my swollen red lips.

"What?" I asked in a daze.

He looked into my eyes. "I missed you."

"I missed you too but..." I ran my hands through the shorter silky strands.

He chuckled. "It will grow back you know."

"Um, hi, Evie."

I twisted from my straddled position to see Travis standing in the doorway with an amused expression.

"Hi, Travis." I flushed and tried to struggle to my feet.

Jared, sensing my efforts to take flight, wrapped his arms around me and held firm.

I gave up with a huff. Jared, happy with my lack of mobility, turned to Travis. "What do you know?"

Travis folded his arms, looking just like Jared had a few moments ago, but his expression was worried. "Frank says Sarah Jenkins is the sister-in-law of Joseph Farrell who is the recently deceased brother..." he glanced pointedly at Jared "...of Jimmy Farrell."

Oh my God, was he *that* Joe? I didn't know he'd died. Jared hadn't mentioned anything. My hands gripped tight on his shoulders. "He died?"

"Yeah," Jared murmured. "Shit!" His voice grew louder. "Do you think he was following Coby in Evie's car or following Evie?"

"Fuck. I don't know. It could be either," Travis said unhappily.

"Why would he be following me?" I asked in confusion. I didn't even know the man.

"Coby and I were both on scene at the time Joe was shot. He may think Coby shot Joe and is tailing him, or I did, and he's after you because you're my girl," Jared explained. He stood up and set me on my feet. "If he was smart enough, he'd just go underground, but it's possible that he's looking for payback."

Travis nodded his agreement as Jared paced the room in full business mode.

"I'll get Evie home soon and stay with her. We need a schedule to have someone on Evie at all times until Jimmy is located. Tell Frank to call Mitch. The police will need to be notified. I want everyone to drop everything that's not urgent and get on to finding this bastard." He swiped a hand down his face. "Shit."

"Shit is fucking right," Travis muttered.

"I'll be right back, babe. Wait here and don't worry. We'll have this bastard locked up by days end." Jared bent his head and with a brief touch of his lips to mine, disappeared through the door behind Travis.

Chapter Eleven

It was early, the sun just rising, and it was not a time of day I was overly familiar with or fond of. I won't deny I enjoyed the quiet, but I was tired and the ability to get back to sleep had died a slow and painful death as I lay staring at the ceiling. Jared had been working around the clock for a week, and Jimmy was still at large. Not wishing to wake him, I sat on the front balcony of our duplex sipping a cup of tea and reflecting on the past week.

We'd played two shows, one at a place called *The Cathouse* and one at *The Forbes,* a shopping trip with Mac and Tim, nothing heard from Gary the Jettison Records scout, and a whole week of having Jared in my bed. It wouldn't have been half bad, but considering every moment that I wasn't with Jared I had either Coby, Travis, Henry, or Jake stuck to me like glue, it gave me an idea of how it must feel to be one half of a conjoined twin. I appreciated the sentiment that it was done in the name of keeping me safe, but blankets were less smothering, and the weight of concern surrounding someone following me left me slightly breathless whenever I allowed myself to think on it.

I felt the air stir as Jared came up behind my chair. He swept my hair over my shoulder and pressed a soft kiss to the back of my neck that sent cool goose bumps travelling along my skin.

"Morning, baby," he murmured, yawning as he moved over to sit in the deck chair to the right of me. Hair mussed from sleeping, he smiled at me lazily, and I let out a long, quiet breath. His chest was bare but he'd slipped on the pair of jeans he was wearing last night.

"What are you doing up so early?"

I took a sip of my tea and waved my hand at the horizon before I answered. "I wanted to watch the sunrise."

He looked out at the brilliant pinks, oranges, and soft blues before raising one eyebrow, looking back at me sceptically.

"Okay," I said on a sigh. "I couldn't sleep."

"Come here," he ordered.

I shifted and crawled into his lap, breathing in his warm, male scent as I rested my head on his shoulder.

"Evie, I'm sorry. I've loved every minute of you being here, but I feel responsible for what's happening with Jimmy. It's been a good idea to lay low until he's found, but maybe we can relax things a bit." He rubbed his hands up and down my back in soothing motions. "We still haven't had that talk yet either."

That was ages ago. Damn the man, he had the memory of an elephant.

"We don't have to do that now," he said, sensing my sudden urge to flee, "but you need to know that I want you with me—permanently. I'm happy to wait for you to catch up, but it doesn't mean I'm not going to do everything I can to make you want to take that jump because I'm right there with you." He leaned in to kiss my forehead. "I know you've been hurt in the past, and I can't promise that I'm never going to make you angry or upset you, but I wouldn't ever do it deliberately. Just give us a chance, okay?"

Without waiting for a response, which was good because I needed a moment to think about what he'd said, he held on to me and stood up. The fact that this amazing, beautiful man wanted *me* was thrilling, and I knew I wanted him just as much. That was never in doubt. I just wasn't ready to let those last, final pieces of myself go. That fact he was willing to give me time gave me some measure of peace.

Carrying me into the bedroom, he tossed me on the bed and crawled up and over the top of me to lean down and press a kiss on my lips.

"I want you every minute of every day. You make me crazy," he whispered as he nipped and licked his way down my neck before sitting me up to take off my camisole. He pushed me back down and finished his trail down my chest, peppering little kisses across my ribs as his hands ran up and down the length of my thighs. I moaned at the touch, and in response, his tongue traced a hot path along my hip bones.

He paused and met my eyes. "I think we should go on a date."

"A date?" I repeated. My conversational abilities were at a disadvantage while his tongue and hands were caressing my skin.

"Yeah a proper date, just the two of us. We can go out for dinner, a movie, have some quiet time together away from everyone else. What do you think?"

He peeled the silk shorts slowly down the length of my legs, my breathing becoming shallow as his mouth moved between my thighs. What did I think? He was asking me to think?

When he'd finished the long drawn out process of doing wicked things to my body, we had another water conserving shower, and I was now in my wardrobe searching for something to wear. Since we'd signed on with Marcus to a regular, lucrative spot at the White Demon, Henry had decided to buy a car, and Jake, he and I were going car shopping today.

I pulled on my grey cuffed shorts with the hot pink pinstripes, a pair of silver sandals, and a plain white fitted shirt and trotted down the stairs to find Henry and Jake sitting around drinking coffee and munching toast while Jared was sliding on a pair of shoes.

I gave Henry and Jake a dirty look. "You didn't make me any toast?"

Henry and Jake had the good grace to look guilty as they munched heartily.

"Babe." Jared walked over to me. "You shouldn't eat that," he said. "It's white bread, full of preservatives. Anyway, I gotta make a move."

He kissed me gently on the lips, and I closed my eyes to savour the press of his body against mine.

"Evie?"

"Yeah?" I sighed as he pressed another kiss on my lips.

"You've parked me in."

"Oh right." I opened my eyes, slightly dazed. "You boys ready to go?"

Without waiting for an answer, I picked up my handbag and keys off the kitchen counter and waltzed out the door. I could do a drive through breakfast grab on our way to wherever it was one went to buy cars in Sydney. Henry and Jake would get absolutely nothing.

"Shotgun," Henry yelled at Jake as they both tried to muscle each other out of the way, literally jamming themselves in the front door as Jared stood impatiently behind them.

"You bunch of wankers," I called out as I got in the car and put the window down. "Get in the car before I leave without either of you."

Jared and I shared a look of disbelief before he gave them both a shove out the door. He mimed that he would ring me as he folded his long sexy body inside his Porsche, gunning the engine impatiently as Henry and Jake ran back inside to get their wallets and phones. I backed out the drive and idled on the curb so Jared could get going, and he gave the horn a toot as he headed off in the opposite direction.

We drove along towards the direction of Parramatta Road as my stomach growled menacingly. "You two can suck it for not making me toast. I'm going to Macca's and neither of you are getting anything."

"Why would we? You heard the man. It was white bread. You know you can't eat that rubbish, Sandwich."

All I could manage was an attempted swat at Henry's head in response because I was trying to drive.

Ten minutes later we were back on our way with Henry and Jake munching burgers, so I made Henry feed me pancakes dripping in syrup as I drove. My phone buzzed a message and Henry picked it up on instinct, long used to me having him answer my messages while I was driving. He did refuse to the other day, though, when Jared was getting particularly amorous while stuck in Adelaide, and I'd asked Henry to text something about where I wanted to put my tongue. Apparently, that was beyond the call of duty of a male best friend, but he'd refused to believe me when I told him I was only kidding.

"It's from Mac," he said, pre-empting my question. "She wants to know if you did your test this morning. What test?"

I rolled my eyes. "What test do you think? Tell her to let it go."

Henry snorted and dutifully texted back. "Is she still going on about that?"

I groaned. "Yes and I am so over it. We need to find Mac a hobby. Marcus needs to give her a good—"

Henry cleared his throat loudly, cutting me off before I could unwisely ruin the rest of our day. We were starting to think that Jake had a slight *Mac Crush* because of late, whenever we mentioned Mac and another guy, Jake got all tense and went on a rant—not a rant directed at Mac, but about whatever he chose to rant about at the time. It just seemed the correlation between the two, Mac and another guy, rant, Mac and another guy, rant, was starting to become slightly obvious.

I sent Henry a grateful glance as my phone buzzed again. Henry sucked in a loud breath as he read the message.

"What did she say to that?" I grinned at him.

"It's not from her. It says 'Buckle up bitch.'"

My mouth fell open in shock and the car jolted as I fumbled gears.

"Who the fuck sent that?" Jake demanded from the back seat before I had a chance to ask the same question.

Henry's brow furrowed in worry. "I don't know. It's a blocked number."

He passed the phone back to Jake while I drove so he could have a look.

I glanced in the rear view mirror to see a silver Camry, not unlike the one Coby described was following us a week ago, sitting right on my tail.

"Uh, guys?"

They were busy talking amongst themselves and ignored me. Meanwhile the Camry driver was speeding up to ram us, and my breath started to short out in panic. Did the idiot really think ramming a Hilux with a Camry was going to have us coming out worse off?

"Guys!" I yelled impatiently.

The Hilux gave a lurch which suddenly had their complete attention.

"What the fuck?" Jake yelled.

Both Henry and Jake swivelled around to look out the back window.

My panicked glance into the mirror showed the Camry had backed off and my towball had added some nice damage to its front fender.

"We just got rammed by a tossbag in a Camry," I said in disbelief.

"Goddammit! It's that Camry cocksucker that was tailing you a week ago." Henry shook his fist angrily out the window.

"Henry! Jesus, you're not helping."

"Shut up, Sandwich. He's coming back again. Speed up."

My glance confirmed Henry's words. I pushed my foot hard on the accelerator, my knuckles white on the steering wheel at seeing the car pick up speed right along with us. Jake snatched the phone back off Henry and began dialling.

"He's getting close, Evie. Plant your fucking foot," Jake shouted at me as he glared out the back window, phone firmly to his ear.

"I'm trying to plant my foot, but I'm hitting traffic dammit," I yelled, feeling another lurch as we shot forward. "I can only go so fast."

At that moment, I was busy regretting those pancakes. I could feel them rolling around in my stomach, and I swallowed frantically as I changed gears.

"Turn here," Henry shouted.

Barely slowing down, the tyres squealed as I made the left turn where Henry indicated and sped down the road, the Camry still hot on our tail.

Jake was talking rapidly. He moved the phone away from his mouth and spoke, "The guys said to turn around and head straight for the police centre. It's only ten minutes in the other direction. They've got your phone on GPS, Evie, so they're on their way."

I did what Jake said, and the Camry didn't deviate from our tail the entire time while he stayed on the phone.

"Turn here," Henry shouted again, and I hooked a right turn and shot out onto a dual lane road. The Camry followed our turn and sped into the lane beside us, trying to push us off the road.

I risked a proper glance at the driver. "Oh hell no."

"Oh hell no what?" Henry threw out.

I interrupted Jakes blow by blow phone account of our situation. "Who do you have on the phone, Jake?"

"Jared," he replied.

"Tell him it's definitely Jimmy in that car. I recognise him from the photos they showed us a week ago." I shouted the last part because the idiot pushed us up and over the curb as we sped down the road. I heard someone behind us honking their horn.

Henry grabbed hold of the dashboard at the reckless jolt. "Fuck."

"Oh my God, Henry, this bastard thinks he can ram us in that piece of shit he calls a car?" I yelled.

I'd somehow managed to tightly lock all the panic, disbelief, and shock away as I fought to keep the car under control, but the anger had overwhelmed me and spewed out in a sudden fiery burst.

Almost on autopilot, I felt myself jerk the steering wheel to the right, tyres squealing as I rammed my car back into his. Jimmy wobbled a bit and backed off in order to gain control. Adrenaline pumped through me from my driving manoeuvre until I felt light-headed.

"Jesus Christ, Evie, that was fucking awesome!" Jake shouted from the backseat.

"I know, right?" I yelled, contemplating my future career as a rally car driver, kicking serious ass as I spun gravel around tight mountain corners.

Unfortunately, my reckless driving didn't appear to deter Jimmy because the Camry was gaining ground, even with some serious dents to the left side of his car.

Muffled shouting came from the back seat. "What the hell is that?"

Jake held up my phone and put it on speaker "….. and tell her to stop playing car games and head towards the fucking police centre. Right the fuck now!"

It sounded like Jared wasn't as impressed by my driving as Jake and Henry were. In fact, he sounded downright pissed off, and maybe even a little scared.

I didn't have time to think about my actions as we flew down the road. Coming the other way, we passed a police patrol car with lights flashing, sirens wailing, followed by Coby and Travis in Coby's own Hilux, then Jared's Porsche. My mirrors showed them executing squealing u-turns over the cement median strip in the middle of the road. Random cars lurched out of the way and came to a dead stop in a giant pileup while they took up procession behind the Camry.

"Evie!" Henry shouted. "Lights! Red ones."

My focus back on the road showed a set of orange lights a hundred metres ahead had changed to red. A panicked glance told me no turns were available before we'd reach the huge four way intersection. My new driving style was rally car and tight turns, not fucking red lights.

"Jared?" I shouted at the phone, having no idea what to do.

"Evie, fuck," I heard shouted and then a fumble. "Hang on, Mitch is going to try and shoot out the Camry's tires."

"Jesus!" Henry yelled. "Can that even be done? What if he hits us?"

"He won't," I heard Jared yell. "Just make sure you all have your seat belts on."

I started slowing down as I reached the red light, my heart pounding in my chest, my hands shaking as I downshifted gears. I was trying to keep a grip on the dread forming a tight ball in my stomach, but I felt it unravel and tears climb my throat. There were no cars in front of me, and as I slowed to a stop, I noticed the Camry behind me was *not* slowing down.

"He's not slowing down!" I yelled.

To my left another car, already ahead of me, was stopped at the lights so there was no room to move. I couldn't attempt a red light run because cars were flying through the intersection at a deadly pace.

"Christ, does this guy have a fucking death wish?" Jake shouted.

Panicked, I shouted at the phone. "Jared, why isn't Mitch shooting out the tyres?"

His voice bellowed out from the phone in a frantic, pain-filled burst. "He can't, Evie. It's not safe anymore, and it's far too late. FUCK! Brace yourselves," he shouted desperately.

We all swivelled to the back window to see the Camry much too close.

"Henry," I whispered, meeting his eyes.

His hand reached out to grasp mine and squeezed tight. Jimmy finally hit his brakes. I saw the back end fishtail slightly as though he finally realised the outcome of him slamming in to the back of my big ass Hilux would not go in his favour. Our car took a massive hit as it heaved forward, the Camry crumpling into the tailgate.

The violent lurch had my phone flying out of Jakes hand and hitting the front windshield, causing a small crack before landing on the dashboard. For a brief moment, I felt okay, shaky, but okay, until Jared's wild scream could be heard from the speaker. "Evie, get the fuck OUT OF THE CAR!"

The impact from the Camry had pushed us a full car length into the busy intersection. Cars flew by dangerously. Out of my peripheral vision, I saw the cavalry screech to a stop behind us, descending out of their cars, running for us. I was making a fumbled frantic move for the door handle when I saw a truck bearing down towards us with nowhere else to go, honking his horn loudly, then everything went black.

I woke in a room I immediately noted was not my own. My blurry eyes couldn't focus as the sound of beeping pinged through my head like an out of control ice pick.

I turned my head left and found Jared sitting in a chair, fast asleep. He looked rumpled, worn out, and slightly vulnerable in a way that made me want to reach out and run my fingertips tenderly down the side of his face.

I shifted to sit up and do just that, but the pounding in my head began escalating, leaving me to wonder how much I'd had to drink last night, where I ended up, and what type of hangover it was that I was suffering from. I'd never experienced anything of the like before, and I here I thought I'd categorised every type of hangover that ever existed.

"Jared," I croaked out.

He didn't move. I cleared my throat.

"Jared," I managed a bit louder.

The effort overwhelmed me, and I closed my eyes. I thought that maybe I just needed to eat, but when my stomach rolled over feebly, I began to worry.

"Baby?"

My eyes blinked open. Jared was standing over the bed and he took my hand in his.

Looking around the strange room, I asked, "What's going on?"

Why was the room so bright and where were my sunglasses?

"Baby, you're awake," he whispered and without letting go of my hand, he weakly sank down into the chair.

"Yay me," I muttered feebly. "My head is splitting open. What did we drink last night?"

I felt myself drift away before I could catch his answer. When I stirred again, the afternoon sun was still shining brightly, and Jared was sitting on the bed drinking a coffee.

"Where am I?"

His brow furrowed as he focused his eyes on mine. "You don't remember anything? Hang on, I'll buzz the nurse." He reached over to the back of my bed and pressed a button on the wall.

"Nurse?" I whispered.

Jared put his coffee down on the side table and leaned in, pressing a kiss to the top of my head before he spoke. "You're in the hospital, baby."

Oh shit. It flooded back to me in all its painful, panic inducing glory. Jimmy. The Camry. The truck.

"Are Henry and Jake okay? Jared, what…?" I trailed off and didn't even finish my sentence before I felt myself drift away again.

When I came to later, the sunshine had faded to night, Jared was gone, and there was a young doctor standing at the edge of my bed, scribbling in a chart.

"Genevieve." He smiled at me when I stirred.

He looked far too young to know what he was doing, but I smiled back anyway because he looked kind and friendly with his soft grey eyes and fine blond hair.

"Evie," I offered.

"Okay, Evie," he repeated and smiled at me again. "How do you feel?"

"Like I've been hit by a truck."

He moved to the side of the bed, leaning down to flash a pen light in both eyes. I cried out in pain as the out of control ice pick made a re-appearance, and the doctor patted my arm reassuringly.

"Sorry about that, Evie."

I closed my eyes for a moment and whispered that it was okay. Then I heard what appeared to be a party coming from somewhere down the hallway: loud voices, shouts of laughter, arguments. Someone even yelled.

I noted the tag pinned to the doctors white coat. "Dr. Reed, are you having a party?"

He shook his head as his lips tugged up at the corners. "Sorry, Evie, but that *party* out there..." he nodded towards the door "...happens to be all on you. Your friends and family are out there."

Of course they were. This didn't surprise me in the least. I get injured and end up in hospital, and they turn it into some kind of excuse to get shitfaced and disturb an entire ward full of bed ridden and critically ill people.

"No," I denied. "You must be mistaken. I have no friends or family. Whoever they say they are, don't believe it. In fact, you should tell them all to move their party on elsewhere."

He grinned. "I think the nurses are likely about to do just that."

"When can I leave?" I asked, struggling to shift my body into a comfortable seated position.

He placed his hands on my shoulders and gently pushed me back down on the bed. "You're not going anywhere yet. You've suffered a severe head injury. This is the first time you've been alert in almost three days."

Three days? I lost three days? I should be hungry. When my stomach growled in response I knew everything was going to be okay.

"What day is it?"

He stood there scribbling in my chart. "It's late Sunday evening."

I closed my eyes. That meant we missed the show at the White Demon. Shit. This meant another three days of missed pills. Double shit. I told Jared I was unreliable.

He looked up at me, pen poised. "Do you remember what happened?"

I nodded.

He scribbled some more in his chart. "Good."

161

He tucked the chart away and came over to stand by the bed, clicking his pen before slipping it into the pocket of his white coat. "Is there anything I can get for you?"

"I'm kinda hungry so something to eat would be nice, thanks."

"Okay." He checked his watch. "Dinner will be around soon."

I didn't mean hospital food. I meant real food, but I didn't bother to correct his assumption because I couldn't imagine him arranging a takeaway run with one of the nurses.

"How about I send a couple of your visitors in and tell the rest to come back tomorrow?"

"Yes, please."

"We've booked you in for a scan, so I'll be back for you in a few minutes, okay?" He smiled kindly and left.

More shouting came from down the hall, and after a few moments, Coby and Henry rounded the doorway. They both looked tired and wrinkled.

"You both look terrible," I announced.

"You should see yourself, Chook," Henry muttered.

I ran my fingers through a snarl of hair at Henry's words, and Coby leaned in to kiss my forehead. Henry took up the other side of the bed and grabbed my hand.

"Thank God you're here." My stomach growled its agreement. "I need food. Where's Jared?"

"We sent him home to shower and change his clothes. He was starting to stink the place out and scare all the nurses," Coby told me.

Thinking of how he looked when I first came too, I asked, "He's not coming back, is he? Please tell him I'm fine and to get some proper sleep okay?"

"I can tell him," Coby agreed, "but it doesn't mean he'll listen."

I faced Henry and when I noticed his arm in a sling, my eyes whipped to his in a panic. "Henry, your arm!"

"I'm fine. It's more precautionary," he assured me. "I'll be back on the guitar in a couple of days. I was lucky and just cracked my elbow. You smashed your head."

"Well, there's no point in doing anything half-assed now, is there?" I said dryly.

"You did a pretty good job," Henry said reassuringly. "The truck clipped the front bumper of the car on the driver's side and spun us around. You hit your head on the side window on impact. A smaller car and we might have been crushed."

"Jake?"

"Jake's fine," Coby replied. "Not even a scratch."

"Typical," I muttered bitterly to Henry as I leaned up a little to wrestle with a pillow. "Look how I ended up, and you two come out of it dancing the hokey fucking pokey."

Coby helped adjust my pillow, and I flopped back down gratefully. "Thanks, Coby. How is my beautiful car? Will she live?"

Coby shook his head. "I'm sorry, Evie, but she didn't make it."

I couldn't take any more. The tears began trickling down my face faster than I could wipe them away.

"It'll be okay, honey." Coby rubbed at my arm soothingly. "We've already arranged a new one under your insurance. It's all taken care of."

"It's not the same," I choked out. "Please tell me Jimmy came out worse off than me?"

Henry and Coby shared a look that told me that definitely wasn't the case.

My eyes went wide. "He's still out there, isn't he? After all that, he got away? How did that even happen? That's it. Your names are officially changed to *Jamieson and Valentine: Assclown Consultants,*" I growled in irritation.

"Evie!"

"Sorry, I'm sorry. I didn't mean it. I'm just pissed off because all this happened, and he's still out there. It's just this continual black feeling that I can't shake off."

"It's alright and yes, Jimmy got away," Coby confirmed irritably. "Everyone was busy working to get you all out and then the ambulance came and with so much going on, he managed to get away."

"Visiting hours are over," Dr. Reed interrupted from the doorway. "This young lady is due for a scan."

"We'll be right outside if you need us, okay?" Coby reached out, squeezing my shoulder wearily before heading for the door.

I turned my head to Henry and whispered quickly. "Go get me a burger and chips Henry, please? I haven't eaten in three days."

"Tomorrow, Evie, I promise. It's too late now," he said quietly so only I could hear. "I just want you to know that I didn't let go of your hand. When I saw that truck right there. God." He shuddered. "I wanted to take your place, and then Jared was there the second the car stopped. You had all this blood running down the side of your face and you weren't moving." Henry let out a deep shaky breath, and I squeezed his hand reassuringly.

"What about the truck driver?"

"Fine, just in a bit of shock I think."

Dr. Reed finally came into the room, clearing his throat.

"Burger. Chips," I whispered fiercely before Henry could leave.

He gave me a wink and let go of my hand to follow Coby out the door.

When I woke later, having had my scan and a shower, Jared was sitting by the bed looking fresher in clean clothes, damp silky brown hair against his neck, and freshly shaven. His eyes were intent on my face, and I flushed at the thought of him watching me while I was sleeping.

"Jared," I said, blinking hard. "You shaved?"

There was silence as he ignored my question, and when he spoke, his voice was almost a whisper. "Why didn't you get out of the car?"

My mind flashed back to the truck bearing down, my hand shaking and seemingly unable to move, fumbling on the door handle.

"I was trying to," I replied, "but I couldn't get to the door handle fast enough. I don't know. It all seem to happen so slowly except for that truck."

He stood up at my words, putting his hands in his pockets and walking over to stare out the window into the inky blackness. "You gave us all a scare, Evie. I thought we were gonna lose you. I can't remember ever feeling so terrified." This time his voice shook and it made my insides churn.

I didn't like hearing it in his voice and tried to be positive. "Well, I get to go home tomorrow."

His eyes softened on my face. "That's good news, baby." He approached the side of my bed, taking my hand in his and gently running his thumb over my palm. "It's not too soon, is it?"

"Nope. The scan came back all clear, so they've recommended bed rest at home, but otherwise I'm okay. Well, as okay as I'll ever get, anyway," I joked.

"I'll make sure you get rest," he said, relief overtaking his voice and he squeezed my hand tightly.

I flipped back the sheets and patted the bed in invitation. "I've been watching old re-runs of Friends on the tiny hospital television, and that Tom Selleck really rocks a moustache. Shame you went and had a shave," I said in mock sadness as I gazed at his upper lip. "You'd look hot with facial hair."

He chuckled as he crawled into the skinny hospital bed and snuggled up against me, his arms wrapping around me while we both struggled to get comfortable. With his strong arms holding me, he rested his chin on the top of my head for a moment, running his fingers gently through my hair with his eyes closed tight.

"Not gonna lose you, baby," Jared vowed so quietly it almost couldn't be heard. Then he relaxed his arms and bent his head to meet my eyes with a faint smile. "Don't cut my hair. Grow a moustache. You trying to turn me into your Hairy Parry?"

I laughed. "No! I was just teasing." I ran my fingertips down the side of his face until I reached the dimple in his smile. "It wouldn't do to cover this up now, would it?"

"I could say the same for you and clothes."

"Jared!"

He chuckled against my mouth, so I linked my fingers around his neck and bit his bottom lip gently. He ran his tongue across my lips, and at the soft touch, I opened my mouth to let it move against mine. My hands travelled across his wide shoulders, down his chest, and slipped under his shirt, running them across the warm, hard ridges beneath. His body was strong, his skin warm, and touching it kept getting better and better. He made me feel safe, wanted, and treasured. No one had ever made me feel that way before, and I wanted him to feel the same. I wanted to erase the fear in his eyes and replace it with heat and desire. Within the tight confines of the bed, his hard body pressing against mine, I couldn't restrain myself and inched my hand inside his jeans. He groaned and snagged my wrist.

"Evie, we can't. Not here."

The fire was starting to light in his eyes. His breathing deepened and seeing that, knowing the fear was changing to desire and it was me doing that to him, had my throat growing thick. There was no way I was stopping now.

"Yes we can," I insisted with a slow smile.

I tugged my hand out of his grasp and slowly unzipped his jeans, rubbing the hard bulge that strained against his boxer-briefs.

He sucked in a shaky breath. "Someone could walk in."

"No they won't. The door is closed," I murmured as I licked my way gently along his neck, my hands gripping the hot, hard length of him as I moved my hands firmly and lovingly along the silky skin. "You make me feel so cherished, Jared. So cared for. I want you to feel the same. I love touching you, just let me touch you."

"Oh, baby," he whispered, closing his eyes as he swallowed hard. At my words, he went from caring that someone would walk in the door to pushing himself harder in to my hand. He moaned my name, his voice hoarse, and when he came, he buried his face into my shoulder and bit down on my neck. I shuddered at the heat swirling in my body from his teeth on my skin, and tears welled up in my eyes at how good it felt to have him wrapped around me. The depth of my feelings for Jared were only getting deeper, and right at that moment I knew that even a lifetime with his man would not be enough.

Chapter Twelve

We were smack bang inside the heart of the Sydney Police Centre, sitting in the designated waiting area. I'd dressed in what I considered was appropriate police interview attire: a mustard coloured pencil skirt and short sleeve black knit top with my hair a loose knot of curls at the nape of my neck.

I smoothed my skirt nervously. Having Jared sitting next to me, the warmth and comfort of his shoulder down to his thigh pressed against mine, helped keep my breathing deep and even. Various police type personnel eyeballed Jared and I curiously, and I fidgeted in my seat, texted Mac and Henry continuously, and watched suspicious wrongdoers with equal parts fascination and apprehension.

I met Jared's eyes when he took my hand in his and squeezed it tight. He smiled at me, soft and reassuring, and I exhaled slowly, feeling the tension in my body ease.

It wasn't like the gritty award winning cop drama I'd expected. People looked neat and tidy as they sat about their desks. No shouting detectives, urgent team huddles, or perps struggling to escape from handcuffed confines as they spat on the floor in anger. The overall mood was the only thing worth noting. The atmosphere was rife with irritation as piles of paperwork, in the space of twenty minutes, continued to pile higher or simply shifted to another pile.

Jared suffered my enthusiasm with quiet patience as we waited for Mitch. Mitch was going to formally take down the information relating to the dodgem car skirmish with Jimmy. Sitting there, I reflected back on my date with Jared two nights ago.

I had been standing under a steaming hot shower wondering, now that I was better, how I could manage to keep taking advantage of my injury. Having people wait on me hand and foot was unheard of, and I decided I liked it so much I wanted to keep the dream alive a little longer.

Mac had barged in to the bathroom and dragged me out of the shower.

"What are you doing?" I hissed.

She reached in to turn off the hot spray and threw a towel at me.

"Shut up. You've been in there forever. You're a prune."

"There's nothing wrong with being a prune," I said snootily in defence of pruned people everywhere as I dried myself off.

"Come on," she said and shoved me out the door and into my bedroom. "Let's get you dressed."

"What are you doing, Mactard? I can get myself dressed."

She blinked her wide eyes at me, her shrug exaggerated, once again aiming for nonchalance and falling far short of the mark. "You're injured, Sandwich. I'm just trying to help you."

I looked at her suspiciously but nodded in agreement. "Yes, I'm injured..." I feigned a wince and a hand to the temple for added believability "...but you're acting shifty."

"Now, now, don't be like that." She waved at the bed where a new black shift dress was laid out neatly. "Look, I bought you a lovely new dress."

"You've been shopping without me again? Why is it okay for you do that to me, but if I do it you, you unleash the hounds of hell?"

She sighed. "Sorry, Evie, but you were in the hospital, and I needed to cheer myself up."

I huffed. "Nice to see you looking out for yourself."

"Hey, I bought this dress for you!"

"Thanks, Mac." I arched an eyebrow. "And you didn't buy anything for yourself?"

"Why are you being so snarky? You usually love it when I buy you stuff."

"Christ, Mac, slap me, would you?" I hissed out a breath and tried to let the rabid feelings go. "I don't know why I'm feeling out of sorts. I think it's delayed shock or something. Sorry."

"Don't worry about it, Sandwich. You're allowed a free pass after getting your head mashed in by a truck. Sit down on the bed. I'll do your hair and face nice for you, okay?"

I shrugged on my robe, and she proceeded to blow dry and straighten my hair until it fell like a like a sleek waterfall down my back. I heard voices downstairs and someone started playing my favourite Lana Del Rey CD.

"What's going on down there?"

"Nothing," Mac replied, dragging my makeup bag over to start working on my face.

"Turn it up!" I shouted down the stairs when my favourite song came on. Someone must have heard me because the volume kicked up a notch, and I sighed in pleasure.

"Mac, are we having a party? Because I'm a bit tired."

"Of course we're not," she reassured me. "We're just going to have a quiet dinner, that's all. I thought you might want to look nice after being confined to your bed for so long."

"Oh. Okay."

I was a little disappointed. A party was what I'd been expecting and gearing up for since being dragged out of the shower. A little "welcome home from hospital we're glad you didn't get dead" kind of affair would have been nice.

She finished dusting the blush across my cheeks and sat back on her heels. "All done," she said, admiring her efforts. "Now hurry up and put that dress on. I want to see you downstairs in ten minutes." She stood up and left, shutting the door quietly behind her.

When I slipped on the short, silky black dress and wandered down the stairs the duplex appeared empty. "Hello?"

Jared walked out of the kitchen in jeans and a fitted green vintage t-shirt that matched his eyes perfectly, and I decided then and there I needed to buy a set of sheets in rich emerald green.

"Where is everyone?" I asked.

"You look beautiful." He took my hands in his and pressed a kiss on my lips. "I thought that since we never got to have our date, and you're not quite up to going out, we could do it here. I kicked everyone out."

I looked at him in wonder. "You did that for me? And cooked for me?"

I racked my brain and couldn't think of a single time that someone had cleared a house and cooked a romantic dinner for me.

My heart filled with admiration at his thoughtful effort, and I bit down on my bottom lip in an attempt to fight the tears that sprang to my eyes.

He shrugged modestly. "Mac might've helped a little. Drink?"

"Yes, please."

I followed him to the kitchen, and he poured two glasses of chilled, white wine, handing one to me, and picking up the other.

"To you, Evie," he said, lifting up his glass, his green eyes soft as they met mine. "The bravest, funniest, sexiest woman I have ever met."

I flushed at his praise and sat my glass down to take his hand in my own. "Thank you, Jared. For being there."

"Don't thank me, Evie. I'm always here for you." He smiled before adding seriously. "I wanted to throttle you when I heard you were trying to run Jimmy off the road, but what you did..." His voice was unsteady as he trailed off and cleared his throat. "I admit I was impressed at your driving, but don't try that again. I don't think my heart could take it. Though even with that reckless manoeuvre, you managed to stay calm and controlled. If you hadn't, it could have resulted in something worse, something that doesn't warrant thinking about. You kept yourself alive and Henry and Jake safe, and I'm so proud of you. I care about you *so* much."

With our fingers still linked together, he lifted them and pressed a gentle kiss to the back of my hand. Then he leaned forward, ducking his head and pressing a kiss to my throat. I closed my eyes at the sweet touch, my pulse pounding rapidly where his lips met my neck. I opened my eyes and Jared stepped away, leading me over to the table filled with flowers, candles and a delicious looking dinner of...

"Pizza?" I squealed in disbelief and let out a laugh. "You made pizza! How did you know it was my favourite?"

"I asked Mac," he said.

Bless you, Mac. I gave it a suspicious look and immediately noted the parts that belonged to Jared. "Is that pumpkin? And spinach?"

"Just because its pizza doesn't mean it can't be healthy," he said, winking at me as he held out a chair for me to take a seat.

I chuckled at his words and sat down, taking a swallow of wine. I could at least see the excessive amounts of cheese and pieces of prosciutto that Mac obviously had a hand in.

We chatted quietly over dinner and wine as my favourite CDs kicked over in a random shuffle. "My favourite wine, favourite food, favourite music. What are you buttering me up for, Jared?"

He came around from the table and pulled me up with both hands, leading me to the lounge room. "Your body obviously, and all the wicked things it does to me." He winked and a slow song kicked over. "Dance with me?"

After a slow dance about the room, which was more of a sway after two bottles of wine, Jared let go of my hands to sit down on the couch. He crooked a finger at me and plastered a sexy grin on his face. "Come here, I want to do dirty things to you."

Unable to resist his offer, I rushed towards him, tripped the corner leg of the coffee table, and managed to tackle him on the couch. We rolled to the floor with a thud. "Oops," I whispered. "I think I might have had a little bit too much to drink."

He chuckled as he lay on his back with my body over his. "Well, at least we're on the floor."

I blinked to focus on his face. "Why?"

"Because Mac made me promise at least ten times that I wouldn't do you on the couch or she'd never be able to sit on it again."

"Do me?" I snorted.

"Her words, not mine," he said, reaching up to run his tongue along my neck and I leaned into it. He moved me onto my back, and I was pinned underneath his weight as his hands ran up my outer thighs, sliding the silky skirt of my dress up and around my hips along the way. I moaned at the feel of rough hands on smooth skin. When his hand slid inside my knickers, I closed my eyes with a shaky breath and tilted my head back, wrapping the length of one leg around his hip. His touch was feather light, skilled and perfect. I felt like I could have stayed there under the weight of him forever.

My handbag buzzed in response to a recent message, startling me out of last night's memory and bringing me back into the Police Centre. I squirmed my legs together, flushing, and Jared gave me a wicked grin, knowing exactly what I was thinking about. As I reached for my phone in a quest for composure, my eyes focused on Tate storming towards us as he glared daggers at Jared, shoulder holster and badge on display.

At that moment, I finally understood what people meant when they said, "Careful what you wish for." We were about to become worthy of an award winning cop drama. I watched all eyes in the building swivel to follow Tate as he passed by.

"Goddamn you, Jared," he shouted when he got close.

Jared stood up quickly, anger radiating from glaring eyes that were cold and hard. The entire floor went silent, apart from my phone which was still buzzing madly. I ignored it, my eyes remaining riveted on the scene unfolding before me.

"Back off, Tate," he growled.

Not again, I thought with unease, though at least this time I wasn't wrapped in a sheet.

"Answer your damn phone, baby," Jared said irritably without taking his eyes off of Tate.

Tate pointed a finger at Jared's chest. "Don't you speak to her like that, asshole. I knew I shouldn't have left her with you. You almost got her killed!" His voice raised with each word.

I quickly switched off my phone without checking my messages and stood. The entire floor watched with blatant interest. A fake cough rang out from the back of the office as I leaned in to make our discussion more private.

"Tate, You're being unreasonable."

Jared spoke calmly. "He's not being unreasonable, Evie. He's right. I did almost get you killed."

I looked at Jared as if he'd grown another head. "What?" I sputtered. "That's ridiculous."

"It's not. That son of a bitch wouldn't have gone after you if it weren't for me." Jared's expression was pained as he pulled in a deep breath.

"You don't know that. I could've been targeted because of Coby. Besides, who knew the man would do something like this? No one is placing blame anywhere for this." I turned to Tate with a fierce eyes.

"The fact is that shit happened and you almost got killed. Now that's something I have to live with," Jared said.

My pulse quickened in a slight panic, and my hands gripped my bag tightly. I didn't want him carrying that type of burden around with him.

"You don't have to live with that. I'm okay, Jared. I'm fine."

Jared frowned, his eyes still hard, his voice firm and unwavering. "It won't happen a second time, Evie. I'm not gonna sit by and watch you get hurt again."

I dropped my arms and Tate interrupted us by taking hold of my hand. "Let's go, sweetheart," he said as he glared at Jared.

I wasn't sure why he was being so antagonistic towards Jared. The two of them had punched it out of their systems in true caveman fashion, so it should have been over.

"Get your hands off her," Jared ground out, his body tense.

Tate wisely let go of my hand. "She needs to make her statement, Jared." He turned to me and nodded his head. "Let's go."

Jared folded his arms unhappily. "Where's Mitch? He said he'd be taking care of this."

"He's been held up. Said for me to make a start without him."

Wanting to avoid another scuffle, this time in public with half of Sydney's finest watching, I picked up my bag to follow Tate.

Tate pointed a finger at Jared. "You can wait here."

For a moment, Jared's look of disbelief outweighed the anger. "Tate, we're consulting on the case. I have every right to sit in on the interview and hear the formal statement."

"And you will." Tate smirked. "When it's typed up and we fax it to your office."

"It's all right," I assured Jared and leaned in to give him a quick kiss. "It won't take long. I'll be fine."

He returned my kiss quickly. "Come get me if you need me, okay? I'll be right here." He glared warningly at Tate. "You keep your hands off her."

Tate rolled his eyes and as we both walked down the length of the long hallway, I felt a burning crawl up my back as every set of eyeballs in the room tracked our movements. He led me into a small windowless meeting room at the back of the second floor that housed a surprisingly nice office table and four black chairs.

Walking in behind him, he turned and shut the door and took my hand, pulling me in close.

"Evie..." he reached out to run his hand down my cheek "...I was so worried about you."

I jerked away immediately. "Tate, don't."

He sighed in frustration as he moved away, slapping a thick manila folder on the table and nodding towards a chair. "Take a seat."

When I sat down, he was leaning up against the wall, hands in his pockets, running his eyes over the length of my body before meeting my eyes.

"I could kill him for getting you caught up in this," he said angrily.

I frowned up at him as he stood there. "Why are you blaming him for this?"

Pushing off the wall, he came over to sit down at the table. "Because he's reckless. Joe didn't need to die, and now Jimmy is out there and after you. Are you okay?"

Tate's disparaging comments towards Jared were like a slap, and I fisted my hands at my sides, fighting the urge to jab a finger in his chest with my next words.

"Whatever Jared did saved the lives of two young kids, and last I heard, it was the job of the police to round Jimmy up and put him away. Jared and Coby have a team out there working tirelessly around the clock, losing money and sleep, to not only find him but cover my ass at the same time and keep me safe. And I'm fine by the way."

Tate replied by rubbing his hands over his face and exhaling loudly. With his hair mussed and shoulders slumped, he looked tired and worn down. "Can I get you a drink or something before we get started?"

My face softened. "A cup of tea would be nice. Thanks, Tate."

"Won't be a sec." He stood up and stuck his head out the door, murmuring to someone before sitting back down.

"Aren't you going to record the interview?"

As he opened the thick manila folder, pen at the ready, he pointed up towards the camera in the corner of the ceiling. I ran through everything, stopping every so often to answer one of his questions. We paused halfway through for a young man who came in with tea and biscuits, his movements hurried. He stopped quickly to catch my eye with a brief smile, and then rushed back out the door before I could return it and say thank you. When we finished the interview, Tate handed me a mug shot that Jared had already showed me a week ago, asking me if I was able to identify him as the man in the Camry.

"That's him," I confirmed, taking a sip of my tea.

As I handed back the photo, the door opened.

"This looks cosy," Mitch said to Tate as he walked in, taking in my now curled up position in the chair as I sat munching biscuits and sipping tea.

Mitch looked just as tired as Tate, showing the same furrow in his brow that Jared had. He also had the same golden skin and green eyes that ran through the Valentine family, though his hair was dark brown, almost black, and cut in a short choppy style, the ends going every which way as though he'd run his fingers through it a thousand times.

"We were just wrapping up," Tate advised.

"Get anything new?" he asked him as he came over and leaned down to kiss my cheek. "Hey, beautiful," he murmured in my ear.

"Hey, Mitch." I gave him a warm smile.

Tate cleared his throat at our exchange. "Nope. Not that we expected to."

Mitch ran his hands through his hair in frustration. "Goddamn asshole must think we're a bunch of fucking pu...ah pansies," he corrected for my benefit. He shouldn't have worried. I lived with a bunch of people who spoke Pottymouth as a second language, though the p-word wasn't one bandied about often, so his considerate behaviour was appreciated.

I frowned, remembering the nasty text from Jimmy that Henry read out and asked, "What about the message he sent. You can't trace it somehow?"

"Jared's already had it checked out, honey, and just like we thought, it came from a disposable," Mitch replied.

I raised my brows in question. "Disposable?"

"Just a cheap throwaway phone, Evie. We can't trace it," Tate expanded.

"Great," I muttered under my breath.

Chapter Thirteen

"Jared," I said in a hurry, "it's not what you think, you don't—,"

"Fuck. Save it. I should have known better, really, it was stupid of me to think you would be different."

He rushed to the front door, swung it open, and stalked out, slamming it shut behind him.

I sucked in painful breaths while everyone watched me in silent shock, apart from Mac who was looking at me with narrowed eyes.

How had it come to this?

Since everything seemed to be on an up hill swing, something needed to happen. The laws of the cosmos dictated balance. The universal scales of life were off kilter, and now I needed to be brought back down to earth where I belonged.

The day started with Sydney suffering under the throes of a heatwave. Mac and Henry lounged on recliners, moaning about the stifling humidity. Cam who came to visit from Melbourne, and I moaned in hunger while we watched a movie.

Mac's phone rang, startling us out of our heatwave coma. With her legs dangling off the side of the chair, she pulled it out of her pocket, sighing as she looked at the screen, and promptly disappeared up the stairs. She came down the stairs so fast she took a stumble at the last leg and fell in crumpled heap of twisted body parts, not a trace of lethargy remaining. I rushed over to help pick her up off the floor, and despite a little wincing as she struggled to her feet, she blurted out the reason for the phone call. I almost knocked her back over when I heard Gary Gilmore from Jettison Records wanted us in that very afternoon.

During a late lunch, we met Casey for the first time. He had recently returned from overseas and was assigned bodyguard duty for our trek to the city to see Gary. It wasn't exactly his brand of excitement since it didn't come with a shoot-out and a car roll or two, but we were enthusiastic enough to practically be doing cartwheels.

The seven of us (the band and Cam) were squished around the dining table eating hot chips and chatting excitedly when the knock came at the door. While Henry got up to answer it, I quickly scooped the rapidly dwindling pile of chips onto my plate ignoring shouts, frantic scrambling, and complaints which included words like *greedy bitch* and someone saying, "Your ass could have its own postcode." I was pretty sure that one came from Mac, and giving her the laser death stare took all my attention, so I didn't expect to find my plate empty.

"You greedy seagulls!" I yelled.

"Us seagulls, Evie?" Frog raised his brows incredulously.

"Damn straight." I reached across to grab a massive handful of chips off his plate and shoved them into my mouth with smug satisfaction. Unfortunately, the mouthful was so huge I couldn't even chew it properly, leaving me thinking I'd either have to spit them out or wait for them to break down.

An amused male voice spoke near the table, suspending my dilemma.

"Did I miss lunch?"

Looking to the direction of said voice, I blanched, thinking that Jensen Ackles had somehow taken a wrong turn and materialised in our dining room in Sydney, Australia.

"Jesus Christ," Cam mumbled, obviously arriving at the same conclusion.

Henry introduced him around the table as Casey, and when his blue eyes fixed on mine, I merely nodded politely, struck speechless and only partly because my mouth was full of chips. I chewed frantically and swallowed a mouthful so big I felt it ache on the vertical downslide.

"Ready to go?" he asked.

Casey raised his delicious eyebrows as the three of us girls looked at him in silence. Could eyebrows even be delicious? I assumed so because his were.

"Uh..." I managed.

Mac nodded.

Cam sat staring silently.

Later that afternoon, as Casey waited in reception, we found ourselves sitting at a boardroom table in expensive high backed cream leather chairs, fidgeting nervously just as we had been for the past half an hour. My hands gripped the arms of the chair fiercely, fingernails digging in, while I sucked in short, sharp breaths. Mac kept giving me odd looks, but I could barely afford her a glance since I was physically restraining myself from getting down on my hands and knees to kiss the thick, plush carpet in a giddy frenzy of gratitude.

The tinted floor to ceiling windows of the June Grady building let in a sunny glare. Already sweaty from anxiety, I was left wishing I had some tissues to stick under my armpits. I evened my breathing by focusing on the iconic view of Centrepoint Tower and the Harbour Bridge.

"Evie," Mac hissed. "Fix your hair."

I didn't quite catch what she said because I was too busy gagging a little. Was I really going to ralph all over the creamy expanse of carpet? Did I really need to eat that supersized caramel sundae right before we got here? Cold shivers racked my body, and I felt I was suffocating under a haze of fear. What if I cocked this up? It was an entirely possible scenario because I cock up most things. It would be on my tombstone. *Here lies Genevieve Jamieson, strangled by a giant sheet because she cocked up her life.* Too much rode on this meeting, not just for me either, which made it worse. I risked a glance at Frog and Cooper, then Jake, Henry, and Mac, who still gave me odd looks and tried to catch my attention. They looked just as freaked out as I was. Frog had a sheen of sweat lining his forehead. Cooper's beautiful olive skin was so unnaturally pale the tattoo under his shirt that climbed around the side of his neck stood out in stark contrast. Jake clenched his jaw, and Henry was counting to a hundred; because from across the table I could lip-read him silently saying, "...eighty-five, eighty-six, eighty-seven."

I started bouncing my leg up and down. I knew I should have gone to the bathroom even though I went before we left. Was that a scuff on my shoe? I was about to reach down to wipe it off when Mac snapped at me, drawing my attention back to her.

"Evie," Mac said through clenched teeth.

"Mac," I hissed back. "What is your problem? You've been on everyone's case all afternoon. We know how important this is. Stop reminding us."

The guys all nodded their agreement. Just as I sat back to take a deep calming breath, Gary Gilmore walked through the door, swiftly closing it behind him.

We all sat up a little straighter, and I smoothed the creases that had formed on my shirt from my seat belt. I'd actually considered leaving it undone to keep my shirt wrinkle-free, but somehow I didn't think that would fly in the face of an accident. Fancy explaining to some stern copper the reason I'd flown out the front window of the car, smashing myself to smithereens in the process, was because I hadn't wanted to ruin my shirt.

Mac glared at me and pointed to her head.

What? I shrugged.

She shook her head back in a silent *whatever*.

"Sorry to keep you waiting," Gary said as he walked hurriedly over to one of the chairs and quickly sat down, dumping a folder on the table in front of him. "I got held up at the studio. Sins of Descent are in the middle of their world tour, and we've been busy putting together a selection of supporting acts to put forward for the Australian leg in February because Menace pulled out."

We looked at each other with wide eyes. Sins of Descent was one of top bands in the world. They currently had three songs in the top fifty Billboard Chart. They were musical gods, and their lead singer, Ethan, had been voted second sexiest male singer, only behind Adam Levine.

Gary looked at all of us and sat back in his chair, steepling his fingers, as his assistant David came running in with a coffee. David had kindly offered us drinks when we arrived, but we'd all declined for various nerve related reasons.

"I'm Gary Gilmore and I head up the A & R Department here at Jettison Records. We're in charge of discovering talent, which you seem to have quite a bit of." He smiled at us. We stared back, hanging off every word. "Thanks for coming in at such short notice."

We murmured polite responses.

"We've called you in because I liked what I saw when you played at The White Demon Warehouse a little while ago, and I think you may have what we're looking for. However, what I think and the label thinks don't always align, which means it's up to my department to convince them you're worth the investment, so that in turn, leaves it up to you, as the talent, to convince me to take that risk on my reputation."

Gary sat back to let us absorb the words while he took a sip of his coffee then waved his hand about. "I'll run through a bit about our label shall I?" He went on to talk about the various departments. The Art Department would be involved in album covers, displays, advertisements. Marketing handled everything involved in releasing an album. Promotion made sure the artists got air time on radio stations, television spots on stations like MTV, and scheduled various interviews. He went on to talk about producers, sales, publicity, and label liaisons until it swirled around in my head dizzily.

"Today, I'd like to get a bit of background about yourselves, what instruments you play, how long you've played, what artists influence your music, and what direction you see the band taking."

We all nodded so he would know we were listening.

"Then," he continued, "we'll set up an appointment for you down at the studio so we can get two or three songs recorded. I'll take that, along with some video of a live performance, and if the label is happy to go ahead, we can start talking contracts."

We went around the table discussing our musical backgrounds as Gary asked questions, eventually handing over some paperwork to Mac.

"Mackenzie, you're the band's official manager?"

She confirmed that she was and reached for the papers across the table.

He nodded towards the pile. "That paperwork should have all the information for the recording studio. Where they are, who you need to talk to, what's involved. The contact information on there is for Marty Jennings. He's who you'll need to talk to about scheduling. The studio is pretty backed up I'm afraid, so I would suggest you ring today. At the least it will give you time to put the songs together that you wish to put forward. I've included a selection that I think might be appropriate."

He looked at all of us. "Any questions?"

I scrambled through my brain for something to ask so I wouldn't look like the dumb mute I'd been throughout the entire meeting.

"What kind of contract might we be talking about?" Henry asked, sitting back in his chair.

Gary directed his answer to all of us. "We usually look at about a four to five album deal. That means you have to produce those records under our label alone. We don't usually stick a time frame in there, but we don't want albums to drag out forever. If you manage to debut a popular album, you could fade into obscurity if you don't back it up with something reasonably soon. The whole purpose is to keep your name out there, but our publicity and promotions department can work with you on that."

We all nodded and murmured appropriately at his explanation.

"Well if that's all..." he stood up "...I'll get my assistant David to see you out. Mac, you have my contact information if you need to be in touch. Thanks for coming in."

He shook all of our hands politely, and David materialised to usher us all out the door, pressing the lift button for us before returning efficiently to his desk.

First into the lift, I saw myself in the mirror and blanched. A giant strand of my straightened hair, which I thought was tucked neatly behind my ear, had somehow managed to do a double loop and pin itself back the other way so it flared out crazily in to the air. God! Gary must have thought I was a complete twat.

"Mac," I shrieked, madly brushing the offending tuft of hair back to where it belonged. "Why didn't you tell me about my hair?"

Mac let out a huff as I frowned at all of them through the mirror in the lift and patted it back into place.

"Didn't notice, Evie," Jake said.

Frog and Cooper just shrugged.

"Evie," Henry muttered as we made our way out of the lift and into the hideous heat.

"What?"

"We're about to hit a real live recording studio for a potential signing and your worried about a strand of hair?"

Frog picked me up and whirled me around crazily, and then a group hug had us dancing about wildly and accidentally jostling the annoyed and sweaty pedestrians who had the misfortune of getting in our path.

It was cause for a celebration, and Casey had the thankless task of detouring to a supermarket so we could stock up on party essentials. Mac busily texted everyone we knew in Sydney to invite them over while I strolled the aisles alongside Casey. Thankfully he didn't share Jared's health food affliction. He didn't so much as glance at the giant pile of food I loaded into the trolley, nor did he appear to notice that every woman we encountered embarrassed themselves trying to get his attention.

Later that night we were two hours into the party, and I'd barely seen Jared for more than two minutes because we were surrounded by friendly well-wishers that were anxious and curious for details.

The crowd mingled on the back deck and yard, eating the piles of marinated chicken wings and munching from Mediterranean platters. There were giant pitchers of sangria and beers piled high in the surrounding eskies.

Finishing up a song at the request of the group, Henry leaned his guitar against the wall while I kept strumming slowly, sitting on the edge of the deck table, feet on the seat. Much to everyone's amusement and laughter, I finished off with a limerick.

There was once a young lady named Mac

Who had an unusually large bum crack

"Evie!" Mac screeched.

She got it wedged in the loo

So she screamed like a shrew

And passed out in a panic attack.

"Do me, do me," Tim yelled.

"Okay, okay," I agreed with a chuckle. "Let me think."

I paused for a moment, then grinned.

There was once a young man named Tim

Who in actual fact was really quite dim

He lifted weights and got hurt

When he tried to flirt

And perve on all the hot guys at the gym.

Much to everyone's disappointment, Jared came over, sat my guitar down, and picked me up off the table. "Come, my sweet poet." He grinned at me. "Let's go somewhere more private."

I wrapped my legs around his waist, flushing in embarrassment as he carried me off amidst loaded catcalls and shrieks of laughter. The stairs must have been too far away because we somehow found our way into the pantry, backed up against the shelving, between flour and unopened packets of red lentils. Jared yanked my head back and began sucking and biting his way up my neck to my lips in a heated frenzy.

"Can't get enough of you, Evie," he muttered and my hips jerked as he tugged at my earlobe with his teeth.

I felt it when he pulled back to look at me. His lids were heavy, his eyes serious and steady. His hands ran slowly up my outer thighs, stopping to rest on my hips where his fingers dug in. His look made me feel like I was the only person in the world who mattered.

It was a look I never wanted to see him give to anyone else. The jolt of possessiveness shook me so much I almost shoved him away.

"What?" I asked him to cover the sudden loss of breath and the shaking in my palms.

"Are you okay?"

The pantry door rattled. "Evie?"

"Won't be a sec," I called out to Mac.

"Okay, well everyone is starting to leave."

We peeled ourselves apart, and Jared smoothed down the wrinkles on my clothes with tender hands. Leaving Jared in the kitchen, I hit the lounge room to say my goodbyes. There were only a few people left when the shouting started. Mitch and Jared were in the kitchen with each other having what appeared to be a yelling match.

Jared stormed out, brow furrowed and fierce eyes glaring. "Tell me it isn't true, Evie."

I looked at him in confusion. "What isn't true?"

"You and Tate."

What the hell? My mouth opened and closed like a fish with the confusion becoming no clearer.

"The other day, at the station," he clarified.

All eyes swivelled to me, and I heard Mac suck in a breath.

Mitch came out and I spared him a glance.

"Evie," he muttered, not quite meeting my accusing eyes.

"Mitch, what did you say?" Fury was bubbling close to the surface, and I could see Mac waiting for it to spew over.

"We reviewed the interview footage today, and I might have mentioned something about you and Tate." He shrugged an apology.

"Tell me, Evie," Jared shouted. "I want to hear you say it."

Awkward tension tied the room in knots. People didn't know whether to leave or stay and began an awkward shuffle for the door.

"You're overreacting," I ground out.

He glared at me accusingly. "Did he touch you? Did you let him?" His tone went from angry to broken, and I scrambled to get the words out before I caused him any more pain.

"Jared," I said in a hurry, "it's not what you think, you don't—"

He cut me off. "Fuck. Save it. I should have known better, really, it was stupid of me to think you would be different."

He rushed to the front door, swung it open and stalked out, slamming it shut behind him.

I sucked in painful breaths while everyone watched me in silent shock, apart from Mac who was looking at me with narrowed eyes.

I made for the stairs with blurry eyes, in shock at how quickly Jared turned into just another asshole. How could he look at me like I was his whole world in one moment, and the next, believe something about me that wasn't true without talking to me first? If he didn't trust me, then it was likely I didn't matter to him half as much as I was starting to believe. His actions were proof that protecting my heart should have been my number one priority. When would I ever learn?

Chapter Fourteen

It had not been a good week. Not that I'd expected it to be all sunshine and daisies, but we had studio time to plan for, and I'd be damned if Jared being an asshole got in the way of all that happiness. I hardly slept without him there, I was being a high maintenance bitch, and if Cadbury wasn't my middle name, things would have been a lot worse, and not just for me.

J: Evie, please answer your phone.

Delete.

J: Evie, I'm sorry. I managed to get the full story. Please can we talk?

Oh you did, did you? Nice of you to wait until after your asshole episode and skank assumptions to realise I'm not a cheating bitch.
Delete.

J: Look. I understand you're angry but just let me explain.

I don't think so.
Delete.
I received a message from Mitch the next day.

M: Sorry, Evie. It's my fault. I didn't see the actual footage. One of the detectives here was obviously exaggerating by saying that Tate was all over you.

What could I say? I would have thought Mitch knew me better than that, but he was looking out for his little brother after all.

E: That's okay, Mitch. I'm not angry at you, just at Jared for choosing to believe it.

In the heat of the moment, Mac was, surprisingly, supportive.

"Honestly, Sandwich, all men are wankers. Henry excluded," she added quickly when he flipped her the finger. "It's a wonder they can find their own dicks what with them being stuck about on their heads all the time."

However, two days later her tune started to change. "Maybe you should talk to him."

"Why should I, Mac?"

"Because there's more to it than what you realise and maybe if you spoke to Jared, it might clear a few things up."

I thought back to my *chat* with Coby.

"It's not just you I'm worried about."

"What does that mean?" I'd asked.

Coby had sighed and waved his hand. "Nothing."

"You're keeping something from me."

"It's not my place to tell you, Evie."

"Why couldn't I manage to settle for a nice quiet unassuming dork that pecked me on the cheek as he headed off to his nine to five office job?" I wailed.

"Evie," Mac snorted. "Don't be ridiculous. You used to walk right over the top of Hairy Parry and Beetle Bob. They bored you silly."

"They weren't boring, Mac. I did like them you know, and yes, they might have been safe, but I didn't use them."

When Jared messaged me again a week later, I didn't delete it in light of Coby and Mac's words.

J: Can I see you?

I sent a reply off quickly before I could change my mind.

E: Okay, but not here.

The duplex was full and as much as I appreciated the support of my friends, I wasn't in the mood to have them involved in our conversation.

J: Come to my place. Travis isn't here.

He messaged me the address and an hour later found me pulling into an allotted visitor park outside a converted warehouse apartment complex in Woolloomooloo.

Jared buzzed me up to the top level and led me in to a beautiful loft style apartment with double height ceilings, massive windows, a huge open style dining room, a kitchen, and a lounge room. The kitchen was right in the middle, separating the two rooms with wide caesarstone benchtops and stainless steel appliances. There were doorways off to the side, which I imagined led to the bedrooms and bathroom. Big glass doors led to an outdoor deck that was perfect for entertaining. The whole place was painted white with a feature red brick wall and decorated in *man*. No girly touches here. As I wandered through the room, I glanced at photos here and there in an effort to avoid looking at Jared and moved to one of the giant windows where I could view the famous Finger Wharf where Russell Crowe supposedly lived.

"Evie, who drove you here?"

I turned to face him and sighed. He looked tired, but even wearing just an old pair of faded jeans and a shirt with a big tear in it, he still took my breath away.

"Jared..."

"Evie, Jimmy is still out there. Shit. Just...don't do that again, okay?" He sighed. "Drink?"

I latched onto the subject change. "Yes, please."

He poured us both wine and led me over to the couch. Once I'd arranged myself comfortably, he took a sip from his glass, sat it down, and took hold of my hand.

"So, here's the thing," he began without wasting time on small talk. "Jessica was the girl I was going to marry."

"Oh." I snatched my hand away, thinking that maybe a bit of conversation beforehand would have been a good idea to soften that particular blow. "How lovely for the two of you. Am I standing in the way of that?" I asked.

Jared and Jessica had a much better ring to it. Their celebrity name would be Jarica, pretty in a sort of ghetto-ugly kinda way.

"No," he said, grabbing my hand back. "She died."

"Oh, Jared, I'm so sorry," I blurted out, horrified at my insensitivity. "I can be such a thoughtless bitch sometimes. I'm sorry." I gave his hand a squeeze.

He squeezed back before letting go to rub his hands down the front of his jeans. "That's okay. You didn't know."

"What happened?"

He picked his glass back up off the coffee table and sank into the navy leather couch, fiddling with the stem of the glass rather than taking a sip. "I met her when she moved to Sydney from Perth. Her dad had been relocated for work. She was only a little thing with short blonde hair and brown eyes, but she was trying out for our high school mixed soccer team anyway. I was inside the six yard box and going for a hat trick when she got in the way and the ball slammed into her jaw and sent her flying. I got ribbed for months after that, but it certainly got her attention," he said with a chuckle. "She asked *me* out after I'd bruised her jaw all purple and green, said she liked my powerful inside curve kick."

I didn't know anything about soccer, and for a brief, selfish moment, I felt jealous that this girl had shared something with Jared that I would likely never do.

"Anyway, we'd been together for three years, and about two years after we started uni, she began acting strange. Not ringing or coming around as much, being secretive, taking phone calls in another room. At the time, we were so busy caught up in part time jobs, assignments, and group study, I didn't think too much of it. Then a few months later, she started getting really sick: tonsillitis, constant infections, tired all the time. When she came down with pneumonia and was hospitalised, they diagnosed her with a rare type of leukaemia." He paused to take a sip of wine and ran his fingers through his hair. "It progressed so bloody fast. Three months later they said there was nothing they could do for her, that she had anywhere from two to four months left, and sent her home. It was awful and I felt like I couldn't do or say the right thing."

Tears filled my eyes at the pain in his voice, and I blinked them away, watching him rub a hand down his face. I couldn't imagine what it was like to watch someone lose their life, right in front of your eyes, and know there was nothing you could do about it. Knowing the type of person Jared was, feeling useless would have cut him deeply.

"Apparently, it was time for death bed confessions, and she admitted to sleeping with someone else," he said bitterly. "Not just some one night stand either. This was a relationship that had been going on behind my back for a whole year and only ended when he moved away."

She cheated on him? On *this* man? Disbelief and anger were conflicting emotions, and I tried to keep my thoughts from travelling down the path where it was wrong to speak ill of the dead. Oh God, this was why he didn't trust *me!* That hurt. It fucking hurt knowing I was paying for something she'd done. But then wasn't Jared paying for the actions of others from my past? Did that mean it hurt him too? I didn't know what to think, but I did know I wasn't the only person in this relationship carrying scars on the inside.

I took his hand back in mine, giving it another squeeze, encouraging him to finish.

"I felt so fucking stupid. I still do to be honest, thinking back on it makes my insides feel all twisted. How could someone be such an idiot to not notice something like that going on for a whole year?"

I shook my head in disagreement. "I think the question should be 'Why was she such an idiot?' Did she ever say?"

He nodded. "She tried to tell me she was in love with the both of us and how could she choose? What was I supposed to do, Evie, when she told me? Be the asshole boyfriend who dumped his girlfriend of three years when she had maybe two months left to live? How was I supposed to forgive that before she died? I couldn't leave her, and I felt so angry and sad and fucking stuck. I couldn't tell anyone either. How could I when she had so little time left? She died about three months later, and I felt like a heartless bastard at the funeral when all I could feel was anger because the past year and a half of my life had been a complete lie."

Leaning forward, I sat my drink down on the coffee table with a loud clank, and then I turned around and straddled his lap, running my palm gently down his cheek. "Jared, right until the end, you were with her. I can't even imagine how it must have felt to do that, but I know you wouldn't have forgiven yourself otherwise. Maybe she lost your respect for her actions, but you never lost respect for yourself."

He slid his arms around my waist and locked his eyes on mine. "Thank you, Evie. I know my past is no excuse for overreacting the other night and storming out on you, but for what it's worth, I'm sorry. It's just..." Jared paused and let out a shaky breath "...you mean so much, so much more than anyone ever has, and that's fucking scary."

My throat grew tight at his words, and at that moment, my admiration and respect for Jared was immense. Shitty things happened to good people all the time, and it was how you dealt with it that mattered. Despite the emotional cost, Jared had acted with so much dignity and honour, it left me wondering what he saw in me. The way I'd dealt with the shitty things in my life was so very different. Jared knowing that *my* actions were disappointing and shameful was scary because then maybe I would lose his respect just like Jessica.

"You mean a lot to me too, Jared, and your apology? Taking the time to explain something so painful just so I could understand your actions is worth more than you realise." His eyes remained on mine as I spoke and I rested my hands on his chest and pressed a soft kiss on his lips before pulling back.

"Jessica is part of your tattoo, isn't she? A reminder about how being true to yourself is being true to others."

He nodded, breaking eye contact and turning his head to stare at the darkening sky through the window. "Part of it. I hated that I felt like our time together was a lie, but it also made me realise I didn't love her like I thought I did. Not because of her actions, but before that. Maybe I just wanted to love her, and if I had been honest with myself and realised that, then maybe the whole shitty mess wouldn't have happened."

"I think you shouldn't be so hard on yourself. Of course you loved her. Maybe not in the way you think you wanted to, or should have, but sometimes it's hard to know what is in your heart."

At my words, his gaze returned to mine. "My mind knew, Evie. It just didn't fucking tell me what I wanted to hear." He hesitated. "Speaking of hearts....Are you going to tell me about Asshole Kellar now?"

"I'd probably have to start with Wild Renny first," I muttered.

My stomach growled angrily, and I checked my watch to see that time had gotten away. Jared eyed my stomach before asking, "Wild Renny, huh?"

"Yeah," I replied with a heavy sigh, not in the least looking forward to reciprocating the sharing process. "Maybe you could feed me first?"

"What would you like?" he muttered, staring at my lips.

His fixation was getting me hot. "You, for starters."

The corners of his lips tilted up, and his green eyes glittered. "Yeah? I'm just the entrée? What's the main course?"

I squirmed on his lap. "Well..." I drawled out.

"Wait," he chuckled. "Let me guess, Mr. Chow's?"

I blinked at him in surprise. "How did you know?"

He gave me an exasperated look. "Coby does happen to be one of my closest friends you know. He told me all about you and your Mr. Chow fetish."

"Yeah? Well who doesn't have a Mr. Chow fetish? Besides, I heard all about the fetish the guy who works at Mr. Chow's has for your ass," I nodded knowingly.

He tugged at the knot of hair at the nape of my neck so it unfolded down my back in a mass of waves. "Who doesn't have a fetish for my ass?" he joked, his fingers threading through my hair.

Later, after dinner arrived, we sat at the solid oak dining table drinking iced tea and eating honeyed chicken with a side order of steamed dim sims, steamed vegetables, and rice.

Jared pointed his chopsticks at me. "Wild Renny." His eyes bore into me, prompting me to spill.

I swallowed my mouthful of chicken, feeling my insides tie themselves in knots. "Right," I mumbled, wondering how to begin.

Jared knew my dad had disappeared and Mum died, but he didn't know the full story, so that's where I started, telling him how Ray had deserted us, Mum was always working hard, the car accident, and my party.

"I don't remember the months after Mum died much. You know that feeling you get when you're just waking up? When you're not quite conscious but you can feel your dreams slipping away? I felt like that. Constantly. That was when I met Lorenzo Rossi, or Renny."

I took a swallow of tea as Jared sat across the table, chewing thoughtfully and watching me as he listened.

"He was the typical bad boy, eighteen, longish black hair, black eyes, tattoos, and a black Triumph Thunderbird motorcycle."

Jared nodded. "Sweet ride."

"I know, right? By that point I was starting to lose the surreal feeling, that dreamlike state I'd been drifting in, and that meant anger was slipping its way through. I didn't like being angry. At the time, I didn't realise it was perfectly normal to feel anger at a parent for dying and leaving you behind. I just knew that it was there and that I didn't understand it. Being on the back of Renny's motorcycle took me back to that dreamlike state, and going back there felt so good. It felt even better at night. I could tilt my head back and watch the stars, feel the wind in my hair and everything twisting around inside me would disappear."

I pushed the vegetables around on my plate a little to make it look like I was eating them. "Trouble was that being with Renny didn't make anything better. It kinda got worse. The anger wouldn't go away, and it was like the more I pushed at it, the stronger it got." Tears worked their way from my throat, and I swallowed them back down. "It just wouldn't let go, and I hated myself for it."

I took another sip of my drink to compose myself. "Renny introduced me to tequila, which at the time I thought made those night time motorcycle rides feel even better. Coby tried to pull me out of it, but he wasn't a dad and he was dealing with losing Mum too. Nothing I ever did back then was fair to him. God, I knew the way I was acting was wrong. Even at the time I knew, but I couldn't stop, and Renny made me feel so good after everything had left me feeling so bad. Six months of skipping school, disruptive behaviour, and drinking excessively ended on a four day drunken bender where it was all I could do to remember my own name. Coby and Henry had tried ringing and messaging constantly, but I didn't even notice, and my phone eventually died. The bender finished with an evening motorcycle ride down Melbourne's Highway 31, tequila bottle in one hand, the other wrapped around Renny. When I felt the bike swerve I was suddenly airborne..." Jared closed his eyes as though to brace himself "...and while I don't remember anything after that, the accident investigation report suggested Renny simply went off the road. I was lucky, Jared, that I actually woke up in a hospital. Lucky to be alive. Renny managed to walk away, and he did it so well that he checked out of the hospital the next day without even a backward glance."

Ray leaving, Mum dying, and then knowing Renny walked away so easily had hurt like nothing I could ever imagine. I swallowed the feelings of abandonment the memories still managed to evoke.

"Well that wasn't the end of it. Social services turned up and put Coby through the wringer because he was my guardian and supposed to be looking after me. So he almost lost me twice. That's just how twisted and selfish I can really be."

"Fucking hell," Jared muttered. I chanced a glance to see he'd stopped eating. His elbows were on the table as he held his hands together, resting them against his forehead as he stared at his plate.

When he looked up to see me watching him, I expected to see disgust in his eyes for my actions, but all I saw was sadness in his pained expression.

"Evie, baby, you were so young and going through so much. How can you expect yourself to have known how to deal with something like that on your own? I would think acting out is normal, maybe not as wildly as you did, but you didn't have the support network there that so many people have. Don't blame yourself anymore for how you acted, okay? The main thing is that you came out the other side, and I have you now." He smiled to reassure me.

"Maybe," I murmured.

"Though I'm not sure my heart can take hearing any more," he muttered.

"Well I haven't got to Asshole Kellar yet," I pointed out.

He stood up and made for the kitchen. "I know. I think I'm gonna be needing another drink first. A real one. Beer?"

I shook my head and Jared got a beer out for himself and topped up the iced tea in my glass. Before sitting back down, he leaned over and pressed his lips to mine, coaxing me with his tongue until I opened my mouth to let him inside. The kiss was sweet and soothing and nothing like the hard and fiery ones we shared earlier.

"Okay," he said after pulling away, and sat back down, picking up his beer. "Sock it to me."

"James Kellar was a drug pusher." I was all for ripping off the bandaid this time. He did ask me to sock it to him after all. Jared winced and downed a huge swallow of beer. "Not that I knew that at the time," I added hurriedly. I *was* trying to pull myself together after Renny, and I didn't want Jared to think I was deliberately turning to harder, more mind numbing endeavours.

"He was older, twenty-five to my eighteen. I thought he was such an improvement over Renny, different, and he really looked to have it together. I was trying hard to make an effort. I stopped drinking except on weekends, improved my grades at school, and was finally dealing properly with losing Mum, so I thought maybe I was capable of making better choices. Kellar had plenty of friends and owned his own house. He had a beautiful car, a 1967 Shelby Mustang in gun metal grey with these big black racing stripes. He loved that car like it was his baby. Looking back I think I loved it more than him too." I tried to lighten the moment, but Jared didn't look amused so I hurried on. "Well I didn't know it at the time, which was really stupid, but I didn't know anything about drugs, that he was slipping pills now and then in my drink. I thought I was just getting tipsy because I'd lost my alcohol tolerance. It wasn't until later when I thought about it that I realised I hadn't been drinking all that much, just maybe one drink, two if I was lucky."

"Fucking hell, Evie," Jared bit out. "The house, the car, the people constantly coming and going... How obvious did it need to be?"

"Jared, I was eighteen and I'd never been exposed to that level of the drug chain before. Despite all the wild, stupid things I've done, drugs are actually something I've never touched, so how would I know? You're trained to see this kind of thing." I actually didn't have a clue if he was trained to see that kind of thing at all, but it sounded good.

He relaxed his clenched hands. "Shit. Sorry, it just pisses me off that he did this to you."

"You and me both. So one night we were having a party and there was a raid on his house. Unfortunately, whatever he'd slipped into my drink that night was particularly strong and thank God for the raid because the cops found me climbing up the third balcony railing in an attempt to fly and caught me before I went over."

Jared's golden skin went sheet white, and he held up his hand to indicate he needed a moment. "Please tell me they caught the asshole?"

He closed his eyes in relief when I nodded.

"But not before I watched him squeal out of the driveway in hail of gravel and gunfire like a really bad James Bond movie. I'd like to say that was the last I saw of him, but the police came by several times, and I had to testify against him in court."

Jared stood up and took our plates to the sink as he spoke. "So both of these two bastards broke your heart and almost got you killed and now..."

He trailed off into silence, as though lost in his own thoughts.

"And now?" I prompted.

"Now I..."

I got up from the table and moved into the kitchen, frowning when he didn't meet my eyes. "Now you what, Jared?"

He leaned up against the kitchen bench and folded his arms, wincing as he rubbed at his chin. "Nothing, baby." He unfolded his arms and reached for me, pulling me close. "I'm just glad you're safe."

Chapter Fifteen

After leaving Jared's loft the next morning, my health took a fast downhill slide by the time I reached the driveway of our duplex. In light of Jimmy, he followed me home in his car, and after waving him off, I weaved unsteadily into the house and promptly sent him a message.

E: Dying. Was it an attempt on our lives by Mr. Chow or are you ok?

J: Baby, I'm fine. Want me to take you to the doctors?

Of course he was fine. Mr. Chow's manager probably slipped something in the food that somehow only killed off females, thus removing me from the equation and allowing him to make his move.

E: No. Thanks though. Will see how I am later.

Jared had left this morning for what he said was a busy day, no doubt interrogating suspicious witnesses with his unwavering stare and coordinating million dollar ransom drop offs. I wasn't going to interfere in that.

Mac and Henry still asleep left me free to hit the shower and towelling off, I promptly found myself either about to lose my entire stomach to the bowels of the toilet or die. Dying, at that point, seemed the much preferable option.

Henry banged on the bathroom door. "Evie, are you okay?"

"Peachy," I called back feebly and curled myself into a ball in the bathtub, hesitant of venturing too far from the toilet that was now my new best friend.

"What's going on?" I heard Mac ask Henry outside the bathroom door.

"I don't know. I think she might be sick."

"She can't be sick." Mac sounded horrified. "I just got off the phone with Gary. They're doing video footage of Jamieson live at the White Demon tonight."

My stomach pitched terribly at that unfortunate piece of second hand news, and I pulled myself up from my wedged position in the bathtub to retch violently in the toilet again.

"What's going on?" Cooper asked from the hallway.

I flushed the toilet and sank back down into the bathtub.

"Maybe she's pregnant?" Mac sounded hopeful.

"Bugger off," I moaned.

"Evie, are you okay?" Frog asked.

The doorknob rattled.

"Is it locked?" Jake whispered.

Was the entire world coming over to see me brought low?

Later that day I ended up at the doctors getting an anti-nausea injection. Halfway through our set at the White Demon found me fading fast, and with one song left to go, I was hanging onto the ledge of what felt like a fifty foot drop below. Unfortunately, the day wasn't yet done with kicking me in the ass.

"One last song for tonight, beautiful people," I said into the microphone and winked to Mac and Jared as they stood by the edges of the crowd and watched on with concern.

Suddenly a sharp, searing pain contracted my stomach, and as I doubled over in agony, a loud shot rang out, cutting through the hush of the crowd.

Everyone froze, then someone screamed. "He's got a gun!"

"Fuck!" I heard Jake yell out, and before I even had time to blink, I found myself tackled to the floor under a huge, sweaty mound of muscled man. Any other time I might have appreciated the situation, but unfortunately it was Jake I found myself pinned under, not Jared. Not to mention the pressing concern of a gunman on the loose who had been, as I started to lift my head, apparently aiming in our direction.

"Stay down," he ordered furiously. "Son of a fucking bitch shot out my goddamn bass drum."

Somewhere to my right, I heard Coby yelling and risked a peek to see Henry, Frog, and Cooper being hustled off the stage.

The chaotic crowd rushed towards the exits at the right of the building, and I managed to see Jared pushing through them, heading for the front of the stage.

"Are you shot?" I thought I heard him say.

I blinked.

He managed to get closer, and I flinched at the fury on his face. "Are you shot?" he yelled at me.

I shook my head. "No."

He started to reach for me when Travis let out a shout.

"Jared, to your right, three o'clock!"

All eyes swivelled to the direction of the street. A tall blond man pushed through the side exit and shoved a gun in the back of his pants.

"Fuck!" Jared yelled. "Go that way, Travis!" he indicated to the other side of the crowd with his arm. Reaching around his back, he pulled a handgun from the waist of his jeans, engaged the slide, and checked the safety.

"Jake," he barked. "Get Evie to the back room. Now."

"Wait," Jake yelled as I started sliding off the front the stage. "Where's Mac?"

"She was headed for the back room with Coby," Jared said over his shoulder as he took off in a sprint towards the exit, all long muscled legs and furious intent. Pulling out his phone and dialling, I watched him close the distance like he was flying.

I evaded Jake's grasp and ran after him to the street to watch the scene unfold before me.

Jared was sprinting hard and fast down the slope of the street, phone gripped to his ear as he shouted into it. The blonde gunman was losing ground, but not easily and my eyes caught Travis running equally hard down the opposite side of the street.

"Should we take a shot?" Travis yelled to Jared.

"No," Jared yelled back, dodging two drunk pedestrians weaving about the street in obvious search for a cab.

I cringed, seeing a red hatchback fly out of a laneway which stopped the gunman in his tracks. Jared and Travis gained on him, and he flew around the back of the car and into the middle of the road. I almost died a little as he pulled out his gun and aimed it at Jared.

"Back the fuck off, man," he yelled and Jared ducked behind the nearest car as the man wildly pinged off a shot.

It was like something out of *The Bourne Identity*, and I watched in disbelief as a drunken pedestrian stopped to snap a photo on his phone.

"Evie. Fuck." Jake grabbed my arm and yanked hard. "Get inside."

I shrugged off his arm as Travis stopped, lifted his gun, and aimed for the blond man's leg, firing off a shot and missing as the man started to run down the side of the road.

"Holy shit!" Jake stopped yanking on my arm to watch the scene unfold. We had to squint just to make it out because they were now at the very end of the street.

The gunman was heading for the busy intersection. People on the corner started screaming and scattering as he ran through them, waving his gun and shouting for everyone to move. Travis cut through the intersection and four lanes of traffic, sliding off a small, compact car and hitting the ground hard.

Jared sprinted on as Travis scrambled to his feet to catch up. He was yelling something, but he was too far away to hear.

The blond gunman was obviously tiring. He started an awkward sprint across the road, trying to dodge a hooning taxi that was flashing its lights. Jake and I watched in stunned silence as the taxi screeched to a stop, and the gunman went sprawling across the hood in a flurry of arms and legs and off the other side.

Onlookers screamed and Jared flew across the road, tackling the man to the ground as he tried to get to his feet.

We could see the taxi man railing his fist out the window as Jared rolled the gunman over, cocked back his fist, and smashed it in the man's face. The gun in his hand went flying, and Travis picked it up as he reached them, flicking on the safety and tucking it in the back of his pants.

Jared stood up, shoving the man to his feet and yanking his arms behind his back. He was frogmarched off the street into a side alley, Travis following close behind as pedestrians looked on with shocked bewilderment.

A dark blue sedan screeched to a halt at the front of the alley, police lights flashing from the front and rear windows. Mitch and Tate exited the vehicle and rapidly disappeared into the alley.

We waited, our eyes peeled to the alley entrance, and five minutes later a black Subaru squealed up to the side street and Casey subsequently got out of the car and disappeared into the alley.

Finally reaching breaking point, I turned and promptly lost the two crackers and glass of ginger ale I'd forced down before the show in the street.

Changed into a white tank top, cotton shorts, and hair still dripping wet from a shower, I paced the lounge room back and forth like an OCD sufferer in the throes of a meltdown. Water droplets flung from the dripping strands at each turn, showering those who couldn't be bothered to move from my path.

I stopped suddenly when Coby hung up the phone. "Well?"

He stood up and tossed his phone on the dining table where the Rice Bubbles were playing cards. I felt like picking up the deck and flinging it in a wild hissy fit because Jared was out there and they were playing poker.

"They have the shooter in holding," he reassured me.

"Thank fuck," Henry muttered from his prone position on the floor.

Sprawled out like a starfish on the couch, Mac lifted her head. "And?"

"Everyone is fine."

Mac seemed to sag in relief and closed her eyes, but unlike her, I knew there was more.

I folded my arms. "And?"

"It wasn't Jimmy." He began checking the locks on the windows and the front door, and I heard him say something about a perimeter check under his breath.

"What?" I asked loudly.

"Nothing. Everyone should get to bed. Evie, honey, I'm gonna stay here the night, okay? Just throw some blankets and pillows on the floor of your bedroom."

I pointed my chicken flavoured rice cracker at him. "It wasn't just some random crazy assclown, was it? It *does* have something to do with Jimmy, and he had someone aiming for me."

Henry stopped his lunatic channel flicking, the Rice Bubbles put down their cards, and Mac opened her eyes until we were all eyeing Coby silently.

Coby put his hands on his hips, looking annoyed. "Okay, yes. Jimmy wasn't the shooter, but he was the one who arranged it."

I flopped my backside on the couch at Coby's confession, landing on one of Mac's legs. "Bloody hell."

"Christ!" Henry yelled, tossing the remote at the wall. "The bastard is still in the picture, and he's shooting at her now? This shit is getting so much worse. That asshole needs to be found."

Coby nodded. "You don't need to tell us that. Jared, Travis, and Casey are out there right now along with the police, and we'll have everyone working around the clock until Jimmy is picked up. Everyone please just go to bed, okay? We'll know more in the morning."

I was sitting a set of sheets and blankets on the bedside table when Coby came in and sat on the edge of the bed wearing a pair of Henry's sleep pants.

"How are you feeling?"

While I didn't feel like I would be eating properly any time soon, the nausea which I'd sworn felt like it would hang around until the end of time was gone.

"Better. Thanks, Coby."

"Maybe we need to send you away until Jimmy is off the streets."

"You're kidding, right?"

I shook out the fitted sheet and tucked it over the air mattress Jake had set up on the floor while Coby was in the shower.

"No, I'm not kidding."

He picked up a sheet and started helping me.

"Coby we have a shot at reaching everything we've ever dreamed of, and if you think I'm going to bugger off to some warm tropical island and drink piña fucking colada's all day, then you've got a screw loose."

"I don't know, I think it sounds kinda nice right about now."

"Coby!"

He grabbed my arm from where it was busily stuffing a pillow into a pillowcase. "Stop. Just fucking stop." He shoved me over until I was sitting on the bed, and then stood back to rake a hand through his hair. "If you think I'm going to sit by and leave you as a target, then you're the one with loose screws. Dammit, honey, I almost lost you twice. I can't take that shit again. I'm scared okay? Fucking scared and I'm not the only who feels that way." He blew out a shaky breath. "I won't lose you."

"Coby, I understand your reasons, I really do, but I'm not going to give up everything I've ever worked for because of some assclown lunatic. I'm sorry, I just can't and I won't."

I finished tucking the pillowcase on and chucked the pillow onto the makeshift bed.

"Do you have some grand plan to go out in a blaze of glory? Because this isn't the movies, Evie, and you don't come back from a bullet in the head."

Tears threatened to strangle me, and I choked them back but when I spoke my voice trembled. "You're my brother, Coby, and I love you so much, but you put yourself in danger for your job every day and not once have I ever told you to give that up. Please don't ask me to give up my dream."

He pulled me to my feet and wrapped me in hug so warm and so comforting, the tears I'd been swallowing down reached my eyes. I squeezed back as hard as I could, but I felt one spill over.

"Okay," he agreed, "but I know you. Just please promise me you'll be safe. No reckless moves, no silly risks." He pulled back and held his hands tight on my shoulders as he looked at me intently. "If this is what you really want, I'll beef up security. No going anywhere without either, Jared, Casey, Travis, Mitch, or me attached to you like fucking velcro. Velcro, okay?"

I nodded. "Okay."

He sat down on the air mattress and climbed under the sheet. "Now turn off the light and get into bed."

I did both, all the while hearing him grumble under his breath about not knowing how I managed to talk him into this shit.

Coby's phone buzzed, and after a pause, he called out softly from the floor. "Evie?"

"Yeah?" I mumbled from under the white fluffy covers that were smothering me in a soothing, comfortable way.

"I'll be gone by the time you wake up in the morning, but Jared will be here, okay?"

"Okay, thanks, Coby. I appreciate you all taking such good care of me."

It was silent for a few moments.

"Coby?"

"Yeah?"

"Be safe."

"Always."

Chapter Sixteen

I woke the next morning feeling like an old, wrung out dishrag. My head was fuzzy, and my stomach, having finished eradicating whatever bug invaded my system, churned with anxiety. It let out a feeble grumble for food, but the events of last night rushed my head, leaving me shaky and not in any rush to move, let alone get up and make breakfast.

Peeking over the edge of my bed, I found Coby gone. I felt equal parts relief, because I wasn't up for a rehash of last night's chat, and worry, because a shooting had now entered the equation. Seeing it all from this perspective made it that much harder knowing that Coby and Jared were out there dealing with this type of thing every day.

Voices could be heard from downstairs, but oddly enough, I hadn't been disturbed. The bedroom door suddenly opened, and Jared's head poked through. Seeing me awake, he came in and shut the door behind him, the door clicking shut. He still looked tired, and I couldn't remember a time where he hadn't looked tired since the whole Jimmy thing began.

He started slowly peeling off his t-shirt and jeans as he stalked towards the bed, and I sat up on my elbows to watch the unwrapping.

"Feeling better?"

I nodded silently because now that Jared was here it was as though the sun had broken through the gloomy clouds hovering above. My tummy, sensing the rapid transformation, began to grumble in earnest, so I promised it good tidings if it would just shut up and let me enjoy the moment.

Clad now in nothing but a pair of black boxer-briefs, he knelt on the end of the bed and playfully tracked his way up on all fours until he was hovering above me.

His eyes locked on mine, turning hard and sombre, and I wondered what was swirling behind their green depths. Not leaving me hanging, he gently brushed the hair off my face with one hand. "I would never forgive myself if something happened to you."

"I'm okay." He didn't look reassured, so I leaned up and kissed his lips softly. "Really." I placed a hand on his shoulder and let it trail down his bicep, revelling in the feel of his hard body. "You didn't message me last night. I was worried."

He took in my reproachful frown with a pleased expression. "You were worried about me?" A cheeky grin lit his eyes and getting off the bed, he rummaged in his jeans, pulled out his phone, and pressed a few buttons as he stood by the bed.

"What are you doing?"

He shrugged innocently as my phone buzzed.

I gave him what I liked to think was an intimidating glare and picked it up.

J: Baby, I am ok and wishing I was in bed with you right now.

My eyes whipped up to his, the glare rapidly shifting to desire, and I smiled slowly as I began pressing buttons.

E: Thanks for letting me know. I wish you were too, but alas you aren't, so I will have to begin without you.

The playful smile died upon his lips as he read my message. He lifted his eyes to mine, and I sucked in a breath as their heat damned near singed my skin off. He threw his phone over his shoulder and pounced.

I giggled as his mouth swooped down on mine, smothering my laughter as he kissed me thoroughly. He pulled back, slightly breathless, and did a quick check of the time.

"We've only got ten minutes."

"Seriously?"

I sighed as his lips travelled down my neck and his hand skimmed around my hip, trailing down until his fingers slid inside my knickers. "I don't have anything scheduled. We have all day."

He shifted and pulled my shorts off impatiently. "You've got shit to do today."

"I do?"

He nodded and kissed me quickly, pulling back to remove his own underwear.

As his lips found mine, I ran my hands up and down the smooth skin of his back, bringing them around to push at his chest until I'd managed to roll him over and straddle his lap.

"Fine," I growled, peeling off my top as he grabbed my hips, fingers digging in when bare skin was revealed. "But I'm in charge."

He grinned wickedly, pulled me down, and rolled me back over. "Sometimes, I let you think you're in charge, but there's no time for pretending this morning, baby."

I should have pushed him off the bed, but in one fell swoop, he hooked his arm under the knee of my right leg, lifting it over his hip, and I sucked in a breath as he slid inside. After our allotted time was up, Jared collapsed his weight on top of me and rolled us back over. "Now you can be in charge."

I wanted to laugh at his antics, but as I put my hands on his chest and looked in his eyes, I felt my heart pound fearfully knowing that I was slowly falling in love with him. The fear must have left me looking pale because Jared gave me a quizzical look.

"Are you sure you're okay?"

I let my breath out in a slow whoosh. "Yeah."

He moved one of his hands from my hip to rub gently across my belly, his eyes tracking the movement before they met mine. "Baby, you're not pregnant, are you?"

I held my breath at his soft words and the care he took in touching me. I shook my head and when he swallowed and looked away I could have sworn it was disappointment I saw on his face. "Just a tummy bug, so no cause for alarm."

In light of last night's chat with Coby, I changed the subject by taking a pre-emptive strike about being told to pack my bags for safer ground.

"Jared, you should know that I'm not going anywhere."

He slapped me on the backside, not hard, but not soft either. "Yes, you are...to the shower. Quick," he ordered.

I glared down at him. "Don't flip me off. You know what I meant."

His eyes went fierce. "I'm not losing you, Evie."

"No, you're not. I'm just telling you—"

"I spoke to Coby this morning," he interrupted. "I know there's no point in trying to change your mind so rather than—"

The front door slammed loudly and a "yoohoo" interrupted our little talk. I jumped in shock from my straddled position and flew off the bed, my legs tangling in the sheets as I fell to the floor with a thud.

Jared let out a shout of laughter, gasping as he peered over the edge of the bed. "Are you okay?"

"Oh my God," I hissed. "Why didn't you tell me?" I scrambled to get off the floor and made a mad dash for the wardrobe, flinging the door wide and racing inside. "Where's my robe?" I muttered as I flung clothes about wildly. I careened back out the door. "Where's my goddamn robe?"

Jared pointed to the chair in the corner as he untangled the sheet, pulling it up to his waist and propping a pillow behind his back.

"Is anyone there?" The voice appeared to be trekking its way up the stairs.

213

"You are so dead," I said, pointing a finger at Jared furiously as I made a grab for the robe off the chair.

"I tried to tell you to get in the shower."

I tied the belt and flung open the bedroom door to make a break for the bathroom when Jenna pulled back in shock, arm raised at the ready to knock.

"Evie, honey," she said softly.

I opened my mouth to both speak and hustle Jenna down the stairs when Jared beat me to the punch.

"Hi, Mum." Smiling wide, there wasn't a trace of embarrassment on his face.

She looked around me and her eyes widened as she took in her bare chested son sitting in my bed, busily tapping away on his phone. He looked comfortable, his demeanour practically shouting that my bed was a place he visited naked on numerous occasions. While this might actually have been the case, shoving it in his mother's face was not currently on my list of things to do that day. I resisted the urge to close my eyes and ooze into a burning little puddle of mortification on the floor.

With a delighted smile, she said, "Hi, honey."

"I uh...Jenna, how nice to see you," I stammered and turned to glare at Jared when I heard his chuckle.

"You too, darling..." her gaze drifted from Jared to me and then back again "...you too. I'll just wait for you downstairs shall I?"

Without wasting time to blast Jared for being an insensitive man-bastard and not telling me about his mother's imminent arrival sooner, I made that mad dash for the bathroom and caught Henry running in before me, slamming the door in my face.

"Dammit, Hussy," I shouted and banged the door down, willing him to appreciate my desperation.

"Too slow, Sandwich," I heard him sing-song as I stormed back to the bedroom.

By the time I'd showered and slapped on a bit of mascara, blush, and strawberry lip gloss, it was close to nine. The heat already stifling, I braided my hair and dressed in a pretty lemon sundress with thin straps and delicate white crocheted lace trim and headed downstairs to find out what *shit* I was supposed to be doing today.

I found Jared on the phone in Mac's office out back, so I left him to it and headed for the kitchen, catching Jenna clucking away busily in our linen cupboard as though doing a stocktake. When I reached my destination, Tim was loitering by the sink, and the kettle was boiling.

Tim chattered away as I ate my Coco Pops, talking about last night's shooting incident for at least half an hour and finishing by telling me that he, Jenna, and I were off to get some Christmas shopping done today. I had no idea how Jenna had managed to convince Jared that going shopping was a brilliant idea in light of the shooting incident, but she was his mother after all. I decided I would watch her closely today to see if I could pick up any Jared handling techniques.

I also decided a battle plan was in order and began writing down some gift ideas. I'd only managed a few things at the Paddington Markets, and with Christmas only two weeks away, I needed to get organised. As I gnawed on the end of my pen, I contemplated what on earth to buy Jared. I never got around to giving him the surprise present I'd picked up, but that was before we were together. Now, I wanted to get him something that was a bit more girlfriend appropriate.

Thinking Tim might know, I interrupted his chatter. "What should I buy Jared?"

I tapped at the list with my pen in time to the mad bop of my hips as music played in the background. I started to chew the pen again as I contemplated my list so far. "Tim?"

Tim's chatter died a quick death.

"Tim?" I frowned and turned my head.

"Uh, Evie..."

I followed the direction of his eyes and saw Casey leaning against the kitchen bench, arms folded and looking amused. I pulled the pen out of my mouth before it fell and straightened up, watching his grin get wider.

I smiled. "Hey, Casey."

Tim said nothing which I thought was a bit rich. I mean, Tim worked for him after all. Surely, he'd gotten used to the way Casey looked by now. I hadn't and still managed to say hello.

I elbowed Tim.

"Casey," he managed feebly and I rolled my eyes.

"Cuppa?" I asked Casey.

"Uh, yes please," Tim stuttered.

I looked at him incredulously. "Not you, dweeb. Casey. You're supposed to be the one making it. The kettle's been boiling on and off for the past half an hour."

Tim came alive, pushing off from the bench as he suddenly found his voice. "Oh my God, are you retarded? Dean is the dweeb in our relationship, Evie." Dean was Tim's boyfriend, and at a muscle-bound six foot two, I highly doubted that Dean was the dweeb in anything.

I turned to him with a grin. "Oh yeah, if Dean is the dweeb, what does that make you?"

He smoothed his hair. "I'm the badass," he said and then paused, "but I can't talk about it."

I refrained from pointing out that he already was. "Why not?"

He looked at me in disbelief. "Because the first rule of being a badass is that you don't talk about being a badass. Period."

"Why do you get to be the badass? I can be badass!" I retorted.

"Uh, honey, see? If you were badass your status would already be revoked because you're talking about it." He nodded knowingly. "Besides..." he waved his hand over at Casey who stood there watching our interaction with apparent fascination "...have you seen the people I work with? It's practically automatic qualification into badass status."

I rolled my eyes. "What's a girl gotta do then? I've been involved in a high speed car chase, rammed a Camry off the road, been in hospital with a head trauma, slept with a badass—several times in fact—my brother is a badass, I've been shot at, and potentially scored a contract with Jettison Records. If that doesn't qualify my membership to the badass club then I'm forming my own." I folded my arms, letting my eyes narrow threateningly as I clenched my jaw.

Ignoring my look, Tim let out a little shriek that had Casey flinching. "You've almost got a contract with Jettison Records? Oh my God. Why didn't anyone tell me?" He turned to give Casey a vicious look and Casey shrugged. "No one tells me anything," he hissed.

With no tea or coffee in our immediate future, I reached over past Tim to flick the kettle on to re-boil, all the while Tim continued on his merry way with his little rant.

"Yes, thanks," Casey said, arms folded, still leaning up against the kitchen counter.

I looked at him stupidly. "What?"

"Coffee," he prompted.

"Right," I muttered and pointed at Tim. "Make yourself useful Tyler Durden."

He pulled a face. "Who the hell is Tyler Durden?"

"Fight Club," Casey interjected and I grinned at him.

Tim nodded. "Okay, I can be Brad Pitt."

I kissed him on the cheek and patted his shoulder reassuringly. "Of course you can."

He pointed the teaspoon at me threateningly. "Don't patronise me."

I held up my hands. "Dude." I turned to Casey. "Jared's out in the back office."

He rubbed at the back of his neck uncomfortably. "I'm here for shopping duty actually."

"Seriously? What did you do in a past life to deserve that?"

He chuckled. "Somebody doesn't like me, or..." he looked me over in a way that made me feel my sundress wasn't enough coverage "...maybe they do?"

Jared rolled into the kitchen, freshly showered, and slapped Casey up the back of the head. "Heard that." He leaned over and planted a swift kiss on my lips. "Where's my mother?"

I folded my arms and arched a brow. "Why, Jared, you sound a wee bit scared. Shall I go get her?"

He cleared his throat. "No, no, I've got to get going. Walk me out?"

I nodded, leaving Casey and Tim to the kitchen as I followed Jared to the door. He pulled me in close, and I rested my hands on his chest. "Don't be fooled by Casey's looks babe. He's the meanest, toughest, and smartest son of a bitch I know. He's also a good friend, so I know he'll take good care of you."

I wasn't surprised. The man had rolled his car and walked away. That was pretty impressive in my books.

"Him being with you is the only reason I'm letting you go out shopping okay? Make sure you stick to him like—"

"Velcro, yes, I know." I nodded and waited patiently for his lecture to continue. My eyes started to glaze over as he went on a bit more before tuning back in.

"...and make sure you keep your phone switched on at all times."

I nodded at that very important piece of information, wrapped my arms around his neck, and tugged him down for a kiss. He ran his hands down my back and cupped my ass, pulling my hips in tightly against him.

"Be safe," he whispered against my lips.

"You too," I whispered back. "You'll be back for dinner?"

He nodded. "I'll be back for dinner," and with that, he opened the door and left and I walked back to the kitchen to get my cup of tea.

"I can't believe neon is back in." Tim held up a hot pink shirt with a glittery heart plastered over the front of it. "Fucking neon..." he shook his head forlornly "...next thing you know everyone will be wearing plastic mesh shoes in *outrageous orange* and singing 'wake me up before you go-go.'"

He paused for a moment to shudder, and I snatched the shirt out of his hands. "Oh my God." I showed it to Jenna. "This is so cute!"

Jenna nodded in agreement. "It is cute."

Tim looked like he was about to burst into tears, and I chuckled. "Seriously, Tim, it's for Jake's four year old niece. It's all about pink and nothing but the pink. She'll love it."

He took a deep breath through his nose, lips pressed flat. "Fine," he muttered, "but I don't have to watch you buy it." He turned away as Jenna and I moved to the front counter to pay for our things.

As I was reaching for my purse I got a message from Mac.

M: Can you hit the supermarket on the way out? I'll send through a list.

We walked out to find Tim chattering away to Casey, who was standing at the entrance of the store, arms folded, nodding vaguely as his eyes continually swept from left to right without actually appearing to move at all. "And so Dean told me to stop being ridiculous because Eric and his brother couldn't care less. Then with half the people coming being vegans it's turned the whole thing into..."

Casey grabbed my arm in what appeared to be welcome relief and tucked me close as we started to move along again. I leaned up to whisper in his ear. "Casey, we need to somehow ditch Jenna. I need to get her Christmas present, and I don't want her to know."

He stopped and turned around to face Jenna and Tim behind us. As I was still tucked to his side, he dragged me around with him in an awkward shuffle. "I have to visit the men's room. Unfortunately, that means Evie has to come with me." He gave me a convincingly apologetic glance. "How about we meet for lunch somewhere in ten minutes?"

I cleared my throat loudly and gave him a look. I planned to buy Jenna a pair of rose gold earrings to match the pretty bangle I'd seen her wear on special occasions, and I was lucky if it wouldn't take me all day.

Casey rolled his eyes. "Okay, twenty minutes."

"Alright," Jenna agreed. "What does everyone feel like for lunch?"

"I could do Mexican. There's that new place that just opened that makes yummy fresh tortilla chips and salsa." I smacked my lips.

Tim shuddered. "We're not doing Mexican, Evie. My insides would go into complete revolt. I vote Yum Cha. I need some steamed dim sim."

I shot Tim a withering look. "Some badass you are if you can't handle Mexican food."

"I'll have you know—"

"Enough," Casey growled, looking as though being flayed alive would be enjoyable right about now. "Jesus. We'll meet at the café we stopped at for coffee on the way in, okay?"

Realising he had just about reached the end of his patience, we quickly agreed and peeled off in different directions.

I held up a pair of solid small hoop earrings to one ear and rose gold studs with intricate threads to the other. "What do you think, Casey?"

He shrugged noncommittally and I turned back to the assistant and sat them down on their casings. "What about those drop earrings there with the diamonds?"

He opened the tray and got them out. "These are forty millimetre and eighteen karat gold. The diamonds are point five carats each." He held them up to my ears, and I felt his fingers brush my cheek a little. "Are they for yourself? The rose gold compliments your beautiful skin and those gorgeous dark eyes of yours."

Confident the assistant was simply flirting to help the sale, I battened down the hatches in preparation for a shameless price negotiation and gave him a brilliant smile. Casey, thinking the man was flirting, tucked me back into his side and glared at him in irritation. "We'll take them."

"Casey, I haven't decided yet," I argued. I turned back to the assistant. "They're for my uh..." I paused. Did I say boyfriend's mother or mother-in-law? It wasn't like we were married, but "boyfriend's mother" didn't feel enough to encompass the relationship we had.

"Mother-in-law," Casey supplied before I could say any more.

The assistant rang up the sale and twenty minutes later found us sitting in the café with Jenna and Tim, Casey with his back to the wall and my chair pulled closely to his side.

We placed our order for lunch, and Jenna, having taught Mac everything she needed to know on how to spend money, pulled out her shopping list and turned to me. "Do you have your list?"

I picked up my handbag and sat it on my lap. Casey sighed in exasperation as I repeatedly jabbed him with my elbow while I dug around in its hidden depths. It couldn't be helped. We were sitting so close I may as well have been in his lap. I gave an apologetic smile.

"I just have to get those shoes we looked at for Mac and then I'm done."

We chatted until the waitress returned with our sandwiches, and I heard my phone beep a message. I pulled my handbag back up on my lap to dig for my phone and Casey sighed.

"It's probably Mac with the supermarket list she said she'd send through."

I frowned at the blocked number and opened the message.

Hello, beautiful Evie. I like your new male accessory. What a collection you have. You certainly managed to land on your feet after last night but not to worry. Your day will come.

My breath hitched as I fumbled the phone with clammy hands and it dropped to the floor. Casey picked it up and promptly read the message, a frown marring his brow.

"Fuck." He pulled out his phone and started dialling.

Jenna patted my hand soothingly. "What is it, honey?"

221

I showed them both the message.

"Frank," Casey said into the phone as he indicated for all of us to round up our things and move out. I looked forlornly at my sandwich as we were ushered out the door, Casey throwing some cash on the counter on our way through, continuing his phone conversation.

Chapter Seventeen

Christmas day was spent at Steve and Jenna's house by the barbecue and pool since Christmas in Australia was in the middle of summer and hot. The food was kept simple with grilled steak, cold roast chicken, and salads. Presents were unwrapped and Jared loved the coffee machine I'd bought him so much, I spent the next hour making him espresso until he was completely buzzed.

Jared bought me a beautiful pair of diamond stud earrings that I specifically remember eyeing in the jewellery store with Casey, and I made a mental note to message Casey later to say thanks. Later that afternoon, Jared answered a knock at the front door of his parent's house and returned with a big white box. It was tied with a bright red bow, and I squealed with delight when Jared said the box was for me.

I was lying out by the pool in a cushioned deck chair and sat up as he set the box at my feet. "Who's it from?"

"Just open it, babe."

Everyone crowded around and waited for me to open it, Coby and Mac swimming to the pool edge and resting their elbows on the sandstone pavers as they watched. I gave them all a suspicious look when I heard an odd sound and quickly pulled the ribbon apart and took off the big white lid.

I let out a shout when a pair of big brown eyes attached to a ball of soft reddish brown fur and a wagging tail yipped at me. Tears filled my eyes and I brought my hands to my cheeks in disbelief as I raised my eyes to Jared's.

"You remembered," I whispered, thinking back to our text message conversation of years before.

"Babe," he said softly, a smile curving his lips.

E: Do you have any pets?

J: There's golden orb spider that hangs out under the eaves of our deck. Does that count?

E: It only counts if he has a name.

J: His name is Gideon the Gold. He's very fierce.

E: Sounds a bit pompous to me.

J: Don't go hurting his feelings now. He's also very sensitive. What about you?

E: No. I argued with Mum the day before my sixteenth birthday for a dachshund puppy because I'd always wanted one.

He knew she'd died the next day, so I had left the obvious unsaid.

I reached into the box and picked up the tiny bundle of fur, cuddling him against my chest as he squirmed and wriggled, his sandpapery little tongue attacking my cheek. The puppy got passed around excitedly until I eventually plopped him on the grass.

Mac got out of the pool and flopped down next to us. "Oh, my little baby boy," she crooned as the puppy wriggled excitedly and climbed all over her. "You are such a cute little man, oh yes you are." She gave me a meaningful look. "Everyone knows a puppy is a trial baby."

I could see Jenna's eyes twinkle at this statement, but she still shook her head at Mac. "I can't wait for you to have kids, my darling, if you think it's as simple as raising a dog."

Mac frowned at her mum as she stood up and wrapped a beach towel around her waist. "Of course I don't."

Jenna picked up an empty tray and headed for the kitchen. Mac followed. "You know if Jared and Evie have a baby then you'll leave the rest of us alone." Her chatter continued as she followed her mum to the kitchen until I couldn't hear any more.

Jared crouched next to me on the grass and we watched the puppy for a moment as he did some business before stopping to chew on some grass. "So what are you going to call our little man?"

I sipped my drink thoughtfully. "Peter."

"Peter?" he laughed.

I grinned. "I have a thing about dogs having human names."

He ruffled my hair. "Yeah? Why is that?"

"Because it's cool. Look at him, he's already got serious street cred." Peter had his paws up against a small tree, yipping at a tiny garden lizard that scurried away for its life. "Already taking down the creatures of the neighbourhood."

We watched as he made a swift move for Jenna's vegetable garden and yanked out a carrot with immense delight. He began barking and dancing around the orange vegetable as though waiting for it to jump up and join in his playful game.

"Oh shit," Jared muttered. "Peter!" Peter stopped and looked at us. "Would you look at that? He already knows his name."

The next morning found us in the loft, waking to a shredded couch cushion, a nasty unmentionable on the timber flooring in the corner behind the dining table, and the little Christmas tree I'd set up a week ago on its side. Bits of tinsel lined a festive yet damning trail towards the bathroom from where Travis let out a shout. I immediately scooped Peter up and headed for the safety of the front door.

A pair of chewed shoes, a shredded roll of toilet paper, numerous inside unmentionables, and a week later, I stood stiffly in the studio dressing room for a photography shoot for Jamieson.

Because Jimmy was still at large, apparently he was some sort of super villain with the special power of invisibility, Jared and Peter had accompanied us and were waiting out in the lounge area while the five of us stood in the dressing room getting ready.

I pulled the shirt off the rack that was listed with my name and held it up dubiously. "Uh, hmm, do you think there's more to it than this?"

The light of the window had the sun shining right through the sheer fabric. It was white, with a collar and buttons up the front, almost like an office shirt, but the sleeves had gathers up the sides to the elbows and tied with little red bows.

Henry shrugged at my question.

"For once I wish Mac was here," I muttered.

Mac wished she was too, but it was party season which meant we were booked solid. This left her channelling Ripley under the drowning weight of work and us running for our lives whenever we hit her sights. Even Peter, who had rapidly climbed the aggressive ranks of the doghood on our street in just the past week, scampered out of her path.

Bec, a short, fine-boned lady with spikey hair, who looked far too young to be the capable stylist she appeared to be, poked her head in the dressing room. "All set?"

"Um, no." I waved the shirt about. "Is there something I'm supposed to be wearing underneath this?"

"Nope. That's it, no bra either please." She left, shutting the door behind her.

Frog and Cooper let out matching shouts of laughter as I stood in disbelief.

"I'm sorry, but did she just tell me to get naked?"

"Pretty much." Cooper smirked as he took his own shirt off and threw it in the corner. "Get your gear off."

Frog shrugged. "Just ask Bec if you can wear something else."

"I can't," I wailed. "This is our first proper photo shoot. I don't want to set the precedent of being labelled a prima donna."

The four boys slid on their provided jeans and stood around bare chested. In minutes they were done. I'd been worked on for *hours.*

"At least get the pants on, Evie, then I'll go get the stylist for you and see if she has something else," Jake offered.

"Thanks, Jakie," I said gratefully.

I reached for the shorts on the rack and slid them on as he headed out the door. They were black leather, short, and matched the shirt with their gathers up the sides and thin red ties finished in a bow dangling down my legs. A pair of flat heeled, calf high, brown boots sat by my meagre clothing offering to complete the look. Having come out of hair and makeup, my hair was huge, tumbling down my back in wild waves. Liquid eyeliner gave me sex kitten eyes, and someone had spent at least half their lifetime painting temporary tattoos up my left forearm and left side of my torso.

Jake returned with Bec who was looking harassed. "Problem?"

"Well..." I paused, hesitant to be the cause of further harassment. "I'm not sure about the whole shirt with nothing underneath thing. I mean, it's a really nice shirt," I tacked on hurriedly, "but—"

"You don't want your boobs on camera," she finished for me.

"Not particularly," I muttered, wondering if that made me a giant prude.

Maybe it did, but didn't these things come back to bite you later in the ass? I planned on having kids eventually. They didn't need to be blinded one day while performing an innocent Google search for photos of their mum in her heyday.

She put her pixie like hands on my shoulders and turned me towards her. "This is completely professional and you can trust us, okay? We're going to have you positioned so that nothing here..." she pulled a hand away to gesture at my chest "...will actually be seen. You'll be able to tell there's nothing on underneath, but you won't quite see what that is. You'll retain your modesty while still enabling the photo to look sexy as hell. Is that okay?"

I nodded at her explanation and changed, safe in the knowledge that my future children would be unscathed from embarrassment.

Emerging from the dressing room, Jared did a double take and called me over.

"Uh, babe..." With my arms crossed over my chest, he gave my shirt a pointed glance. "Is this a low budget photo shoot?"

What was he talking about? Porn?

"What?"

His eyes flicked to the guys who were standing around without shirts as they waited for me. "They can't afford to clothe you all?"

I chuckled as Peter tried to climb my boots and kept sliding off and explained to him what Bec had told me. "Trust me, Jared." I even added my apprehension about my future children and not scarring them for life.

"Yeah?" The corners of his lips curled up slightly. "How many kids you planning on having?"

"Two," I announced.

I'd thought about this a lot. One of each so I could take my daughter shopping while my son went off to do some sort of sporting activity with his dad. Terribly stereotypical, but this was my little fantasy, and I could have whatever I wanted. Though said fantasy may not bode so well if Jared and I ever headed down that path together. Jenna had three boys before she finally got her little Mactard.

I visibly shuddered and Jared frowned, picking Peter up and tucking him under his arm. "Only two?"

"Why? How many are you planning for?"

"Four."

"Four?" I shouted. Maybe four was normal in his world, but in the real world that shit would not fly.

"Ah, any time you're ready, Evie," John, our photographer, cut in.

I sucked down my panic and turned to John with a brilliant smile. "Be right there."

Jared eyed my outfit with irritation. "I'm gonna take Petie outside, okay? Leave you to it."

Jared left through the side door, and John had me sit on a chair in front of a white backdrop while the boys watched on. "Just a couple of single shots to start with," he advised.

He pushed my legs around a bit until my calves were spread out but my knees still close together. "Now lean over. I want one arm here," he murmured and put my right elbow on my leg, "and the other here," and put my left elbow on my left leg, "but cup your face with your left hand."

He went back to his camera after he'd finished prodding me into a human mannequin and took a quick couple of shots. He muttered a bit with Bec, and she came over to fiddle my arm and hair around a bit.

"Now pout your lips just a little and look to the left of my shoulder. Put your left arm down."

Click, click, click.

He walked over and showed me some of the images on the back screen of his camera, and I saw Bec was right. You couldn't see anything but the mere suggestion gave the shot a sexy vibe.

"Sex sells," John grinned at me. He went back to the camera set up on his tripod and clicked away a little longer as he called out directives.

"Guys in the shots now," he called out. "Lights, Andy."

Frog, Cooper, Jake, and Henry moved in as John's assistant, Andy, started fiddling with the lights until I was blinded as they cast huge shadows on to the white backdrop.

"Evie, in the middle please. Jake and Henry, on either side. Frog and Cooper, I want you sitting straight-legged in front, hands on the floor behind you. Andy, come grab this chair out of the way will you? Right, Evie, face me. Henry, I want you facing Evie. Put your arm across her chest. Jake, stand slightly behind. I want your arm slung across her back shoulder."

Click, click, click.

229

More directives, a bit of fuss with everyone's hair from Bec, and a pat at some shine.

I didn't whine but this wasn't my idea of fun. I was starving but couldn't eat anything for fear of ruining my made up face or spilling something on the tattoos the poor artist had sweated blood and tears for. Not to mention it was hot and sweaty under the bright lights that were aimed our way.

John decided he would alleviate that particular problem by telling me to lose the shirt.

I balked. "Um, sorry?"

"Evie?"

"Yeah?"

"Won't see anything okay?"

I turned around when the hive of people were removed from the room and unbuttoned my shirt, sliding it off, wondering what the hell I was doing and hoping I could trust John like he said. I tucked my arms across my chest modestly and turned back around as the guys all looked everywhere but at me.

"Right," John walked over and grabbed the shirt out of my hands and tossed it over on a chair, rubbing his chin in contemplation. "Jake or Henry," he muttered. "Henry's pretty, but Jake's bigger." He kept muttering to himself, and I laughed at the comment.

"Oi." Henry elbowed me.

"Frog, Cooper, I want you both standing," John ordered and rubbed his chin. "Evie, I want you and Henry facing each other and in close. Put your arms around his neck. Henry put your hands in the back pockets of Evie's shorts. Jake, face me but I want you to put your elbow on Evie's shoulder and rest your head on your hand, cross your leg over. Frog, next to Jake but face the other way, looking at me. Cooper, next to Henry please. I want you to fold your arms, chin up, face me."

We all shifted into the requested positions, and Henry's eyes hit the ceiling as I awkwardly pressed my bare chest against his and slid my arms around his neck. It felt wrong, like I was hugging my brother.

John went back to his camera.

Click, click, click.

"Evie, head up a little."

I glared at Henry as he gave me an odd look. It wasn't like I hadn't gotten down to my underwear in front of the boys on numerous occasions in backstage dressing rooms, but having my naked chest mashed all over Henry's had never been on my bucket list.

"You better not be enjoying this."

"Evie, look at me please. Henry, I want you to keep looking at Evie," John ordered.

I looked at John.

Henry smirked. "Please, Chook, it's like hugging a man."

Jared chose that inopportune moment to return through the side door with Peter, and by inopportune I meant extremely shitty timing if the unhappy expression on his face was anything to go by. I didn't blame him. If I found him hugging a half-naked girl for some photo, I'd be more than unhappy. I'd likely be blinded by the haze of red flooding my vision.

Click, click, click

"Chin up, Jake. Frog put your hands in your pockets."

Click, click, click.

"Jake, I want you to shift so your front is pressed against Evie's back and look at me. Frog, Cooper, both move in closer."

After an eternity, whereby man had evolved into space aliens and buildings had been levelled under the melting of the Arctic, John announced that we were done.

By the time I removed the gunk from my face and body and re-dressed, the boys were peeling out of the parking lot in my Hilux, and Jared was leaning by his Porsche waiting, hands slung on the loops of his jeans, black Raybans covering his eyes. Peter was happily chewing the grass at his feet, oblivious to the tense vibe I felt emanating from Jared.

I watched him carefully as I walked over, feeling an odd little nudge that scratched the back of my mind. Nothing serious but I was left with the feeling that maybe this thing with Jared and I was moving a little too quickly.

I adjusted the strap on the bag hanging over my shoulder. "So…"

Jared folded his arms in case the tense vibe wasn't enough to warn me of an impending argument, so I sat my bag on the hood of the car and leaned up against it so our shoulders were touching, but we weren't looking at each other. "I knew this girl once, Katja. She went to the same uni as us, majoring in economics. She was, I always thought, both smart and stupid. Smart because she had a GPA that wiped us all out of the water. She was like the rain man of aggregate supply and demand." I bit my bottom lip and frowned but couldn't expand further because economics was not my strong suit. "Stupid because she dated this guy who liked to tell her what to do."

"Evie—" Jared interrupted with a sigh.

I looked sideways at his frown. "Let me finish. She didn't have much in the way of money or family support, so she worked nights and weekends at Revival, a topless waitress bar in the city, telling her boyfriend she was waitressing at a normal restaurant," I explained. "One day he found out, and when she got home, he cracked her across the head so hard that she fell, hitting her head on the corner of the kitchen bench. She never woke up."

I felt all the anger swirling around Jared deflate as he turned around to face me, his legs on either side, straddling the length of me. "Evie, I'm sorry about your friend, but what are you trying to say? You think I'm going to hurt you?"

I grasped his forearms. "No! My point is I don't want to be the type of person who feels they have to hide parts of their life from someone because they're being told what they can and can't do. I know…" I raised my voice when he started to protest. "I know you didn't say a word about the photos. I know you were going to though, so I just wanted to put that out there. You need to trust the decisions I make for my career.

Sometimes you might not like them, maybe sometimes I might not either. Just please, trust me, Jared, and if I'm ever unsure about anything I'll talk to you about it, okay?"

The corners of his lips turned up. "So you have no grand plans to do a naked Playboy spread wrapped around Henry?"

"No!" I practically shouted. "God, Jared, he's like a brother. Besides, Henry said it was like hugging a man."

Jared laughed and put both hands on my boobs. "These? Feels like a man?" I gave him a mock glare and smacked his hands away. "I hate to break it to you, baby, but I think he was only saying that to make you feel more comfortable."

Satisfied the situation had been diffused, my stomach growled loudly. "Can we go now? I could eat a small country."

"Yeah?" He opened up the passenger door for me to hop in. "Which one?"

"China," I declared, winking at Jared with an easy smile.

He moved around the front of the car and folded himself inside the driver's side, passing a wriggling Peter over to me before he roared the car to life. "What are you trying to say now, you want Mr. Chow's?"

"I see my efforts aren't lost on you."

He shook his head at me as we peeled out of the studio car park. "Babe, no time. I have to get back to work after I drop you home. How about we pick up some sushi on the way?"

I made a face before covering my eyes with my giant sunglasses. "Only if it's got tempura chicken in it."

Peter licked my cheek so I could only assume that when it came to the battle of food, he'd already chosen the winning team. Smug, I reached for my phone to message Mac to see if anyone else was hungry.

Chapter Eighteen

"Come on, asshead," Mac began bashing the bathroom door down with renewed vigour. "What is taking you so long? You're going to record a song, not a bloody music video."

The bathroom door whipped open, and Jared and I, wrapped in towels, made our way out, epic trails of steam flowing out the door behind us in big foggy clouds.

Jared smirked at Mac as she took in our towel clad state with pursed lips. "Seriously? That shit is not cool." She pointed to my room. "That is what your bedroom is for."

Mac was still operating under the guise of Ripley, so figuring my water conservation speech would be lost on her, I followed Jared into my room and shut the door behind me with a giggle.

"And hurry up!" Mac yelled after us. "We have to leave in ten minutes."

I giggled again as Jared ripped my towel off and threw me on the bed.

Mac must have heard my giggle because she yelled at me once more. "Do you want to be late and come across as an unprofessional bitch?"

I slid off the bed with a sigh. "Mac's right, I need to get dressed and you need to get to work."

I picked Jared's jeans up off the floor and threw them in the direction of the bed where he sat down and started checking the messages on his phone.

"Any news on Jimmy?"

He threw it on the bed with a frown as he picked up his jeans. "Nope," he muttered unhappily.

I hadn't had any new messages from him in a while and the police had scaled back the search to minuscule proportions. Jared and Coby, not taking any chances, had not scaled back in their efforts to have me covered at all times. This was both re-assuring and smothering at the same time. Not one to complain, okay I complained a little, I tried to make sure I didn't make the job too hard on them.

"Who's on velcro duty today for the recording studio?"

Jared stood up as he pulled on his jeans. "Travis. He should probably be here by now."

I picked out an underwear set that was white with a pink and green floral pattern and slid them on. "Okay," I muttered and disappeared into the wardrobe to throw on a pair of yellow capris, a white tank top, and strappy silver sandals. I came back out tugging a brush through my hair, and Jared gave me a quick kiss. "Good luck today, baby."

"You too."

He turned, ruffled Peter's floppy brown ears, said, "See ya, little dude," and left.

I scooped up my bag in one hand, Peter in the other, and headed down the stairs.

Seven hours later, no joke, seven long freaking hours to record two songs, I sat in the control room with Marty, the engineer, Travis, and Jake. We were listening to the final version after Marty had finished working mixing magic so mystical even I had no idea we sounded that good.

Jake's beat was hard, heavy, and fast, and I could feel it pound through every fibre in the room so it felt like someone was jumping up and down on my chest. Henry's guitar ripped sweet and clean through the beat, and shivers hit my spine a little as my voice kicked in, husky and full.

I rubbed at my arms, and Marty grinned at me knowingly. "You guys are fucking ridiculous. This stuff is the shit. I knew you when, yeah?"

He pressed a button on the console and leaned down, talking into the live room. "We're wrapping up in here, dudes," he spoke to Frog, Henry, and Cooper. "Time to pack it up."

Frog gave the thumbs up.

"So we weren't booked in for another month Marty. Lucky to get squeezed in sooner, huh?"

Marty put a copy of the CD of our two songs into a casing. "Well you didn't hear it from me, but there wasn't a last minute cancellation. Someone got bumped."

"What?"

Did he mean like someone got offed? I know I liked to claim badass status on a regular basis but the lingo sometimes left me in the dust.

"Yeah, kicked down the schedule."

"Oh," I muttered. Marty wasn't speaking Badass after all.

"You sayin' that someone got pushed back so we could be squeezed in? Why's that?" Jake asked.

"Well..." he peeled off a label and fixed it to the CD "...you might have heard that one of supporting acts for Sins of Descent pulled out of the Australian leg of the tour in February."

Jake and I nodded because Gary had mentioned this to us at our meeting.

"A friend of Matt, the lead guitarist, saw one of your songs on YouTube from one of your Melbourne festival appearances and sent it to him. Then Matt heard through the grapevine you were on the verge of signing with Jettison and put you forward to play for them on their tour here in Oz. So anyway, in case you haven't noticed, Gary has been scrambling to get your shit together: photos, recorded music, whatever. Also," he continued as Jake and I sat on the edges of our seats, mouths and eyes wide open, "if they do that, Jettison is gonna wanna get a single out in early March to promote you ASAP, plus a music video and more photos. You sons of bitches are going to be busy as fuck if you can pull this off, *and* after hearing your shit today, I think it's a fucking shoe in." He spun his chair and flung the CD in my lap with a grin. "But..." he tapped the side of his nose "...you didn't hear that shit from me."

When we arrived home, I raced to the kitchen sink, filled up an industrial sized glass of water, and guzzled it down so fast I felt an aching pain follow its path.

"Sandwich?" Mac called out from the lounge room where I'd whizzed past her. "You okay?"

I bashed at my chest a little to ease the pain.

What had I done to deserve something so potentially momentous to happen in my life? Sure, I could sing. Sure, our band together was pretty awesome, but let's face it, I was a selfish person. I spent too much money on frivolous things, I could be petty, I made terrible decisions, and my life hadn't been spent volunteering at the local animal shelter. It was only the other day that I was complaining when we were having cake because Henry cut Mac's slice way bigger than mine.

I heard Mac ask Travis what my deal was. Her voice drowned out when I ran the tap for another glass of water.

I took a sip and focused on my breathing. I could do this. I could. I deserved this.

Why else would good things be potentially coming my way? I was kind... Dammit why is this so hard? What else?

I could be polite, to those that deserved it. I was a loyal friend because sometimes even when I *knew* Mac was in the wrong, I still defended her to the death (unless I was the one in the 'right' party of course, then it was on for young and old). I may not have volunteered at the animal shelter, but I did give them hefty yearly donations. I could afford to do it because Mum had left behind so much money, Coby and I didn't really know what to do with it all. Truth was I couldn't really bring myself to touch mine because it didn't feel right. Maybe I would leave it for my kids. My two kids.

Mac came into the kitchen when I finished my water, exchanging it for wine as I got the bottle out of the fridge.

"I'm going to sponsor a child for World Vision," I blurted out as I sat the bottle on the counter, my stomach sloshing like my insides were at sea from all the water.

"Okay," she drawled out as though I was a crazy person she was trying not to startle.

I got some glasses down from the above cupboard. "Wine Travis?" I yelled.

I didn't hear what he said because I began talking again without waiting for a response. I poured him a glass anyway.

"And those bears that are all caged up over in Romania," I continued with determination. "There must be something I can do. Maybe we can raise some money and descend upon the WSPA?"

She took hold of the wine glass I shoved at her chest. "You want to visit Romania? Do you even know where that is?"

"Of course I know where Romania is. Seriously, do I look that stupid?"

She smothered a laugh. "Well…"

"Oh shut up," I hissed. I paused for a moment to think, taking a sip of my wine. "It borders the Black Sea, and Serbia and Ukraine."

"Is it even safe to visit there right now?"

"How would I know? I haven't consulted my daily friendly travel guide today."

I sat my wine on the counter and opened the fridge door to examine the contents. According to Henry, it was my turn to cook dinner tonight, and usually that coincided with there being no food in the house. This usually meant having to conjure a mealtime miracle with only an orange, two eggs, a tin of creamed corn and a packet of chicken noodle soup from nineteen-ninety-four.

"So are you going to tell me how it went today because frankly, I'm not getting good vibes. Did you run over a cat on the way home?"

"Travis drove."

"Did Travis run over a cat on the way home?"

"Hey!" I heard Travis pipe up from the couch.

Travis sat up and shuffled tiredly into the kitchen, and I immediately felt bad. It was no doubt he had a million things to do, but instead babysat my ass all day long after likely working half the night. His clothes, usually cooler then even Jared's, looked wrinkled. I'm sure he used to have a life once that included things like manly sporting activities and well, the like.

I gave him his wine and a sympathetic smile. "Stay for dinner?"

"Sure. Whatcha making?"

"Hello?" Mac almost shouted, waving her hand in front of my face.

"What?"

"Oh hang on." She frothed with sarcasm. "I'm just going over here to have a conversation with this wall because it's less likely to provide a nonsensical reply and more likely to tell me what happened today than you are."

I gestured to the wall in a go ahead hand wave and watched as she sucked in a deep breath.

"Where's Hussy?" she asked.

"Next door with the Rice Bubbles."

I pulled out an onion and a chopping board and began slicing. Travis sat up on the bench next to me which was nice. I liked to have company while I faffed about in the kitchen. It made the whole task more like a social activity rather than a chore.

My phone beeped a message.

J: How did today go?

"Ah, I don't think so."

Mac, reading over my shoulder, snatched the phone out of my hand and tossed it into the lounge room.

"Mac!"

I went back to slicing the onions.

"Evie!"

"Okay." I popped a pan onto the hot plate and added some olive oil. "Oh, the CD is in my bag. You should go put it on."

"It's done?" Mac rummaged through my bag on the dining table and plucked it out. "How many songs did you get through?"

"Just two," I told her as I tossed the onions in the pan and stirred them around.

"Can I help?" Travis asked.

"Absolutely. You can help by sitting there and relaxing."

Mac cranked up the music to body pounding decibels. My phone managed to cut through some of the noise. "What do you think? Get my phone."

"It's awesome and no. Finish telling me about today first."

"Marty is a mixing genius." I sliced the rind off the bacon. "Is it safe to give raw bacon rind to Peter Travis?"

Travis raised his brows. "What do you mean safe? Like would he choke?"

Mac shrugged. "Could he choke? Google it."

"Maybe I should just grill it for him?"

"Grill the rind?" Mac repeated.

"Well, yeah."

Travis laughed. "You're going to grill bacon rind for your dog? Bet Jared would love that."

"Listen up, people." I pointed my little chopping knife meaningfully at Mac and then at Travis. "All Jared needs to know is that the bacon in this pasta is rindless okay? No telling him where the rind went."

I flipped on the grill and added some pasta to the boiling pot of water I had going as Travis's phone rang.

"'Lo? Yeah, here, in the kitchen. No that was Mac. Uh huh. I think she said pasta carbonara. Hang on, I'll check." Travis put his hand over the speaker. "Jared's on his way over. Wants to know if you need anything for the salad."

Um, I hadn't planned on making salad. I spun around and rummaged through the fridge. "Ahh, lettuce, tomatoes. Oh, I'll do a Greek salad. Tell him to get some olives and feta, too, please."

Travis relayed the message and gave Mac a stern look before speaking to me as he placed his phone back in his pocket. "You know, you really need to answer your phone when Jared gets in touch. He was worried for a minute." He folded his arms to emphasise the seriousness of his point and Mac look suitably chastened.

"Sorry," I murmured.

I finished putting the pasta together as I told Mac about our day at the recording studio. "Anyway, the big news is that mixing miracle man Marty revealed Sins of Descent might be considering us as one of the supports for the Australian leg of their world tour."

"Holy shit!" Mac shouted. "Holy shit!"

She picked up her wine and did a fast waltz into the lounge room and back. Peter, sensing fun, roused himself from the couch and barked at her feet. I slipped him a grilled piece of bacon rind when he hit the kitchen.

"Well it's only gossip, Mac, but Marty's grapevine is probably pretty solid. He reckons we're a shoe in. Don't say anything though," I tacked on hastily. "He was telling us on the down low."

Jared arrived, finding Mac doing a mock serious waltz around the lounge room, albeit this time with me. I stopped so he could plant a hard kiss on my lips, and then he dumped a shopping bag on the kitchen counter.

"What's going on?" he asked Travis.

I abandoned Mac for the kitchen and started rummaging through the bag to make a start on the salad. "Skim milk feta? Are you serious? I didn't even know there was such a thing."

Jared reached in the fridge and pulled out two beers, handing one to Travis. "So, how did it go today?"

I told the story of our day over again and before anyone could mention the tour, I hustled Jared into the pantry, shutting the door behind me.

"Private chat, huh?" Jared grinned as he pushed me into the shelving.

"No, I'm serious."

He started peppering little kisses along my collarbone. I tilted my neck and my breath came out on a long sigh.

"So talk."

"I can't when you're doing that." His mouth had moved up to tug on my earlobe and I moaned.

"Okay." He pulled back just a little. "What's up?"

My heart descended a little from cloud nine. Just because an invitation for the tour may be imminent, Jimmy being out there would surely make security almost impossible.

"Well..." I took a deep breath "...you see..." I mumbled the rest in a rush, "it misht be poble ther weir goiw on touw,"

I cringed slightly with an awkward scratch of my head before peeking up from underneath my lashes.

Jared looked amused, the corners of his lips curved up in that half grin of his. "Ah, what?"

I fidgeted with an unopened packet of brown rice while I looked everywhere but at his face. I'd just recently finished informing him, in a polite way, that he couldn't tell me what to do, but in matters of security and Jimmy, he was the expert, so I needed to take his opinion on board. "It might be possible that we're going on tour."

"Are you for fucking real?" I looked up again and started at the grin splitting Jared's face wide.

"Uh, yeah?"

"When? Where?"

"Next month, supporting Sins of Descent across Australia."

Reaching up to tuck my hair behind my ears so he could see my face properly, he stilled as shadows fell across his eyes, changing them from brilliant emerald to a dark forest green. "Well, baby, that's all kinds of awesome, but next month?"

"It's nothing yet. Just a rumour from Mixmaster Marty, but apparently his grapevine is like, solid."

"Mixmaster Marty?"

"The guy who did our songs at the studio."

Jared nodded thoughtfully, and I held my breath as I waited for his response. "It's not much time really, is it? For you to prepare. Could you manage it?"

"We'd be replacing another band, so yeah. We just have to step in is all."

He nodded again and rubbed his chin, his mind ticking over. "We'd have to be in charge of your personal security, but I'm sure we can work something out."

My heart lifted. "Really? So you'd be cool with this?"

He put his hands on my hips and pulled me close. "Well, I wouldn't say cool because keeping you alive is something I happen to take very seriously. Let's just say it's doable, and I'll deal with it because I know how important this is for you."

The boys must have descended from next door because the chatter got loud and someone started cranking our CD, all two songs of it, loudly again.

"Can we eat already?" I heard Henry yell from the kitchen.

I ignored them as I wrapped my arms around Jared's neck. "You know," I whispered, "you're important to me, Jared."

As I pressed my lips to his, the pantry door busted open, flooding the little room with brilliant light. I shielded my eyes as Mac bore down on us, finger jabbing at us fiercely.

"Seriously? There's food in here. This shit is not cool. What are you, rabbits?" She stalked away muttering something about bedrooms being completely underrated these days.

I giggled and we shuffled out because Jared was behind me, arms wrapped around my front.

My phone buzzed and I picked it up with a grin.

I missed giving you your xmas present. Hang tight. Better late than never, Songbird.

The grin slid from my face.

Chapter Nineteen

"Goddamn fucking fucker," Mac growled as she ripped the rollers from my hair with such savagery that even Coby visited the bathroom to make sure I wasn't being tortured to death.

"Ouch," I yelped for the five hundred and sixty-third time, give or take a few. I put my hand to my scalp to see if I was haemorrhaging blood. "Give it a rest, Mac."

Mac had been on a rampage since the latest message. It seemed I wasn't the only one not enjoying the threat Jimmy hung over my head with such sinister delight. How he couldn't be found I did not know. All I knew was that it needed to be done because I had a weight on my chest that sucked the breath out of me. I worked at keeping it to the back of mind, but now and then it just spilled over.

"You're trying to tell me what to do?" she growled, dumping another roller in the sink.

I shrank back a little in fear as her hands reached for my head. "No," I squeaked. I changed the subject. "So tell me again what Gary said to you on the phone."

My neck snapped back as another roller ripped free. "I told you, asshead. He didn't. You know it's gotta be about the tour though."

Mac was referring to the meeting we had lined up today with Gary. He hadn't, according to Mac, revealed any details about said meeting except that I should come alone. Mac thought this was odd, as did all of us, because if anyone should be meeting with Gary, it should be her, not me. That was the way the industry worked, right? You had your people talk to their people. Well Mac was our people. Mac liked being our people. She excelled at being our people.

Mac yanked the brush through my hair and picked up the hair spray.

"Fingers crossed it's about the tour," I choked out from under the haze of toxins that enveloped my face. "Mac, can you imagine what it would mean for us if we did this tour? God, it wouldn't just be a foot in the door, it would be like Goliath's boot kicking us into the stratosphere of Planet Success."

"What?" She gave me her "you're an idiot" face as she tweaked a few strands of hair around my face. "Stop talking Klingon. Some of the shit that comes out of your mouth." She shook her head.

"It would be a really freaking big deal," I spelled out for her with a roll of the eyes.

"Really? I wouldn't have guessed that."

Jesus. I *was* nervous and stressed about this meeting, but now I couldn't wait to get out the front door.

Mac took a step back to view her handiwork. "All done. Go get dressed."

I left the bathroom for the bedroom where my outfit had been laid out on the bed by Mac. I gave a deep sigh knowing any attempt at dressing myself for such an important meeting would have been thwarted anyway.

I slid on a lace panelled yellow miniskirt in a flirty a-line style and tucked in a printed silk camisole with thin straps with a frilled front in shades of hot pink, purple, mustard, and cream. Once again, Mac had managed to pair two items together that I would never have realised worked. The look was finished with a pair of metallic gold strappy wedges, gold accessories, and a slick of hot pink lipstick.

I turned to Mac. "How do I look?"

"You look like a shimmery golden ray of magnificence."

My mouth gaped open at the uncharacteristic nicety. "I do?"

She nodded. "You do."

"Well, alright then," I muttered, feeling unexpectedly buoyed by Mac's mood upswing.

"Thanks to me," she tacked on.

An hour later, I'd waved goodbye to the boys as they pretended not to be nervous about the meeting. Henry was coolly plucking at his guitar, but his knee bobbed up and down like a pogo stick. Jake was twirling his sticks like he was King Cool, but his face was carefully blank, and Frog and Cooper were abnormally subdued.

Coby pulled into the rounded drive of the hotel, and that was about when the butterflies launched their attack on my insides.

He pulled the key from the ignition and gave me a questioning look. "Why is the meeting at a hotel?"

I shrugged. "Why is the earth round? Why does peanut butter taste good with celery?" This last part I'd found out a week after my first shop with Jared when there was nothing left in the house to eat apart from vegetables and a jar of crunchy peanut butter.

Coby shook his head with a grin. "Smarty pants."

"Well, don't ask me questions I can't answer."

"I guess that means I shouldn't talk to you at all." He tugged on a curl of my hair with a wink, and then got out of the driver's side, passing the keys to the valet, and we shuffled in closely, Coby's hand guiding my back. I gave my name to the man behind the long marble reception desk and smiled politely. He asked for identification, and I flipped open my purse like I was the FBI.

He looked at it, then at me. "Thanks," he offered politely if not a little snootily.

I flipped my purse shut and wedged it back in my giant bag as Coby rolled his eyes at me.

What? I shrugged at him.

My phone beeped a message as Reception Man announced us via the phone and handed over a pass card for the lifts. "Lifts are to your left, top floor, room 4501," he offered with another polite, yet snooty smile.

I dug for my phone as Coby hit the button for the lift.

J: Make this meeting your bitch, baby.

Jared was gone when I'd woken up this morning, but Peter was snuggled close as though he'd been tucked in before Jared left. I'd rolled over and snapped a photo of the two us, snuggled and sleepy-eyed and messaged it off. Jared had replied by calling us his two lazy babies. His reply had filled me with warm fuzzies.

E: I wouldn't do it any other way.

The butterflies did a pretty pirouette as the lift shot up, and I folded my arms and tapped my foot nervously.

Coby gave me a look. "You're not nervous, are you?"

"Absolutely not," I lied. Acknowledging the nerves, Coby had always told me, gave them a voice.

"Good to know."

I checked my hair in the lift mirror after receiving a previous Gary meeting flashback. The curls were sitting neatly with no bits of hair doing crazy backflips. All was good.

We arrived at the top floor, the lift dinging our arrival. Coby took my hand, walking out first, but before we could go any further, he stopped and I almost slammed into his back.

He let go of my hand and turned to face me. "You know, honey, I couldn't be more proud of you right now if I tried. You talk as though you don't deserve this..." he held up a hand as I attempted to interrupt "...but you've worked so hard for so many years. I know if Mum were here—"

"Stop." My voice wobbled as I dabbed the corner of my eye carefully. "Thanks, Coby, but no going down the Mum path, please, or the waterworks will loosen my eyelashes, and for some reason, eyelash glue is not something I packed in my giant bag of tricks today."

Coby raised his eyebrows. "Okay."

We started moving along the hallway again, reaching room 4501 where out front stood Gigantor. He was big and wearing all over black. His hair was also black and short, and he looked mean. I waited for Gigantor to growl at me. Instead, a grin split his face wide, transforming it from "I'm gonna end you" to "Hey, how's it goin', buddy." It wasn't aimed at me though; it was aimed at Coby.

"Coby, my man."

"George, buddy." They shook hands and leaned in, doing that whole "I'm not really hugging you but it's good to see you" back slap type thing.

Gigantor George. There was no doubt I could pick it.

"Whatcha doin' here, man?"

Coby rolled his eyes towards me as though irritated beyond belief. "Babysitting. You?"

I successfully resisted the urge to slap Coby on the back of the head for turning from loving brother to Asshole Man in the blink of an eye.

"Same, man, same."

George turned to me, his deep voice a rumble. "You must be, Evie."

I nodded politely and held out my hand.

He took it, his big hand swallowing mine. "George." Letting go, he gave a brief rap on the door and opened it slightly, nodding his head at me. "Go on in. You're expected."

I stepped through. Coby went to follow but George stopped him with a hand to the chest. "Dude."

Coby raised his brows. "That's my sister, George."

George nodded his understanding, but didn't give an inch. "Orders. Evie only."

Coby shook his head in disagreement. "I go where she goes."

George shook his head in further disagreement. "Then she ain't goin' in there."

I felt a sliver of concern. Coby was a big dude, but George was a colossal dude.

Coby paused for a moment, his eyes on George. "I trust you, George. You guarantee she's safe in there and I'll wait out here."

George uttered his guarantee with all seriousness, and I finally made it inside with a click of the door behind me. Before I had time to ponder what that was all about, someone spoke my name.

"Genevieve."

"Evie," I amended, mouth working on autopilot because Matt, the lead guitarist of Sins of Descent, was walking through the twin doors of the suite's bedroom. Not only that, he was talking to me, and he knew my name. My feet felt stuck to the floor, so I stood waiting as he headed towards me.

"Evie," he repeated. He held out a hand as he got close, and my hand reached out to take his. It was a nice hand, warm with long fingers capable of great things. With a guitar of course. "I'm Matt. You might be wondering who –"

"Uh...no, well, yes...no. I mean, I know you."

I cringed internally for cutting him off, but the words just came out with my authorisation. Not only that, my conversational abilities appeared to have reached an all-time low.

He smiled, amused. It was a nice smile, attached to nice face. Not a gorgeous one, but striking—longish black hair, green eyes, lean—like the rest of him. Clad in black skinny jeans and a tight fitting white shirt, he had colourful tattoos winding up both arms. "Okay. Sometimes it's not good to assume people know me because then I just sound a bit conceited."

He stood there, looking at me, assessing my worth maybe? Was he waiting for me to speak? I tried to form something that would make sense.

"I thought that—"

"Maybe we should—"

I flushed a little and apologised. "You go."

He waved his hand at the couch. "I was just going to say that maybe we should sit down."

Sitting was good. "Okay."

I urged my legs to move, and we shifted to the plush coral couch and both sat down. I wiped my sweaty hands down my skirt in the pretext of smoothing wrinkles while Matt sat on the edge, elbows resting on his knees.

He jumped back up. "You want a drink? Sorry. I get so used to people doing that shit for me."

"Uh, okay. Sure, thanks."

"What would you like?"

"Diet coke if you have it."

He moved to the kitchenette and flicked the kettle, reaching up to the top cupboard for a mug and then to the mini fridge for the drink.

I offered a thanks as he handed it over, and he went back to making himself a coffee. "Um, not to sound rude, but I thought I was meeting Gary?"

"No, that's cool. The meeting was really with me, and Gary said he'd try to make it if he had time." He glanced up at me. "Sorry for the slight subterfuge, but I wanted to meet you, and I didn't want anyone to know I was here. That way I could slip in and out of the country without any fuss."

He finished making his coffee and carried it to the couch.

"Aren't you in the middle of touring?"

"Yep. We just hit New Zealand for two weeks, then we're holidaying there for another week before we get here."

"Where were you before New Zealand?"

We managed a conversation where I actually made sense, and Matt happily chatted about the tour and the people he'd met and some of the crazy things they'd been up to. We even became friendly enough for me to snap a photo of the two of us and message it to Mac. An avalanche of messages swamped my phone immediately, and I had to take a few moments to reply to all the questions.

"Anyway..." Matt sat his empty coffee mug on the table "...you're probably wondering what you're doing here?"

We had an idea thanks to Marty, but I tried not to let that show.

"One of our supports had to pull out of our Australian leg unexpectedly. I want, *we* want, Jamieson to take their place." As though expecting some sort of ridiculous rejection, he rushed on. "I know it's only three weeks away, but we can help with whatever you might need. You should be able to just slot right in. We've seen footage of you live, and I listened to the CD from Marty the other day. We think you could do this. What do you think?"

What did I think? Hmmm… I think—

"Well don't answer now. Talk it over with your guys, and then let me know, okay?" He picked up my phone off the table and punched a few buttons before sitting it back down. "My numbers in there, call me direct tonight. Honestly, pulling out so close to our tour here is all kinds of fucked up, but what's worse is that we had no backup plan."

Seriously, Matt, the lead guitarist of Sins of Descent, just put his mobile number in my phone. That shit was cool. Who needed Snoop Dogg?

"Okay," I replied with a big smile I couldn't hide. "I would pretty much think it would be a big fat yes though."

Matt returned my grin. "Fuck yeah. Let's run through the details?"

"Um, hell yeah."

"Okay. Let's order up lunch first, though. I'm fucking starving. Who's that outside, your man?"

"Oh God no, that's my brother." In the interests of being professional despite the fact it might cost us the tour spot, I added, "He's also my security."

"Security?" He gave me a questioning glance.

"Yeah. I've sort of got a stalker that's trying to well, bump me off."

I said sort of because coming right out and saying "There's an asshole following me around, waiting for his moment to kill me," sounded well, worse.

"Fuck, Evie. Hang on…" He answered his ringing phone and walked over to the window for a moment while he talked before returning. "That was Gary. He's not gonna be able to swing by, but he said to mention he'll call Mac tomorrow morning about the tour if you're all happy to go ahead. Anyway, that really sucks. We get that kinda crazy all the fucking time. Price of fame, you know. Our security is pretty tight, but we'll pass on the info to you because no doubt you'll want to bring your own along."

Relieved that security didn't appear to be an issue, I spoke to Coby and he left, trusting I was safe with George in attendance. I had to promise I wouldn't go anywhere, and he said he'd return later to collect me.

Nearing the afternoon when we'd finished running through just about everything possible, I remembered the small twinge that had tugged at me back at the photo shoot and took the opportunity to speak to Matt about it.

"Matt, can I ask you a personal question?" He nodded, so I continued. "Well, I was just wondering, being famous, all the late nights performing, long days recording, and always being on the road..." I paused for a moment to think about how to form what I was trying to say "...how does that work with relationships? I mean, obviously it's not easy, but you can make it work, right?"

He cringed a little and rubbed at his chin just enough to make me think maybe I shouldn't have asked. "I'm probably not the best person to ask that question, Evie."

"Oh, sorry."

I fidgeted with the hem of my skirt.

"No, it's not that. I don't mind. It's just that if you're hoping to hear happily ever after, it hasn't happened for me. If you want me to be honest, well, it's more than just not easy. It's fucking hard work. The hours are long, and performing takes you away more often than not. That's just the first hurdle really. Get famous and you've got PR telling you who you can and can't be, add paparazzi to the mix, catching you in compromising positions, making it into something that it's not, creating rumours and jealousy. Then you spend your time defending your actions and the person you are. Constantly second guessing people around you. Do they really care or if it all went away tomorrow would they still be by your side? After all that, it gets exhausting and well, lonely. Even surrounded by people, you can still feel really alone. Music has to be your world to want this kind of life and to live it because it's what gets you through all that shit."

While it was always good to hear the truth, his words left me feeling cold. I could understand the reasons behind Jared's reaction to thinking something more happened with Tate than what it did, but I was left feeling anxiety for our future together, especially after Matt confirmed all my doubts.

Matt glanced at my ring finger. "Well, I'm assuming you're asking because you've got a partner?"

"Yeah," I muttered. "We've known each other a long time I guess, but it's still in its early stages."

"Frankly, Evie, if it's still in its early stages, you're probably better off leaving it there. Suddenly being introduced to this life is harder than living it. This guy, it is a guy?" I nodded. "He's probably used to having you all to himself. Soon you'll have guys all over you, literally, and that's just walking down the street. Handing you their number, putting you in compromising situations, and he'll be sitting off watching it all, seeing it in papers, watching while people control your life. If you don't think he's the type of person who can deal with that, then..." he trailed off with a shrug and the cold feeling only got worse.

Chapter Twenty

I viciously yanked another weed out of the little cottage garden by the back deck and tossed it over my shoulder. The garden was pretty, but heading towards overgrown, deserving much more than I could offer it. My green thumb was more brown, and weeds, being wily imposters, made the task of determining friend from foe twice as difficult.

I sat back on my haunches to rest my noodle arms. The dirt had somehow evolved into cement like proportions which meant my recently purchased trowel from the homeware's store was getting dirty. I had to buy it because it was hand-painted pink with white and yellow daises.

Unwinding the hose, I turned it on and clicked the spray handle to mist, aiming it at the garden bed in the hopes it would loosen the dirt.

"What the fuck are you doing?"

Startled, I turned at the question. Forgetting I was holding the hose, it turned with me, and I misted Henry.

"Shit." He leaped back, the unexpected shower providing me with an entertaining impromptu dance.

"What does it look like I'm doing?" I asked, wondering if stupid questions were going to be the order of the day. I wasn't in the mood but I couldn't imagine there was ever a mood that happily entertained stupid questions.

He gave me a scan, taking in the dirt encrusted singlet top, grass-stained shorts, and pile of hair that had likely progressed from this morning's rats nest to something that would now scare small children.

"It's eight in the fucking morning."

Finished misting, I clicked off the hose and let it drop at my feet.

"Thanks for the update, Henry."

I resumed my crouching position and yanked what I assumed was another weed and tossed it at his feet.

He threw up his hands in exasperation. "Fuck it. It looks like you're up. At eight am. Weeding the garden. So I'll repeat, what the fuck are you doing?"

"Jesus, someone get this man a medal because he just answered his own question."

I threw another weed and we both watched it hit Peter in the face. Since Peter considered himself Aslan, and the backyard his Narnia, he wrestled with it, chewing savagely until it was a pile of defeated green mush at his feet.

"Har har. Talk, Chook, or I'll throw you to Peter, and he'll chew you up and spit you out."

I paused and took Peter in. Dribbles of green mush lined his chin, his eyes were freakishly fanatical, and his incisors were slightly bared from his hardened battle. "I'll take my chances."

I knew I was in for my own battle when Henry dragged a timber deck chair out to the grass and sat down. Reclining comfortably, he ruffled Peter's head when Peter began chewing viciously on the leg of the chair.

"What happened?"

I swallowed the sick, hollow feeling that crept up my throat, but it didn't descend. "We're over."

"What?" Henry sat forward in shock. "You and Jared?"

"No, me and Ryan Gosling," I said sarcastically. "Unfortunately, Ryan told me that every day we were together was the greatest day of his life and he'll always be mine. I told him he was a loser and to get lost."

"Ah fuck," he muttered.

Ah fuck was right, so I nodded.

He sat back in his chair. "Tell me."

I thought back to last night. We had played at the White Demon. It was our last show before we went on tour and three weeks after I'd met Matt. Sins of Descent were playing a song, a surprise for the crowd to generate some publicity for the tour. It was a busy night. Word had got out the famous band was in the building. Lines snaked out along the side of the building and down several blocks. Fights broke out, the police were called three times, people were arrested. It was a huge success.

Matt and I were catching up, holed up in the backstage dressing room having a drink. I was nervous. I was about to head out and introduce their band to the frenzied crowd. We stood up from our chat, and Matt gave me a tight hug. One hand rested on my head as I tucked it under his chin, the other around my waist. I returned the hug because I had no romantic feelings towards him at all, and Matt seemed lonely, not lecherous.

Then Jared had opened the door, and there was no other word for how he looked other than hot. His hair had grown again, sweeping over his eyes, and the longer it grew, the lighter the ends got. He was wearing his dark vintage Calvin Klein jeans and a fitted black Led Zeppelin US 1975 tour t-shirt. I loved that shirt. I needed to buy the girl version.

His eyes found us and his brows furrowed together creating a fierce glower. Arms folded over his chest, accentuating his biceps, he stood in a wide legged stance which evoked images of pistols drawn. Jared pissed off was a sight to behold.

Wisely, I pulled myself out of my daze and pushed Matt away, thinking no matter how harmless our situation it still didn't look good.

Then Jared spoke and that thought became a realisation. "Would you mind getting your fucking hands off my girl," he growled.

I made an attempt to diffuse the situation. "Jared, it's not what you think."

"Yeah?" His voice raised a bit, not sounding like my attempt had performed its intended miracle in the least.

Jared nodded his head towards the door. "Get out," he said to Matt.

Matt raised his brows at me in a "See? I told you so" expression, but he left, making sure to glare at Jared on his way out the door.

"Jared," I turned to face him fully. "I'm not Jessica. You're gonna have to learn to trust me."

Jared, his lips pressed together in a thin line, did not look delighted about me bringing Jessica into the conversation. "You think I don't trust you? It's everyone else I don't trust. You gotta learn not to put yourself in situations where people take advantage of you."

"Oh I do, do I?" I folded my arms, copycatting his stance as my snit started to take hold. "You think I'm stupid enough to let people take advantage of me? You think I can't take care of myself, recognise the real people from the frauds?"

"Baby, you don't understand—"

"No, you don't understand, Jared." I unfolded my arms and reached for the door behind him. "But I don't have time to explain it to you right now."

He put a gentle hand on my arm to stop me and spoke softly. "Is this what you've been stewing on for three weeks? Because I've felt you pulling away from me since the first time you met that asshole. What did he do to make you start shutting down?"

It was true.

Since my chat with Matt, I freaked out as the cold feeling took hold little by little and began closing myself off. It wasn't even deliberate, simply an instinctual type preservation, yet I could still feel myself doing it.

"Shit," I muttered. "I have to go."

It was later, after the show finished, that it came to a head in a manner that was both messy and downright hostile.

The boys, Henry, Jake, Frog, and Cooper were lost to the bar, completely wankered and in no condition to know where they were or if they had a name or even a home. Mac was missing in action, and it appeared so was Jared. I sat myself down at a private table between Matt and Travis with conflicted emotions. Excited, because we had a tour in two days, and edgy because of Jared. I noticed, as I glanced around, female eyes were trained on me with resentment, so I smiled a little smugly. I *was* sitting at a table with one of the hottest bands of the moment, and Travis, and if I didn't take a moment to bask in the glory just a little, my female membership card would have been revoked.

Travis leaned over. "What's going on with you and Jared?"

"Nothing," I lied.

"Doesn't look like nothing." He turned his head towards the bar to indicate where Jared had now re-appeared, wedged between Henry and two blonde skanks.

"Fuck." My first instinct was to wade into the pile of bodies and throw a hissy fit big enough to rival a Britney Spears meltdown. Then I realised my reaction was in complete alignment with Jared's earlier assumption. Would this be our life now? Constantly defending ourselves to each other?

Jesus.

I threw back a shot, set down the empty glass, and picked up my beer chaser.

"I can't do it," I admitted to the table.

The table didn't respond, but Travis did. "Can't do what?"

"Relationships. Jared and I." I shook my head and sucked the beer down as though it was last call at happy hour. Realising that I didn't want to be the only one sober, I put down my now empty beer glass and reached for Travis's drink.

He stilled my hand and I paused to give him a look that told him I really needed that drink.

"Don't say that, honey. Don't." His lips were tight and he looked unhappy.

"It's only going to get worse," I declared.

Travis looked even more unhappy. "Evie, don't cut him loose. You'll break his fucking heart. Just give yourselves a fighting chance. Talk to him in the morning when alcohol is out of the equation okay?"

Travis ran his fingers through his hair and huffed out a breath, glancing towards the bar and at Jared. "I don't wanna see him hurt, and watching him shut down over the whole Jessica farce was fucking torture. With you, Jesus, it would be even worse. When you get back, we'll have Jimmy out of our hair and everything can go back to normal."

"Even worse?" I repeated.

"Yeah. He never loved her like he loves you."

"Jared loves me? How do you know?"

"Come on, Evie, it's him you need to talk to about this shit, not me. Okay?" Travis exhaled loudly and ran his fingers through his hair.

"You know going back to normal after the tour isn't an option," I pointed out. "We're on the verge of signing a major record deal, and we're about to go on tour with one of the hottest bands alive. If we don't fuck this up, when we come home people are gonna know us, and life's gonna be different. We'll be recording more songs, doing interviews, more shows, more tours, music videos." I waved at the Sins of Descent members crowding around the table laughing it up and drinking. "This shit is our life, and we choose this. We live for this. How does a relationship fit into all that?"

Travis shook his head impatiently at everything I said. "You make it work, Evie. It's that hard and it's that simple."

This time, when I reached for his drink, he didn't stop me, so I downed it too.

That was about when I felt a hard wall press up behind me, heavy hands coming to rest on my shoulders. I knew it was Jared, not because I had eyes in the back of my head, but because I knew the feel of his hands and the sweet clean scent of his skin, even over the smell of alcohol so strong it damn near seeped from the walls.

He leaned down close to speak and his warm breath against my ear gave me shivers until his words sunk in. "Out of all the chairs in this place, and after what just went down between you and me, I find you sitting here, next to *him*."

I half turned in my seat, incredulous, my voice loud enough for the whole table to hear, and I didn't care one bit. "You aren't going to tell me where I can and can't sit now, are you?"

He lifted his arms from my shoulders, straightened, and took a step back. "Damn straight."

I stood up carefully because three drinks thrown back in rapid succession wasn't for the weak. Then I raked him over with a scathing glance that was, unfortunately, fuelled by alcohol. The table went silent and rather than embarrass myself by turning into a screaming basket of drunk trash, I hissed quietly. "We need to talk."

Matt, eyeing our conversation with a knowing look, turned to face me in his seat. "I warned you, Evie."

My eyes widened and I shook my head to indicate he should shut up, but my non-verbal warning was foolishly unheeded.

"This is what fucking happens. Better now than later." He waved his hand towards Jared dismissively.

Turning towards Matt, Jared unfolded his arms. They were now tensed by his side, fists clenched, knuckles white. It wasn't looking good for Matt, and before I could open my mouth to speak, Jared beat me to it.

"What the hell did you say to her?"

All eyes at the table swivelled to Matt, including mine. "Nothing she didn't need to hear."

I closed my eyes at the reckless statement.

"Let me guess..." Everyone turned back to Jared and his seething tone. "Three weeks ago, you stuck your fucking nose into business that wasn't your own. You did this by spouting a load of bullshit, and it must have been bullshit because you don't know me from Adam. Then that bullshit you spewed got her so wound up she shuts down and can't even talk to me about it. Are you happy now? Is that your mission? To make other people as miserable as you? Because you let that shit fester inside her and sat back for the fallout. Tell me, because I really want to know, exactly what it was that you *fucking said to her?*" The last part ended on a shout, making me flinch and effectively silencing the tables surrounding our already subdued huddle.

Matt had stood up in the middle of Jared's rage. "I fucking told her that she's better off without you!" he shouted back.

That was when Jared had cocked back that clenched fist of his and slammed it in Matt's face.

"Holy shit!" Henry's voice startled me out of last night's recount of events and back to the dirty pile of weeds at my feet. "Where was I when this happened?"

"I told you, Henry. You were wankered at the bar."

I grabbed the nearby bucket and started shovelling in the pile of weeds. It wasn't easy because Peter was running through them like it was a sprinkler on a hot day. I paused a moment to admire his joie de vivre.

"Well, what happened after that?"

"I told him we were over and to leave."

"Did he?"

I nodded because watching him leave made my chest hurt and remembering it made it hurt worse. "Yeah," I muttered.

"Have you heard from him?"

My phone had remained determinedly silent. No sweet or funny messages from Jared and no angry or appeasing ones either. "No," I whispered, putting down the bucket and wrapping my arms tightly around my knees.

"Now *that* answers the question."

I tilted my head to look at Henry. "What?"

"Of why you're up at fucking eight in the morning weeding the garden. Right. I'm going to get a coffee, and when I get back, you're going to tell me what Matt said to you, and we're going to sort this stupid shit out."

I picked the bucket back up and went back to shovelling the weeds into it with determination, Peter dancing and barking at my feet. When Henry returned, he shoved a cup of tea in my face and growled at me to "Sit the eff down."

I sat. Henry sat.

"Talk."

I talked.

Henry summed it up. "So basically what you're telling me is that some guy—"

"Matt is not just some guy. He's got experience in this kind of life."

"Don't interrupt me. Some guy tells you the life of a rockstar is a rocky road and all relationships lead down the path to Shitsville. Rather than voice your concerns to Jared, your boyfriend and the man you've known for how many years..."

"We were only together for—"

"That wasn't a question." Henry's voice steamed over mine. "You listen to some guy you've known for like...a day. Then, when the going gets a little hostile, which mind you, I too would punch a guy out if he stuck his nose in my business like that, rather than act like a normal person, you put your silly 'I'm a fucking idiot' hat on and tell Jared to get lost?"

I was still riding the tails of anger, but as he spoke, I felt a sinking sensation in my stomach that evolved into a dull thumping ache in my heart. I'd said I'd never hide anything from him, so why didn't I just talk to him?

"This is the first guy you've been with that I actually like, but I don't think you see him, like really *see* him. He's wanted you since the moment you both met, but you were so swamped in your pile of emotional dork bullshit you couldn't see the light. Now you two finally get your shit together, and not even waiting until you reach the first hurdle, because every relationship has hurdles, you create one out of thin air just so you could dump him before he breaks your heart. You'd be lucky if Jared would take back a lunatic like you. Tell me this, did it work? Because from where I'm standing, you're already in love with him, so you've already done what you were trying to avoid doing and gone and broken your own heart anyway." Henry leaned forward in his chair as he spoke the words that cut deep. His eyes were hard and angry and directed at me.

I took a gulp of scolding tea, and it burned my tongue. I felt it scorch all the way down but it didn't hurt half as much as knowing that Henry was right. My actions were rash and thoughtless and when I'd woken up it felt like Wile E. Coyote had dumped an anvil over a cliff and it had landed on my chest. Is that why I'd done what I did? I thought I'd let go of all the fear, but maybe I hadn't. Obviously, I hadn't because the going hadn't even gotten tough before I got going.

"Fuck," I muttered.

I dumped my tea on the outdoor table, raced inside to the kitchen, grabbed my phone off the bench, and raced back out to the chair. In a panic, I started to randomly punch numbers in.

"What are you doing?"

"I don't know," I wailed. "I don't know what the hell I'm doing, Henry. I need to ring Jared. I need to sort this shit out. What did I do? Henry, God, if you weren't so wankered last night this wouldn't have happened." I pointed my finger accusingly at his chest to make my point. "You weren't there like a best friend should be while I lost the plot."

Henry snatched the phone out of my hand, calmly went to my contacts, and dialled Jared's number before handing it back.

I stood up and started to pace, holding the phone to my ear, feeling my stomach churn.

"I feel sick," I muttered.

It went to voicemail and I hung up the phone, closing my eyes at the sound of his voice. I already missed hearing it and missed him. Knowing he wasn't mine anymore and the fact that it was on me made it all the worse.

"Voicemail," I muttered. "Can't say what I need to over voicemail. Shit, Henry."

Over the next two days, Jared's phone continually went to voicemail, so I didn't text. I'd never *not* been able to get in touch with him. He always, *always,* made himself available to me. I felt like I should have been stripped naked and marched to the town centre and taken ten public lashings to atone for my sins. I cuddled Peter late into the night while he reclined on his back, snoring heavily and consistently, his furry belly heaving up and down. He liked to keep his little front paws propped over the sheets and his head shoved half under the pillow to avoid any light. He was now the survivor of a broken home. This meant he needed to be spoiled to appease my guilt, but I wasn't sure how to do that considering he pretty much had run of the house already.

The night before we flew out to kick off the tour, we had a minor celebratory dinner, just the six of us, out on the back deck with the barbecue.

Henry stood up, holding a beer, and cleared his throat. Everyone went silent to listen, all assuming it would be a pre-tour pep talk. However, Henry turned until he was facing me, his eyes finding mine.

"So everyone by now knows that Evie was operating under a mental deficiency the other night, and what I want to know is—"

"Jesus, Henry, we did this speech yesterday morning. Are we seriously going to re-hash it?"

Henry finished taking a pull of his beer and sat it down carefully. "Tell me this, Evie, have you spoken to Jared?"

I pushed the food around on my plate. "You know I haven't spoken to Jared."

"And why is that?"

"Because when I ring it keeps going to voicemail, asshead. That's why." I passed off a piece of sausage to Peter along with pat.

"Have you left a message?"

Looking away, I answered quietly. "No."

"What was that? I didn't quite hear you."

"No!" I shouted.

Peter flinched and I immediately gave him another piece of sausage.

"We all love you." He waved his hand around the table and everyone nodded their agreement. Mac glared because she was still in the throes of anger from my actions. "We all care about you. We're all here for you." The last comment was said with a pointed glance at Mac. "But Christ, Evie, look at you. You look like shit, you're not eating, and…and…"

Mac entered the conversation. "And your shoes don't match your freaking pants."

All eyes swivelled to assess my silver sandals and mustard coloured capris as though we'd suddenly teleported into an episode of Project Runway.

"Jared's a hothead," I told them.

Everyone was silent, as though processing my announcement and wondering what it had to do with my fashion faux pas.

"You're stubborn," Jake responded.

"He leaves wet towels on my bedroom floor," I pointed out.

Mac snorted. "It's a wonder he can find clear floor space to leave it there."

I glared at Mac, evaluating her sanity. "I'm tidy. You're the one that leaves my clothes in chaos, you…you chaos merchant," I hissed.

"Stop getting off track," Henry ordered.

I held up my hand and rattled off each finger. "He's opinionated, overbearing, violent, arrogant…" I finished with what I considered the death blow. "And he wants four kids."

Even Mac sucked in an audible breath at that last one.

I nodded at her.

266

"Yet you still love him anyway," Henry offered softly.

I pointed my fork at him. "Damn you, Henry."

"Stop trying to convince yourself that it's not going to work."

"Newsflash, Henry. He's not answering his phone. I don't need to. It's already over."

"The man's not an idiot," Frog offered.

All eyes swivelled to Frog, and Cooper expanded upon Frog's statement with a shrug. "What he's trying to say is that only an idiot wouldn't fight for you, Evie."

Frog nodded.

"Okay, I'm over this conversation. Evie, get upstairs, ring Jared, and leave a message this time. We don't wanna see you 'til it's done."

At Henry's order, I stood up, picked up my plate in one hand, Peter in the other so he was tucked under my armpit, gave them all a glare so frosty icicles should have been forming off their interfering eyelashes, and exited the deck.

Contrary to popular opinion, the fact that my calls kept going straight to voicemail told me that Jared was not going to fight for me. As I picked up my phone, I flopped across my bed sideways and wondered how long it would take for the anvil to go away.

Deciding not to try ringing again, I sent off a text message instead. I thought it fitting really, like the circle of life. We began via text, we finished via text. Sort of like live by the sword, die by the sword, only less dramatic really.

E: Current popular opinion is that I am a daft idiot. This is not news. I was the one talking about trust, and in the end, I didn't trust what you and I had together. I'm sorry.

I left off the clichéd "maybe one day we can be friends" part. In some part because that would've turned my whole message into lame rubbish, but mostly because I wasn't sure I could handle being friends with Jared after everything that had come before. I would likely bitch slap the next girl he started seeing into next week, and that would just be embarrassing and awkward for all involved.

Because our flight left at a cringe-worthy time in the morning, I switched off my phone, set my alarm, tucked Peter into the sheets, and drifted to sleep listening to the song *Africa* by Toto. I liked to listen to this song on repeat under times of great distress because it was better than a shot of Berocca. It was one of my most embarrassing and best kept secrets, along with my love of Rupert Grint from Harry Potter.

Chapter Twenty-One

The next morning I woke looking hideous enough to earn myself a best actress Oscar. Charlize Theron from Monster was staring back at me in the mirror, only with darker hair and more of it. The only way to pull off the Oscar was to transform back to golden swan in the blink of an eye, so there I was at dawn, once again pulling out my arsenal to perform magical deeds.

After much pounding down of the bathroom door, a minor scuffle over the last two slices of bread between Mac and Henry, another chewed stiletto unearthed from the lounge, forcing Peter to run from Mac's laser death stare, and another scuffle between Jake and Mac for the front seat (Jake won), we finally hit the road to the airport by way of Steve and Jenna's place to deliver Peter. I was driving, Frog, Henry, and Cooper were in the back with Mac unhappily wedged between Frog and Henry. Peter was on Jake's lap, head stuck out the open window, ears flapping like Dumbo and mouth wide open because he was trying to eat air.

Peter was being dropped off at their place for the duration of the tour before we hit the long term airport car park, meeting up with Coby and Travis, my personally designated security for the tour. Jimmy's messages hadn't died off, but they hadn't escalated either. No recent attempts on my life led me to believe that he'd either given up or was just happy to drag the process out to epic proportions, but the wait for something to happen was mentally exhausting.

Handing over Peter was a bit traumatic; the past two days of emotional vulnerability had secured our bond. Jenna, obviously up to date with the whole "it's over between us" Jared situation, kept eyeing me with grief-stricken disappointment, clearly stuck in the throes of a major grandparentdom setback. I offered her reassuring nods and smiles, a giant box of Peters things (Peter didn't travel light), and a long list of instructions for his care. Peter was fussy and liked routine. Offering a quick goodbye and a teary cuddle with both Jenna and Peter, I rushed back to the car, and we squealed off to the airport.

Later that morning found the eight of us touching down in Perth, the other side of the country along the west coast of Australia. As we leisurely coasted down the street in a black limousine towards the stadium we'd be performing in that night, a long line of people already snaked down the designated pathways. Spying the limousine heading for a side entrance, the crowd started squealing and shouting. Clearly it was a major quandary as to whether they should risk their head start in the line and attach themselves like barnacles to our car or keep ferociously to their line, thus securing the best standing spot in the mosh pit later that night.

Mac and I giggled and I lowered the window offering a wave so they would know to keep to the line, and it was just the support act. I was startled when I heard shouts of "Oh my God, that's Jamieson!" and "Evie!" and "That's Hottie Henry!" People started to surge and I paled. Inside, the limo went silent in shock, so I hastily put the window back up. Everyone eyeballed each other in disbelief.

"Holy shit," Henry muttered.

Mac tittered. "Hottie Henry?"

My eyes were wide. "How do they even know who we are?"

"Who cares? Did you see how hot those girls were?" Cooper's eyes were still glued to the window. "Perth is the fucking shit."

From then on, we were introduced to the world of touring and waded through the thousands involved in putting together such a massive production. There were tour managers, production managers, stage managers, engineers, guitar techs, lighting techs, pyrotechnic techs (basically about four thousand, seven hundred and twenty-nine different types of techs, give or take). Then there were the engineers, security, merchandise crew, and caterers.

We pulled up and piled out to the sounds of Sins of Descent doing their sound check. Mac said ours would be last so we could keep our instruments set up on stage since we were opening the show.

Gary arrived and started walking us to our backstage area. I asked about the fans outside.

"Evie, did you see the giant billboards?"

I shook my head.

"I don't know how you missed them. They were from your photo shoot. We've been advertising your band for this tour the past three weeks very seriously. Did you know your YouTube festival appearance views have gone up over one thousand percent already? People are going to start recognising you now. Speaking of which, we need to talk about your contract. Jettison is keen to have it signed and are getting the papers drafted as we speak."

I stopped short and felt Mac smack into my back. Gary, not realising we were no longer behind him, kept on walking along.

"Mac, did you hear that?"

"Yes. God! We knew it was coming, but holy shit!"

In a moment of situational elation, I was still a daft idiot operating under a pile of emotional grief and Mac was still the bitter third party and festering ill will, we managed to come together in an excited hug.

"Evie!" Gary shouted from further down the way.

"Oh, Sandwich," Mac muttered, gently brushing a rogue curl off my face and tucking it behind my ear just like Jared always did.

I gave Mac a bittersweet smile before I turned, rushing to catch up to Gary. He was waiting to introduce us to the sound engineer for our sound check.

Later that night, after the sound engineer gave us the "good to go" thumbs up, we caught up with Sins of Descent, which included several looks of the disgruntled variety aimed Matt's way from Henry, Travis, and the like. Then we piled into our dressing room where the guys began getting ready, and I commenced faffing about in my robe, busily building myself into an epic state of panic. My excuse was that I was already emotionally crippled thus an easy trigger. The fact that Mac's usual hardcore Ripley status was on the verge of desertion in her own brand of anxiety simply made me panic even more.

"Pull yourself together," Mac wheeze-hissed.

Mac wasn't being overly sensitive, it wasn't her style, but she knew me, and that entailed knowing any particular type of kindness right at that moment would only make my current state of mind worse.

I struggled to get a hold on my nerves. "I'm trying,"

I closed my eyes to speed along the calming process, but all I could visualise was a stadium filled with tens of thousands of screaming people. If that wasn't bad enough, we were hitting Brisbane next, and it was sold out to over fifty thousand. Well it wasn't bad *bad;* it was bloody brilliant, but right now I was living through tunnel vision and my only focus was the panic.

I was on my own with hair and makeup. Mac had shit to do. I finished dressing and was only ten minutes late when I arrived at the side entrance to the stage and found Mac. I couldn't believe that I was here in this moment. I wanted to savour it but without Jared at my side, his quiet strength soothing me, his sexy eyes heating me, and his words making me laugh, it felt hollow.

Seeing tears sheen my eyes, Mac reached out and took my hand. "I'm sorry for being an asshead, Evie. I was so damn mad at you for being an idiot that I don't think I've been able to see straight for two solid days."

"It's okay Macface, really." My voice was soft and small. "I was the one that posed the question to Matt, so don't bear him any ill will, okay? It's just…Henry was right, which is scary considering he's the retarded relationship bastard. I *am* scared of getting hurt, and with Jared's short temper, it freaked me out, especially considering Jessica. I mean, after what he went through with her, why would I expect him to trust me? I know he says he does, but sometimes his actions made me feel like he didn't, you know?"

"Have you heard from him?"

Jared was not, from past experiences, a game player. This meant if he wanted to talk to me, he would have. I wouldn't have wanted to talk to me either, so the fact that my phone still remained silent was both expected and devastating all at the same time. Despite all that, I still waited all day for him to call.

"No." I let out a deep sigh.

Mac looked like she was having a light bulb moment. "Have you heard from *anyone* today?"

I stood in silence while it was Mac's turn to give me a moment. She used the moment wisely to ogle the myriad of hot man flesh that shifted about all around us, moving equipment, speaking into those walkie talkie things. Not an ungrateful person, Mac was very appreciative of all the men surrounding us. I also noticed the men happened to be equal opportunists, and Mac should have been blinded by the searing looks being continually swept her way. Was I invisible? I offered a bright smile and a wink to the next man that walked passed us and watched his eyes widen. The man turned, walking backwards to watch me, and collided with Henry as he came up behind him.

"Dude!" Henry held up his hands politely as the man stumbled.

"Sorry," he muttered and scurried away.

Mac narrowed her eyes at me. "What was that?"

I shrugged my shoulders innocently but then grinned. "Just seeing if old Evie still has the goods."

Henry joined our huddle, catching my comment to Mac. "Jesus, Sandwich, if you had any more goods, that huddle over there would be thinking they'd found a new religion." He indicated to three guys in the corner, all holding official clipboards and eyeing us. One smiled suggestively when I glanced their way.

I fluffed my hair a little. Not because I was interested, but a little bit of attention thrown my way when I felt about as wanted as pile of elephant poo on a hot summers day was a lift of the spirits. "Well, at the rate I'm going with Jared, it looks like plenty of the male population might just get their chance," I mumbled unhappily.

"Stop going off on a tangent, Evie, and answer the question." Mac smoothed her perfect waves. How they managed to look so perfect after her afternoon of busting balls, I didn't know.

"Tangents are good," I offered. "They keep life interesting. What was the question?"

Mac rolled her eyes. "Never mind. I'll be right back."

I moved quickly out of her way as she shoved passed us. Mac was a woman on a mission as she charged away, muttering something into her headset. Many sets of male eyes stopped to watch her ass undulate its way out the door.

"What's up with her?" Henry asked.

"What's not up with her? What's up with you?" I gave him a once over. "What's up with that shirt?"

He looked down at his tight black Linkin Park t-shirt. "What about it?"

"Can it get any tighter? Can you breathe?"

Henry smirked. "I'm speaking to you, aren't I?"

My gaze travelled further down to his skinny black jeans and returned the smirk. "Your jeans are even tighter. It's a wonder you're speaking and not squeaking." I waved my hand over the ensemble. "Are you trying to communicate something with that outfit?"

Henry looked a little uncertain and ran a hand through his tousled white-blond locks. "Well, yeah. Why? What's it communicating to you?"

"It's saying, 'Hi. I'm Henry. I have pecs and a tight ass that won't quit.'"

Henry paled. "Fucking Cooper."

I laughed and leaped on him. He caught me as I wrapped my legs around his waist. "Kidding, Henrietta. Geez, you're a soft touch tonight. You look hot. I'd do you. Maybe. Well, no way, but you know..."

He laughed, spun me once, knocking a random techie, and apologised.

"Gee thanks, Chook. I think."

He set me back on my feet when Mac returned. "Hold out your hand," she barked at me.

I eyed her with suspicion. "Why?"

She was in a huff about something and snatched my wrist with her long taloned fingers and yanked my arm up, slapping my phone into my palm. "That's why."

I shrugged. "Um, I don't get it. How many words? Can I buy a vowel?"

After taking several deep breaths, she spoke. "You're on in ten. Now turn your phone on, Sandwich, before I slap you."

"Oh," I muttered, feeling a couple of pieces short of a full puzzle. I switched my phone on. "I don't think I switched it on after I turned it off last night."

The moment my beloved little phone beeped back to life, it buzzed through a mass of messages which included a voicemail from Jared recorded only half an hour ago. Holding my breath, I went straight to the message and held the phone to my ear.

"Baby," he spoke softly. Just hearing his voice directed at me, calling me his baby in that soft sexy rumble was enough to release the pent up flood, and I burst into tears. The salty wetness slid down in streaks, leaving a trail of destruction upon what was previously a perfectly made up face.

"Now?" Mac muttered. "You've kept yourself together for two days and *now* you choose to fall apart?"

"Shhhh, I'm trying to listen."

"I got your message. We can talk about it when you get back, but if you thought I was letting you go that easily, then you thought wrong. I just wanted to tell you—" I frowned as he was cut off. Tell me what? He must have pulled the phone away, but I could still hear. "Fuck, are you sure?" Someone yelled and I pressed the phone tighter to my ear as though it would help me hear better, but I only made out muffled shouting and something that sounded like "Go, go, go!" A car roared to life and he came back on. "Shit. I've been trying to ring you all day," he shouted into the phone as the roaring got louder and voices could be heard yelling.

I looked up in a panic as I listened, searching for Coby. He was standing near the edge of the stage, ten feet away, on his phone, pacing. Travis next him, on his phone too and looking on edge. Shit was going down.

"We've located Jimmy. I can't talk now. I'll have to call you back later."

The message ended and I tossed my phone to Mac as I made a fast beeline for Coby and Travis, feeling myself hyperventilate at the thought of Jimmy shooting at Jared right this very moment.

"Now?" Mac yelled again after I filled her and Henry in on the brief message when they followed behind me. "You fall apart and this shit goes down tonight of all nights?"

It was now Mac's turn to look like she was ready to toss her cookies. I watched in fascination as she sucked the panic deep inside until her outer layers appeared calm and unruffled. It was fascinating to watch, and I constantly wondered how she did it. The transformation complete, she grabbed me by the arm and muscled me all the way back to the dressing room where Jake, Cooper, and Frog were still in various states of undress.

She eyed the Rice Bubbles in disbelief, and I had a passing moment of reprieve with her wrath focused elsewhere. "You three lazy assheads aren't ready?"

Jake paused in the act of pulling on his shirt as he copped an eyeful of my wrecked face. "Sandwich, honey, you okay?"

I sniffled a little because I was being offered a sympathetic ear.

"She's fine," Mac announced before I could open my mouth. "You all just get out there. You're on in like a minute."

Frog and Cooper finished dressing and hustled out the door, but Jake paused for a moment, his concern for me warring with his need to get far away from Mac.

My eyes urged him to save himself. "I'm fine, Jake," I offered. "I'll see you out there."

He acknowledged my communication with a nod, and he turned and left.

Mac, her lips tight, worked quickly and silently on my face.

"Mac?"

Her eyes found mine and softened slightly. "This is his job, Evie. He's gonna be okay. Now *your* job on the other hand..."

"I can do this," I lied with fierce determination.

"You can." She gave my head an affectionate pat and plopped the mascara back in the bag with a loud clack. "You're like the little engine that could."

"Do you think—"

"Yes I do," she interrupted. "He adores you, Evie. He won't give up on you. Just..." she paused for a moment "...don't you give up on him either, okay? Now, you, us, this whole thing, it's huge. One day, Sandwich, we'll look back and..." Mac's voice hitched and she sucked in a breath.

With her arms folded and eyes on the floor she looked so vulnerable that I stood up and pulled her in for a hug. "Oh, Mac."

Taking deep breaths, Mac stood back and smoothed a hand over the slinky gold satin bodice of her corset top. "Right, enough of the emotional retardedness, Sandwich. Let's pack it all away for another day. Everyone's mother and their hot son are out there waiting for us, well, for you."

I stood up. "How do I look?"

She grabbed the super-hold hairspray and gave my strands a once over, ensuring my waves, big enough to rival Optimus Prime in impressiveness, weren't planning a disappearing act and gave me the critical once over.

"You look like a goddamn rockstar." She gave me a shove. "Now get out there and act like one."

"You want me to act like a rockstar, Mactard, and I assure you there won't be any liking it on your part," I warned as we walked through the dressing room door.

Matt pulled me up short by standing in my way, and Mac glared. It was obvious that whatever respect Mac had for Matt, which was pretty high with him being almost as big as Lady GaGa, was now lower than the crust of the earth. The mighty had fallen in Mac's book of mighty people, and once again, I felt bad for being the instigator of really bad things.

"Now?" She growled at him. "You have to do this now?"

I was in agreement on that one. I couldn't even begin to describe the many ways that made this a really bad time, not to mention there was a crowd big enough to rival a Boxing Day sale riot waiting for me to get out there and give them everything I had, which right now, honestly didn't feel like much. I'd avoided Matt since the whole PunchGate incident and feeling bad, I knew I needed to apologise but I had yet to figure out what to say.

I asked Mac to give us a minute, and she offered a final glare before stalking away fiercely.

I turned back to Matt in the awkward silence. "So..." I muttered, trying and failing at not giving him the once over. His clothes held the perfect amount of worn-ness required to look like it was something he'd sat around in for three days straight and still looked sexy at the same time.

"Evie," he muttered back, returning the once over and finishing at my hair with widened eyes. "You look ahh..."

"Thirty seconds!" Mac yelled from somewhere far away.

I felt a slap and grab hit my ass as Ethan, Sins of Descent's lead singer, rushed by. "Good luck, sexy ass," he said over his shoulder with a wink, disappearing before I could form an irritated response.

I rolled my eyes at Matt and he responded with a grin. "Matt, I'm so sorry."

His gaze turned rueful. "You're sorry? Me and my big fat mouth. I was looking out for you, Evie, and I took that way too far. It's just... I wished someone warned me back when, you know? Now, I've screwed shit up for you, haven't I?"

"You? I hold the Oscar for screwing shit up, Matt."

He laughed and scratched the back of his head. "Alright." He held out his hand. "Friends?"

I took the hand with a smile. "If you're lucky."

"Sandwich!" I heard screeched.

I let go and Matt offered a good luck along with a back slap and headed off in the opposite direction. I met Mac and the boys at the side of the stage. My eyes found Coby and Travis next to the huddle. Coby gave me a simple nod to let me know all was okay, at least for now, so I straightened my back and joined the huddle.

"Right, time for a pre-show pep talk, girls." I went around the huddle and eyed each and every one of them. "I hope you're all wearing your big girl panties tonight."

"Who needs underwear?" Cooper threw out with a wink which caused all our eyes to widen.

Cooper thrust his chin out. "Have you seen the chicks out there? Who wants to waste time with that?"

I barked out a laugh when I saw his shirt. It was white and as tight as Henry's. A rainbow coloured arrow wound its way down until it was pointed directly at his crotch, with big letters saying "Let's all go to Candyland."

I grinned. "Cooper, your shirt is the shit!"

Henry gave me a dirty look. "Are you fucking kidding me?"

I shrugged.

"Right. Can everyone hear that crowd out there?"

We all paused nervously for a moment to take in the thunderous roar made from tens of thousands of eager fans waiting impatiently for something, anything, to happen.

"That is the sound of victory, my young grasshoppers. That is the—" I gagged a little. "Shit, I think I'm gonna ralph."

Mac grasped my shoulder in the huddle, her fingers digging in tightly.

"Deep breaths, Sandwich, and hurry it the fuck up."

I sucked a few in as I looked around the group, watching the boys all looking a little green and doing the same thing. Knowing that they felt the same way, that we were all in this together, calmed me a little.

"Okay, I had a fabulous big speech all planned." I didn't really but it made me sound good. "But there's no time for grand words right now. This might feel like right now is our moment, but we've had a million of these moments, just smaller crowds, stepping stones to bigger things. This is just another stone along the paved pathway to greatness."

"Evie!" Mac shouted impatiently. "You're rambling."

"Right," I muttered and wrapped it up. "Let's go kick ass."

We made our way up the side steps of the stage and walked out to the thunderous roar. While the lights were bright enough to singe your retinas, it hadn't quite gone dark, so the thousands upon thousands of people were still easily visible and seemingly eager to get the music happening. Behind me, my boys took their places, and three giant screens formed a half circle behind them. The two on each side had a giant photo from our photo shoot: my naked body plastered all over Henry, the boys all looking sexy and shirtless. The middle screen was showing current video feed, and I could see myself, larger than I would have ever wanted to, moving towards the microphone in the middle of the stage.

Chapter Twenty-Two

Mac's eyes, panicked and worried, met mine as I made my way off stage for a quick breather between sets.

It was Jared. I just knew. My steps faltered and I moved towards her feeling like I was wading through mud until I stood before her, not breathing, just waiting.

"Jared's been shot," was her words.

I let out a shaky breath and seemingly on autopilot, I shifted away and began searching the side of the stage for my phone.

"Did you hear me? What are you doing?"

"Where's my phone?" I muttered.

"Evie!"

I stood and yelled at her. "Where's my goddamn phone?"

Mac, never one to put up with any lip from me, silently pulled my phone from her pocket and handed it over.

I slid the unlock key and ignoring the messages that still flooded the screen after having it switched off for twenty-four hours, I began dialling Jared's number.

No answer.

"Talk to me Mac. Where's Travis and Coby?"

"I don't freaking know anything," she replied with a voice full of worry.

Mac grabbed my hand and tugged me back towards the stage.

"What are you doing?"

She stopped to face me. "Evie, I'm sorry. I shouldn't have told you, but how could I keep it from you? And now you have to get back up there. You were only supposed to be off for a couple of minutes."

"Are you high? I can't get up there. I need to get on a plane. I need to get home."

My phone beeped a message and I clutched it in my hands like a lifeline.

I can only hope he lives long enough to see you die first.

I felt my face drain of colour, and Mac snatched the phone out of my hand.

"Fuck!" she shouted so loud several people stopped and stared. "Fuck!" she shouted again, not caring about said people staring. "We need to find Travis and Coby. Scratch that. I need to find them. You get back out on stage."

"Mac—"

"No, Sandwich. Right now there is nothing we can do until we know something, so get back out there until we do."

I reluctantly did what I was told, and after what felt like two years had passed, we wrapped up our set. I remained backstage while the stage hands scurried around to take down our equipment and setup for Sins of Descent.

By that time, Coby and Travis had returned, so I made a beeline straight for my brother. He picked me up until my feet left the ground and squeezed hard enough to bruise a rib or two. "Evie, you were amazing!"

"Coby," I wheezed out and he let go. "Jared?"

"Fine. He's fine," Coby reassured me and I sucked in what felt like my first real breath in an hour. "Just winged on the arm, couple of stitches."

The relief had me giddy, but it wouldn't stop the worry until I could see the damage for myself. "Did Mac show you the message? What about Jimmy?"

Coby shook his head in frustration and my heart sank.

"Foiled again? Who does this guy think he is? I can't believe it! How does this happen?"

The man must have made an alliance with the Teenage Mutant Ninja Turtles and was hiding out somewhere in the sewers, popping up just long enough to send me his sinister little messages or take pot shots at us.

I didn't wait for an answer from Coby because I was too pissed off to be patient and also because I didn't really think he could provide one. Instead, I got my phone back off Mac and sent Jared a message.

E: What, still applying for Wolverine status?

To my relief, the reply was immediate.

J: Anything is worth keeping you safe.

Not anything. *It's not worth your life Jared*, I thought to myself. I typed out a reply.

E: Are you okay?

J: Be better when you're home.

E: Come to our Sydney show?

J: Wild horses, baby.

His words released the tension that had held my body tight and left me thinking that maybe things between us might actually be okay.

283

We kicked off the tour, and it was the busiest and most exhausting time of my entire life. Between sound checks, performing, promotional interviews, after parties, and catching sleep wherever possible, I'd realised it was a blessing in disguise. The attachment I'd formed to Jared was more powerful than I could have imagined, and the whirlwind of the tour left me with no time to wallow.

We still managed to do what we did best, which was message each other every day. On our trip to the city of Brisbane, Mac snapped a photo on my phone of Henry and I on stage, the crowd cheering behind us, and I messaged it to Jared.

E: The tough life of a rockstar.

J: You look hot, babe. Next time send video so I can hear your voice.

Two days later, I got a photo of Jared and Peter sitting on his couch at the loft, white stuffing suspiciously hanging out the side of Peter's mouth.

J: Good news is that Peter is now hanging with me. Bad news is I need to go shopping for new couch cushions.

I laughed, feeling light and happy, and set the photo as the background on my phone.

A week later, we hit Melbourne's Etihad Stadium for a record crowd capacity of over fifty-eight thousand people. This was our home city before moving to Sydney, so we had plenty of supporters and fans backing us for the two shows we performed there.

Uploaded onto YouTube was a video of one of our songs played at Melbourne's Etihad, so I messaged Jared the link to it.

E: Here's your video.

Ten minutes later.

J: How did you know that song is my favourite?

I knew because I'd seen his eyes darken intently when I'd played it the night we'd had our scout.

Four days later, we landed back in Sydney and went straight into sound check, then directly to our dressing room, where it took an hour to get my Rockstar Goddess face on because my hands shook with the thought of seeing Jared that night.

By the time I'd slipped on the outfit I'd first worn at the Florence Bar, courtesy of Mac, he hadn't arrived. By the time I hit the stage, he still wasn't there. Eventually, I gave up craning my neck towards the right side of the stage because it was likely the audience would start thinking I was having a stroke. Just as I drew in a deep breath to begin crooning our final song of the night, I succumbed, peeked over, and there he stood. He was watching me with a faint smile on his face, arms folded as he leaned casually against the panelled wall.

I missed my cue and if you saw how good he looked and knew the instant feeling of being complete after two weeks of feeling slightly disconnected from reality, you wouldn't blame me. I twirled my finger at the band to indicate they should keep up an instrumental until I found my place.

Henry meandered close as he plucked at his guitar, and I held the microphone down and threw an apology his way as he glanced at me questioningly. I nodded towards the side of the stage, and Henry followed my gaze. Understanding and relief filled his face, and he stepped back, fingers still moving like lightening up and down the strings without missing a beat.

Not missing my cue a second time, I crooned out our final song. When the final note rang out, security detail flipped out when I jammed the microphone back in the stand and jumped off the front of the stage. I stood in the gated area that had formed a barrier between us and the masses, and the crowd squealed when I reached out for hands, chatted to locals, and got my photo taken numerous times. The band followed suit, and our posse of security did not look pleased. Soon after, a strong muscled pair of arms encircled me from behind, lifted me up to the cheers of the crowd, and walked me over to the back area of the stage.

I was set down gently but still in their grasp, so I twisted around, and if possible, Jared's arms circled me tighter when my eyes hit his. The connection in that moment was immediate, and I knew, after all this time, I finally *knew* there was no more avoiding and no more lying to myself or anyone else. I really did love this man, belonged to him like no other, and no matter what that meant for my future, whatever we had in the now would remain with me all of my life.

"Evie," he whispered and tucked that rogue curl behind my ear in a gesture so familiar, so loving, tears pricked my eyes.

I palmed his cheek, brushing my thumb softly across his bottom lip.

"Jared," I whispered in return, my lips now mere inches from his own.

He closed the gap and his lips pressed against mine, soft and hesitant at first. I gripped both sides of his head and mashed my lips hard against his, wanting to get closer because it wasn't enough. He groaned at my impatience, and his mouth opened under the pressure, our tongues swirling together until completely immersed in his touch, I forgot where I was.

When he pulled away I would have stumbled had I not been held so tightly in his arms. "Sorry I didn't get here sooner."

"You're here now."

His brow furrowed. "I know...but I can't stay. We're in the middle of an investigation, and Casey is going overseas in a couple of days for four months." His hand caressed my hair gently. "I'll meet you back at the after party, okay?"

I nodded and he made to leave. "Wait!" I grabbed his arm as he started to turn. I didn't know what I wanted to say, only that I wasn't ready for him to leave, so I stood mutely for a moment. "Do you ah...know where the after party is?"

He took hold of my hand. "Florence Bar Mac said. That right?"

I nodded and he let go of my hand and turned to leave again.

"Um..."

He stopped, waiting patiently, not for something intelligent I hoped, while I tried to think of something else to say.

Jared looked faintly amused as he stood patiently. "Baby, you okay?"

Realising I was being silly, I informed him I was fine, planted a swift kiss on his cheek, and shooed him off with a quick wave.

The corners of his mouth tilted upwards, and he tapped a finger to my nose. "See you, Evie."

He turned and I watched him leave until his tall form disappeared from view, happily unaware that the next forty-eight hours would be the most critical of my entire life. If I had known in that one moment that the next time I saw Jared he'd be looking at me as though I'd crawled out from under a rock, that he would be telling me he wished he'd never met me with the burn of regret in his eyes, I wouldn't have let him go.

Later that night, I sat in a booth at the bar wondering when Jared would arrive and decided to send him a message.

E: I miss you.

I didn't get a response, and immediately wished there was some way I could retract it. Was it too much? Putting myself out there wasn't easy, especially considering my past mistakes, and my stomach rolled with uncertainty.

I tucked my phone back in my bag and turned to watch Mac flirt with the bar manager, Jack, at a nearby table. I grinned at his dazed appearance. I hoped something came of it because I could see myself having fun with that—Jack and Mac. Their celebrity name would be McJack. I got my phone back out and sent a message to Mac, watching her fight a grin as she flicked open the text and read it.

E: You two would be McJack.

I watched her type out a response, and my phone buzzed a few seconds later.

M: You do realise you're sitting by yourself don't you, Nigel?

E: Nigel? Original much? You two together sound like a drive through burger.

I chuckled to myself and saw Mac give out an embarrassing snort of laughter when she read my reply. My phone buzzed again, and I was surprised because I didn't see her text a response. My heart quickened when I saw Jared's name.

J: Miss you too. Be there in an hour.

The uncertainty disappeared, replaced with butterflies at the knowledge I would see him soon, and I felt a brilliant smile light my face. I took a sip of my metro just as Ethan slammed down a tray full of shots on the table.

"What's with the sexy hot grin, sweetheart, and why are you all on your lonesome?"

"Nothing," I replied and waved at the empty booth seat. "And no one wants to sit with me because I'm lame and boring."

"Rubbish. Everyone loves you. You must be giving *fuck off* vibes."

I raised a lofty brow. "If I am, they don't seem to be working on you."

"That's because no one ever tells me to fuck off, sweetheart, so I wouldn't know that particular vibe if it came up and bit me on the ass." He grabbed two shots off the tray, handed one over to me, and held one for himself. "Now have a shot because these are for the two of us. We singers have to stick together because no one knows how tough we really have it."

"We have it tough?"

"Of course. We're stuck up the front. We have the microphone. The pressure is on us to make friends with the crowd, get them on our side, make them want to hear more. Now suck it back," he ordered.

I shrugged and did just that, my eyes watering like I'd chomped down on a green chilli. He watched me drink it down with a grin before he did his own.

"Not trying to kill me off, are you?" I wheezed out and thumped my chest as though that would somehow alleviate the burn. "One more show left to do first."

He handed over another shot, and I attempted to delay its burning descent by making conversation. "What's the go with Matt? I haven't seen him hook up with anyone during this tour of Oz, and there are so many gorgeous girls at these after parties."

We both looked over to Matt who was near the bar, chatting animatedly to Jake as he waved his drink around.

Ethan gave me a funny look, sitting his shot back down before drinking it. "He's into guys, Evie. You knew that, didn't you?"

"I...what?"

"Gay, Evie. Matt's gay." He spelled it out as though I was five years old.

My mouth flew open and I gripped the table in shock. "Oh." How did I not know this? I peeled my fingers away in order to suck back another shot.

"I thought you knew this. You two are friends, aren't you? Yo, Matt!" Ethan hollered.

Matt glanced up and caught Ethan's nod to join us.

"What are you doing, Ethan?" My eyes darted nervously around the room as I felt the urge to flee.

"Clearing the air."

Matt reached our table and picked up a shot. "Shots, huh?" He sucked it back before slamming the glass back on the table with a slight hiss.

"So, Mattie," Ethan drawled out. "Our Evie didn't realise you were batting for the boys."

I practically clenched my butt cheeks in embarrassment. I quickly picked up another shot off the tray and sucked it back.

Matt flushed a little and scratched at the back of his neck, a habit I noticed he did when nervous. "Well, I'm not really out to the whole world." He shrugged at me as though in apology.

"Well I don't go announcing 'Hey, I'm Evie and I like guys,' so there's no expectation for me to think you should. I was just surprised that's all because...well..."

Matt gave me a curious look. "Because why?"

He tossed back another shot as I answered him. "Well, because I've seen a lot of publicity of you with other girls."

"Yeah that," Ethan muttered. "That's our publicity department for you. Making things never really seem quite what they are because they think we might lose sales. It's fucked up bullshit."

The puzzle pieces clicked into place and nodding, I stood up to visit the bathroom. "Whoa," I mumbled as I wobbled. I grabbed for the table and Matt grabbed for my arm to hold me steady. "Those shots crept up on me, I think."

I stepped forward unsteadily and Matt and Ethan shared a look that seemed to communicate something without saying anything at all.

"Dance with me," Matt murmured in my ear, tugging on the arm he hadn't let go of.

I readily agreed and he led me out to the dance floor where I wrapped my arms around him tightly like a lifeline because if I didn't, I was pretty sure I would ass plant on the floor.

"Evie," he bent down and whispered in my ear. "Are you all right?"

I looked up into his midnight eyes and tried to focus, but all I got was blurred vision and unresponsive limbs. "Actually, I'm not so sure I am."

He ran an arm gently down my back until his fingers touched mine and he tucked my hand in his. "Come on. Let's get out of here."

I nodded blankly. "Fresh air."

That was the last thing I remembered because it felt like only a minute later I was blinking sore, gritty eyes open in a strange bed in another hotel room. I moaned, holding my head at the movement and frowned as I took in the room. Weren't we back in Sydney? Why wasn't I at home?

I felt a warm, male body stir and roll over at my movement, wrapping an arm around me. A warm, *naked* male body. What the hell? I sat up hastily and looked down to see Matt lying there sleeping peacefully. His hand slid down at my sudden movement and gripped my hip possessively.

I almost shrieked in horror and slapped a hand over my mouth. Quickly, I slid my legs over the side of the bed, wincing at the hideous hammering that pounded my skull. I panicked when I realised I was only wearing my two little black scraps of underwear and my heart sank. I racked my brain but I couldn't remember a thing. All I knew was that this wasn't me. I wasn't the person who went out and drank and just slept with anyone.

I flew off the bed and raced to the bathroom, throwing up the entire contents of my stomach. Oh God, what had I done? In less than twenty-four hours, I'd lost the one thing that had come to matter more to me than anything. The thought left me empty and weak and sinking into a tight ball on the floor, I pressed my forehead against the cold tiles and sobbed until there was nothing left.

Chapter Twenty-Three

A warm hand brushed at the skin of my back.

"Evie, I…"

I weakly pushed up off the floor, feeling like a giant wrecking ball had taken a few aims at my head. I wiped at my face and imagined that Matt was probably thinking he'd somehow stumbled onto the set of a horror movie.

Wearing nothing but a small hotel towel perched precariously about his hips, he helped me up until I sat on the edge of the bath. I watched him carefully as he ran a washcloth under the tap and began wiping gently at my face. He looked how I felt: pale, red eyes, unsteady, and wincing at every movement.

"What the hell happened, Matt?" I croaked out.

He paused to look at me, frowning, confused. "I don't know."

Random snippets flittered through my head: the bar, Ethan, shots, Matt. Matt! Matt was gay!

He turned back to the sink and I grabbed his arm, stopping his movement. "We couldn't have done anything, right? I mean, you…you're gay, I remember our conversation."

He cringed. "I don't know."

"You don't know?" We both winced at my voice which hit a frequency so high it should have been inaudible to anyone but dogs.

What I did know was that I needed to find my clothes and my phone because everyone would be frantic and wildly furious. If I wasn't already wishing the wrecking ball pounding my head had taken me out quickly and quietly, the wrath of Coby and my friends would be enough to have me wishing for a speedy death.

I stood up and immediately pitched forward. Matt grabbed at me and between the two of us we managed a shuffle back into the bedroom.

"Where are my clothes?"

Matt chuckled. "I'm not answering that on the grounds that I don't want to keep repeating myself. Sit down, I'll go look."

"No," I pushed away from him. "I'll look. You go find your own."

As I shuffled out to the front room of the suite, Coby and Travis burst through the hotel door. I jumped and the fright had my stomach rolling.

"Holy shit!" Travis was taken off guard by my involuntary leap, his eyes trailing over my almost naked appearance.

The relief on Coby's face was immediate as he did a full body scan for potential injuries. "Evie, thank fuck," he whispered, his whole body seeming to sag.

Spying my skirt and top on the floor, I made a grab for them just as Coby seized me, yanking me in for a hug so tight I could feel him trembling.

"God, honey. I thought we'd lost you. I've never been so scared in all my life."

He pushed me back to glare into my eyes, and I waited for the wrath of hell to rain down upon me but before he could open his mouth, Matt came out of the bedroom, hair mussed, slipping on his jeans in a scene that made me want to melt into a little puddle of nothing and ooze quietly out under the door.

Both Travis and Coby looked instantly furious, and I wondered if my day could get any worse.

"Get the door right now, Travis," Coby ordered, fists clenching tightly to his sides.

Travis moved to the front door at the speed of light, but even that wasn't fast enough to waylay Jared, who a second later burst through it.

Besides looking frantic, he also looked completely and utterly exhausted, and the sight had tears stinging my eyes.

I grasped the edge of the couch as I felt the room tilt, realising that yes, my day could get worse. Just like Coby, Jared's eyes did a rapid scan of my body for potential injury. Seeing none, the relief vanished from his face when his eyes shifted to Matt who was still in the process of casually buttoning up his jeans. His eyes swivelled back to me in my underwear, then back again to Matt, and I saw comprehension dawn in his eyes.

"You goddamn motherfucker," he ground out at Matt.

If I'd thought Jared was a sight to behold when he last faced off with Matt, it was nothing compared to how he looked now. Now, his eyes were cold and his face was carefully composed and completely blank, the whites of his knuckles the only tell-tale sign of his fury.

Perhaps Matt was either too jaded or a bit daft because he stopped buttoning his jeans and simply folded his arms with a smirk. I could only conclude he had a death wish.

In the blink of an eye, Jared rushed him.

"Jared, no!" I called out in panic.

Travis grabbed Jared about the waist as Coby moved to stand between him and Matt, and I felt immediate relief that certain violence had been avoided.

Unfortunately, my relief was short-lived because while Travis held Jared back, Coby turned to Matt and slammed a fist in his face. "Stay the hell away from my little sister, you fucking asshole."

Oh. My. God.

During the scuffle and before the situation could deteriorate any further, if that was possible, I quickly slipped my clothes on.

Jared shoved Travis away in irritation as Matt held a hand to his jaw. Coby stood looking slightly satisfied, and I returned to grasping the edge of the couch like a life preserver.

"Fuck!" Jared roared and I flinched as he slammed a fist in the wall. Then he stood there, his back to all of us, head tilted to the floor, breathing hard. I wanted to close my eyes but they were stuck watching his body radiate pain as he struggled for control. He turned and pointed a finger at Matt. "You're not worth it."

His body shifted to face me and his gaze was so carefully constructed, and so empty, I couldn't breathe. "Neither of you are." He turned and walked out the door.

Hearing his words, seeing him walk out the door like I was nothing, had me feeling like my life was circling the drain. I wanted to hide, I wanted to cry, and I wanted to yell at him to let me explain. I ran out after him.

"Wait!" I called out to his retreating back.

He stopped but didn't turn around. His shoulders moved up and down as though he was taking deep breaths, and when he did eventually turn, his face was still blank.

"Jared, I…it's not what you think."

I hadn't made a joke but he laughed anyway, and I hated how the sarcasm sounded on his lips.

"Really? It's not what I think?" He rubbed at his jaw. "Did you find it amusing that I trusted you? Because I never thought I would trust anyone again until I met you. Not once did I ever doubt my feelings for you or the absolute faith I had in putting those feelings in your hands, until now. Christ, Evie." The hand that was rubbing his jaw now moved over his face, and I stood silently, each word feeling like a poisonous dart as I waited for him to finish. "I can't remember the last time I slept. I was out, *we* were out all night looking for you. I thought I was going to lose my mind thinking Jimmy had finally gotten his hands on you but…" he waved his hand towards the suite door "…here you were, sleeping with someone else."

"Jared, please," I whispered, wrapping my arms around myself as tears climbed my throat.

He looked at me in disgust, and the last time I could ever remember feeling so low was the day my mum had died.

"Did I really mean so little?"

"He, I…Matt. I didn't…"

"You didn't what?" He spread his arms wide. "You didn't fuck him? Is that what you're trying to tell me?"

I hesitated. "I…" Struggling to remember the events of last night, I couldn't offer anything. It would have been impossible for anything to have happened, I would've known, and Matt was gay. I needed to tell Jared, and even though it wasn't my place to share Matt's private business, in this situation I was sure he would understand.

"I would have given you the world, done anything for you, but you were always too scared to take that final step." He sighed and rubbed at the furrow between his brows. "You know what I wish? I wish that I had never fucking met you," he whispered, raking his gaze over me from top to toe and back up again, making sure I could see the insult in his eyes.

Before I could say anything, he turned and left. This time I let him go because even though some days I felt like I could move mountains, today was not one of those days.

Feeling completely drained, I sank down against the wall of the hallway as the look on Jared's face played on repeat inside my head.

Travis walked out and took in my pathetic huddle, my head on my knees, my hands wrapped around my ankles. I knew his first instinct was likely to slap me into next week for doing whatever he thought I did to his brother, but as he crouched down to eye level, the concern furrowing his brow must have won out over anger. "Come on, Evie. Let's get you out of here. Go get your bag, okay?"

He gently brushed his hand down the side of my head before he stood back up.

I pushed up off the wall but my limbs struggled to respond. In fact, it felt like I couldn't breathe, and I slumped uselessly back against the wall, taking shallow breaths as my panicked gaze hit Travis's.

"What the hell?" he muttered under his breath and crouched back down in front of me. "Show me your eyes," he ordered and looked into their red dilated depths. "Oh hell no. Fucking hell! Have you taken anything?"

"I, drugs? What? No! The hardest thing I've ever taken in my life is a Panadol."

Well unless you counted the times that Asshole Kellar slipped whatever the hell he did into my drink, but that wasn't voluntary. Panic over the whole situation must have blinded me to the same symptoms, and adrenaline must have kept me going, because now I was crashing. Hard.

"Coby?" Travis shouted. "Get out here."

He slipped an arm under my back, one under my knees, and lifted me up. Feeling woozy but safe, I huddled into his chest and gratefully closed my eyes. I wanted to be angry, but my energy levels had reached critical flashy red light status and that image of Jared was still stuck on repeat, ensuring I wouldn't forget the pain.

"What is it?" I dimly heard Coby ask.

Travis sounded grim as he cradled me gently to his chest. "She's been drugged."

I tried to lift my head to speak to Coby and tell him I was okay, that I was sorry, but I couldn't move.

My eyes were slits as I watched Coby slam his fist against the wall in anger, jaw ticking as he struggled for control. At that moment, I hated myself for what my actions had done to him. Our lives had not been easy: Dad taking off, losing Mum, him taking responsibility for me only to watch me slowly self-destruct. Now it appeared to be happening all over again. He pulled out his phone and began dialling, and I closed my eyes again because the agony in his expression was enough to make me want to howl.

After a moment, he spoke. "Jared's phone is off. Can you get her to the hospital for me, Travis? She needs to be checked over. I want a blood test so we've got the means to lay this fucker out."

I heard him whisper something further in Travis's ear, but I couldn't make it out. All I knew was that what he said was cause for Travis to grip me tighter in his arms, and I felt a shudder rip through his body.

He rumbled something, feeling the soothing vibrations against his chest, and next thing I knew I was being placed gently in a car.

Travis climbed in the driver's seat, started the car, and negotiated his way out of the parking lot.

I stared blankly out the car window as I spoke. "I saw Jared last night. At the stadium," I whispered. "I never felt anything so right in all my life as what I felt when he was there. I love him so much, Travis. You know that, don't you?"

I turned to face him, and he shot me a sympathetic glance as he drove.

"Sweetheart, everything will work out. I promise you. I don't know how you managed to slip out last night without one of us noticing you. We all feel responsible, so don't place the blame on yourself. You were drugged so I would imagine you didn't even know you'd left. It's our fault. This is on us because we were supposed to be looking after you."

I heard my phone ring, interrupting my intended reply, and I reached for my bag while Travis fumbled in his pocket. He pulled out my phone and handed it over with a shrug.

"We found it on the table at the bar. That's why it took so long for us to find you. We couldn't track you through your phone."

I glanced at the display, noting an unknown number.

"Hello?" I mumbled.

The sinister voice that answered left me reeling. "Hello, Evie."

I let my breath out in a whoosh and when Travis gave me a questioningly glance, I put the phone on speaker.

"Jimmy? Is that you?"

Travis swore under his breath, yanking the steering wheel hard left and pulling off to the side of the road. He put his finger to his lips, and I nodded to indicate I understood he wanted to listen quietly.

"Yes, you remember me? Good. This must be a nice surprise for you."

Oh yes, a lovely surprise because remember when I thought my day couldn't get worse? I was ready to tell him to go dip himself in a pot of boiling oil, and then throw my phone out the window, but Travis rolled his hand to indicate I should keep talking.

I nodded back in reply. "I...ahh..." What does one say to a sinister stalker? *How are you? What are you up to today? Any murder plans or kidnapping on the cards? Yes? Oh good, let me know how that works out for you.* I decided to keep it simple. "What do you want?"

"I'm so glad you asked me that, Evie. I wanted to welcome you home from your tour. I've missed seeing you."

Thoughts of him seeing me literally had me gagging, and Travis reached out and took my hand, squeezing it tightly in support.

"Have I lost you, Evie? Still there?"

I nodded in response even though he couldn't see me. "Yes, yes I'm here." My voice trembled and I hated that Jimmy could hear the fear in it.

"Good. You know, with you being surrounded by your goon squad and the tour and all, I haven't been able to give you the Christmas gift I promised you."

"I don't want anything from you, Jimmy." I wanted to kick the dash of the car as anger overtook the fear and I glared at the phone.

He let out a shout of laughter. "Well, I'm afraid it's too late for that."

I glanced at Travis in panic and his hand gripped mine tighter.

"What do you mean?"

Jimmy gave a loud, dramatic sigh. "Are you saying you don't remember last night? I'm not surprised." He chuckled. "I must say, having the drugs slipped into your drinks I was hoping you'd slip out all on your lonesome, and I'd finally get my hands on you, but no," he snarled, starting to sound angry, "you had to stumble your way out with that pierced, tattooed loser. Tell me, have you moved on from Jared so quickly?"

I sat there in blank shock. "That was you?"

"Of course it was me. Thought it was a nice touch after I read about what happened between you and that James Kellar all those years ago.

What would have been nicer was if there was a nice high balcony where you could have had your second chance and finally got it right."

"James Kellar?" Travis mouthed at me with a questioning glance.

I shook my head at him in reply, and my body, though completely worn down, still managed to shake in anger.

"You stupid asshole," I shouted. "If you think—"

"Now, now," he interrupted. "No need to be an ungrateful bitch. I only wanted to make sure you were happy with your present. Now that I know, I can tell you you'll get the rest of it tonight. I can't wait, can you?"

He hung up and I threw my phone at the dash, wishing for a quick, effective teleportation to the fluffy white cloud that was my bed. I had a serious urge to bunker down until my next life was upon me.

My phone once again began a mad buzz, and I picked it back up to see it was simply notification of a flood of messages and missed calls which right now seemed like a mountain I was unable to climb. I threw the phone back at the dash and glanced at Travis.

His jaw was clenched and if I had to determine the expression on his face, I would liken it to really fucking unhappy. I placed a gentle hand on his arm as he gripped the steering wheel tightly. "Hey."

He jolted, as though a million miles away. "Sick of this shit," he muttered. He pulled out his phone, dialled, and held it to his ear. "Coby," he said after a moment. "No, we're not there yet. You need to get Matt down to the hospital too because the drugs were from Jimmy. Yeah, I know, could be he got dosed too." He paused for a long moment. "No shit? Well he's promised something else for tonight, so we need to meet with security. No, he didn't, but it's their last show of the tour so you'd think he'd—" Another long pause. "Roger that."

Travis hung up and carelessly tossed his phone to the dash, meeting mine in a joint huddle of rejection. Pulling back out into traffic, he spoke as he concentrated on the road. "Are you okay?"

"Not really."

"Coby said Matt told him that a tray of shots were the only drinks you two shared so—"

"Ethan!" I blurted out. "He bought the tray of shots."

Was he somehow in on the whole thing? That didn't make sense.

"*So* Matt spoke to Ethan and Ethan told him that a man by the bar handed him the tray of shots, telling him it was your drink order and could he take them over to you."

"Do you think it was Jimmy that gave him the actual tray?"

Travis nodded as pulled up at a set of red lights, indicating to turn left. "Either him or someone he's paid off. We've got someone heading over there to see about getting footage from the bar's security cameras."

We were both quiet for the rest of the drive to the hospital, and twenty minutes later, I was sitting on the edge of a hospital bed in the emergency department. Travis sat in the corner murmuring quietly into the phone that now appeared to have become surgically attached to his ear since we vacated the car.

When the privacy curtain flung open and Matt stalked in, Travis quickly ended his call and stood, slowly unfolding his glowering, six foot four inch intimidating frame out of the chair.

Matt ignored him, instead, focusing on me by looking me over carefully. "I want to talk to, Evie. In private," he said to Travis without taking his eyes from mine.

Travis didn't budge and I took a brief moment to appreciate his glaring stance because the take charge Valentine men were always a sight to behold.

"It's okay, Travis."

He nodded and slowly closed the distance between himself and Matt. "I'll be right outside, Evie." He trained his eyes on Matt in silent warning as he left.

"You okay?" Matt asked.

I cringed at his reddened jaw. "Am *I*?" I huffed out a brief laugh. "What about you? You'll be glad to see the back of me. I keep getting you into situations where you come out of it with a punch to the face.

Unless, uh, violence is your kinda thing? I mean you don't seem to possess the natural, inherent capacity for fear like most people do. Fear can be a good thing, you know," I joked. "Keeps you alive."

He snickered quietly. "Sorry. I can't help it. Jared reminds me of someone I used to know."

"And that makes you antagonistic because?"

Matt did his whole scratch the back of his neck, nervous habit thing and let out a big sigh. "Because the someone I used to know is...was someone I loved and he..." Matt stopped and I saw actual tears form in his eyes. "He..."

Matt sagged against the side of the bed and the most I could manage was a brief shuffle to get close and wrap one arm around his defeated form.

"You don't need to say any more. I get it now. I'm sorry."

The silence for a few moments was comforting.

"I'm sorry about last night, Evie. It's coming back to me little by little. The way you acted straight after the shots immediately had Ethan and I on edge. That's why I pulled you up for the dance. I wanted to keep an eye on you and also see if I could pinpoint anyone watching you by moving around on the dance floor without being obvious. Honestly, I was only looking out for you, but after we hit fresh air outside, I just felt so out of it. How we got back to my suite, I don't really know. I vaguely remember peeling off my clothes, crawling into bed, and passing out, so I can assure nothing happened. No offence, but what you've got doesn't do it for me at all. That combined with heavy drinking and drugs, well, I wouldn't have been able to get it up for anyone."

"You were looking out for me, Matt, and you have nothing to apologise for. I'm the one who's sorry. Coby told you about Jimmy?" Matt nodded so I continued. "We can't seem to shake him off because he keeps going underground. I've been starting to think he must be living in the sewers." I mustered a smile.

Travis came back in. "Talk's over guys. The nurse will be here in a couple of minutes."

303

Matt nodded, gave my shoulder a reassuring pat, and said he'd see me tonight before he left the room.

"Travis—"

Travis held up a palm to cut me off. "Evie, you should know I heard your entire conversation. I'm supposed to be keeping an eye on you so the other side of the curtain was the furthest I was willing to go. Sorry for the lack of privacy but right now that's the least of our concerns."

"So you know about Matt then?"

He nodded.

"Well he's not out to the world, Travis, so please keep that bit of information to yourself."

Travis looked a bit insulted. "Do you think I'm gonna go to the nearest tabloids, Evie? Relax. I'm telling Jared though."

"Have you spoken to him yet? I don't have my phone. I left it on your dash."

"Fuck, sweetheart." Travis's eyes flared irritably. "You need to keep your phone with you at all times okay? We've told you that before."

The curtain whipped open again and this time Coby strode in. Reaching my side, he rubbed my back gently as he asked how I was doing. Telling him I was doing much better, he still ordered me to lie down.

When the nurse came in, she commanded Coby and Travis to leave, not looking the least intimidated when they both folded their arms and didn't budge.

She eyed the two massive specimens of man and let out a sigh as she turned to me. "How did you get so lucky? Not just one, but two of them. Bit greedy, aren't you?" she said with a wink.

I chuckled thinking it would probably bring on a stroke if Jared and Casey put in an appearance as well. "You haven't seen the rest of them."

She gave me a look of disbelief as she tied a tourniquet around my bicep in preparation to take a blood sample. "There's more of those? Honey, I am your new best friend."

"I could always do with more friends," I offered.

She swabbed the inside of my elbow with an alcoholic wipe. "So what are we testing for today?"

Coby spoke up, sparks firing in his eyes. "She was drugged last night at a bar."

"What time was that?"

Everyone looked at me as they waited for an answer, and I started to feel light-headed as I racked my brain for the time. "Um.......maybe about one...ish?"

The nurse wrote something down before she came at me with a needle.

"Sweetie," she said, looking sympathetic. She frowned at both Coby and Travis before she leaned close to my ear, lowering her voice until I strained to hear her. "Do we need to do a rape kit?"

My blood instantly ran cold and then hot as I flushed uncomfortably. "No! No...nothing like that happened."

She turned to look at Coby and Travis again. "Maybe you should leave," she asked pointedly, obviously thinking I was unwilling to admit anything with the two of them in the room.

Coby shook his head stubbornly and the nurse sighed.

The curtain shoved open again, and Mitch walked in looking tired and rumpled, his detective badge clipped to the waistband of his worn jeans. His eyes immediately found mine and they softened with concern.

"My God," the nurse barked out, and everyone jerked at the sound, including her. At her sudden movement, I feared the needle in my arm would snap clean in half and my blood would spurt out in some horror movie parody. "You were right, there *is* more. How many more? You need to pre-warn unsuspecting females about these types of things."

This was true and I would have voiced my agreement, however, I was too busy cringing in pain.

She mumbled an apology and began to fill another vial full of blood. How much was she going to take? I wanted to shout for biscuits and orange juice STAT before I started to fade away.

After she finished harassing me with medical devices, and after I'd told Mitch everything I could remember, twice, Coby took me home so I could sleep off the effects of the drugs. I spoke to both Mac and Henry before I dozed off, promising I would be in the best shape of my life to perform the last show of the tour at the Sydney stadium tonight.

In the early afternoon, Peter's loud snoring woke me, and I could hear rummaging sounds in my wardrobe. Rubbing at my face as I struggled to surface into the real world, I heard a strange muttering that sounded suspiciously like "My God, Mac was right."

When Tim bustled out of my wardrobe with an arm full of clothes, I flopped back down on my pillow, groaning at the return of the wrecking ball.

He dropped the clothes all over my bedroom floor and went rushing to the bedside table to hand over some Panadol and water.

"How are you feeling?"

I rubbed at my forehead wearily. "A hundred percent."

He forced a laugh, peppering me with questions while he fussed for a few moments before disappearing back into my wardrobe, only to return with another load of clothes.

"What are you doing?"

"Performing miracles it seems."

I set the glass of water on the bedside table and sank back into the downy depths of the doona. "Oh?"

"Mac was right. We need to go shopping."

He plucked a shirt out of the pile with the caricature of a person drinking a beer and held it up as though it was going to bite his face off. "'Rehab is for Quitters'? That has *got* to go." He shuddered with distaste and flung it across the room.

"Hey," I mumbled. "That was a present from Frog."

He held out another one and squealed. "'Come to the Nerd Side. We have Pi?' That is just weird! And lame. How many of these vile things do you have?"

"That one was from Hairy Parry. The rest are all from Cooper, so you can't throw them away, Tim. Trust me, I wear the shirts he buys me around the house all the time. He'll notice if I suddenly stop. What are you doing anyway?"

"A clean out for the Salvation Army by the looks of all this rubbish." He eyed the piles distastefully as he made his way back into the wardrobe. "This might work." He came back out holding a gold coloured silk camisole with shoestring straps. "I'm under orders from Mac to get you dressed and in Rockstar Goddess mode for tonight," he explained. He laid the camisole on my bed and disappeared again. "Go and get in the shower."

"We've got ages yet," I whined and bunkered down, Peter snuggling close as he angled for a belly scratch.

Tim emerged long enough to throw me a withering look. "Have you seen yourself? Trust me, we need all the time we can get."

"Fine," I growled and whipped back the covers. "But I'm wearing what *I* choose to wear."

As I stalked to the bathroom, I was pretty sure I heard him mumble something that sounded like, "Not in this life time."

Chapter Twenty-Four
MAC

I stood off to the side of the stage next to Coby and Travis and watched Evie strut and chatter to the mammoth crowd of Sydneysiders crammed into the stadium. You couldn't tell the shit she'd been through with the way she grinned and bantered with the audience, dazzling them with her sexy smile and glorious hair.

I grinned smugly to myself as I took in her outfit. Tim had come through, just like I knew he would. Her caramel hair hung down her back in her trademark glossy waves, and her skin glowed underneath the gold coloured strappy silk camisole. He'd teamed it with a thick gold arm band that encircled her bicep and a pair of vintage indigo Ksubi skinny jeans that I'd given her last winter when I realised, to my absolute devastation, they did her better justice.

My gaze moved to Jake as they hit the intro into the next song of their set. The conceited, egotistical bastard was shirtless again, as usual, and the muscles in his arms and chest rippled powerfully as he hammered the drums. Whatever it was about him rubbed me up the wrong way, and I knew he felt the same because whenever I got anywhere near him, he turned into a complete asshole. I gave him a good glare, not that he was watching, but it did make me feel a little better.

My gaze moved over to pretty boy Henry as he hunched over his guitar, his fingers moving along the strings like he was born doing it. He'd tried to teach me several times how to play, but I was a complete boob when it came to music, and after a while, he gave up, lacking the patience of trying to turn me into a musical genius. Maybe he thought I felt a bit left out of the whole music vibe, but I was glad I wasn't in the middle of it. Standing out there while a bazillion people watched you? No thanks. I was confident and outspoken, but I'd rather sit around a dirty campfire in the middle of the Congo and converse with snakes while chewing on alligator steaks than walk out in front of that.

My thoughts turned to next week. The band had two weeks off to recuperate before they had to get started on the songs they were planning for the first album. While they would all be busy sitting on their asses, I had meetings to arrange with all sorts of departments, bookings to sort out for studios, plan a music video, press events to respond to, and photo shoots. I also had five interviews lined up for potential assistants to help me deal with all the crap. One of them looked promising, the rest not so much. I had all my hopes on the promising one, so I'd set her interview up first.

I pulled out my phone to check for messages. Nothing. Damn you, Jared. Where the fuck are you?

As the band wrapped up the song, Evie turned to give me a questioning glance. I knew she was waiting for me to tell her the minute we'd got hold of Jared. I hid the worry from her because the moment I showed any concern would likely be the moment she fell apart. Evie depended on me to keep it together, so I shrugged, but I saw the anxiety and disappointment flitter across her face before she tucked the emotions away and forced a smile.

That's my girl. She knew how to pack it away and get the job done.

She was perfect for Jared. Her demeanour, so radiant and cheery, brought out Jared's playful side, and offset his tendency to be too serious, yet she was capable enough to pull it all together when she needed to. I loved both of them and could see the love they had for each other. When they were together, Jared couldn't take his eyes off her, and Evie's would shine. It was mushy, heart-warming stuff, not that I would admit it, but now, seeing them like this was painful. Deep down I was worried. I didn't want to see Jared alone and Evie full of regret for not taking a chance. Unfortunately, between the two of them, they were about as useful as a fart in a thunderstorm when it came to sorting their shit out. I was tired of standing back and letting them bumble around like twats. It was about time I interfered, well, interfered more than I already had. Truth was, I couldn't wait to be an aunty. Aunty Mac had quite the ring to it, and the pink frilly outfits I'd already been eyeing wouldn't buy themselves.

Whipping my phone back out, I dialled Jared's number again. Straight to voice mail. I wanted to scream with frustration. I wasn't worried about Jared physically; I knew he could take care of himself. My brother was smart, quick, and packed a shitload of muscle. I was more worried about what was going on in his head. When Evie arrived at the stadium earlier, I'd managed to pull her aside and got the lowdown on last night and this morning's events, right down to the last word and expression on Jared's face which just about broke my heart. Afterwards, she looked tired and worn out, and I regretted dragging her through all that again. Now my brother was out there thinking bad shit, and no one could freaking get hold of him to sort the whole sorry mess out.

Travis was standing next to me on the side of the stage. "Heard from Jared?" I asked.

Travis pressed his lips in a flat line as he checked his phone and then shook his head. "He'll be okay, Mac."

"I know, Travis. If only he would just check in so we could sort this freaking mess out."

"He'll show up," Travis said patiently.

I think my brothers sucked all the patience genes out of my mother before I was born because I didn't have a single one in my body.

"Yes, yes. I know he will eventually and love will prevail and I'll finally get my little niece, but I'm not the most patient of people, Travis."

He snorted. "No shit."

"So any idea of what you think this Jimmy asshole might do tonight?"

He shook his head in frustration. "Nope. Every single person who has walked into this stadium has gone through detectors, not to mention we've got sniffer dogs roving the area and bodyguards posted at every single entrance to the stadium. We've done everything humanly possible to ensure Evie's safety. Trust me. He can't get at her in here."

"Trust you, Travvie."

I gave him a quick pat on the back and turned to see Marcus walking up behind me. I raised a brow. "Marcus, what a surprise. What are you doing here?"

He grinned and waved a ticket. "Wanted to see the show of course. Can I...uh...talk to you in private for a minute?"

I glanced around at the stage to make sure everything was running smoothly and saw Jake frowning at me. Typical, the wanker. I frowned back before I turned to Marcus. "Sure," I clicked off my headset. "Just for a minute though, right?"

He nodded.

"Okay, follow me." I led him down the stairs and around the back into the makeshift dressing room.

As I pulled the door shut behind him he grabbed my arm and shoved me up against the wall. "Why haven't you called me?" He growled and planted his lips on mine for a kiss that sucked all the breath from my body. I kissed him back for a moment before I shoved him away, panting hard.

"Christ, Marcus." I walked over to the mirrors and freshened my lipstick, more so to gain some equilibrium than concern over my appearance. I looked at him through the mirror. "I've been busy, you know, with the tour."

He looked a bit sheepish. "Right, sorry. I just thought..."

"You thought what? We're only dating casually, Marcus. I did tell you that was all I wanted when we first went out, right?"

311

He sat down. "Yeah, yeah, I know. That's what I wanted to talk to you about."

Uh oh. He looked nervous. This did not bode good things.

I walked over and sat down next to him. "Marcus, I don't want to be rude, but I really need to get back. Do you want to talk now or some other time?"

He hesitated. "Might be better some other time." He gave me a hopeful smile. "Dinner next week?"

I sighed internally as I mentally reviewed my crammed schedule for next week. "Sure, that sounds good. Can I call you to set up a time and place?"

He nodded and I leaned over and placed a gentle reassuring kiss on his lips.

"Good then. I'll look forward to it," I said and stood up. "Right, I better get back. Come on, I'll walk you back out."

He followed me out and as we reached the stairs to the side of the stage I gave his arm a quick rub, telling him I'd see him soon, and walked up the stairs.

I really liked Marcus and I had nothing against relationships, which should have been obvious with the way I kept trying to shove Jared and Evie together, and one day I even looked forward to having one all of my own. One day. I liked dating. I liked meeting and getting to know different people and not having to answer to anybody. I wanted to keep it that way. Not forever, just for now. Hell, I was still only twenty-four, just a spring chicken by current standards. Besides, finding a man who could put up with a ball busting bitch like me and then go through the gauntlet that was my three older brothers was not the most simplest of tasks.

I reached the side of the stage and took my place next to Travis, clicking my headset back on. Jake caught me with another frown, and I had to put my one free hand in my pocket to refrain from giving him the finger. Dumbass. I couldn't believe he actually accused me of being a maneater. Of all the freaking nerve. I'd never been anything but honest, maybe more than I needed be. Evie had mentioned more than once that I needed a prescription for tact pills. I tried, really, but I was who I was, and if some people couldn't accept that then they could stick it up their hooha. You couldn't like or please everyone right?

A voice crackled in my ear. "Mac? George. I'm at Gate E. There's a delivery for Jamieson."

"Another one? Roger that, George. Let me check the schedule." I flipped through the paperwork on my clipboard. "I can't see anything. Do you know what it is?"

"Just looks like a case of booze. Do you want it scanned?"

"Hang on, I'll check." I turned to Travis. "Another unscheduled delivery for Jamieson," I said with a sigh. "Do you want it scanned? George thinks it's likely just alcohol."

Travis nodded. "Scan it first. Tell George to trust nothing."

I spoke into the headset. "Scan it please, George. Travis said to trust nothing. Then let me know."

"Roger that, Mac."

I plopped my clipboard on top of a standby amp and sat on an empty stool, rubbing at my shoulder with fatigue.

Travis came up behind me and gave my shoulders a quick massage. "You doing okay, little sis?"

"Yeah, God yeah, don't worry about me. I'm just tired and busy. Hopefully, we'll have an assistant by the end of next week, and I can stop chewing off all my lovely manicures from the stress."

The headset crackled in my ear again. "Mac, George, Gate E. We've got an all clear on the delivery."

"Cool, can you have it sent up?"

"No can do, Mac, sorry. We're stretched thin tonight to cover every damn entryway in this joint. Can you come down?"

I sighed. It wouldn't do to not bother with it, even if it was only alcohol, in case it had come from some industry bigwig that we needed to play kissy face with. "Okay, I'll see you in a minute."

The band wrapped up what was their second to last song for the night according to the schedule on my clipboard, and Frog raced over to the side of the stage. "Mac, quick, I need to change a guitar string. Can you run to the supply bag backstage and grab me one?"

"Sure, be right back."

I moved quickly, grabbing the string and heading back to the side of the stage.

"Thanks," Frog muttered as he worked quickly. I checked the stage to see Evie busily joking with the crowd while she gave us the occasional glance to check Frog's progress.

I put my hand on Travis's arm to get his attention. "George gave the all clear on the delivery but they're swamped. I'm just going to quickly whiz down and grab it, okay? Be right back."

He nodded at me once and turned back to watching Evie and the crowd with serious intensity.

I trotted down the stairs at a fast pace, eager to get back and catch at least most of their last song for the night. Evie had changed the line up at the last minute and added a cover song that she'd wanted to sing for Jared. I thought it was a beautiful gesture; it was just a shame that we couldn't get in touch with him before now to see it.

The sound of Evie's voice reverberated throughout the stadium, clear and strong, betraying no hint of her current emotional turmoil. I could still hear her banter as I made my way to Gate E. Frog must have finished fixing his string because I heard her introducing the final song. Dammit, I was going to miss it. I picked up my pace as I heard her voice echo around the damp concrete walls of the stadium exterior, introducing the song *For You* by Angus and Julia Stone, simply saying the song was for someone who was her world. My eyes began to water as she started to sing, and I was thankful she wasn't able to see that.

Arriving at Gate E, there was a man standing out by a black SUV wearing jeans, a black shirt, and a red baseball cap. He was leaning casually against the back of the car, but I couldn't see George.

As I walked through the gate, the man came over. "Yo," he muttered. "You Mac?"

"Yeah that's me. You got a delivery?" I looked around. "Where's George?"

The man shrugged as he opened up the back of the car. "Dunno, mentioned something about a situation at Gate C?"

Crap. I hoped it wasn't something to do with Jimmy. We were all on edge tonight, and with Jamieson playing their final song, were on the home stretch.

I followed the man over to the back of the car, and he took off his cap and turned to grin at me.

My stomach pitched as I looked into the pair of sinister dark brown eyes I'd seen numerous times in mug shots. I opened my mouth, but before I could let out a shout, I felt a sharp, cold, excruciating pain and everything went black.

I mustn't have been out long because when I came to, I was lying in the back of the SUV as it pulled out of the stadium's exit. If I could have screamed I would, but my mouth was stuffed with something that tasted like I'd licked a goddamn dog. I gagged, the urge to vomit was intense, but I worried I'd choke, so I kept swallowing and taking deep breaths through my nose.

Bloody bastard had been so focused and intent on getting his hands on Evie, that no one, not even me, had thought *I* would be in any danger. What a colossal mistake that was. My heart ached for Evie and my brothers when they realised I was gone. Last night without Evie had been a nightmare.

I tugged at my arms but they were bound together behind my back, and I couldn't move. This asshole was not going to live to see another day if I had my bloody way. I mentally slipped on my big girl panties and sucked it up. I wasn't some defenceless little twat. I was a goddamn Valentine, and this wanker had picked the wrong bitch to mess with.

We eventually pulled into a driveway, Jimmy reversing in so the neighbours wouldn't see. I managed to take in my surroundings: a clapped out little white weatherboard house that looked like it was built before the war and had never been cleaned since.

My eyes followed Jimmy as he slammed the car door and came around to the back of the SUV, looking left to right, before he opened the back door.

"Right," he said with a grin most evildoers somehow seemed to master. I wondered if there was some kind of Dummies Guide to being an Evil Murdering Asshole being sold on the black market where he learned his craft. I could see it now: 1. Kidnap victim. 2. Grin evilly, etc.

"Make sure you take in the sunshine and the smell of fresh air, Miss Valentine, because when I get you inside that house, you ain't gonna be walking out alive. I'll be delivering you home in pieces."

I glowered at him fiercely, wishing that my eyes were able to shoot laser death rays at his head. For one moment, the bastard had actually managed to leave me feeling scared, and I hated to be scared. It made me feel weak and useless. One time in primary school, when I was eight years old, some fat little punk had locked me in the supply closest because I'd deliberately tripped him for bullying a friend. It was a sneak attack, so no one knew I was there. After being locked in there for hours, I hadn't been scared at all because I knew Jared would eventually find me, and he did.

This time I *was* scared because I *knew* that Jared wouldn't find me, at least not before it was too late. They'd been out, along with a huge Sydney task force, working on finding Jimmy for months. The likelihood of it suddenly happening in the next few hours was really fucking unlikely.

Jimmy reached in, a knife in his fisted hand, and I flinched. He chuckled as he leaned down and sliced neatly through the ties that bound my ankles together.

Not wasting any time, I rolled onto my back and kicked out with both legs. He grunted as I caught him in the gut, and I struggled as he pinned my legs down and rolled me over on to my stomach. He grabbed my bound hands and yanked me out of the car so hard I felt my shoulder wrench and my stomach roll as tears burned my eyes.

I stumbled as he took hold of my arm and jerked me up the three steps onto the patio and through the front door, shoving me so I fell to the floor. He reached behind and whipped out a gun, pointing it at my head. I whimpered as I lay panting on the floor, trying fiercely to breathe through my nose because of the gag.

He flicked off the safety and loaded a round into the chamber. "Ready to die?"

My vision blurred with tears, and I shook my head frantically. No, I wasn't ready to die, fucktard. As I fought to get to my feet, he backhanded me with the butt of the gun, and I went sprawling face first on to the floor. Black spots swam in my eyes, and I could already feel red oozy blood dripping down my brow.

Jimmy yanked me back up by the arm and dragged me to the left and through a large archway, into what I deduced was the lounge slash dining room of the humble abode. There was no furniture to speak of except for a solitary chair that sat in the middle of the room. Mould riddled the ceiling, paint was peeling off the walls, and the wooden floorboards looked filthy and half rotted.

The chair teetered as he threw me down in it and proceeded to tie my ankles to each leg while I struggled. He then re-tied my arms so they were bound around the back of the chair.

He stepped back with a smile to view his handiwork. "Now, maybe I might be ready for you to die, but first, you have chores to deal with."

I eyed him warily and he reached over to yank out my gag. I wanted to rub at my jaw, but the most I could manage was to suck in a few deep breaths.

"Nice digs, wanker," I spat out. "Save your whole pathetic life to afford this little palace?"

"Mouthy little piece, aren't you? I knew you would be. It's not only Evie I've been watching, but you too. You're a real bossy little bitch. I hate bossy bitches, but that's okay because you'll be dead soon anyway."

"Why are you doing this, Jimmy?"

He laughed as he tucked the gun into the back of his pants, moving to the window to look up and down the street. He turned back to me and folded his arms.

"Come on, Mac, I can call you Mac, can't I?"

"Oh be my guest, please," I said sarcastically.

"Your brother Jared obviously. He killed my brother Joe. So it's only fair that you should die. I'm sure you can see that. You know, I was originally only going to kill the little songbird but, you see," he sighed before continuing, "my brother Joe was a hell of a man, worth more than the two of you combined. So I decided it was in my best interests to kill the both of you, out of fairness of course. The only trouble with that plan was I could never get Evie alone. You on the other hand, well, they must not care much for you if they left you to fend for yourself. I realised that all I needed to do was get to you, and then Evie would come. It's that simple really."

I forced myself to adopt a casual attitude but inside I panicked. Evie was like my sister. Of course she would come the stupid bitch. God, I would kill her myself if she did.

I snorted. "Evie isn't going to come. She's not stupid, unlike you, asshole."

"Oh, but you're very much mistaken, Mac. She will, with you as bait. All I need to do is get her on the phone and tell her where you are. She'll come running like the good little friend she is, and then I'll have the both of you. I'm going to be generous, though, and let you know that I've decided to let Jared live. Hell..." he spread his arms wide "...I'll let all your brothers live. Do you know why I'd do that for you?"

"No, but I'm sure you're going to tell me."

He smiled at me in mock sympathy. "Because then they'll get to live without the two of you. Can you imagine that? I wonder what will happen to them knowing that you both died and it was all their fault."

I closed my eyes as my heart sank. The goddamn fucker was right. I couldn't imagine how my brothers would deal with Evie and I gone. I didn't think Jared would survive it.

"So, tell me, Mac, because I'm really interested to hear, what do you think of my plan? It's good, right?"

I took a few deep breaths before I opened my eyes and shrugged. "I think your plan is kinda lame really. I mean, sure, they're my brothers, but life will go on, won't it? They're strong and capable, quite unlike you, so they'll deal with it and move on with their lives. Can't say you've managed to do the same, but hey, you can't win them all can you, Jimmy?"

His face fell. What did he think I was going to say? That he was some kind of evil criminal mastermind genius? Fucktard.

"Well," he said with a smirk, "I hope you're comfortable, Mac, because it's a long night ahead of you. I think we might just give young Evie a call in the morning. You know, let your brothers freak out and search all night long for you. That will be fun, I think. Then, early in the morning while they're still out chasing their tails after not having slept for days, Evie will be left all on her lonesome. We'll give her a call then, see if she feels like stopping by for a cup of coffee. Whadda you say, Mac?"

I pressed my lips together and glared.

He chuckled and checked my ties to make sure they were secure before leaving the room.

Chapter Twenty-Five
EVIE

I grinned and clapped my hands high thanking the audience for the thunderous ovation. Unfortunately, revelling in the sensation was entirely impossible thanks to my current state of emotional retardedness.

Damn you, Jared. I should be furious at the conclusions you jumped to, but how could I when I would have done exactly the same were the situation reversed? It looked pretty damning, and despite outside sources informing me of Jared's feelings, love was the last thing I was rolling in when he took off this morning.

With a last wave at the crowd, I hit the side of the stage and was immediately smothered in my brother's arms. He lifted me off my feet and spun me around as laughter bubbled out.

"My famous little sister," he murmured close to my ear.

"Not quite, but we're on our way." I grinned as he set me on my feet, teetering a little in the skyscrapers Tim insisted I wear.

"Where's Mac?" I'd seen her disappear just before our last song and it looked like she hadn't returned.

Coby frowned as he glanced around. "Not sure. She'll be about somewhere."

Travis was on the phone, so Coby followed me back to the dressing room where Cooper was handing out beers. In light of last night, I opted for a water before shouting at the boys to listen up. "I have some housekeeping issues to discuss. As we now have two weeks off, we need to re-charge properly, which means *no partying*."

Frog groaned and flung his beer top at me as protests rendered the air.

Jake in turned threw his at Frog. "This is serious shit, Frog."

I ignored the whining and continued. "Come on. If I can do it so can you. Also, the rumour mill informs me that dinner at our place tonight, before the after party, is being catered for by none other than Mr. Chow himself." Coby gave me a wink, and I held up my beer in salute, unwilling to visualise the lengths he would have gone to in order to arrange that particular feat. "So here's to Jamieson. You might all be riding my coattails like a bunch of rockstar wannabes..." I laughed and had to speak louder over the shouts "....but I love you all like brothers. Now hurry up and drink your beer before I start hugging you all as though you actually deserved it."

They cheered loudly. "To Jamieson."

When I stood up to face the mirror and began wiping the heavy makeup off my face, exhausted and ready for nothing more than bed, Travis stuck his head in the door, frowning as his eyes scanned the room. "Where's Mac?"

"We don't know," I answered. "She's not out there?"

He shook his head. "When I got off the phone, one of the roadies was asking me where she was because they're doing the pack up, and they need her."

"Have you tried her phone?" Henry interrupted. "She mentioned a few industry bigwigs were stopping by tonight, so maybe she's caught up schmoozing."

I picked up my phone and tried ringing her but there was no answer. Mac *always* answered her phone. She was as dependable as chocolate was in fixing a shitty day.

Travis opened the door wider and moved into the room.

"When did you last see her?" Coby asked.

Travis paused for a moment and rubbed his chin. "Right before the last song. She mentioned something about picking up an unscheduled delivery for Jamieson. I can't remember her returning."

My body began channelling vibes, really bad ones—ones that set off a churning in my stomach that wouldn't be ignored. By the look on Travis and Coby's face, I was not alone. Meaningful glances were exchanged before the two left the room. Finished wiping my face, I stood up to follow.

Jake, sitting to my left on the couch, snagged my wrist. "Sit down," he growled. "You aren't supposed to be going anywhere without either of those two." He pushed me back down at the same time he stood up. "I'll go."

When Coby, Travis, and Jake eventually returned, all expectant eyes turned their way. If they were worried, they weren't showing it.

"There are thousands of people out there," Travis muttered. "It's impossible."

"Well can't you track her phone?" I asked.

"We did. It says she's here," Coby answered. "We've organised your car. You're all coming home with me. Casey's on his way and Jake and Travis will stay here until we make sure she's safe."

"Fuck that. I'm staying. I'm not leaving without Mac." I folded my arms for emphasis. I might not have the tracking abilities of an undercover FBI agent, and frankly, Agent Provocateur was the only type of agent that meant anything in my book, but I wasn't leaving without Mac.

"For God's sake, Evie," Coby shouted out angrily, "can you just for once do what I ask of you? Do you think they can focus properly on looking for Mac if they have to worry about you bumbling around out there as well? How is that gonna help Mac?"

I hated that Coby was right, apart from the bumbling part of course. I didn't bumble. Pressing my lips together, I began getting all our things together.

Coby visibly calmed down at what I liked to think was my Stepford Wife impersonation, and soon after, we all piled into the limousine that would take us home.

Coby was shutting the door when Travis jogged out. "Wait!" he panted, grabbing the car door and leaning in to speak to me. "Just got hold of Jared."

My heart stuttered. I could literally feel it skipping beats. "You did? Did you tell—"

"I haven't told him anything yet," he interrupted, impatience to get back to badassery type things laced his voice. "He's on his way here. I'll talk to him, okay?"

Later that night, I pushed Mr. Chow's around on my plate because it tasted as appealing as a mouthful of soggy broccoli. It was food wastage at its most heinous, but at that moment, my care factor was buried well below the rocky layer of the earth's crust. I looked around the silent table to see Henry, Frog, and Cooper looking as sick as I felt. Coby was in the back office of our duplex, not even pretending to eat as his focus alternated between the computer and his phone. I gave up and shoved my plate to the centre of the table with frustration.

When my phone starting to ring and showed Jake's name displayed on the surface, I snatched it up like a life preserver and answered breathlessly.

"Evie," Jake responded. Nothing in his voice indicated happy rainbows and pots of gold.

To save repeating the entire conversation, I hit speaker and sat the phone in the middle of the table. "What?"

We heard muffled swearing. "It doesn't look good. The last time Mac was sighted she was headed down to George's gate to collect a delivery, and there's no indication she returned." He paused and we all heard him suck in a breath. "George has been found dead. Shot."

"Chook?" Henry grabbed my shaking hands in his own. I could see him holding them through my blurred vision; I just couldn't feel them. I closed my eyes.

Really? Were we all that stupid thinking I was the only ball in play? If Jimmy had Mac then I'd... I'd what? Somehow perform the miracle of finding him like no one else had managed to do? Damn it all to the great fucking fiery infernos of hell.

I abandoned the phone, the table, and the faces of worry and slipped quietly up the stairs to my bed. The urge to bust out and rain vengeance upon the man warred with the knowledge that doing so would take vital focus away from the search. I wanted to go all Rambo on the situation, strap bullet belts across my chest and line war paint across my cheeks. My only consolation was that Mac's attitude was never say die. If she was trapped in the slippery man's clutches, I could only hope it was after a good eye gouging and a few stabs with the nearest blunt object.

"Jake says that Travis spoke to Jared."

I blinked my eyes open. Henry stood by the bed. His bright blue eyes were lifeless and reddened, and I wondered if this nightmare would ever end for us.

"Yeah?" I offered half-heartedly. I wasn't sure I wanted to hear any more. I'd already been laid out like Wile E. Coyote. Steamrollered to a pathetic pancake on the floor as Road Runner casually beep beeped on by.

He sank onto the bed beside me until he was on his back, folding his hands behind his head to stare at the ceiling. "Apparently, Jared didn't say much in reply, but Jake says the two holes he punched in the wall was answer enough."

I wished *I* was strong enough to punch a hole or two in the wall because I felt the need for a bit of redecoration myself.

When I didn't respond, Henry continued. "Put yourself in his shoes for a minute, Chook. His little sister appears to be in the clutches of the man whose brother he shot dead. Because Jimmy spent so much of his time focused on getting you six feet under, the fact that Mac was on his radar was never an assumption. Months later, Jimmy still can't be found, and now this has happened to make them all look like a bunch of bumbling fools who couldn't find their own ass in the dark. Not only that, the bastard drugged you right under everyone's nose, and after abandoning you and pretty much saying you were the crap on the soles of his shoes, it comes to light that Matt, of all people, was the one who kept you safe. As if that's not enough, he hasn't slept for two days straight, and is likely existing on the power of anger alone."

Henry's summary was enlightening, but I wasn't sure what I was supposed to do with it, apart from the fleeting thought that "You're the crap on the soles of my shoes" might make a good song. "What's your point, Henry?"

"My point is that I'm not sure Jared's going to be able to forgive himself. You need to know this because you're the one who's going to help him do it."

I sighed and rolled over to face Henry. He rolled to face me, and I brushed at the choppy blond hair on his head. "How did you ever become such a retarded relationship bastard, Henry?"

For a brief moment, a cheeky glint lit his eyes, and he gave a mock shudder. "Because living with the two of you is enough to put any sane male off relationships for life."

I used the hand that was brushing at his hair to shove his head. "Maybe those tight outfits you've been wearing mean something after all. You're turning twinkie on us."

"I wish. Men are such simple creatures. We just want sex. Lots of it. The end."

"And the retarded relationship bastard returns," I said dryly with an eye roll.

He snickered until horror filled his gaze.

I reached down to squeeze his hand in understanding. Mac was out there and we were lying here being shitty friends by making jokes, but to be honest, sometimes it was the only way to help the mind cope.

We must have dozed off into a deep sleep after that because when I woke up, Henry and I were still holding hands and the light of dawn was beginning to creep into the room. My first instinct was panic, and I swung my legs out of bed and crept down the stairs to find my phone when I heard it ringing.

I picked it up off the table where it was left last night and answered with a soft whisper, tiptoeing through the kitchen and out to the back deck so I wouldn't wake anyone.

"Hello, Evie."

Oh fuck. "Jimmy?"

My legs wobbled and I sank into the deck chair before I ass planted on the floor.

"Twice in two days. I enjoy speaking with you," His creepy voice ran through my body like ice water. "I won't keep you for long. I just wanted to let you know that I have something of yours."

Red hot rage boiled through me and the urge to throw and break things had my fingers curling into fists. Maybe Jared and I weren't so different after all. "You fucking bastard. Where is she?"

"Relax, Evie," he crooned. "I'm about to tell you."

My heart thumped in my chest as I asked the question that almost had me hyperventilating. "Is she.... is she alive?"

"Of course she is. You don't think I'd kill her, do you? Anyway, she wants to see you, so we thought we'd invite you over for coffee."

He rattled off the address, and I struggled to memorise it as the relief thundered through me. Finally. After so long in trying to find Jimmy, I had his location in my hot little hands.

"Wait, I want to talk to her. I'm not going anywhere until I know she's okay."

There was crackling silence and then Mac's bossy voice came on the line. "Evie?"

"Mac, oh, Mac, are you okay?"

"Shut up and listen to me," she ordered. "Don't come here, Evie. He's just going to kill the both of us. Don't you come here."

I frowned into the phone, feeling sick.

"Do you hear me?" she shouted impatiently.

"Yes, I hear you, Mac."

"Good. This is not a goddamn rescue mission, so you leave Polly alone, okay? I know you, so don't do it. Do you hear me, Evie?" She was screaming into the phone now. "Don't you come for me, you—"

I heard Jimmy growl. "That's enough."

"Goddammit," Mac wailed in the background and my hands trembled violently when I heard a loud crack and then silence.

Jimmy came back on the line, all sense of sinister calm gone. "Get your fucking ass here now, bitch, or I'll kill her. If you tell anyone, ring anyone, I'll kill the both of you. I have a gun pointed at her head right now, and if I see anyone but you, I won't hesitate to put a bullet in her brain. I'll know if you tell anyone because her useless as fuck brothers will be over here like flies on shit, and it'll only take one second to make the shot. Play it smart. I'm giving you half an hour." Then he hung up.

I took deep breaths until an odd calm settled over me. It was almost like drifting at sea, no one around for miles, just the gentle lap of the ocean my only company.

Relieved to find Henry still under a deep sleep, I got dressed in the wardrobe, sliding my legs into an old worn pair of jeans and pulling a white fitted singlet top over my head. Remembering that Coby always told me my long hair could easily be used as a weapon against me, I reached up and plaited it into a quick braid before rolling it into a knot at the nape of my neck. Finished, I slid my phone into my pocket, picked up my shoes, and crept quietly into Mac's room, a single key fisted tightly in my palm.

I swore quietly when I saw Frog and Cooper both passed out in Mac's bed. I tiptoed into her wardrobe, climbing the little step ladder until I reached the locked steel box up the back of the top shelf. I pulled it down and cringed when a loud clink invaded the silence.

"Mac?" Cooper's voice was a sleep filled whisper.

Shit.

I moved back down the ladder and quickly put the box on the floor, opening the wardrobe door.

"Sorry, Cooper." I shrugged. "It's just me."

Cooper exhaled loudly and he shifted up on one elbow, rubbing sleepily at his mess of dark hair. "Any news?"

My heart was pounding in frustration. Damn you, Cooper. Now is not the time for a freaking conversation.

I shook my head.

"What are you doing up so early and in there anyway?"

"I uh....wanted one of Mac's shirts. You know, to make me feel closer to her. Go back to sleep, Cooper."

He nodded and flopped back down on the bed, rubbing his hand over his tired eyes before closing them.

I watched him carefully for a minute before I moved back into the wardrobe. Time was precious now.

I used the key to unlock the box, cursing when my unsteady hands took twice as long. Grabbing Polly, I quickly set about loading her and tucked her into the back of my jeans. Polly was Mac's gun. I'd jokingly called it Polly Pistol one day and the name stuck. Every time we visited the shooting range, Mac always threatened to send Polly to the bottom of the ocean because she was a terrible shot and always ended up owing everyone lunch.

Peeking my head out of the wardrobe, I saw Cooper was breathing deeply with his eyes closed, so I tiptoed back out of the room and down the stairs to the kitchen, picking up my keys with a fist so they didn't jingle.

Letting myself out into the cool, quiet dawn, I felt the air brush my face and looked up into a cloudless sky, wondering if Jimmy would finally have his way today, and I would never see another morning again. I'd gladly let him if I knew it meant that Mac would be safe, that she would live.

Once in my Hilux, I put the keys in the ignition and let it roll quietly out of the driveway, not starting it until I hit the street. As I shifted into first gear, I planted my foot on the gas, not being able to stop now even if I wanted to. Thankfully, my emotions seemed to have taken a vacation as adrenaline took over.

I accelerated quickly through the quiet streets, and the phone I'd placed on the passenger seat started to ring again. I risked a glance as I drove, fearing Jimmy was calling again and jolted at Jared's name on the display. Christ. There was nothing I needed more than to hear the rumble of his voice wash soothingly across my skin. I ignored the call, instead turning up the volume of the CD in the car. The loud techno beat screamed enough distraction, providing some measure of relief from the thoughts running through my mind. The phone rang again and once again, I ignored it. It eventually beeped a voicemail, and when I reached a set of red lights, I turned down the music and put the message on speaker. When the panic and the pain in Jared's voice came through the speaker, I wanted to close my eyes as it washed over me.

"Baby, fuck. I've got frantic messages from Henry and Coby. What the fuck do you think you're doing? Frank has your location on GPS, so wherever you think you're going, Travis and I are right behind you. Just turn around and go home. Turn the fucking car around damn you and *go home.* We need to know you're safe. Ring me, baby, please? Don't do this. Please don't... I...fuck."

The crack in his voice on his last words had me resting my head on the steering wheel, and when I eventually looked up, the light had turned green. I hated that what I was doing was causing more pain, but I wasn't going to leave her alone out there no matter if that meant I was going to be the Thelma to her Louise. No matter what she said, she needed me.

Forty minutes later, I screeched to a halt out the front of a shitty, rundown weatherboard house in the far south of Sydney. Leaving the phone in the car, I made sure Polly was loaded with an efficient, practised movement and slammed the car door behind me.

Equipped with the knowledge Jared and Travis were hot on my heels, I raced up the path to the porch until I reached the front door. Not bothering with the social niceties of knocking, adrenaline had me slamming it open so hard it hit the far wall.

"Jimmy," I screamed as my heart tried to pound its way clear out of my chest. "I'm here, you son of a bitch."

I heard a noise somewhere down the back of the house. I followed it through a huge rectangular archway on my left and into a big open area. Mac was bound to a chair in the middle of it. Her ankles looked raw, blood dripped down the side of her face, and her usual silky hair was in a state I'd never seen before, matted and lank. Seeing her this way was a shock, leaving me cold and breathless.

She looked up at me wearily and shook her head, tears filling her eyes. Usually she would blink them back, but this time she let them fall. "Damn you, Evie," she whispered. "Why did you come?"

"Mac? Oh my God."

Jimmy stepped out from behind a wall as I started towards her.

Mac flinched as he pulled out a gun and held it up against her temple.

"One more step, bitch, and your friend is dead."

I froze and he looked pleased, making me want to smack the expression off his face with a baseball bat.

"So the plan was to have a bit of fun, but unfortunately, I don't think we'll have much time for that. In case you're both stupid bitches and don't understand the plan, I'll spell it out. Today, both of you die."

Jimmy cocked the gun he was holding against Mac's temple. Another tear spilled over and rolled down her cheek.

"Don't. Please?" she begged in a whisper.

Seeing Mac so defeated was completely unacceptable, and I stilled, my breathing harsh in the sudden silence.

This shit ends now.

I locked my nerves down tight and with a hand as steady as a fucking rock, I reached behind me to pull out the gun tucked into the back of my jeans.

Jimmy looked up at my movement, saw me bringing out a gun and without any hesitation or warning, he swung his gun towards me, arm out straight and fired. Twice.

I jerked back, the searing, white hot burn of pain sharp and excruciating. It would have brought me to my knees if the wall hadn't been there to catch my weight. I put my left hand to my stomach as I sucked in deep breaths of panic, feeling the trickle of blood start to seep through my fingers. I heard Mac screaming my name and Jimmy laughing, all through a fog as my vision tunnelled.

Blinking, I focused on Jimmy's face as he put the gun to Mac's head. "You fucking asshole," I said through grunts of pain.

Without any hesitation, I swung the gun up and fired once. The bullet hit Jimmy in the centre of his forehead, and I watched as he hit the ground.

Adrenaline gave out under waves of pain and the gun fell out of my fingers. With my legs shaking and no longer able to hold me, I slid down the wall, leaving behind a thick trail of blood against the filthy plasterboard. My chest fluttered frantically up and down, fighting for a breath against a bubbling sensation that left me feeling like I was choking.

"Mac?" I whispered, feeling the blood pulse over my trembling fingers where they rested against my stomach. The relief at knowing Jimmy was gone was overtaken by slivers of dread that wound its way like tentacles all over my body. "Mac, I'm sorry."

"Fuck you, Evie," I heard her sob. "You are not going to die on my watch. Goddammit!"

Her voice finished on a shout, and I could hear her struggles to get loose from the ties that bound her to the chair. It all began to sound far away, and I started shivering, feeling the cold and shock take over. Closing my eyes, everything narrowed to black.

Hoarse shouting had me coming around, but this time the pain was a dull throbbing. I felt hands running over me, tearing open my singlet, pressing down so hard it made breathing unbearable.

"Fuck!" An agonised roar filled the room. "Where are the fucking paramedics?"

My eyelids fluttered open. Jared was kneeling over me, bare chested, as I lay on the floor. Through eyes that burned painfully, I lifted my head and risked a peek down the length of my body. Jared's shirt, red with blood, was bunched in his hands, his biceps bulging from the pressure of holding it hard against my stomach. On the other side of me, another set of rigid arms pressed a bloodied shirt equally as hard against my chest. My eyes travelled up another bare chest and met the frantic eyes of Travis.

"Evie," Jared said in a broken whisper.

Wincing, I turned my head slowly and met his eyes. Wild and panic-stricken, they locked on mine and when Mac called out "ETA one minute," from somewhere behind my head, he never took them off me.

"Jared," I croaked out and swallowed the bitter, metallic tang of blood.

Tears spilled over and down his face. "Oh God. I'm here, baby. I love you," he said fiercely. "I love you so fucking much. Hang on, okay? You're going to be okay."

His voice was hoarse, but his words were beautiful, and I clung to them as I closed my eyes again. I felt Jared rest his forehead against my ribs, his shoulders heaving with sobs until I thought my heart would break just from hearing it.

Chapter Twenty-Six

Jared was standing by the window looking worthy of a devouring dressed in an old t-shirt and pair of boardshorts, hair slightly damp like he'd just come out of the ocean. Unfortunately, his manner didn't indicate a devouring would be welcome, not that I'd be up to the task anyway. His red, tired eyes, dark circles, and distracted demeanour indicated more of a "get the hell away from me" vibe.

"I have to leave."

Having only just busted out of the ICU, a plethora of tubes removed from my body, seeing more of Jared was the current plan, not less.

"Oh?" My voice came out raspy, sounding foreign to my ears. After the breathing tube had been removed, speech had eluded me for a good two days. "So soon?"

"No." He frowned. "I meant overseas. For work."

"When?"

"Couple of days."

"How..." It hurt to speak but I wanted to ask him how could he leave me? Was work so much more important? Why now? The questions burned on my tongue, but instead I rasped out, "For how long?"

Hands in his pockets, he turned away to face the window, and I braced myself because whenever someone couldn't look you in the eyes, you knew it was going to be bad.

His flat voice bounced off the window and hammered into my chest.

"Four months."

"Four months!" The intended shout came out as a squeak. "Can't someone else go?"

I need you.

Still not looking at me, he replied. "I wasn't forced to go. I volunteered. I'm taking Casey's place."

Why would he volunteer? I put a hand to my eyes as though to push the tears back in that were threatening to spill over.

"Why?"

He drew in a deep breath and met my eyes for one brief, painful moment. "I can't be around you anymore, Evie. Us being together was a mistake and the further we're away from each other the easier it will be." Jared's body was rigid but the stress in his voice was distinct.

I frowned and swallowed through the ache in my throat at him calling us a mistake. Was that what he really thought? Offering no further explanation, his silence became all-consuming, and my confusion evolved into anger. My body tensed as it engulfed me and had me gritting my teeth from the pain it caused my healing body.

"You told me you loved me, I heard you, and now you're leaving me?" My voice sounded raspy and pitiful, and I cleared my throat as I struggled to sit up. "What I did saved your sisters life; and I almost died, but I'm just a fucking mistake to you? You asshole!" My voice rose with my anger, ending with a shout that echoed satisfyingly off the walls of the hospital room.

Grabbing the nearest object, a bottle of water, I pegged it at his head, but my body was weak and sore, and it fell pathetically short of the mark. I watched the lid break off and water spill out everywhere, and right at that moment I felt like that bottle of water was me.

I was starting to wonder if the paramedics that worked rapidly at saving my life a week ago, shouldn't have tried so hard. Their frantic movements and voices were still fresh in my mind.

"What have we got?" A female barked the question as they set their bags down and started undoing clips and zippers.

"Gunshot wound to the chest and stomach," Jared replied.

"Move. Now," Another man instructed. I felt something press at my chest, hands fluttering over me.

"How old is she?" the man asked.

"Twenty-four," Mac replied.

"Any allergies? On any medications?"

"No, nothing," Mac muttered.

"How's the breathing?"

"Shallow. Blood pressure bottoming out, and she's turning blue. Collapsed lung."

"Crap. Starting decompression now. How long ago was she shot?"

"Maybe about fifteen minutes ago," Jared said.

"We need her in ER yesterday."

I had come to again when they were loading me into the ambulance. I could feel the jolt of being guided to the waiting doors.

"Evie!" I'd heard Henry's anguished shout from far away.

"Step back," the curt voice of the female paramedic ordered.

"Damn you, Jared. How the fuck did this happen?" Coby's distraught voice was close, and I felt a hand brush down the side of my face.

The paramedic spoke again. "Just one goes with her."

At the time, I couldn't open my eyes to see what the fuss was about. I was floating high. It felt amazing.

I buzzed for the nurse. She needed to take me back to the floating place. STAT.

"I don't understand why you're doing this." I choked out the words as I slumped back in my bed. I didn't want to look at him, but I couldn't look away. He stood there, so beautiful, almost close enough to touch in the small room, but the distance was now a living thing that pulsed between us.

He cursed and shoved his hands in his pockets, making no move to pick up the bottle leaking water all over the floor.

"Remember both those assholes that almost got you killed? All I wanted to do was keep you safe, but it turned out I was the biggest one of all. I didn't plan on being another asshole in your life, Evie. I never wanted to be that person to you." Jared's shoulders slumped as he stared out the window, the wall propping his weight. He looked defeated and pain lined his eyes, sending a pang through my body.

I looked away quickly, closing eyes so tired they burned. "All I know is that you're leaving me. Just like everyone else who mattered that came before you." I opened my eyes and glared at him. "Despite our misunderstandings, I thought you were so far beyond doing something like this that I actually trusted you. In your eyes, I saw strength and courage and fearlessness, but I guess I saw wrong. I never figured you for a coward. I always thought that was my department, but obviously I'm not...I've never been the best judge of character have I?"

His shoulders slumped further at the words that left a bitter taste in my mouth. I felt the urge to escape the confines of my hospital bed and run away from this new nightmare.

I knew I'd been scared and cautious, but in the end I'd given him my heart, and now the warmth that once flooded my body from feeling treasured by this man was now a cold chill of rejection. I remembered being in my car after I picked him up from hospital, when he'd said that when I wasn't with him it was like someone had turned out the lights, and here he hadn't even left, and it was so dark I thought I'd never see daylight again.

Where was that damn nurse? I pressed the buzzer impatiently, biting down on my lip so I wouldn't beg him to stay.

"Get out." My hoarse shout ripped through the silence and he flinched at the words as though I'd hit him.

Swallowing hard, he nodded, his chest expanding as he drew in a deep, shaky breath.

"I'm sorry, Evie." His deep voice was rough, cracking on the apology, and he spared one more glance at me, his eyes trailing slowly over my face as though to memorise every feature, before he turned and left the room. The door closed with a soft *click* behind him.

The fight left me as I heard his heavy footsteps recede down the hall. I turned my head, my face pressing into the pillow as the tears came, heavy in my throat and spilling over to slide down my face. I could hear my own choking sobs in the empty room and cradled my arms over my stomach, never feeling more empty or alone in my entire life, than I did right at that moment.

When the nurse arrived she stood at the end of my bed, checked my chart, and informed me that she couldn't give me anything more for at least another hour.

My eyes were bruised from tears, my body ached from head to toe, and my voice was thick and raspy. "But it hurts so much."

She glanced up from the page she was busy scribbling a note on. I didn't know what she was writing. I imagined it was something like *patient acting irrationally, proceed with caution,* yet her eyes on me softened with concern. "Do you need the doctor?"

Not unless his or her speciality was in the practice of life reassignment. I shook my head and waited for sleep to give me some peace.

When I woke again, I welcomed the return of the blessed floaty feeling with a loving hug and a warning not to leave like that again. I didn't feel better, I didn't feel worse, but I also didn't feel happy or broken. I just didn't feel. At least for a moment, until, not opening my eyes, I focused on what appeared to be an argument in progress.

Henry growled. "I say we play the song."

"No way!" Mac hissed. "We've been sitting on this for years, asshead, and you're not ruining it for me now."

"Come on. She gets that song out on repeat every time she's suffering through something really bad. It'll help."

I *felt* then. I felt an "oh shit" moment.

"Have you ever listened to the words of that song?"

A pause. "Um…no."

"Maybe it might be too much for her. I mean, how many times has she seen him walk away from her? The song bloody sings about how nothing a hundred men or more could do to take me away from you."

Jesus, Henry. Thanks for making me sound like a pathetic dishrag.

Another pause. "Well…we can't control what she listens to, can we? Why don't we just pack her iPod for next time."

Henry sounded frustrated. "Mac, she's just been shot and you're worried over blackmail material."

"Henry, don't you see? If we start acting all retarded around her and try to be something we think she needs when all she needs is for us to be ourselves, she'll bloody well fall apart."

Upon the realisation I would have to oust my obsession with Toto's *Africa* before it could be used against me, I tuned out, willing them both to leave and take their argument with them.

The next two weeks followed the news that Jared made good on his words and left. The news extinguished the last small piece of hope that maybe he'd stayed, and losing it was like another blow. Casey had moved in with Travis, and Peter moved back to our place. It probably wasn't a moment too soon because although Peter was admirably passionate in all his endeavours, it could be wearing on some. Henry was busy helping Mac with the Jamieson obligations while she dealt with the press, and believe me, the press was *huge*. If we thought touring with Sins of Descent would help our rise to success, then the lead singer of Jamieson getting shot gained us international fame. Gary from Jettison was riding a wave of excitement so high he automatically added an extra zero to the dollar figure on our record contract. Journalists were apparently frothing rabidly to win the all-important first interview. Perhaps I should've thought of getting shot sooner. Who knew?

Eventually I left the hospital, unnaturally quiet and subdued. The only consolation was that it appeared I had the constitution of a Terminator. I'd survived through so much. War could rain down, leaving devastation and destruction in its wake, and I would walk out the other side. That boded well for me in facing the wrath of Coby. If I thought the fires of hell were going to swallow me up and spit me out after the drugging fiasco, busting out and going all Quentin Tarantino on Jimmy's ass was enough to unleash the unholy hounds of hell.

The next three months passed by as though I was in a repetitive dream. Wake up, physical therapy, write songs, go to bed. Intersperse that with interviews, meetings with Jettison Records, and counselling sessions with Jude, and there was my life. I was continually exhausted from being unable to sleep. Every time I closed my eyes, I felt the jerk of bullets hitting my body, I saw Jimmy grinning at me, and I saw blood. Rivers of it. Sometimes I would see it without closing my eyes, and the anxiety had my heart fluttering in my chest and me sucking in short, tight breaths that never seemed to reach my lungs. The anger at Jared for not being there when I needed him most was a slow burning ember that I welcomed. I wanted to hate him, and I wanted to *feel* it. I wanted to shake with the rage, but then I would remember the sweet plea in his eyes and his voice when he begged me to be with him. I remembered the way his lips would curl up and his eyes crinkle when I sassed him. Most of all, I remembered lying on the floor of Jimmy's house and seeing the agony in his eyes as he bent over me, and the fierce desperation in his words when he told me he loved me while tears spilled over and ran down his face. Then my anger would fade to despair, knowing that no one would ever matter to me the way he did. That no man would ever find their way through the broken pieces left behind from a love I'd never have again. Despite all of it, a breathless anticipation would cut through the void whenever my phone rang.

I shouldn't have wanted to hear from him, but I did.

And it hurt.

Each day that passed by without hearing his voice pierced my heart until I had to fist my hands together and dig sharp nails into my skin to direct the pain elsewhere.

"Hey!"

A voice cut through the fog and someone splashed water in my face. I turned to confront the threat, putting my hand in the ocean and flicking water in retaliation with a smile that was forced.

Casey grinned in return. His hair glistened with water droplets from the early morning sun, and tanned muscular arms protruded from his short-sleeved black wetsuit. "Look out, she's cracked a smile, call the paparazzi."

I gave a mock snarl and he laughed.

"That's more like it," he said and then nodded towards the horizon. "Set's up."

Following his gaze, I shivered at the line of waves rolling in. "I can't do this anymore."

"You can. Shut up and start paddling."

Casey was teaching me how to surf as part of my physical therapy because it helped rebuild the core strength I'd lost. Unfortunately, I wasn't quite ready to hit the pro circuit. I was far too busy meeting the ocean floor with my face and eating sand for breakfast. Casey, who appeared to be good at everything, found the whole farce the highlight of his mornings, but I'd rather sit down and endure back to back episodes of *The Nanny* while eating sprouts. At least I'd gained a new nickname—Kook—which was apparently some kind of reference to a newbie surfer. I didn't know if it was complimentary, but I did learn from Casey's surfer mate, Ben, that Casey was a ripper hotdogger, whatever that meant, so I used it liberally and told everyone else to as well.

"Fine, *hotdog.*"

The wave bore down and I turned on my board and literally paddled for my life, feeling the cool water lurch beneath me, each stroke of my arm a gnawing ache in my middle.

"Woot. Go Kookie!"

Grinning, I paused in my paddle to introduce Casey to my middle finger and promptly tipped my board, going down in a crash of limbs, riding the white wash upside down and inside out to the shore. I crawled up the sand on my hands and knees, my board dragging behind me as I coughed out a piece of seaweed.

A warm hand landed on my back and with tired eyes I looked up at Casey's concerned face.

"You okay?"

I flopped down on my back and sucked in life saving oxygen. "Does everyone have it in for me? Even the ocean is trying to write me off."

Casey dug his board upright in the sand and leaned down to remove the leg rope from my ankle. "Don't be like that. You're getting better."

"I know." I let out a painful wheeze. "I didn't eat sand that time."

He gently let go of my ankle with a laugh. "See? More room for bacon and eggs."

I eyed him hopefully and sat up. "You wouldn't tease me, would you?"

He gripped my bicep as he helped me up. "Come on, Kookie. I'll take you to Tilly's. Us surfers need to keep up our strength."

This was true. I ate twice as much for breakfast since I started the whole surfing debacle. I wouldn't ever admit it to Casey, but I always felt better afterwards. Fresher, more alive and, a little less sad.

We picked up our boards and trudged through the sand, dodging the diehard beachgoers setting up their place with competent movements in the early light of day. A few surfers trotted by with a hand wave and shouted greetings like "Yo, brah" and "Hey, Kook." I'd seen the movies and being known as Kook sounded preferable to seeing newbie surfers enduring bloodshed for 'dropping in' on waves. Apparently, I was well known though. Suffering a few bullet wounds in a badass gun fight made me a "hard core babe" and earned Casey lots of back slapping for his "score." Not correcting their assumptions, Casey would just roll his eyes and accept their good natured ribbing.

We reached the outdoor showers, and I peeled the wetsuit down to reveal my bikini underneath. I turned the water on to its one and only setting of ice cold and shivered under the spray.

I turned around and Casey, now down to his boardshorts under the shower next to me, eyed the scars on my torso, and his lips pressed flat.

"Fading," he said, his voice barely audible under the spray of water.

Rubbing at the one on my chest because I couldn't get used to the numb feeling, I turned back around self-consciously. "Yeah."

We finished up, and half an hour later found me sitting at Tilly's clad in a simple pair of short denim shorts and white tank top, wet hair tied messily in a bun on the top of my head. We sat at an outdoor table in the sun, so I was wearing my giant sunglasses as I annihilated a stack of pancakes and bacon.

Casey swallowed a mouthful of eggs. "How's it going with Jude?"

At Coby's request, Carol from their office visited me in hospital with a beautiful bouquet of flowers and the contact information for Jude.

His hope was for the counselling to help alleviate the anxiety I was feeling from the trauma of a life-threatening injury and the distress from taking another person's life.

"He's helping," I answered honestly because every day my breathing got a little easier. "But every time I finish an appointment I need wine, so I think he's turning me into an alcoholic."

He chuckled as I shovelled in another bite of pancakes. "Yeah he does that to all of us."

I swallowed my mouthful and echoed, "All of us?"

Casey shrugged. "With our line of work, it's common to help with the stress of what we do or sometimes see."

I wanted to ask what they sometimes saw but my phone rang, and I answered.

Mac's chipper voice was on the other end. "Marty rang and you're needed in the studio tomorrow." There was a muffled crackle, and I heard her shout, "Just a goddamn minute, asshead" to someone in the background.

I sighed as she got back to me, ranting about something or other that was pissing her off. I gave her my sympathy, simply thankful the tirade wasn't directed at me. Sucking in a breath, she finally asked where I was.

"Tilly's."

I heard her let out a loud whoosh. "Bring me back some mushroom cups, and I'll take you off my shit list for the day."

"I'm on there?" I asked with dismay.

"No, but you will be if you don't bring me back some mushroom cups."

I made the promise to bring some home and hung up. I'd planned on getting them anyway because you didn't go to Tilly's and not get them. They were little pastry cups of heaven filled with mushroom, feta, egg, and finely diced bacon.

Finishing our breakfast, we returned to the beach parking lot, surfboards attached to the racks of our respective cars.

I beeped the unlock button before Casey gently pulled me in for a hug. After a few moments, when he didn't seem inclined to let go, I drew back slightly puzzled, and he softly brushed a hand down my face. "Tomorrow. Same time, same place?"

"Sure. I couldn't do without my daily dose of surf dumping, and the sand is good exfoliation for my face."

He chuckled and moved to get in his car.

"Oh wait. Mac's having a get together at our place tonight. Come with Travis."

His answer was a brief nod before he hopped in his car, backed out, and drove away.

Later that night I dressed in a pair of white shorts and a fitted black t-shirt that had *Badass Bitch* written in silver studs across the breasts. The shirt was a gift from Cooper just last week. I made sure to flaunt it in front of Tim's face at every opportunity, and he played deliberately obtuse and kept telling me to stop parading my "lady bags" in his face.

I sat out on the back deck, nursing a glass of wine, as friends littered the inside of the duplex and the backyard. Coby was manning the barbecue, and Casey and Travis were standing in the all-important huddle that was man grilling meat. As I was still riding the coattails of invalidity, Mac and Tim were the ones in the kitchen dealing with everything else. Frog, Jake, and Cooper were busy chatting to two of our female neighbours. I could see them putting on their best moves. Cooper was leaning close, trailing a finger along the collarbone of one of the girls. Her eyes were wide and she bit her lip as he spoke to her. Not to be outdone, Frog reached out and pulled the other girl down on to his lap and she shrieked with laughter. Jake it seemed, had missed out, but the gazes he kept flicking towards Mac whenever she appeared from the kitchen left me thinking that it didn't bother him at all.

Henry pulled up a chair next to me and sucked down his beer as though it was the elixir of life. When he finished he sat the empty bottle on the table with a lip smack and a sigh. "So…"

I raised my eyebrows in reply.

He looked over at the barbecue pointedly. "What's going on between you and Casey?"

My eyebrows reached newer heights.

"Why?"

"His eyes have been tracking you all night."

My eyes trailed to the barbecue in time to catch Casey glancing away, and I frowned.

"We're just friends, Henry. We bonded over surfing." I would have thought Henry would understand the difficulty in explaining a platonic friendship between a man and a woman. "How many times have we had to defend *our* relationship to other people?"

"Yeah but I don't look at you the way he looks at you."

"And what way is that?"

"Like he wants to eat you alive."

"Jesus, Henrietta. I know people think I have some kind of death wish, and frankly that's not surprising, but have you seen Casey? I need to go back to my dorks." Wistful memories of Hairy Parry and Beetle Bob filled my head.

Henry must have been doing the same thing because he winced in reply.

"Maybe I need to swear off men altogether."

"Maybe you and Casey should just sleep with each other and get it out of your system." I could always depend on Henry with sage advice.

"Is it Groundhog Day? Wasn't it just yesterday you and Mac were pushing me into some kind of...whatever the hell *that* was with Jared? Look how well that turned out, and here you are at it again."

Henry shrugged. "Just saying."

"Well don't. Thanks for the retarded relationship bastard advice, Henry, but that's a really shitty idea."

I ignored Henry for a while, and after we ate dinner, I replenished my wine from the bottle in the fridge. Feeling a slightly wonderful buzz that softened my tatty edges, I shifted out to the quiet of the front yard and sat on the step at the front door as I nursed my glass.

Mac came out carrying a bag of garbage and almost tripped over me. "What the hell are you doing out here?"

So much for the quiet. "I *was* enjoying the peace, Mactard."

"Suit yourself."

She headed down the driveway and threw the bag into the big green wheelie bin just as Casey came out, beer in hand, and sat on the step beside me.

Mac came up the drive, texting on her phone. She glanced up as she reached the stairs and chortled with glee. "Hey, look! It's Hotdog and Sandwich."

Casey groaned and I laughed out loud.

Mac pushed her way in between us. Before heading through the door she added over her shoulder, "Don't be long. There's chocolate cake."

"Thanks for that," Casey said with a mixture of amusement and resignation in his eyes.

"My pleasure, *hotdog.*"

"Kook."

"Hotdog."

He sipped at his beer before resting his elbows on his knees.

"Hey, I've been Sandwich for half my life, but I deal."

"I can take it," he replied, fingers working at peeling the label off the beer in his hands.

My gaze moved from his hands to his lips. Damn Henry for putting the thought in my head because that was the last place I wanted or needed to be. The man was seriously hot but...what? Maybe I should just kiss him. That wouldn't hurt would it? I mean Jared practically threw me back in the ocean, so shouldn't I try to move on?

I sat my wine down in horror. Casey was a friend. What was I thinking? Clearly, I'd had too much to drink. I faced Casey to say I was heading back inside when he took me by complete surprise. Both his hands gripped the sides of my face, and he crushed his lips against mine. His mouth was hot, his lips soft, and when I began to respond, he groaned, moving his hands from my face to slide down my back, pushing me closer. I opened my mouth and let his tongue swirl inside, joining it with my own, feeling heat begin its stealth invasion of my body. I ran my hands up his chest and twined my arms around his neck. In turn, he hands slid slowly around my torso, trailing one up my ribs while the other shifted to grip my hip tightly.

For a moment, it felt amazing, but then I realised I was only receptive to the kiss because it was Jared I was thinking of, his hands I was feeling on my body, and his lips that were burning mine.

I wanted to weep, and when I faltered, Casey tore his mouth from mine, breathless. "Fuck."

I didn't speak, watching him as my lungs sucked in mouthfuls of air.

"I'm sorry. I shouldn't have done that."

"No, I…" Tears pricked my eyes because I let it happen and it felt like I'd used him. "I can't let go. I can't let go of him, and I don't want to, Casey. I'm sorry."

"Shhhh," he whispered. "You don't have to explain yourself, Evie. I get it. Really. We've both just had a bit to drink and done something you weren't ready for is all. If anything, I'm always your friend, and if you ever need me, just say the word."

At that point, I decided Casey wasn't real. He simply descended from the heavens to fool us poor women into believing that the perfect man really did exist and thus continue the eternal chase.

"I always need friends like you, Casey, but that goes both ways."

His hand found my knee and squeezed, sliding in a gentle caress as he removed it. "Of course." He stood up. "Coming in?"

"Yeah, in a sec."

No sooner had Casey disappeared through the front door when Henry found his way to the front step.

I picked up my wine and took a huge swallow, deciding that the time to drink again was upon me. "What, Henry?"

He sat down. "Sorry, Chook."

I waved a hand. "It's okay. I did what you said anyway," I replied, taking great amusement in the way his eyes bugged out at my words.

"Um…that was fast?"

My phone chose that moment to ring and happy to leave Henry hanging, I tugged it out of my pocket. When I glanced at the display, I dropped it like it was a hissing snake.

"What?" Henry looked at me then glanced at the phone. "Oh shit." Now *he* was eyeballing it like it was a hissing snake. "You uh, gonna answer that?"

"I don't know!" My voice was a shout and my eyes widened in panic as they whipped to his. "Should I?"

At my shout, both Mac and Coby appeared at the doorway.

"What the fuck is going on?" Mac asked.

Coby followed our gaze to the phone and then anger lit his eyes. "Christ. What the hell time is it over in the States anyway?"

"Don't answer it," snapped Mac.

The frustration of not having any peace to gather my thoughts had me yelling again. "Would you all shut up for just one freaking second and let me think."

They paused collectively, almost breathlessly, and tension singed the air.

I started to reach for the phone, wanting to hear his voice.

"Evie," Mac said in her best "you better not do what I think you're going to do" voice.

Then it stopped ringing and I missed my chance to talk to Jared.

Everyone held their breath, waiting to see if I'd receive a voicemail. Nothing happened and grabbing my phone, I pushed my way through them and towards the kitchen, making a beeline for the fridge.

I grabbed another bottle of wine and poured as much as I could fit into the glass, sloshing it over the sides as Mac grabbed my arm and hustled me inside the walk-in pantry, shutting the door behind us. She didn't bother turning on the light because it blew again yesterday morning.

Feeling weary I waved a hand in surrender. "Mac, please."

"I…"

"Get to the point." I had an alcohol bath to get to.

"Sorry, Sandwich. I've been such a shitty friend. I don't want to make it all about me, but I just wanted to say that it's been hard for me to watch my two favourite people, both so desperately in love with the other, falling apart, and it hurts. It. Fucking. Hurts." I could hear the tears in her voice and if the light had been working, I would've seen them roll down her cheek. "I know I need to be more supportive, but I thought that… I was trying to just be myself. Thinking if things were normal it might help, but I realised that normal isn't enough. Normal hasn't been the support I thought it would be, and I'm sorry."

There was a painful fumble in the dark where Mac grunted when I elbowed her in the stomach and I yelped when her finger poked my eye, and then we were hugging.

The door busted open and blinking at the flood of light, Henry bore down on us. "Jesus, Chook, first Casey and now Mac. Who else are you planning on assaulting tonight because I have plans."

"You do?" I asked.

"Casey?" Mac asked.

"Casey and Evie had sex," Henry blurted out.

"Um, what?" Mac and I replied simultaneously, mine directed at Henry, hers directed at me.

"We didn't have sex. We kissed."

"You did? When?"

"Out on the front step, just before."

With the light flooding in I caught Mac's open mouthed expression. "You mean after I took the garbage out?"

"I think that the next time Jared rings, you should answer the phone," Henry interjected.

"Oh here we go," Mac said with a grumble. "Advice from the retarded relationship bastard."

"Wait." I grabbed at her arm. "Sometimes he can be an idiot savant about this stuff. Make your point, Henry. Fast," I added. I still had an alcohol bath to get to.

"Remember our conversation that night when Jimmy had Mac and we were talking about Jared, and I told you to put yourself in his shoes?"

Mac, not privy to our conversation, folded her arms, and I nodded my agreement, making a rolling motion with my hand to indicate he should continue.

"What's your point," Mac snapped.

"My point..." Henry frowned at Mac as he spoke to me "...is that he blames himself. He's pushed you away because he can't forgive himself for what happened to you. Remember when you told us that he said he didn't want to be another asshole in your life like Renny and Kellar were? He feels like he's no better than them. So he took Casey's place thinking that was the only way he could keep himself away from you, and he thinks he needs to do that to protect you. From himself."

"But that's...that's..."

Henry finished my sentence. "That's how men roll. I'm not saying what he did was okay because pushing you away and leaving pissed me right. the. fuck. off. I'm telling you so you'll understand that it's not because he doesn't love you. It's because he loves you so much that he's not thinking clearly. Make sure you swallow whatever pride or anger you might be carrying, Evie, and give yourselves a fucking chance. *That* is why I think you should answer the phone if he rings you again."

Henry put a hand on my shoulder, rubbing it up and down my arm soothingly as I wiped at tears.

My mind flickered back to the moment I'd first opened the door and saw Jared standing there. The green eyes laughing, the hair in his eyes, the complete and utter panic I'd felt when I knew he was going to mean something to me, something big. The messages we sent every day. The first time I felt his tongue travel the length of my body. Him running for the car when I couldn't get out. Tackling him to the floor on our first date, then me telling him it was over. Him tucking my hair behind my ears with a curl of his lips, then the pain radiating from his body when he thought I'd betrayed him. The agony in his eyes as he told me he loved me while I lay bleeding on the floor, and the painful sobs that racked my body when he walked out the door and never came back.

I saw it all, the highest of our highs and the lowest of our lows, and as much as every piece was a part of me, I wanted to howl for never getting a chance to live in the middle.

Chapter Twenty-Seven

Jared rang back the day after the barbecue. I'd missed it again, not from indecision this time, but because I was in the recording studio. He left a voicemail, and I'd sat on it all day, breathless, unfocused, and waiting until later when I was alone.

"Baby." The deep rumble of his voice and the term of endearment stirred something inside me until he paused and corrected himself. "Evie. I'm pretty much thinking you don't want to talk to me, and I don't blame you. I'm sorry. I left you and I'm so fucking sorry." I heard him inhale deeply and let it out sharply before he continued. "That doesn't sound enough… I tried so hard to convince myself that I was doing the right thing, but the minute I got on that plane I… Evie, I watched the rose in your skin turn blue. I sat there pressing a goddamn shirt into your chest until I thought I would break. I close my eyes and all I see is you, covered in blood, not breathing, and I can't sleep. I can't breathe. Love was the one thing I had to give you, and I fucked it up. I wasn't there for you. You almost died, and I wasn't there for you… I want you to know I was wrong. That we weren't a mistake, and that I was a coward. I was scared of what being with me had done to you, and I was scared of that happening again. I'm sorry… I think of you every minute of every day."

The message ended and my heart thundered painfully. I'd thrown the phone against the wall and no, it didn't make me feel better. It just left a small dent in the wall and chipped the paint. I'd snuggled back under the doona. Then I'd huffed and flung it back off, getting out of bed to retrieve the phone. Peter growled because he was burrowed under the fluffy covers trying to sleep.

The next morning, before we left the beach, Casey crowded me against the car. "There's no coming back for you, is there?"

I turned my head, saw the waves rolling in, saw the orange hues of the horizon, and I saw a chance to live in the middle.

I turned back and met his eyes. "No, Casey. There's no coming back."

He closed them briefly before he nodded and pressed his lips against mine, quick and soft. Then he smiled, and once again I found myself watching him back out of the car park and drive away.

The next morning there was a brief blurb in the newspaper along with a grainy photo of Casey's lips meeting mine. The small story commented about who the mystery man was and asked if "Evie had finally found love?" They also included a brief summary of the shooting. News must have been light on the ground yesterday if *that* was worth reporting about.

"Did you see the paper?"

I nodded at Mac from the dining table because I had a mouthful of Coco Pops.

"What was that about? I thought you and Casey didn't have a thing, but the proof is on the page."

"No, Macface, the *paper* was indicating we had a thing. I can't explain what that was. It almost felt like a goodbye somehow."

Mac poured some Coco Pops in her bowl as Henry wandered in, sleepy eyed and shirtless, scratching at his head as he yawned.

"So you and Casey don't have a thing?" she asked.

Henry looked confused as he frowned at Mac. "I thought we established that Evie and Casey weren't going to have a thing and that things might be moving ahead with Jared." He aimed his frown at me, his voice harsh. "You told us you were going to find your middle."

I exhaled noisily and narrowed my gaze on Mac. "No, we don't have a thing."

She put her hands up in surrender before opening the fridge door to get out the milk. "Okay, okay. Just checking."

I pointed my spoon at both Mac and Henry in turn, milk flying across the dining table. "You two just worry about your own things."

"But we don't have things to worry about," Henry complained as he flicked the kettle. "Cuppa?"

"Yes, please," both Mac and I replied.

"That's because you're the retarded relationship bastard," Mac informed him.

"So what's your excuse, Mac?" Henry asked, folding his arms and leaning against the kitchen counter.

"My excuse is that I'm too busy to have a thing."

"Argh!" I shouted. "If one more person says *thing*, I'm going to throw my bowl at their head."

"Thing," Mac taunted.

I picked up my bowl threateningly as I half stood, and she squealed and leaped behind Henry's back.

Henry shoved her out of the way. "Jesus, Macklewaine, I almost spilled hot tea all over you."

Henry plopped a cup of tea on the table in front of me. "What's on the schedule today, Mac?"

"Got our music video tomorrow. We need to be there just before lunch because we'll be doing some later afternoon/evening type stuff. So today is prep work for that. Not to mention I've got someone coming tomorrow morning for the assistants interview."

"Yeah?" I piped up. "Who?"

"Quinn Salisbury is her name."

"Cool. Nice name," said Henry.

"I agree. I like the sound of her, Henry, and I need someone desperately, so you keep your eyes off her, okay?"

"Whatever."

Henry gave a salute and took his coffee back upstairs.

The day passed by quickly and the next morning found me having a strange dream where a hotdog was trying to eat my leg. I was holding a gun and telling the hotdog I would shoot it because I was a badass bitch but then it turned into a snake that spoke to me with Snoop Dogg's voice and told me to "drop it like it's hot."

My phone ringing woke me from the ridiculousness that was my mind, and thankful, I reached out from under the pillow to snag it from the bedside table, pulling it back under to answer with a muffled greeting.

"'Lo?"

Peter growled at the noise from somewhere deep beneath the fluffy white confines.

"Did I wake you?" Jared's smooth sexy rumble washed over me.

"Yeah," I whispered sleepily, "but that's okay because I was having a really weird dream."

I told him about it and when he laughed I woke up just that little bit more, realising that I was actually speaking to Jared for the first time since he left my hospital room. Not only that, it felt so damn good that tears filled my eyes even as I chuckled lightly at his laugh. Peter growled again at the noise.

"Was that Peter?"

"Yeah. The phone call woke him up, and he's pissed."

"Tell him I said sorry."

"Okay, but I'll wait until he's in a better mood."

"Sorry for ringing so early, but I thought I'd be catching you after your surf."

"No surf today. Casey begged off. How did you know I've been surfing?"

"Casey told me. You don't surf on your own?"

"No, I don't," I replied. "Attempting a surf on my own would be tantamount to suicide."

He laughed and I figured then that he'd heard all about my relationship with the ocean floor.

"Listen, uh, I was wondering if we could catch up?"

I shifted out from under the pillow, realising I wouldn't be getting back to sleep after this conversation. "Um, okay."

"What about this morning?"

I sat up, breathless. "This morning?"

"I'm home, Evie."

The words sent a thrill through my body that started at my toes and ran the entire length of my body until I was sure my hair stood on end.

"But...you're not due back for another month."

"I know, but you know Casey was originally supposed to do the contract job over there. He's flying there this morning to take over the last few weeks so I could come home early."

I put a shaky hand to my forehead, remembering Casey's words yesterday morning at the beach. The way his eyes scanned my face before he'd gotten in his car. I let my breath out slowly. "Casey's leaving? Today?"

"Yeah, Mitch is dropping him at the airport this morning. His flight leaves in an hour or so. Anyway, I have something I want to show you so did you want to? See me that is."

"I...yeah, but we've got our music video today, so I can't stay long, okay? Give me an hour?"

"Sure. I'll message you the address."

I threw the phone on my bed and bolted for the wardrobe. Flinging clothes about in a panic, I realised I needed Mac.

"Mac!" I shouted, running down the hall to her room. "Mac!"

I flung myself on the bed, landing on top of her. She grunted but otherwise didn't move, so I grabbed her shoulders and shook hard.

"Mac!" I shouted again, this time in her face.

"Fuck off," she mumbled without opening her eyes.

"Mactard, open your eyes. I need you. Help! I'm meeting Jared this morning, and I need something that says *sexy bitch,* but in a casual 'I didn't try hard to look this sexy' way, and it also needs to channel a 'I shouldn't have left you, but now that you're here, I want to devour you' kinda vibe."

Mac opened bleary eyes as I straddled her, hands still clutched desperately to her shoulders.

"What?"

"Mac! Don't ask me to repeat that because I have no idea what I said."

I let go of her shoulders, and she pushed up on her elbows. "Jared's home?"

"Yes, now get out of bed."

I climbed down and holding her arm, began to drag her off.

"What are you doing?"

"I'm trying to get you out of bed, asshead. I need help with something to wear."

"Wait, what? Why?"

"Mac!"

I returned to my efforts and with the core strength I'd worked so hard for coming through, she slid carelessly to the floor.

"Jesus, Sandwich, this better be good." She growled.

"Just hurry up."

Back in my room, she burrowed into my wardrobe, ordering me to put some blush, mascara, and lip gloss on. Finished, I sat on the edge of the bed explaining my conversation with Jared to Mac as she threw clothes to the floor, muttering to herself. Out came a pair of short aquamarine coloured shorts with a scalloped hem and large button detail lining the pockets. Huh, I didn't even realise I owned those. I slid them on and checked the mirror, noticing they showcased the long length of leg, tanned and toned from the hours trudging the sand in my quest to ride the ultimate wave. Okay, it sounded good, but my quest to not face plant on the beach was more accurate. I *was* assured that the ultimate wave would come later.

"Evie, you there?"

Mac was snapping her fingers in my face with one hand, the other was holding out a top.

"Sorry," I muttered. I slid it on. The white, silver studded scoop neck top was perfect—loose to convey casualness, yet covering enough skin to make the length of leg on display sexy rather than skanky.

"Shit, what's the time?"

"No idea, Mac."

"I've got that interview for the assistant this morning. You can't leave now. I want you here for that."

I slid strappy silver sandals on my feet and a thick silver and diamonte bangle up my bicep. "No can do, Macky Wacky."

"Thanks a bunch," she hissed and sent me an icy glare. "Next time dress yourself."

"Mac, I'll be late. Go and get yourself ready for Quinn okay?"

I sauntered down the stairs to the kitchen, added my phone and purse to my handbag, and picked up my car keys when the doorbell rang.

"Mac!" I shouted. "That'll be your interview."

I opened the door to see a young girl in a hat and giant sunglasses. She had a death grip on a leash that was currently restraining a giant Rhodesian Ridgeback from barging through the front door. The dog had a giant white bandage wrapped around his head, making him look earless and completely ridiculous.

"Hmmm, maybe not," I muttered.

"Excuse me?" the girl asked.

"Nothing," I offered her a brilliant smile. "Can I help you?"

"Ah, is Mackenzie Valentine here?" She flushed in embarrassment as she struggled to restrain the giant beast.

"Sure. Come in," I stood back a little to let her pass.

"Mac," I shrieked. "It's for you!" I waved at the couch before I brushed past her to the front door. "Excuse me, I have to go."

I jumped in the car, peeling out of the driveway and planting my foot until I arrived at my destination. Parking the car, I didn't bother with my bag. Instead I grabbed my phone and raced for the entrance, checking the board to make sure I could find where I needed to be. Bingo. Jogging to the right gate number, my gaze searched the crowds until I found who I was looking for.

"Evie," Casey said in shock when I reached him and Mitch.

Hands on my hips, I sucked in a few breaths until I was able to speak.

"You're leaving," I wheezed accusingly as I tried to catch my breath.

"I need to get going." Mitch gave Casey a nod. "See you in a few." Mitch gave my shoulder a squeeze. "See you tonight, sweetheart."

I snagged Mitch's arm before he moved away. "What's tonight?"

"Dinner." At my clueless expression, he continued. "At Mum and Dad's. Mac didn't tell you?"

"No, but I left in kind of a hurry this morning. We start shooting our music video today. I'm not sure what time we'll finish."

"Just come over whenever."

I nodded distractedly as a loud voice came over the PA, announcing the boarding for Flight QF107 to Dallas Fort Worth.

"That's my flight," Casey said.

Mitch left with a wave, and I folded my arms to help hold back the tears as we turned to face each other. "Are you leaving because of me? Because I swear to God, I'm sick of people leaving me. It hurts."

He grabbed my arm, steering me out the way of people trying to get through. "How did you even know I was leaving? Did you speak to Jared?"

I nodded in response.

He let go of my arm. "I'm not leaving because of you. I'm leaving *for* you. You both need each other right now, and this was the best thing I could think of that would help. I'm just trying to be the friend that you need, okay?"

His words only reinforced my belief that the man wasn't real, and my eyes softened on his face.

"Thanks, Casey. I appreciate you doing this for us...so much."

"Yeah? Just don't stuff it up this time."

"Me?" I let out a squeak. "What about Jared?"

Casey picked up his carry-on bag. "I've already warned him."

The final boarding call came for his flight.

"I have to go."

I nodded, and unfolding my arms as tears finally made their appearance, I smiled through them. "I'll miss you, *hotdog.*"

He brushed a gentle hand down the side of my face. "I'll miss you too, *Kook.* Make sure you get Jared to take you out surfing while I'm gone, okay? Don't want you losing all those mad skills of yours."

He grinned and I rolled my eyes.

"Only if you promise to surf with me when you come back."

"Deal. It's no fun surfing without you anyway."

He offered a final wave, and I watched him leave until I couldn't see him anymore.

Chapter Twenty-Eight

Half an hour late thanks to traffic, I pulled up outside a house in Bondi, a pretty beachside suburb north of our duplex at Coogee. Rain had begun to sprinkle, turning the surrounding leafy trees a rich, glossy green. I looked towards the house. It was a large, two storey weatherboard building with a timber porch that bordered the front exterior, a pretty railing, and wide steps leading down to a paved, front pathway. It looked in need of a little makeover, well, maybe a major makeover. The painted timber was peeling, the porch seemed to sag in the middle, and the gardens looked sad and brown. In comparison, the neighbouring houses were well-tended and appealing, and I would have wondered if I had the right house had Jared's Porsche not been parked in the driveway. I parked in the street on the opposite side of the rundown eyesore and turned the car off.

Jared must have been watching for me because he came out to the front porch when I pulled up. Waiting, he stretched his arms to loosely hold the top beam. Biceps rippled and I caught a tantalising glimpse of tanned muscles pulled taut where his shirt rode up. His loose worn jeans rode low on his hips, and his hair, even longer then when I saw him last, hung in his eyes and touched the back of his neck. My thoughts scattered at the sight and in what felt like a dream, I slid the keys from the ignition and climbed out of the car.

He remained unmoving as I began to walk across the road, and his piercing green eyes never left my face. As I got closer, he put his hands in his pockets and slowly made his way down the porch steps.

The light patter of rain dusted my face and flutters caressed my stomach as I watched him watching me. My throat feeling dry, I swallowed before breathing in the clean, sweet scent of rain.

"Baby," he whispered when I reached his side. His hand came out and rested against the side of my face, his thumb stroking across my cheek, looking at me as though I would disappear at any moment.

The moment I felt his touch, the warmth missing from my body flooded through me in a rush, and I knew we would have our middle. Tears filled my eyes and my voice wobbled. "Don't ever leave me again."

"I'm sorry." Tears blurred his vision. He bent his head, almost hesitant, and his lips captured mine softly. I leaned my body into the kiss, wrapping my arms tightly around his neck. Not expecting my enthusiasm, he stumbled, falling back on the top step of the porch. Arms attached, I went with him, somehow managing to straddle his lap. For a brief moment, I feared we might fall through the middle of the sagging timber, and he chuckled at the look of surprise on my face. The sound was low and sexy, and as his crinkling eyes smiled up at me, I burst out laughing. To my horror, the laughter turned into great, heaving sobs, and I hid my face in my hands. Jared's arms came around me, crushing me into his chest as his hands ran soothingly over my back. He crooned soft words interspersed with promises to never leave again as I cried into his neck. Eventually I calmed, and to save face, blamed my outburst on Jude and his ability to put me in touch with my emotional side.

I pulled away and he wiped the tears from my cheeks with his thumbs.

"Sorry."

His hands gripped my hips tightly as his eyes locked on mine. "*I'm sorry.* I couldn't forgive myself for what happened to you. I still can't, but that's something I have to deal with. I thought I was doing the right thing by leaving you. I thought you'd be better off without me, but you're in my heart, baby, and I can't get you out. I don't want you out. I want you in there, and I promise I'll never leave you again, no matter what. Just please forgive me and don't ask me to let you go." His voice was hoarse but his gentle plea was so very sweet. "I love you, baby."

The relief in knowing this man was not prepared to let me go again had me smiling wide. I sobered my face, but a faint smile still remained as I spoke. "I forgive you, Jared, and I don't want you to let me go because I love you too."

"Evie." He breathed against my mouth as my lips rose to meet his again. I felt his fingers, feather light as they brushed down my cheeks and my neck. He ran his tongue across my lips, nipping my bottom lip with his teeth, and when I opened my mouth, he swept his tongue inside. I whimpered as his hands moved firmly down my back, grabbing my ass, yanking me hard against him. He slid one hand beneath my shirt, running his hand up the bare skin as he ground his mouth against mine.

Breathless, I pulled away with a grin. "We're making out on the front porch of someone's house."

"We are." He nodded, the curl of his lips belying the seriousness in his eyes. "And it feels fucking amazing."

"It does."

He slowly slid his hands out from under my shirt and stood, setting me gently on my feet, and taking my hand in his. "Come on." He tugged me up the stairs of the front porch and inside of the house. "This is what I wanted to show you."

With eyes wide, my gaze travelled the interior of the huge, empty house, noting the rundown exterior was nothing in comparison to what was on the inside. The windows appeared welded shut under the weight of filth. Psychedelic wallpaper, that I knew would have Tim running for cover, peeled off the walls. The ratty floor fibres, which could be carpet—it was hard to tell under the layers of crust—were so offensive I wouldn't let Peter put his paws on it, and the kitchen was done in a colour of lime green so bright it could take out an eye.

I blinked. "What a dump!"

"I bought it."

He laughed at my look of horror. Henry had said Jared was so in love with me he couldn't think clearly, and I could only conclude he was right.

"You bought this?"

"I'll show you around. Come on."

"Just promise me I don't have to touch anything and I'm all yours."

He held out a hand. "I promise you don't have to touch anything. Except me of course," he added with a wink.

"Well then, what are you waiting for?" I said gamely and slid my hand in his.

He kept up a running commentary of the house and all the renovations he had planned in his head as he led me from room to room. He wanted to open up the downstairs area into a huge dining and living area with bi-folding doors to a back deck. The deck would lead down to a pool and a pool house on the left and still leave enough room to accommodate a game of backyard cricket. He wanted to extend onto the back to add a study and increase the size of the kitchen. Leading me up stairs so rickety I feared falling through, we moved into what would be the master bedroom. Big windows overlooked the backyard where he said he wanted to add a small upstairs deck, then he led me through the all-important four other bedrooms "for the kids."

"You're really serious about that."

"Yep." A large smile stretched across his face as he nodded.

"Two."

"Four."

I changed the subject. "Why don't you just demolish the house and start again? It's so much work."

He led me back down the stairs. "Because this house has character and charm," he explained. "I want to make it ours babe. I want us to get married in this house and raise a family. It has a great school nearby, and the beach is in walking distance so we can take the kids out, teach them to surf. We can put a pool in, have barbecues…"

I started to tune out in a complete daze because what he was offering was the whole package, and it sounded amazing and I wanted it so, so very much, but...

"... will you?"

"Huh?" I was busy wondering how my career would mesh with this newly discovered dream I decided I needed to have. I tuned into him standing by the back window, his hands in his pockets, his face expectant.

"I'm rushing you, aren't I?"

"Sorry, will I what?"

"Will you move in with me? You and Peter?" He strode towards me as he spoke and took both my hands in his.

"I... it all sounds amazing, and I want it more than anything, really, I just..."

Trailing off, I let go of his hands and moved towards the same window he'd just stepped away from. My eyes stared out into the yard, envisioning Jared and our kids running around the grass, playing cricket, the bright sound of young giggles cutting through the splash of pool water. I could sit out the back in the warm, orange glow of sunset, and strum my guitar and sip wine as I watched them all play. How could I have that and endure touring, night after night, months away from them all? How could I make it work?

"You just make it work, Evie. It's that hard and that simple."

Travis' words came back to haunt me and hope fluttered in my chest. Maybe I really could have it all, it might not be easy, but I was forever hearing that nothing worth having ever was.

"I know you're going to be busy with Jamieson taking off like it is, but I want you with me. When you come home from tours, from your travelling, I want to be the one who picks you up and brings you home, to our home, so you can tell me all about what you did and where you went. Sometimes, I could even juggle my workload and come with you. I want us to spend our days off together at the beach or here working on the house, building it into something we can both share together. Fill it up with kids. I know that babies might still be a while off, but we can make it work. I can take on a safer role at the office. I can be the one who looks after them, or you can if that's what you want. We can make this work, Evie. Say yes."

He took in a deep breath, his eyes watching me with uncertainty.

Fuck it. I wanted this.

I grinned. "Yes."

"Yes you'll move in?"

"Yes!" I shouted.

He whooped and grabbed me, picking me up and spinning me around. "I love you so much, baby." He laughed, unable to contain the joy that was bubbling over.

Tears started leaking out. "Oh God again? Jude has so much to answer for."

"I agree. If you're like this now, imagine what you'd be like pregnant?"

He winked at me and I slapped his arm as he set me back on my feet.

"Hey, wait. What about your share in the loft with Travis?"

"I sold it to Casey while I was still overseas."

"Oh. Well that worked out well, but uh, where are you going to stay with the renovations going on, at the duplex?"

He looked confused. "Well no, here, in our house, with you."

He thought I was going to live here? Now? I looked around, and the hideous, filthy interior only confirmed my suspicions that Jared had completely lost his mind.

"Have you lost your mind?"

"Oh I get it."

"Get what?"

"You're being a princess."

I gasped in horror. "I am totally not. This house is not fit for our dog, let alone us. There's probably a family of rats living in the kitchen, coming out every night to cook on their little rat camp stove and scatter a

few rat poos about the floor before going to sleep in their little rat beds."
I shuddered at the image.

"Evie," he said in his "I'm talking to a five year old" voice. "The point is that we live in it and do it up at the same time. I want to do most of the work myself so it makes sense."

"Okay. Well how about *you* move in, and when you're finished all the work, then Peter and I will join you."

He folded his arms. "God, you are so stubborn. Okay. How about we both stay at the duplex over the next two weeks, and I'll get the main bedroom and the kitchen done, and then we'll move in together."

I nodded. "That could work." I held up a finger. "On one condition though."

"What?"

"My bed goes in the main bedroom."

"Baby, I have missed that bed almost as much as you. Your bed not coming with you is a deal breaker."

I laughed, putting my hands on his hips to yank him close. He bent his head and kissed me, and I slid my hands around him with a moan, slipping them inside the back of his jeans. It was like igniting a fire, and soon his lips were trailing hungrily down my neck, the hard length of him grinding against me as his own hands slipped under my shirt, tracing the warm the skin to my breasts.

"Jared," I panted.

"Mmmm?"

My eyes scanned the whole area of the house but nowhere seemed to fit the bill of what I needed.

His lips moved back up my neck. "I want you so goddamn much."

"Where?" I questioned. "The front porch is cleaner than in here. We can give the new neighbours a show."

His chuckle vibrated against my neck where his head was buried.

"Don't laugh. I'm serious. Wait. The car. Mine. It's bigger."

Suddenly serious, he picked me up. "Let's go."

Plastered all over his front, legs wrapped around his hips, I giggled as he carried me out the front door.

My phone buzzed.

Shit.

"Don't answer it," Jared said, somehow managing to talk, walk, and suck on my neck all at the same time. Who said men couldn't multi-task when it mattered?

"It'll be Mac with a message."

He set me down with a sigh, and I pulled my phone out of my pocket. "Yep, Mac."

M: Get your hands out of Jared's pants and return home pronto. Music video ring any bells?

As soon as I read it, another buzzed through from Henry this time.

H: Chook, Mac's about to blow. Get home ASAP. PS You owe me.

This time I let out a loud sigh. "I have to go. We have a music video to shoot today, and Mac is currently biting the heads of chickens and bathing Henry in their blood."

He laughed. "God, I missed you so much. Okay. Let's pick up where we left off tonight."

I nodded. "Bring your things to the duplex some time today, and I'll message you when I know when we'll be done."

"Okay."

My face fell and he raised his eyebrows.

"What?"

"Mitch said it was dinner at your parents place tonight."

Hands on his hips, he tilted his head back to stare at the ceiling of the porch for a moment as though praying for patience. "Okay, then." His gaze returned to me. "We'll eat and run."

"I can deal with that."

Jingling my keys, I smacked his lips in a loud kiss, turned around, and started down the pathway.

"Baby?" he called out.

I turned around and stared walking backwards as I watched him.

"Yeah?"

"I…never mind."

I stopped. "What?"

"I just wanted to say that I can't remember ever being this happy."

I grinned. "Me either."

When I returned to the duplex, Mac and Henry were in the kitchen chatting to the new assistant Quinn. I was introduced and we talked briefly while I poured a cold drink.

"So tell us," Mac demanded.

"Tell you what?"

"Chook," Henry said warningly from his seated position on the kitchen bench. "She's gonna blow!"

Henry chuckled as Mac tried to push him off.

"Jared bought a house and we're moving in together."

Silence reigned as they both froze.

"Sorry, did you say you and my brother were moving in together?"

"Uh, yeah, I did."

Henry scooted off the bench and folded me in his arms. "Ah, hell, Chook," he whispered in my ear, "we're gonna miss you around here, but I'm so happy for you."

I filled them in on a few brief details as Mac took her turn hugging me. "I love you, you know I do," she told me when she pulled back, "but you know what this means."

"I do?"

She started to chuckle slowly until it escalated into a full on wheezing, tear streaming, hyperventilating moment. "Sandwich," she choked out.

"What?" I shouted.

"Your days of chips and chocolate are numbered. From now on, it's mung beans and grilled chicken all the way."

Henry also started to wheeze with laughter while I stood there ready to leak more tears, fuming at their lack of sympathy.

I flexed my jaw. "Thanks for the support."

Henry waved a hand at me as they both gasped for air, so I grabbed my bag, muttering that I would be in the car waiting when they were ready to leave.

We didn't wrap up for the day until later that evening. It would be the first day of many to get the footage needed. I messaged Jared earlier telling him we'd be late, and he replied saying he'd meet me over there and would take Peter with him.

Everyone having gone ahead, I arrived alone, finding the street almost full. Jared's Porsche was in the drive, the van the boys drove parked in the street, and Mac, driving her mum's old Mazda because she complained she never had the time to buy a new car, had the rear end sticking out in the street, showcasing her impatience of having to attempt a parallel park.

Earlier, I'd changed into a light green maxi-dress, grinning when I'd found Jared's things littering my room. I opened drawers to find his clothes wedged next to mine and shirts hanging in the wardrobe. A small desk filled the corner next to my chair which housed a laptop and nifty little electronic devices that gave no clue as to what they were. His wallet, coins, and random receipts littered the bedside table, and I'd had to sit down and take in a few deep breaths, thinking of how much had changed since I'd woken up that morning.

"Hey, Jenna," I smiled when she opened the door to my knock.

She returned my smile. "Genevieve. You didn't need to knock, sweetheart."

She took the cake box from my hands and folded me in a hug. "Thank you," she whispered.

"What for?" I asked as I pulled away.

"For giving my boy another chance."

While it was touching, and the sheen of tears added authenticity to her words, I could still detect the gleam in her eyes and knew the race for grandchildren had reached new heights.

She pushed me towards the stairs. "Go get your swimmers on, dear. Just about everyone's in the pool."

I could see them all from where I was standing in the kitchen. Steve, Coby, and Jake were by the barbecue chatting in the man grilling meet huddle, beers in their hands while Steve turned steaks. Mitch sat poolside with Tim, Dean, and two girls I'd never met before. Jared was in the pool with Travis, Mac, Henry, Frog, and Cooper. Mac was shrieking and splashing water at the boys, and Peter was barking excitedly, running up and down the sides of the pool, evading Jared as he tried to coax him into the water.

Jenna handed me a large soft beach towel, and I made my way upstairs, bikini in hand. Instead of heading into Mac's old room, I took a detour and went into Jared's. I quickly pulled off my dress and put on a simple black string bikini before poking around in the stuff that still littered the room.

There were framed photos scattered along the dresser of Jared and Mac, Jared and his whole family, and even one of Jared and Casey. There were old football trophies wedged amongst books along the shelves, and I poked at the titles to see what he'd read. When I pulled out an old dog-eared Matthew Reilly book and flicked through the pages, a photo fell off the shelf. I stopped, picked it up, and frowned at an old photo of Mac and myself. It was taken at our uni bar only a few weeks after we'd met, and we were already best friends. We had our arms wrapped around each other as we grinned at Henry behind the camera.

Huh, I'd forgotten all about that photo. I wondered what Jared was doing with it.

I opened the wardrobe door and stood staring at myself in the full length mirror on the back. The scars stood out on my torso like homing beacons. Jared had yet to see them, and frankly, I really didn't want him to.

Unfortunately, this now meant sex would involve me having to wear a shirt. I started to reach for one when I felt someone come up behind me.

"There you are. Mum said you were up here."

Damn. Too late. I watched him through the mirror, eyes smouldering as they raked over my bikini clad form, finishing on the angry, pink scars.

I shifted around him and started to reach for my dress.

"Don't." He snagged my wrist.

"Don't what?"

Jared pushed me backwards toward the bed until my knees bumped the edges and I sat down. He knelt between my knees and pressed a gentle kiss to the scar on my chest and then the scar on my stomach. "Don't hate these. They saved my sister's life. They're marks of courage and bravery, and they are so, so beautiful."

His eyes were sincere and for that I was thankful.

I nodded at his words. "They're proof that I'm a badass, right?"

He chuckled and agreed. "Absolutely."

"Just promise me one thing."

"Anything, baby."

"You have to tell that to Tim."

His eyebrows raised. "I have to tell Tim you're a badass?"

I grinned. "Yep. Hey!" I waved the photo about that was still in my hand. "I found this."

He snagged it out of my hands. "I've been looking for this. Where did you find it?"

"You have? It was sitting on your shelf. How come you have it?"

He sat back on his heels with a smile as he stared at the photo. "Mac sent it to me just after it was taken. In fact, she emailed me loads of photos before I met you and even more after. I feel like I've loved you before I even showed up on your doorstep that day."

That sneaky bitch. How could I be mad at her for her interfering ways?

His green eyes met mine and leaning forward until my mouth was brushing against his, I whispered, "We'll have our middle, Jared, and it's going to be perfect."

Epilogue

I sat on the edge of the bed and ran my hand over my almost naked form. My underwear set was new and pretty: cream satin with coral and lemon roses, lace trim, and a matching thong. My breasts, already a handful, spilled out from the lacy confines, and I wondered how much bigger they would grow.

I skimmed a hand across the taut expanse of my belly knowing it would soon change and felt a flutter at my secret. No one yet knew of the little life growing in there, not even Jared. He always talked of kids, four of them, but right now? We weren't in a rush. Trying for a baby hadn't even hit our radar, so this wasn't planned. I'd taken the test early this morning before my shower, and the news had come as a shock because really, I was on the pill.

Sure there were a just a couple of days missed here and there, okay, there were a shit load of them, but we were careful. Shadows crossed my eyes remembering back to a year and a half ago, when I'd been shot and almost lost everything, including my life. I'd lost an ovary in surgery, and despite having a spare, I was told conception would be difficult. The initial news had me wanting to cry with what that bastard had taken from me, but then Jared left, along with the promise of children, and it became something else I had to overcome.

Jared knew something was going on because I kept smiling unintentionally as I stood at the basin drying my hair this morning. I could already see the radiance in my face with my own eyes. I tried to tell him I was just high on life, but my sudden buoyancy for no particular reason left him sceptical. The sparkle in my eye was from the relief of knowing it wasn't some unidentifiable disease making me feel like death, just morning sickness! The initial nausea had started a week ago, rapidly declining to an all-out hell that didn't just visit in the morning. It stayed all day and kept me company well into the night. Morning sickness, my soon-to-be big, fat ass! This was around the clock, lose your stomach lining torture.

In the past week, Jared watched as my face slowly turned a shade of green so deep I began to resemble the sheets on our bed. I told him it was a wonder he could find me under the covers such was my unsightly camouflage, but he wasn't amused. His concern evolved from a furrow in his brow, that I did my best to smooth away with soothing kisses, into flat-out fear at the thought of something being seriously wrong with me. His behaviour was starting to get a little exasperating. I would wake in the night to find him watching me, unblinking, and then his hand would come out and rub my belly, his touch firm and warm. He would close his eyes as his fingers traced the faded scars, and I knew he was remembering the fear of almost losing me, and swallowing hard at the thought of it happening again. I promised him I would see the doctor on Monday, which was tomorrow, but it would simply be for confirmation now that I'd taken the test.

I inhaled noisily and let it out in a huff. All I had to do was tell him.

"Evie!" Jared's voice carried up the stairs of our house in Bondi.

We'd finished renovating it just over five months ago, and the party that resulted from what was now known as the Epic Renovation was mammoth: caterers, drinks flowing freely, big white tables with Tiffany chairs, a marquee, and a wedding.

I couldn't count the amount of times I moved back to the duplex during the restoration, much to Jared's disgust. No plumbing? Move. No floors? Move. No tiling in the bathroom? Move. It got to the point where I would roar into the driveway of the duplex in my Hilux with my bags, and Henry and Mac would just shake their heads and not even ask. I'd found out the hard way that renovations brought out irritation in people.

Jared soon got tired of my complaints with the hot water system, but frankly, I couldn't see why my whining wasn't forcing him to get anything done. The fact that the system seemed to be set at either Arctic Ice or Fiery Hell, with no apparent in between, and no immediate rush to fix it, was grounds for a hissy fit. Then he got irritated at *me* when I refused to walk on dirt after he ripped up all the floorboards downstairs. *Dirt!* I was sure that was where the rats had set up base camp. We did bomb the place for infestations though. It had involved another move back to the duplex, but with the both of us that time.

Somewhere in between all the irritation and the moving, there was love and a proposal. My birthday party found Jared up on stage with the microphone in front of the hundred odd people at the Florence Bar and me watching on with wide eyes and a hand to my cheek.

He'd been nervous because I'd heard the slight tremor in his voice as he spoke.

"Thanks everyone for coming tonight and sharing Evie's birthday with us."

The crowd of people clapped wildly and all eyes turned as the spotlight hit where I was standing, lighting me up for everyone to see. I smiled brightly and waved my glass in a jaunty salute.

"All of you know how lucky we are to have her standing with us today." That was the point his voice went a little hoarse and tears burned my eyes. I took a gulp of wine as I blinked them rapidly away, and Henry, to my left, took hold of my hand and squeezed.

"But I want you all to know how lucky I am to have her living in our house..." There were titters because it was at a time when I'd just moved back in from having the floorboards replaced. "...sleeping in our bed..." he winked at me, and this time there were wolf whistles and catcalls "...and holding my heart."

My pulse, racing from his words, kicked up a notch when he'd called me over to the stage. I climbed the stairs carefully in the gold skyscrapers and red strapless number Mac had me wearing, and he took my hand in his and drew me close. Then he turned and spoke to me rather than all our friends and family.

"Evie, one time I said to you that when you're not with me it's like someone's turned out the lights." I heard a few drawn in breaths and caught Jenna raising a hand to her chest, a tissue clutched tightly in her fingers. Steve's arm was around her shoulders, rubbing her arm gently as he smiled up at us.

"And when it looked like we were going to lose you, I thought I'd live the rest of my life in the dark."

A loud sob came from the audience. I didn't know who it was because Jared's eyes were locked on mine, and I wouldn't have been able to look away if a bomb had gone off.

"Evie Jamieson." My heart tripped over at that point because I realised what was coming. Jared's chest starting moving up and down a little more rapidly, and his hand around mine squeezed tight enough to almost have me wincing.

"You're the light I can't live without and the only one that has ever held my heart. I want to be the man standing beside you, laughing with you, crying with you, holding you, and loving you. Will you marry me?"

Tears rolled down my cheeks as I said yes. So overwhelmed at his words, my voice was a shaky whisper.

Naturally, no one but Jared heard my response, and there were yells for me to say it louder.

Jared grinned and held the microphone to my lips, and I shouted yes. Then he tossed it over his shoulder and yanked me into his arms. I heard Mac scream, and turning my head, I saw her jumping up and down with Henry. Coby was smiling and Jenna was openly sobbing in Steve's arms, no doubt knowing her dream was getting that much closer.

Jared slid a huge, princess cut diamond solitaire onto my finger, and the boys got up and played *Beneath Your Beautiful* by Labrinth as I wiped at tears while getting twirled around on the dance floor.

After several cut-ins and the band moving on to another song, I found myself in Casey arms.

"Organizing a wedding isn't grounds for me losing a surfing buddy is it, Kook?"

They were spoken lightly but there had been heaviness in his eyes, and for a moment I'd wondered if he was feeling regret. I hadn't given up my quest to hit the pro-circuit, but it still wasn't looking like it would happen any time soon. Unfortunately, I found surfing a bit of an addiction that was hard to let go, and I shared two or three mornings a week in the surf with Casey. Mostly it was horsing around and laughing, but other times I actually caught waves, Casey watching on as I rode them to shore, fist pumping the air like a lunatic.

I snorted at him in response to his words. "You're kidding right? A wedding is just a giant party with food and alcohol. Not much to it, Hotdog."

He raised his eyebrows in apparent surprise at the words that eventually came back to haunt me.

Who knew that it took two hundred and seventy-four different people to put a wedding together? Obviously not me. The weeks leading up to the event had me reeling, between the organizing, the last minute renovations, Tim faffing, Mac frothing, and our first ever released album going platinum, I thought I would lose my mind.

The two days prior to the wedding left me thinking we should have just eloped. It was a hard lesson learned, and I vowed to issue warnings to all other engaged couples I knew to save themselves.

It had started off the day before with Henry, Mac, Tim, Cam, and our new band assistant, Quinn staying over at our house and descended from there.

"Jared!" Mac shrieked as she made her way up the stairs of our house. "I'm going to kill you!"

I barged up the stairs, shoving Mac out of the way on my way past. She stumbled as she hit the wall, and I surged ahead in the advantage. "Not if I get to him first," I hissed.

Henry muscled his way in front of both of us. "Form a line, ladies."

We reached the bedroom in a tussle of limbs to find Jared sitting comfortably on the bed, computer on his lap as he tapped away. Whatever it was must have been important because he had that adorable furrow in his brow. However, this was the day before our wedding and work was not allowed.

I pointed my finger at him accusingly. "You're working!"

Henry pointed his finger at him accusingly. "Where the hell are my barbecue shapes?"

"What did you do with the chocolate?" Mac ground out, flushed in her fury.

Enduring a sleep over at our newly renovated house, they knew to bring supplies.

Jared calmly ignored my accusation as he shut down the laptop, putting it on the side table before raising a brow at me. "Do you want to tell Henry or should I?"

My eyes widened at him, and I shook my head.

Henry turned his horrified gaze to me, looking at me as though I had just run over his dog and crushed all his prized matchbox cars in one hit.

I cringed under the condemning glare and hung my head in shame. "Sorry."

Henry sucked in a breath at the damning admission. "Chook. How could you?"

"You don't know what it's like," I choked out.

379

"Oh, I think we have a fair bloody idea what it's like, but you chose him, and now you have to lump him. It's not right we have to suffer along with you."

"Everyone out," Jared said to the room. "I have to get going soon, and I need to give Evie a proper goodbye."

"No way, Jared. We have shit to do so save it for tomorrow night. Your bag is packed and in the car, and you need to leave now," Mac ordered.

"Mac! Evie!" Tim shouted up the stairs. "The only reason why you two aren't down here helping me better be because you're dead."

Jared and I both looked at each other and sighed. "Fine. At least give us a minute so I can kiss her properly without you all watching on."

"Fine, one minute and that's it," Mac conceded.

Both she and Henry left the room, and Jared turned to me with a twinkle in his eye as he stood up. "I thought they'd never leave."

I grinned as he reached my side. "Me either."

He bent his head and kissed me, soft and warm and slow, like a gentle sigh.

"Will that tide you over until tomorrow?"

"No," I murmured, tilting my head as I tugged at his shirt. "More please."

He chuckled against my lips when a shouting match between Mac and Tim broke out downstairs.

"I left something under your pillow," he said. "I have a feeling you might need it over the next twenty-four hours."

Then he took a step back, tucking a curl behind my ear and tapping his finger on my nose with a warm smile. "See you, Evie."

When I heard his car roar to life and back down the drive, I peeked under the pillow and let out a shout of laughter as Mac's chocolate stash was revealed.

On the afternoon of the next day, I stood outside our yard at the edges of the makeshift aisle, dressed in a Monique Lhuillier blush colored gown. It was strapless with an embroidered corset and an A-line tulle skirt.

My hair had been left to hang down my back in big loose curls, and a fresh flower arrangement sat above my left ear. Coby, clad in a tuxedo, stood on my right, our arms linked. Mac, Quinn, and Cam hovered, dressed in similar style dresses in silk ivory, fresh flowers adorning their hair.

My eyes met Jared's and I watched them travel the length of me, before returning my gaze, the heat in them leaving me breathless. I chuckled, remembering the first day I'd met him, opening the door and seeing that exact same look and fearing I'd burn to a pile of ash on the floor.

At his right stood Travis, nudging him with his elbow and saying something that caused Jared to laugh. Standing next to Travis was Mitch and Henry and the four of them in their tuxedos made for an impressive bunch of masculinity.

I turned to wink at Tim, and at my cue he started the music to begin the walk down the aisle. When the sounds of *Africa* by Toto rang out loud and clear, Mac and Henry let out simultaneous shouts of laughter at the knowledge they'd been thwarted, Mac gasping for breath as guests watched on in puzzlement.

I'd warned Jared the song was coming, and when the music began to play, my heart tripped over watching his eyes crinkle and the corners of his lips curl up in that sexy half smile of his.

"Baby?"

I exhaled softly at the endearment and gave Jared a sweet smile as he came into the room, his green eyes meeting mine. He was wearing my favorite Led Zeppelin shirt today, and I loved how it stretched across his broad chest. I loved wearing it to bed more, particularly when he was away for work, so I could breathe his scent deeply into my lungs. His silky hair had once again reached the perfect length, and as he knelt in front of me, I reached out and brushed the strands from his eyes.

He ran his warm hands up my bare legs, watching them as they trailed slowly up my belly to cup my breasts. I shivered, my skin breaking out in goose bumps at the touch.

His eyes followed his fingers as they travelled along the lace edges and the swell of cleavage above.

His voice came out husky and low. "You're not dressed. I can tell everyone to go home. I didn't want to go ahead with the barbecue anyway with you being so sick. You should rest up for the doctor tomorrow."

We had the family and close friends come for a Sunday afternoon get together. I could hear them out in the yard, Peter barking, people talking, Mac yelling about something. Henry was already playing his guitar, and Travis and Casey were talking with Jenna in the kitchen.

A frown knit his brow, and I caught his hands in mine when he went to pull away, holding them against my belly. My eyes met his again. I went to speak and hesitated.

He rubbed his thumbs over my palms. "Baby? You're getting me worried."

The flutters rising in my body, I answered him. "I'm pregnant."

He froze and I held my breath.

"What did you say?"

"I'm pregnant."

He snatched his hands away, sitting back on his heels and the tears filling his eyes had me swallowing my own.

His voice shook. "You're having my baby?"

I nodded, eyes wide, and he pushed back off his heels and splayed his hands over my stomach.

I tried to fill the silence. "I know it wasn't planned, and we haven't talked about it, and I've got a tour to deal with, and you're busy expanding the security side of your business. It's bad timing and—"

He pressed his lips hard against mine, my mouth opening against the insistence of his tongue as he twined his arms around me, running one down the skin of my back while the other dove into the hair at the nape of my neck. The kiss was hard and full of emotion, and when he pulled away, his breath was ragged. When it evened out, he took my hands in his.

"It's never bad timing for a baby, Evie. Is this why you've been so sick?"

My nod had him letting out a deep breath of relief, then he smiled and the light in his eyes had me pressing my lips together.

"I'm gonna be a daddy."

I nodded again, returning his smile. "You're gonna be a daddy."

"Mum's gonna go ape."

I laughed. "Mitch, Travis, and Mac are officially off the hook."

He picked up the pretty lemon sundress I'd laid out over the bed, and I held my arms up as he slipped it over my head, bending down to press a gentle kiss on my belly as he smoothed the hem down my legs. Then he stood up, taking me with him, and said, "Well, what are we waiting for? Let's go tell them."

The End

Acknowledgements

For my first venture into writing fiction, I want to thank my husband, Dan. Not once did you ever do anything less than encourage me to try. I know that reading books is not your 'thing' yet the fact that you're willing to suck it up and read mine, and a romance no less, warms the cockles of my heart. Don't worry, I won't tell anyone you read a romance book.

A huge thank you to Terrena. How you managed to read every chapter as I wrote it and still managed not to tell me it was a pile of bullshit, I don't know. After four rounds of edits, it's so far beyond what I originally had you reading, that I want to cringe at what it used to be. Thanks for your encouragement and for having my back every step of the way. I hope you know you have mine.

To my group of super fantastic sexy ladies. You are my counselors, my friends, and my cheerleaders. Every day, you put yourselves in my shoes, and I put myself in yours, and we share our lives together. Thank God for all of you.

To Max. What a freaking awesome editor you are. Thank you for sharing your talent and advice. I would tell you I'm thrilled with how much you have helped me and how much I have learned, but you would ask me to tell you what it looks like, so I won't. Bottoms up.

To the book bloggers who have been incredibly supportive from the moment I announced my plans to publish a book. Your enthusiasm and your love of books is inspiring. I cannot tell you enough how much I appreciate your help, and for taking on an ARC from an unknown author. Time is valuable and I thank you for sharing that with me.

Thank you to Sarah at Okay Creations for putting together an amazing cover. It's not just a photo and words, it is a piece of art.

A HUGE thank you to my readers for taking a chance on an unknown author. My book has been a complete roller coaster from start to finish, and I hope it has entertained you as much as it did me writing it.

Finally, a special thank you goes out to all my family. My dad and grandmother, you are still here and I still love you. To my sister, Kirsty, there through the ups and downs that have filtered our lives; life is never easy, but it sure is a hell of a ride. To my beautiful children, the reason I get up in the morning (both figuratively and literally). To my mum, the love will always be there. Chris and Jeff – you are family. To all my friends, thank you. To my CDA, I appreciate all of you, never believe anything less.

Writing this book has been one of the greatest joys of my life and taught me that even though it's scary to take a chance (on writing a book, on love, on a dream, on anything), do it anyway because that's what makes life what it is, and life is too short to sit back at the end with regret for what could have been.

About the Author

Kate McCarthy lives in Queensland, Australia.

Facebook:
https:/www.facebook.com/KateMcCarthyAuthor

Check out Kate's blog:
http://katemccarthy.net/

Follow Kate on Twitter:
https://twitter.com/KMacinOz

Friend Kate on Goodreads:
http://www.goodreads.com/author/show/6876994.Kate_McCarthy

CPSIA information can be obtained
at www.ICGtesting.com
Printed in the USA
FFOW03n0750190116
20599FF